COLD
SPOTS

CREATED BY

CULLEN BUNN & MARK TORRES
STORY   ART & DESIGN

SIMON BOWLAND
LETTERS

D1511455

IMAGE COMICS, INC. • Robert Kirkman: Chief Operating Officer • Erik Larsen: Chief Financial Officer • Todd McFarlane: President
Marc Silvestri: Chief Executive Officer • Jim Valentino: Vice President • Eric Stephenson: Publisher / Chief Creative Officer • Corey Hart:
Director of Sales • Jeff Boison: Director of Publishing Planning & Book Trade Sales • Chris Ross: Director of Digital Sales • Jeff Stang:
Director of Specialty Sales • Kat Salazar: Director of PR & Marketing • Drew Gill: Art Director • Heather Doornink: Production Director
Nicole Lapalme: Controller • IMAGECOMICS.COM

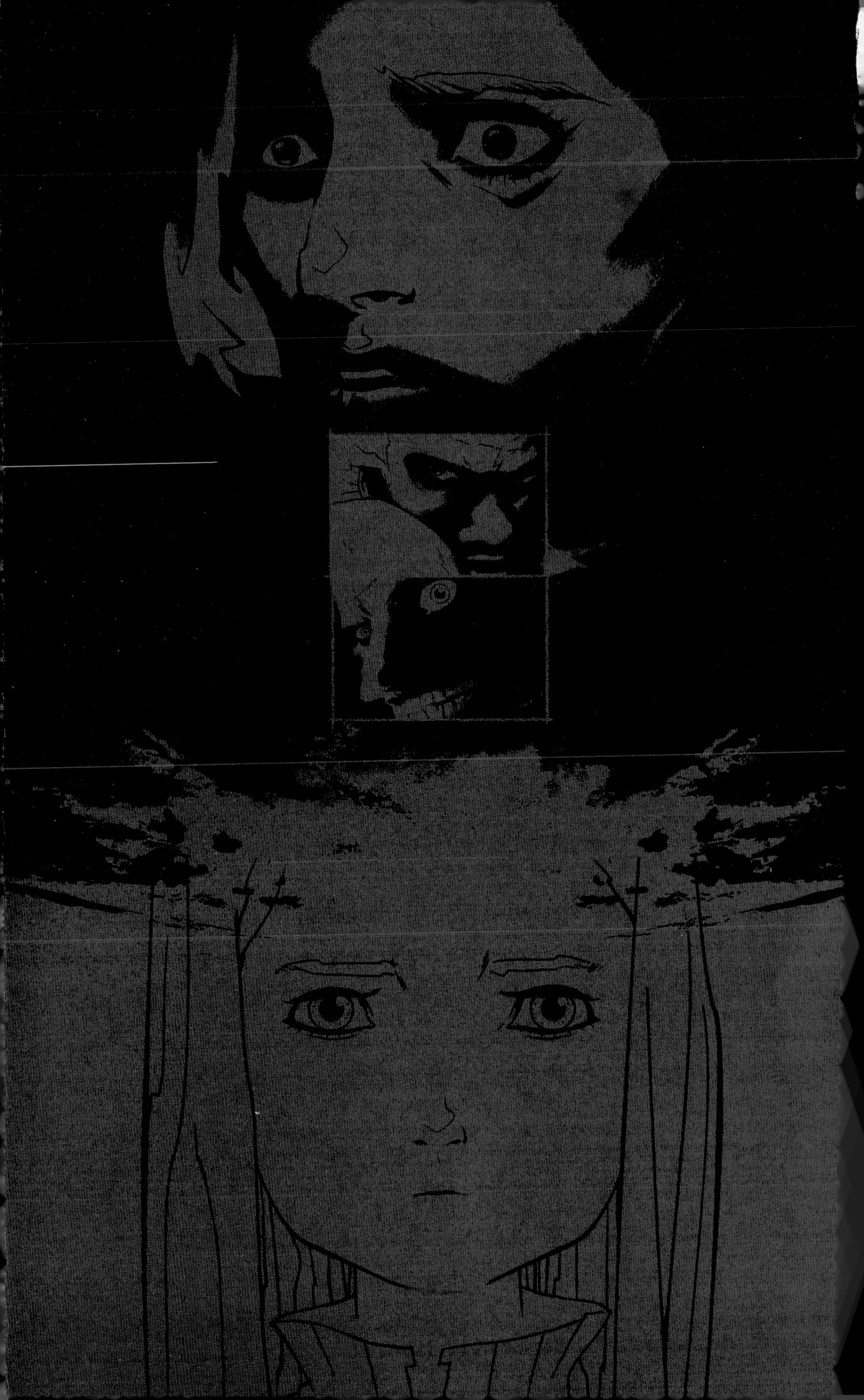

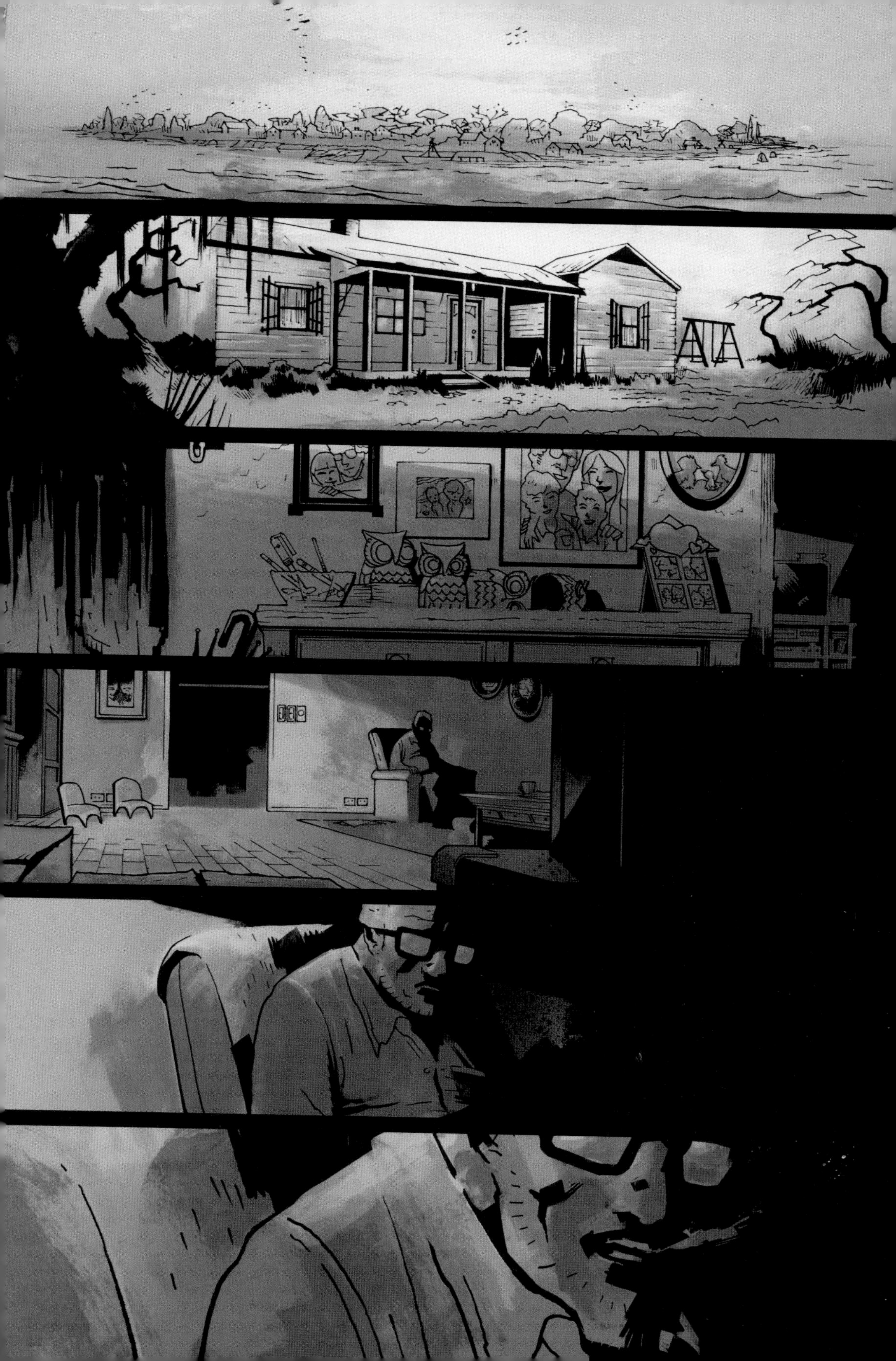

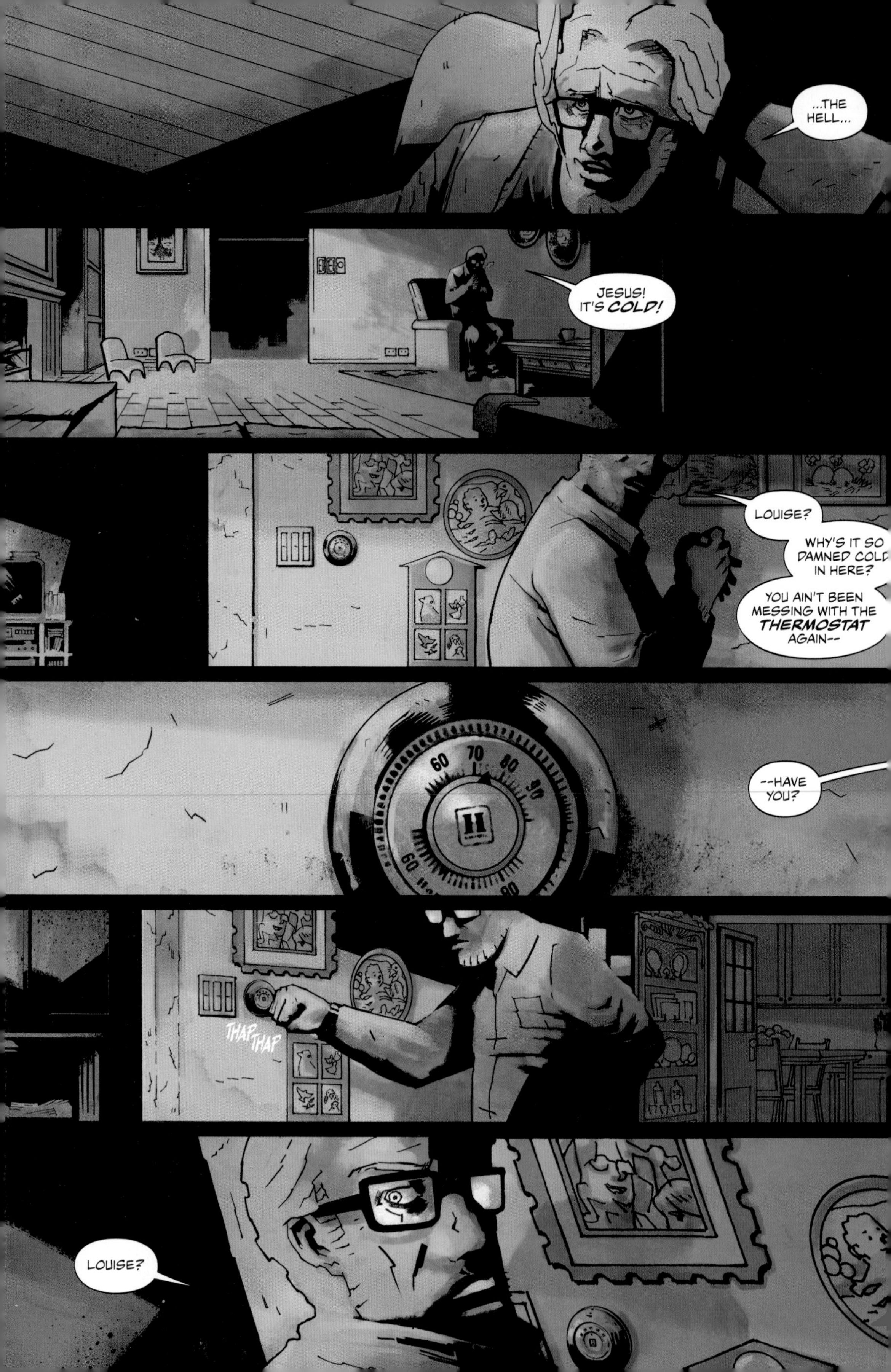
...THE HELL...
JESUS! IT'S COLD!
LOUISE?
WHY'S IT SO DAMNED COLD IN HERE?
YOU AIN'T BEEN MESSING WITH THE THERMOSTAT AGAIN--
--HAVE YOU?
THAP THAP
LOUISE?

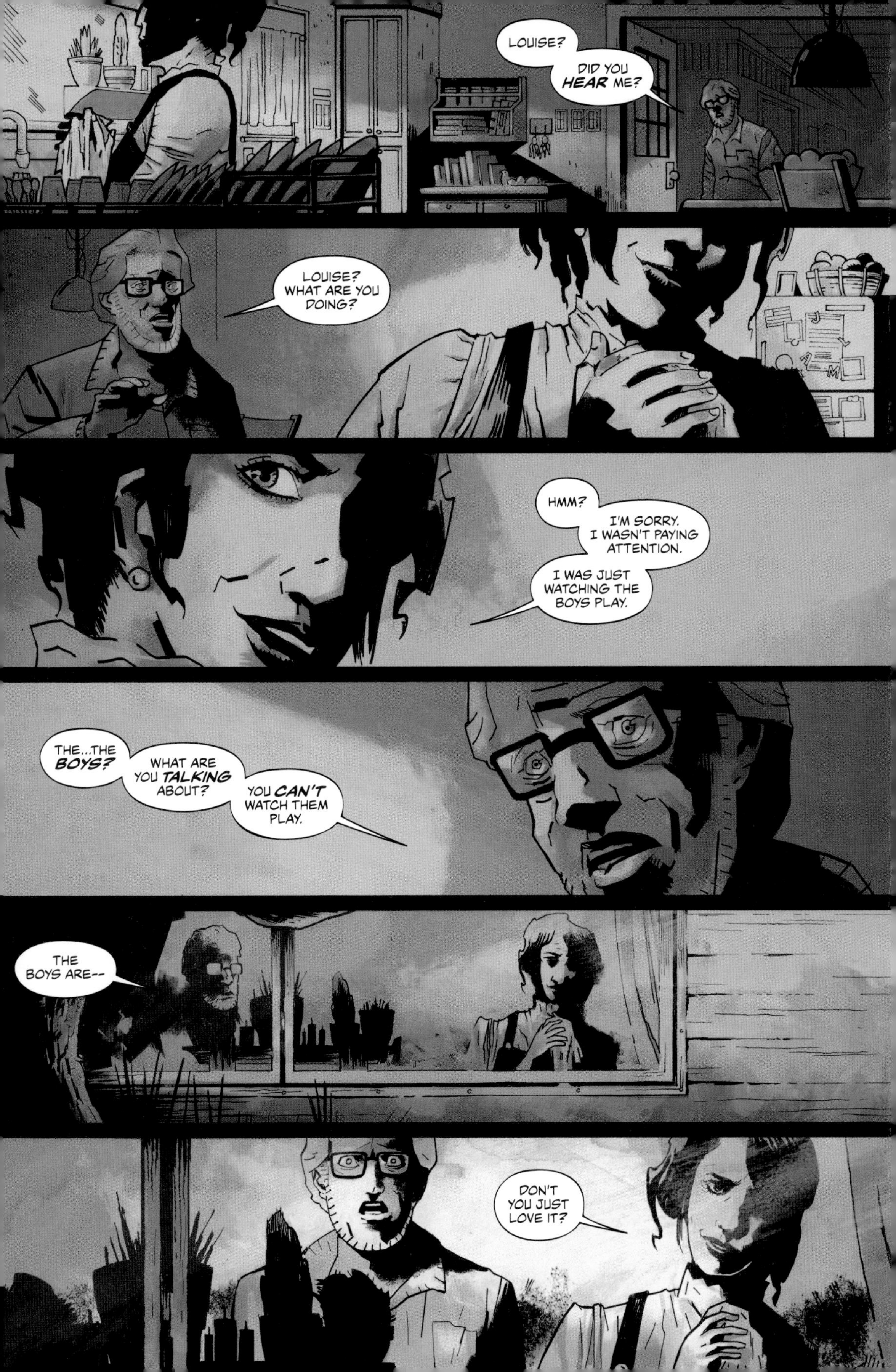
LOUISE?
DID YOU HEAR ME?
LOUISE? WHAT ARE YOU DOING?
HMM?
I'M SORRY. I WASN'T PAYING ATTENTION.
I WAS JUST WATCHING THE BOYS PLAY.
THE...THE BOYS?
WHAT ARE YOU TALKING ABOUT?
YOU CAN'T WATCH THEM PLAY.
THE BOYS ARE--
DON'T YOU JUST LOVE IT?

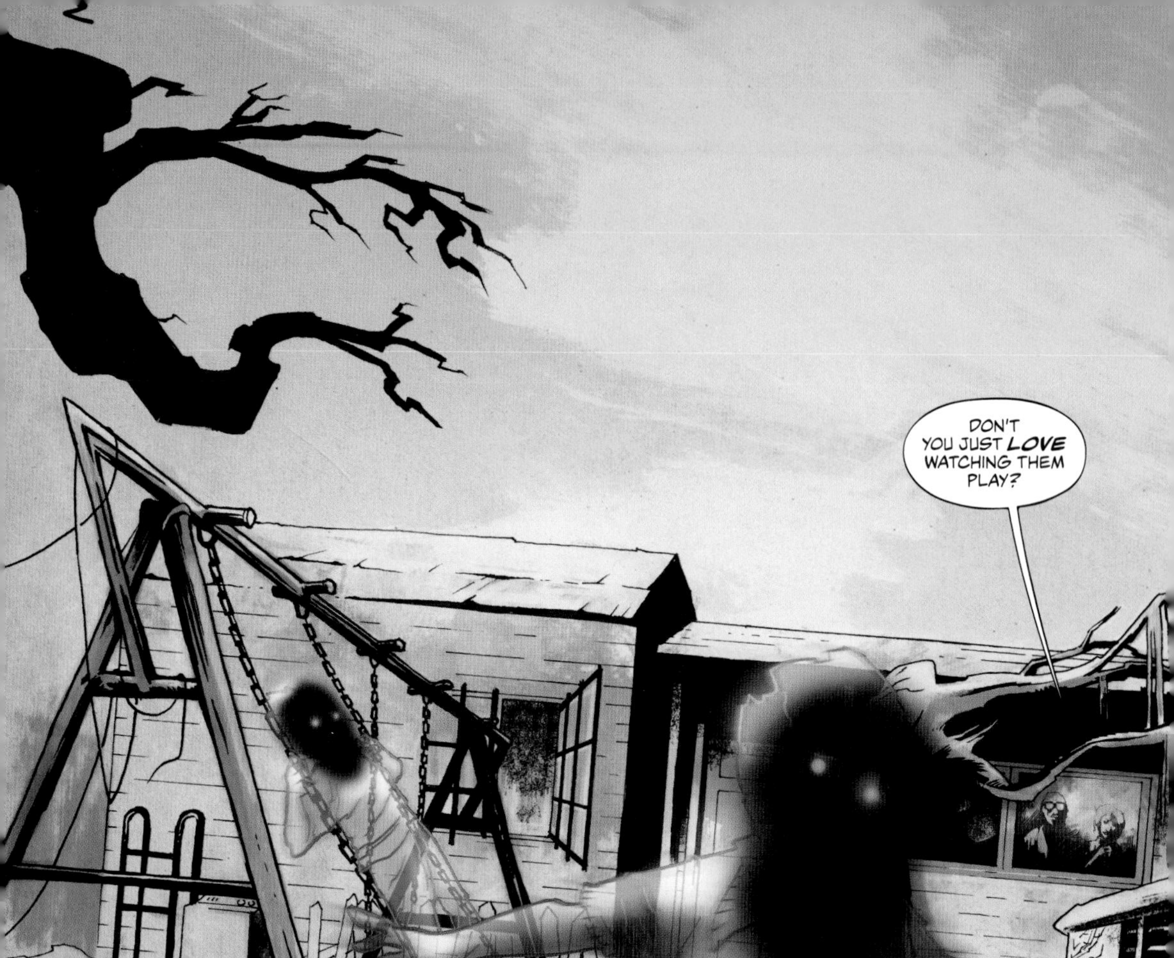
DON'T YOU JUST LOVE WATCHING THEM PLAY?

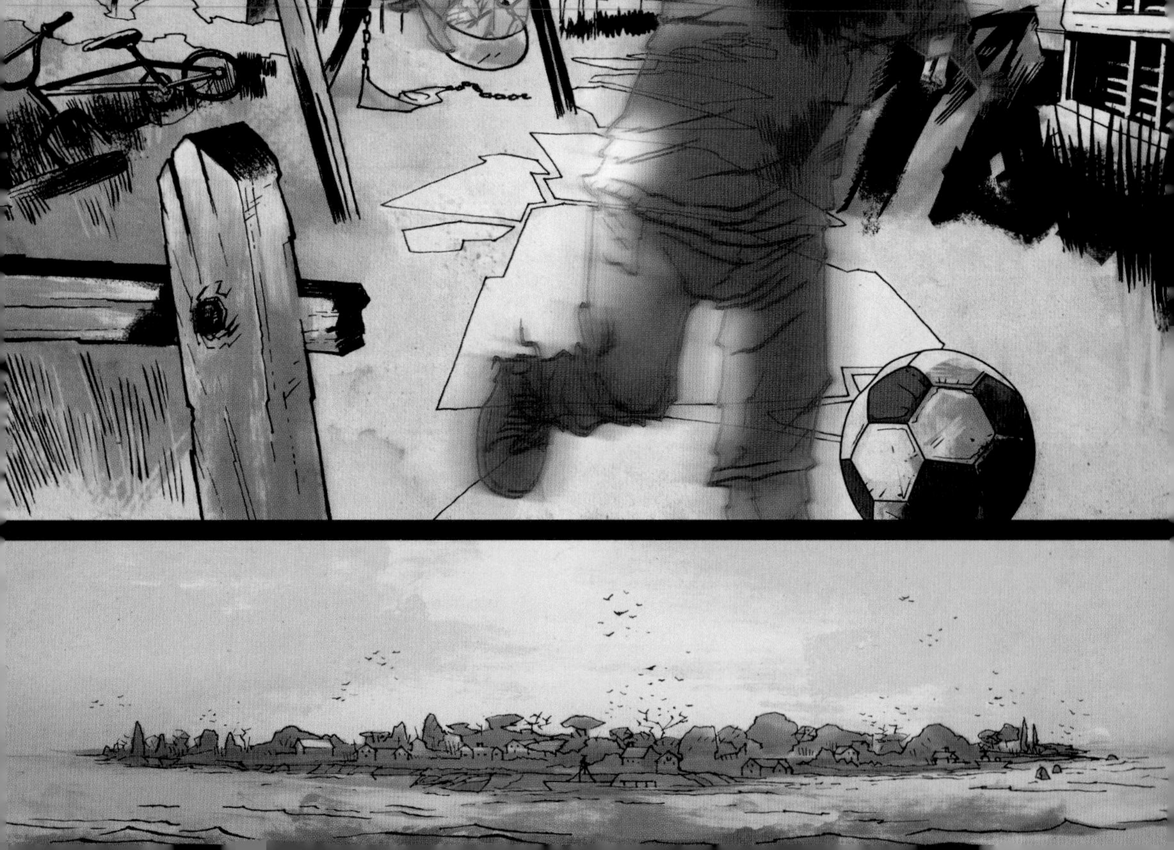

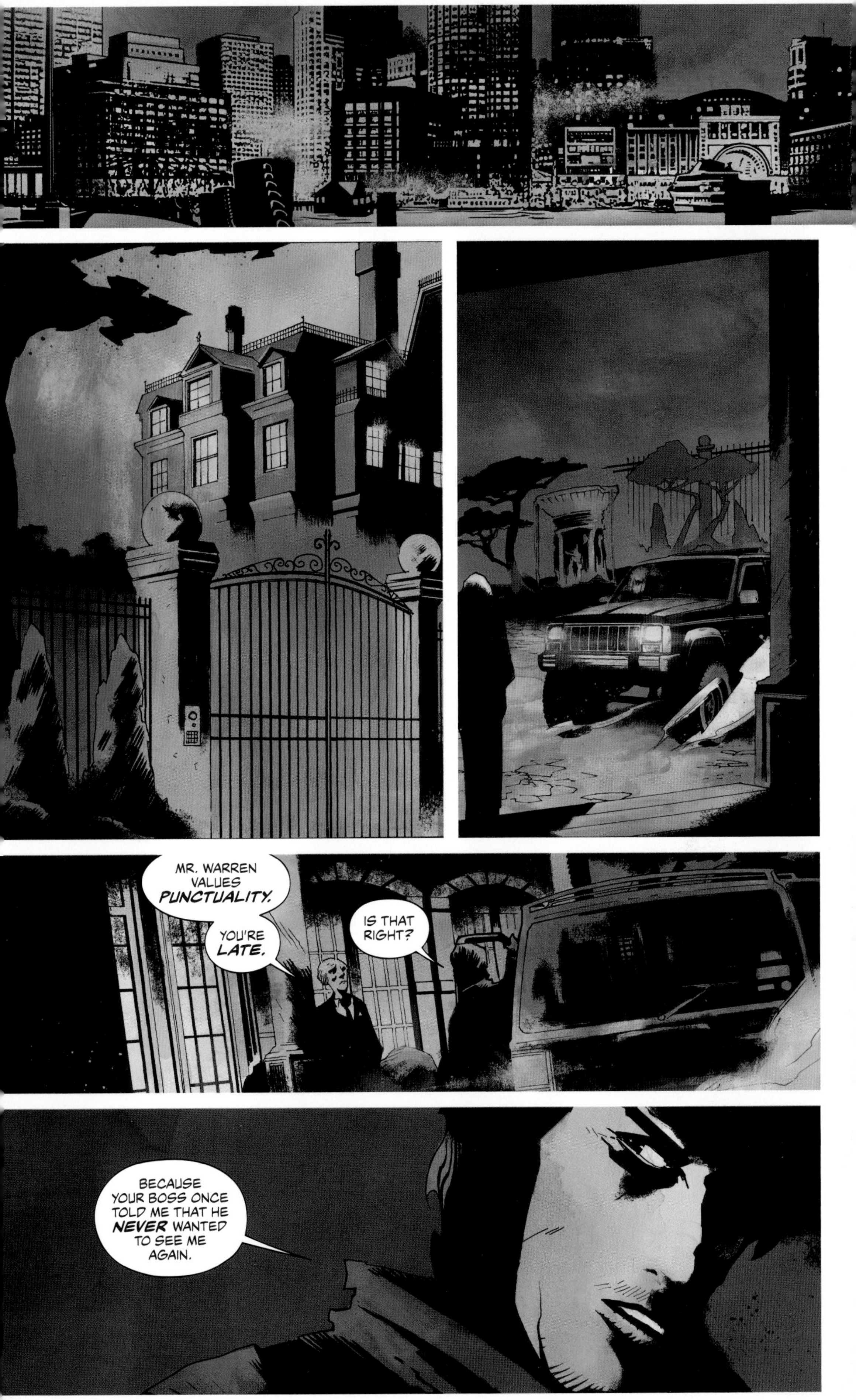
MR. WARREN VALUES PUNCTUALITY.
YOU'RE LATE.
IS THAT RIGHT?
BECAUSE YOUR BOSS ONCE TOLD ME THAT HE NEVER WANTED TO SEE ME AGAIN.

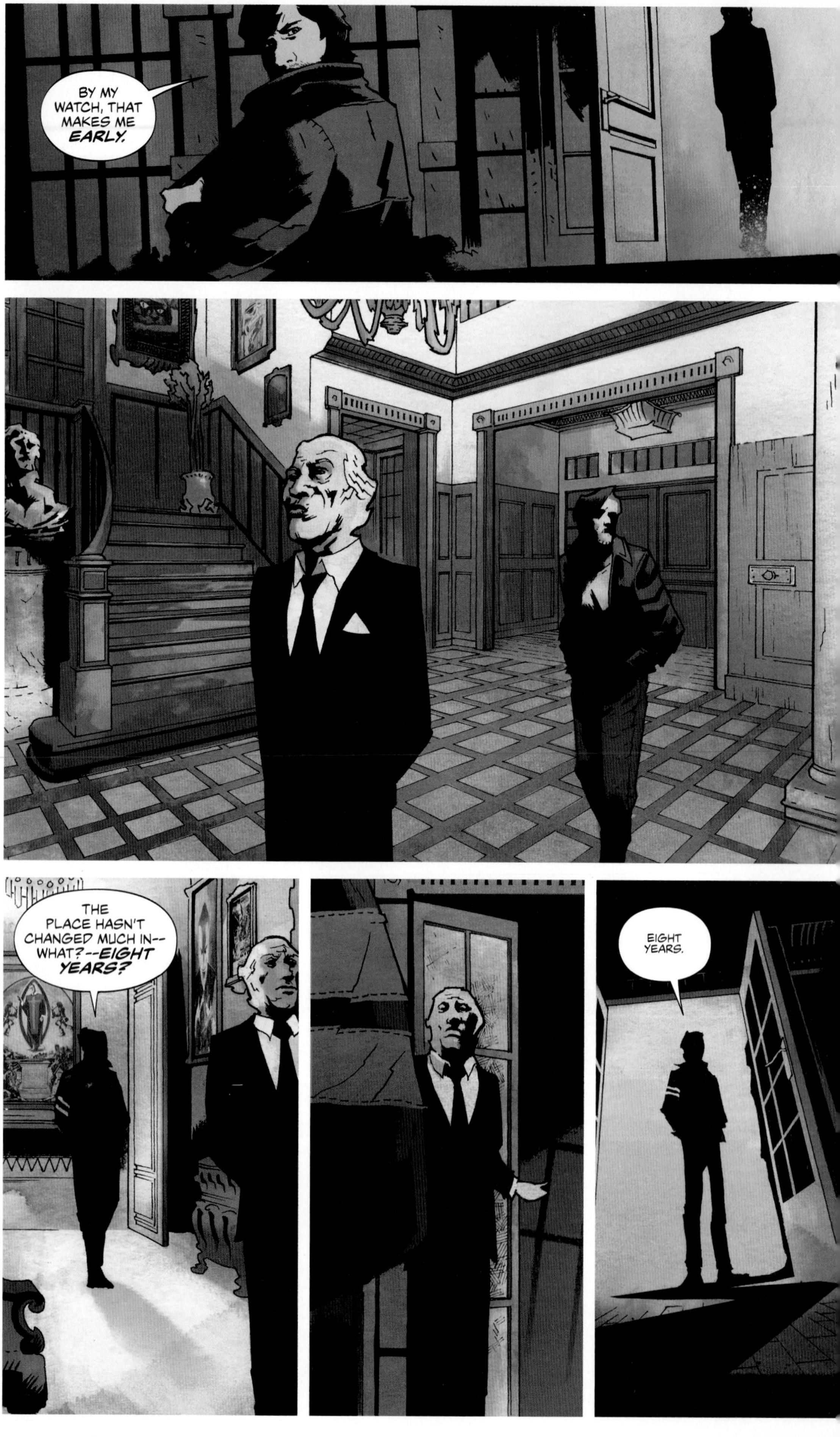
BY MY WATCH, THAT MAKES ME EARLY.
THE PLACE HASN'T CHANGED MUCH IN-- WHAT?--EIGHT YEARS?
EIGHT YEARS.

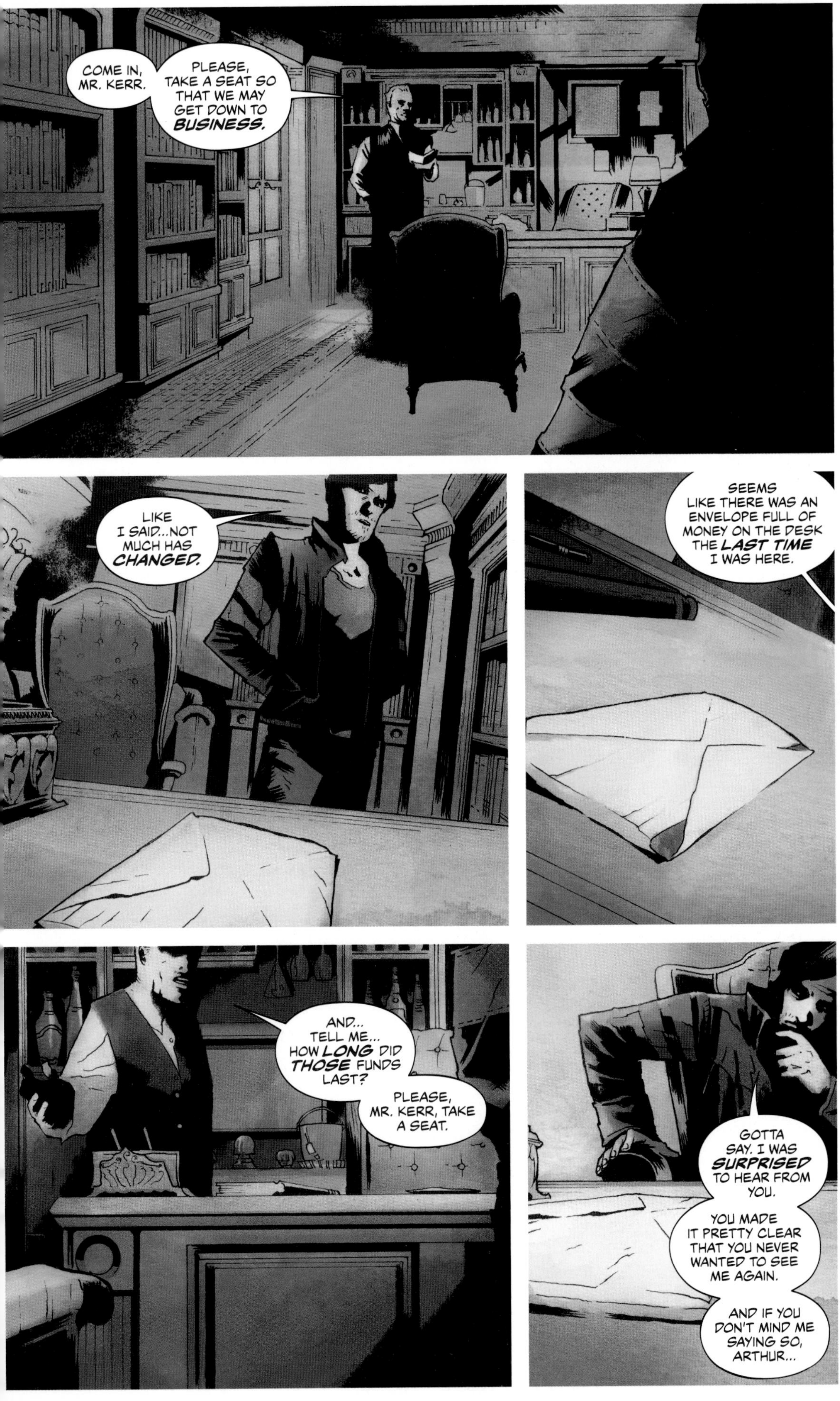
COME IN, MR. KERR.
PLEASE, TAKE A SEAT SO THAT WE MAY GET DOWN TO BUSINESS.
LIKE I SAID...NOT MUCH HAS CHANGED.
SEEMS LIKE THERE WAS AN ENVELOPE FULL OF MONEY ON THE DESK THE LAST TIME I WAS HERE.
AND... TELL ME... HOW LONG DID THOSE FUNDS LAST?
PLEASE, MR. KERR, TAKE A SEAT.
GOTTA SAY. I WAS SURPRISED TO HEAR FROM YOU.
YOU MADE IT PRETTY CLEAR THAT YOU NEVER WANTED TO SEE ME AGAIN.
AND IF YOU DON'T MIND ME SAYING SO, ARTHUR...

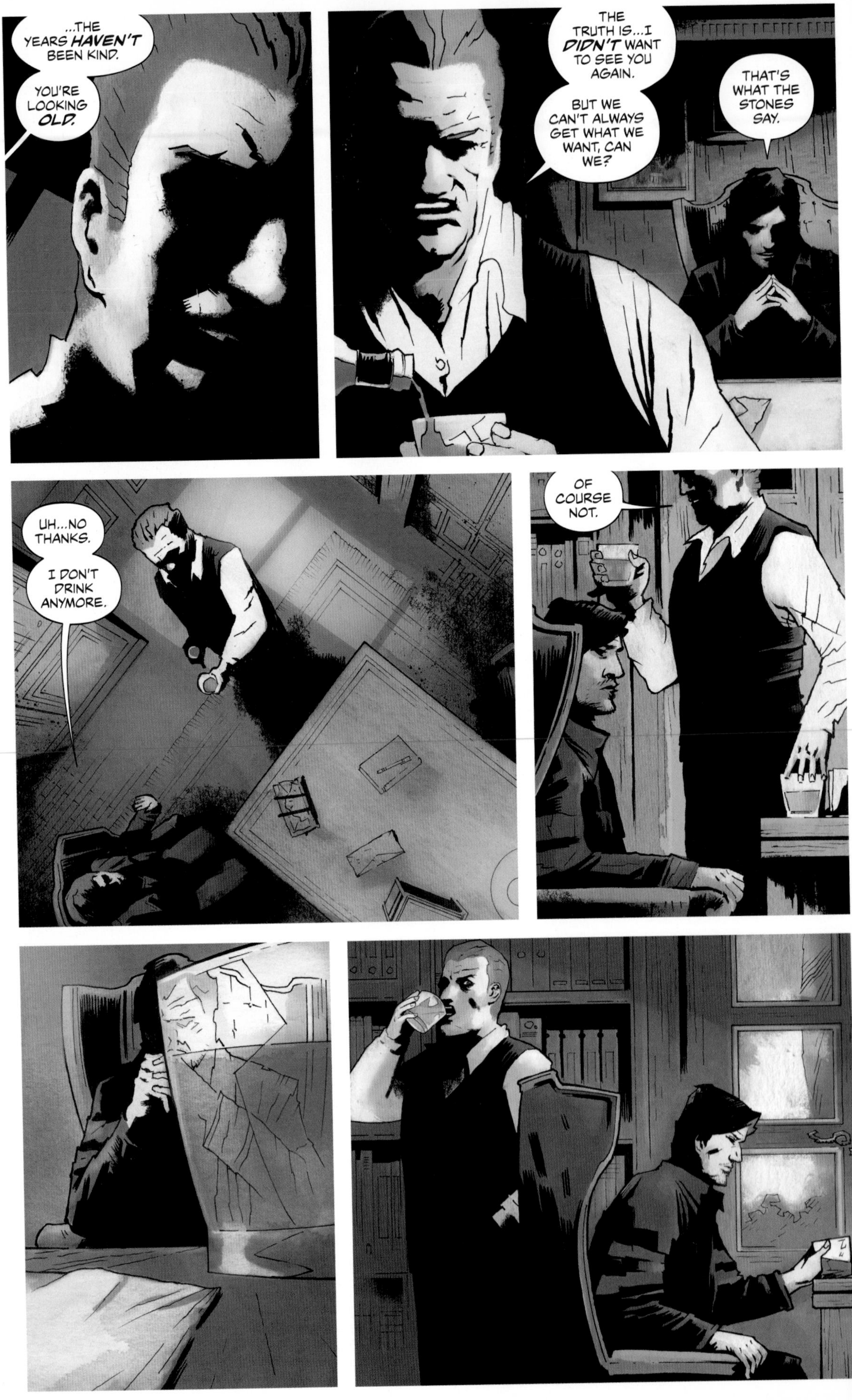
...THE YEARS HAVEN'T BEEN KIND.
YOU'RE LOOKING OLD.
THE TRUTH IS...I DIDN'T WANT TO SEE YOU AGAIN.
BUT WE CAN'T ALWAYS GET WHAT WE WANT, CAN WE?
THAT'S WHAT THE STONES SAY.
UH...NO THANKS.
I DON'T DRINK ANYMORE.
OF COURSE NOT.

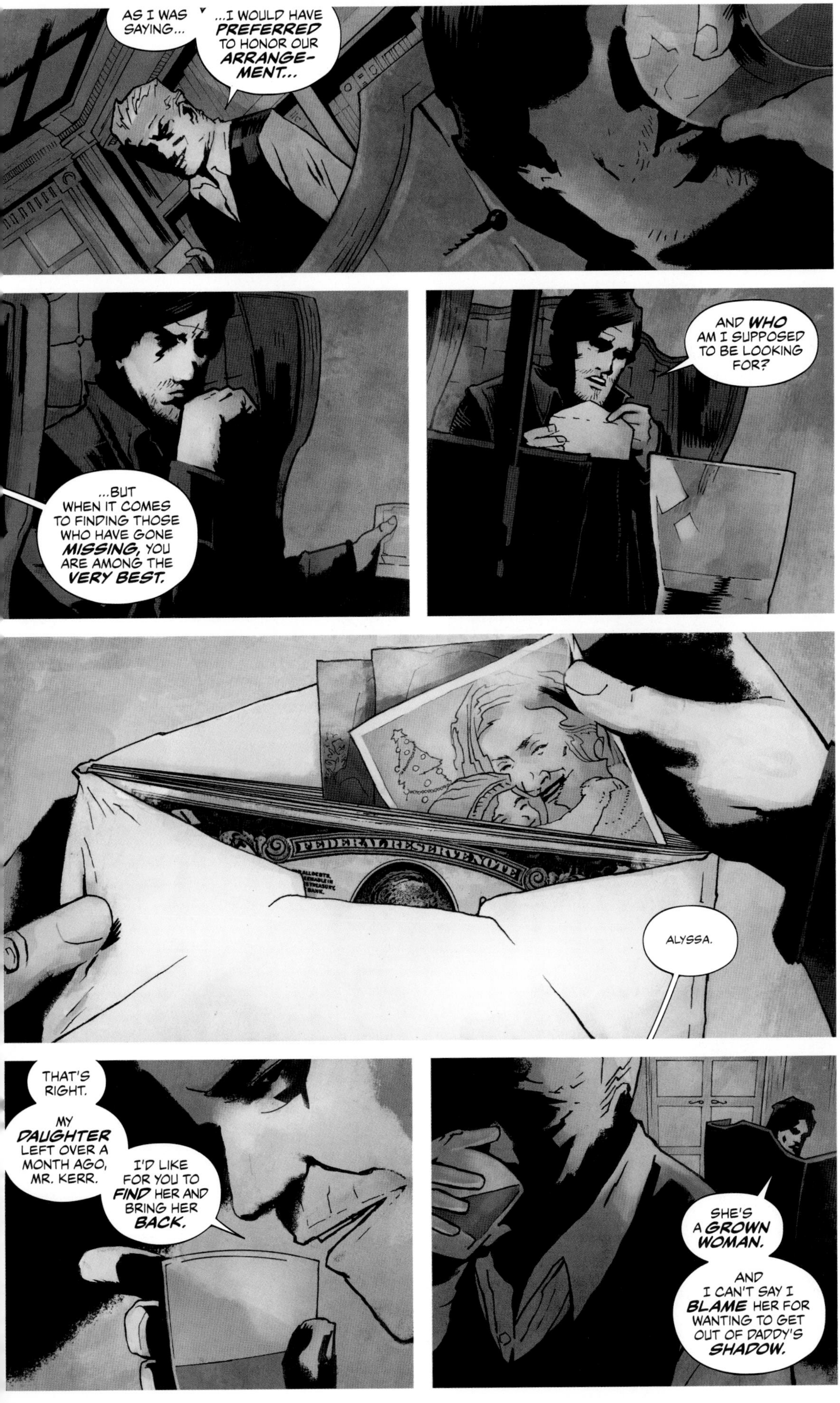

AS I WAS SAYING...
...I WOULD HAVE PREFERRED TO HONOR OUR ARRANGE-MENT...
...BUT WHEN IT COMES TO FINDING THOSE WHO HAVE GONE MISSING, YOU ARE AMONG THE VERY BEST.
AND WHO AM I SUPPOSED TO BE LOOKING FOR?
FEDERAL RESERVE NOTE
ALYSSA.
THAT'S RIGHT.
MY DAUGHTER LEFT OVER A MONTH AGO, MR. KERR.
I'D LIKE FOR YOU TO FIND HER AND BRING HER BACK.
SHE'S A GROWN WOMAN.
AND I CAN'T SAY I BLAME HER FOR WANTING TO GET OUT OF DADDY'S SHADOW.

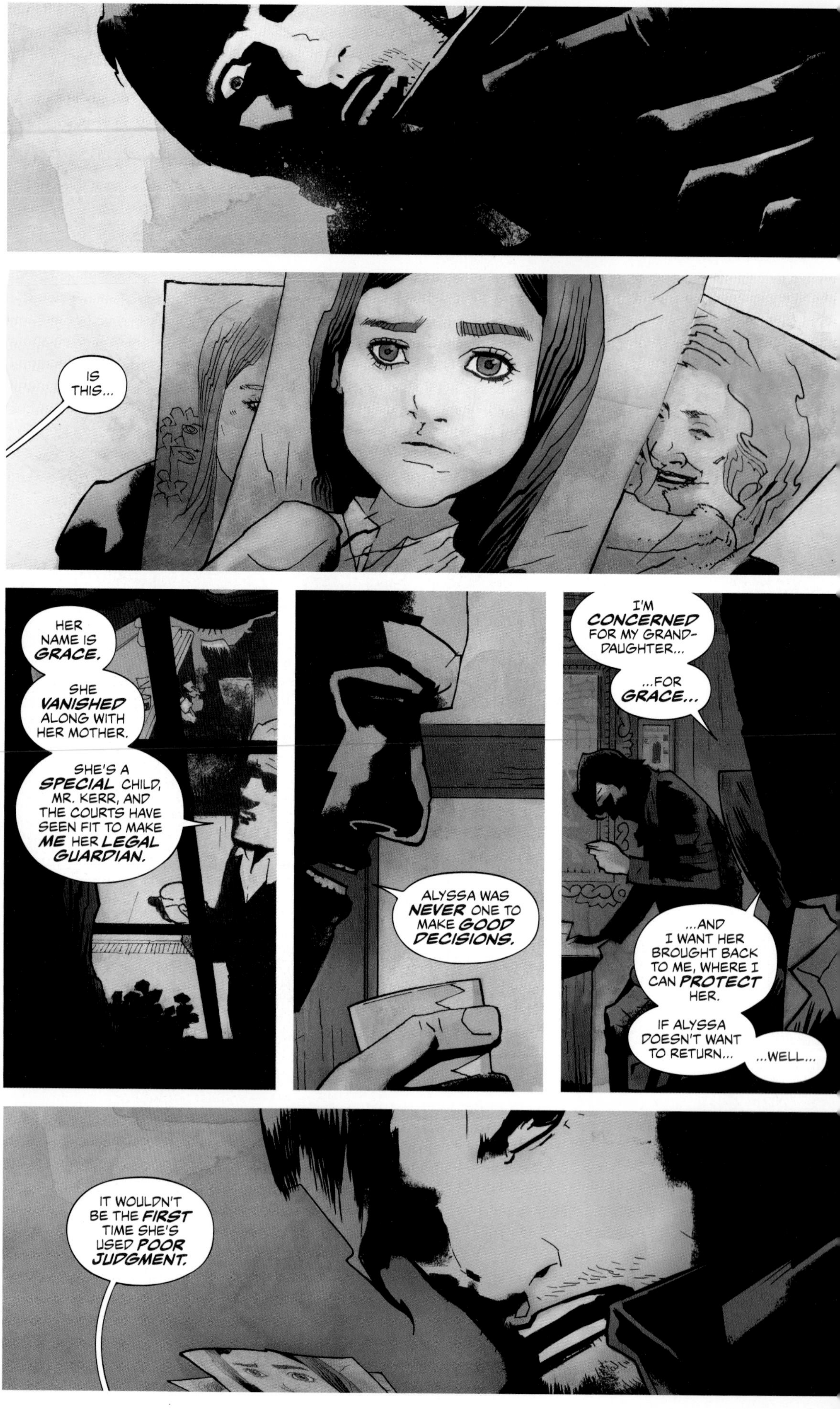
IS THIS...
HER NAME IS GRACE.
SHE VANISHED ALONG WITH HER MOTHER.
SHE'S A SPECIAL CHILD, MR. KERR, AND THE COURTS HAVE SEEN FIT TO MAKE ME HER LEGAL GUARDIAN.
ALYSSA WAS NEVER ONE TO MAKE GOOD DECISIONS.
I'M CONCERNED FOR MY GRAND-DAUGHTER...
...FOR GRACE...
...AND I WANT HER BROUGHT BACK TO ME, WHERE I CAN PROTECT HER.
IF ALYSSA DOESN'T WANT TO RETURN...
...WELL...
IT WOULDN'T BE THE FIRST TIME SHE'S USED POOR JUDGMENT.

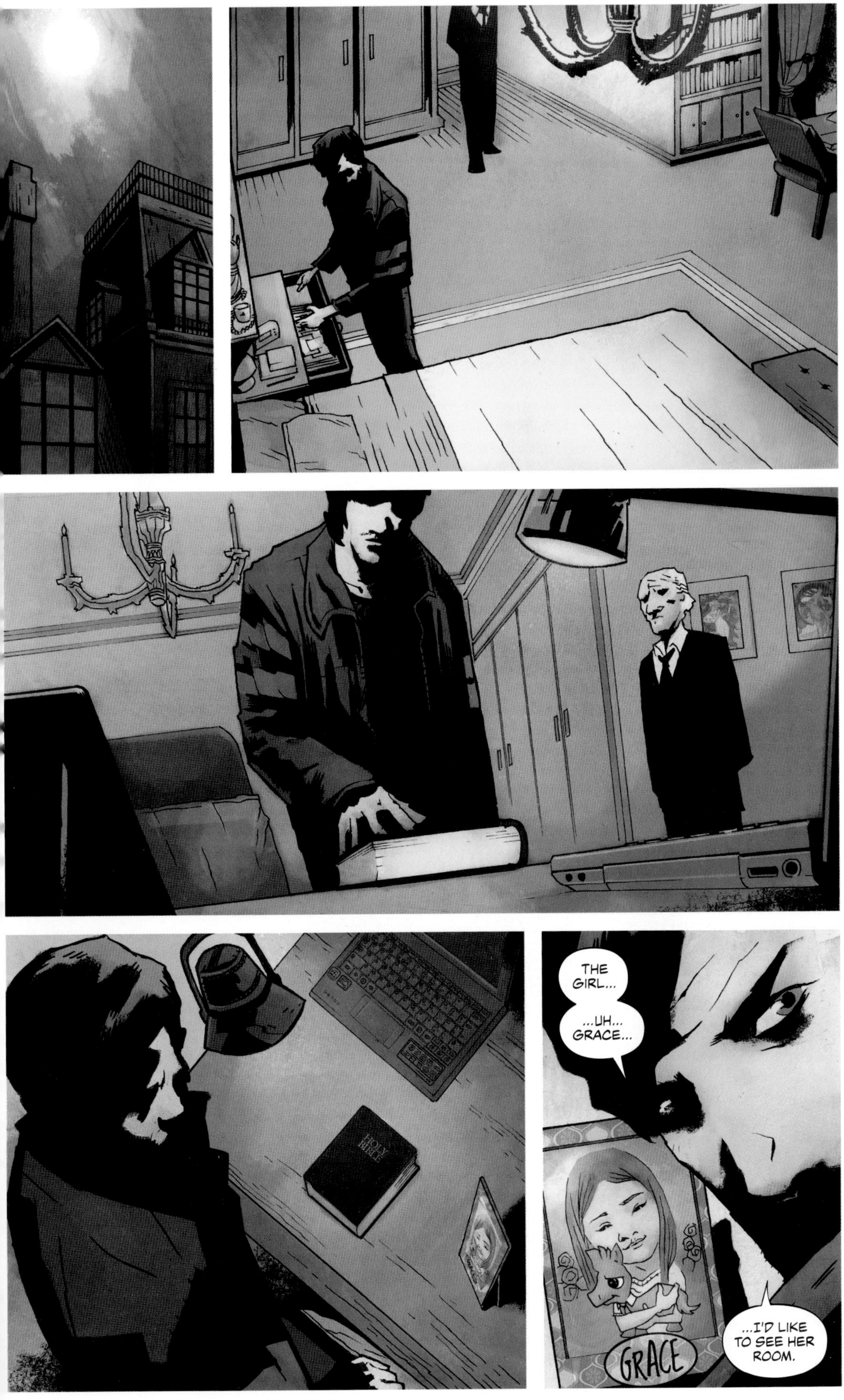
HOLY BIBLE
THE GIRL...
...UH... GRACE...
GRACE
...I'D LIKE TO SEE HER ROOM.

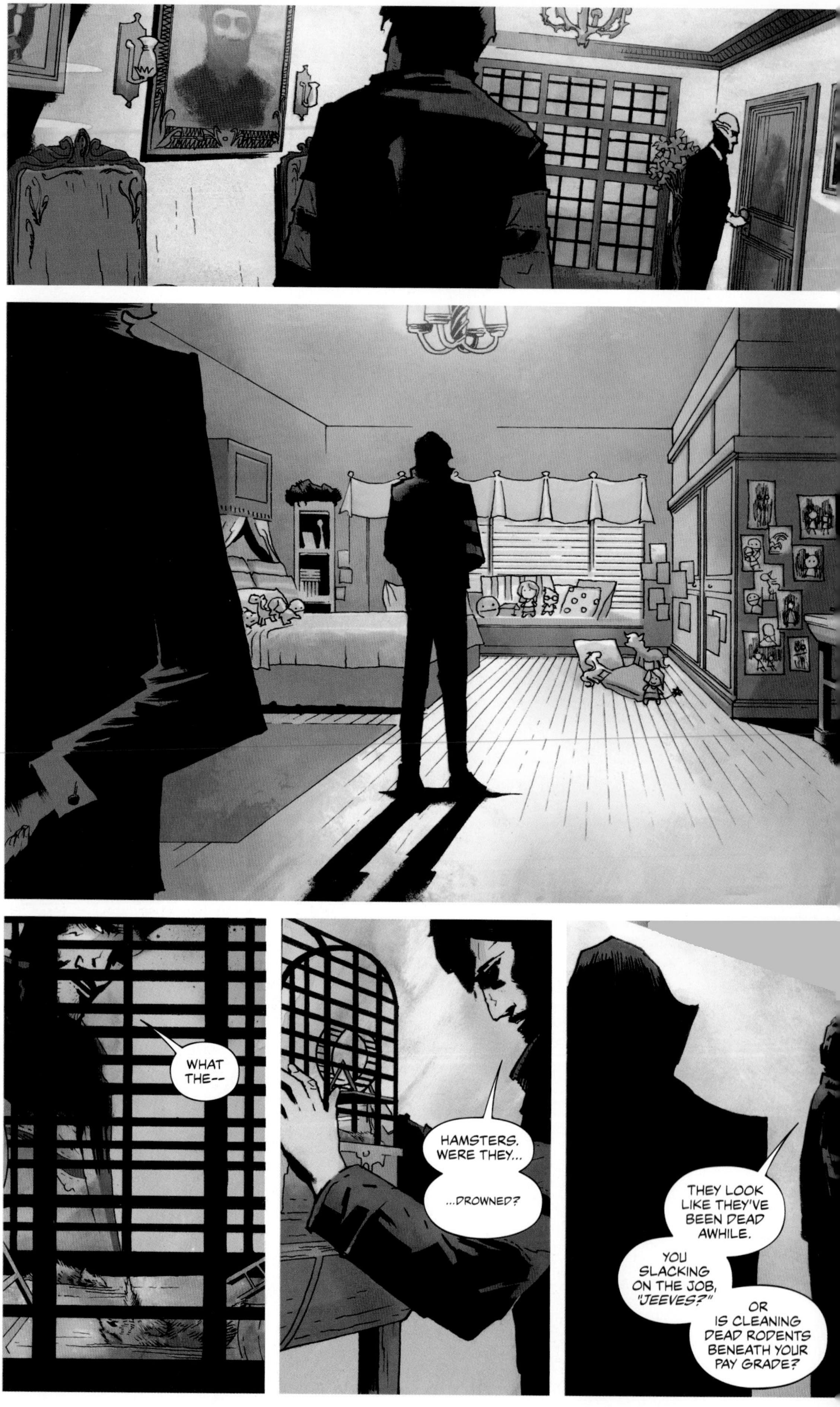
WHAT THE--
HAMSTERS. WERE THEY...
...DROWNED?
THEY LOOK LIKE THEY'VE BEEN DEAD AWHILE.
YOU SLACKING ON THE JOB, "JEEVES?"
OR IS CLEANING DEAD RODENTS BENEATH YOUR PAY GRADE?

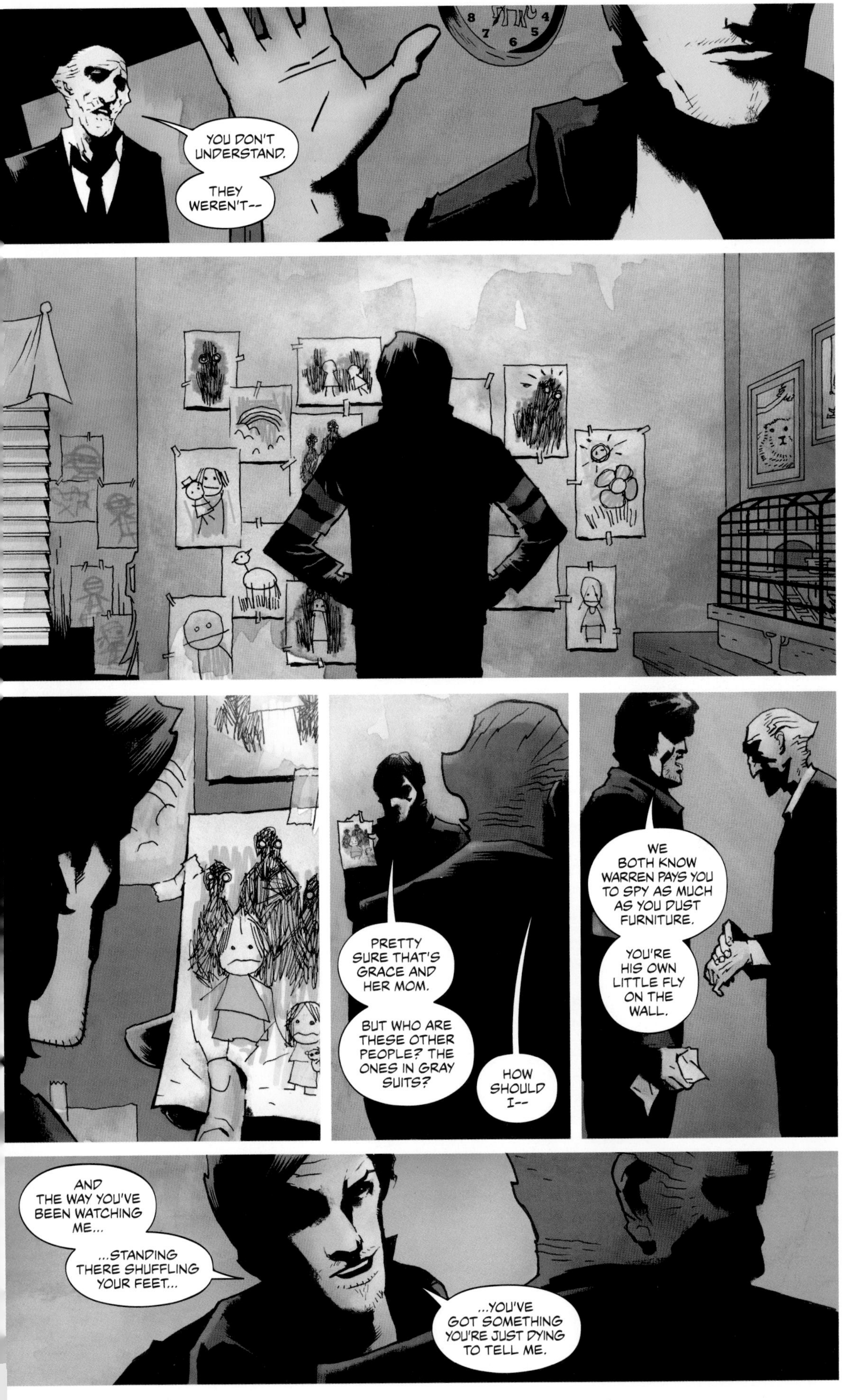
YOU DON'T UNDERSTAND.
THEY WEREN'T--
PRETTY SURE THAT'S GRACE AND HER MOM.
BUT WHO ARE THESE OTHER PEOPLE? THE ONES IN GRAY SUITS?
HOW SHOULD I--
WE BOTH KNOW WARREN PAYS YOU TO SPY AS MUCH AS YOU DUST FURNITURE.
YOU'RE HIS OWN LITTLE FLY ON THE WALL.
AND THE WAY YOU'VE BEEN WATCHING ME...
...STANDING THERE SHUFFLING YOUR FEET...
...YOU'VE GOT SOMETHING YOU'RE JUST DYING TO TELL ME.

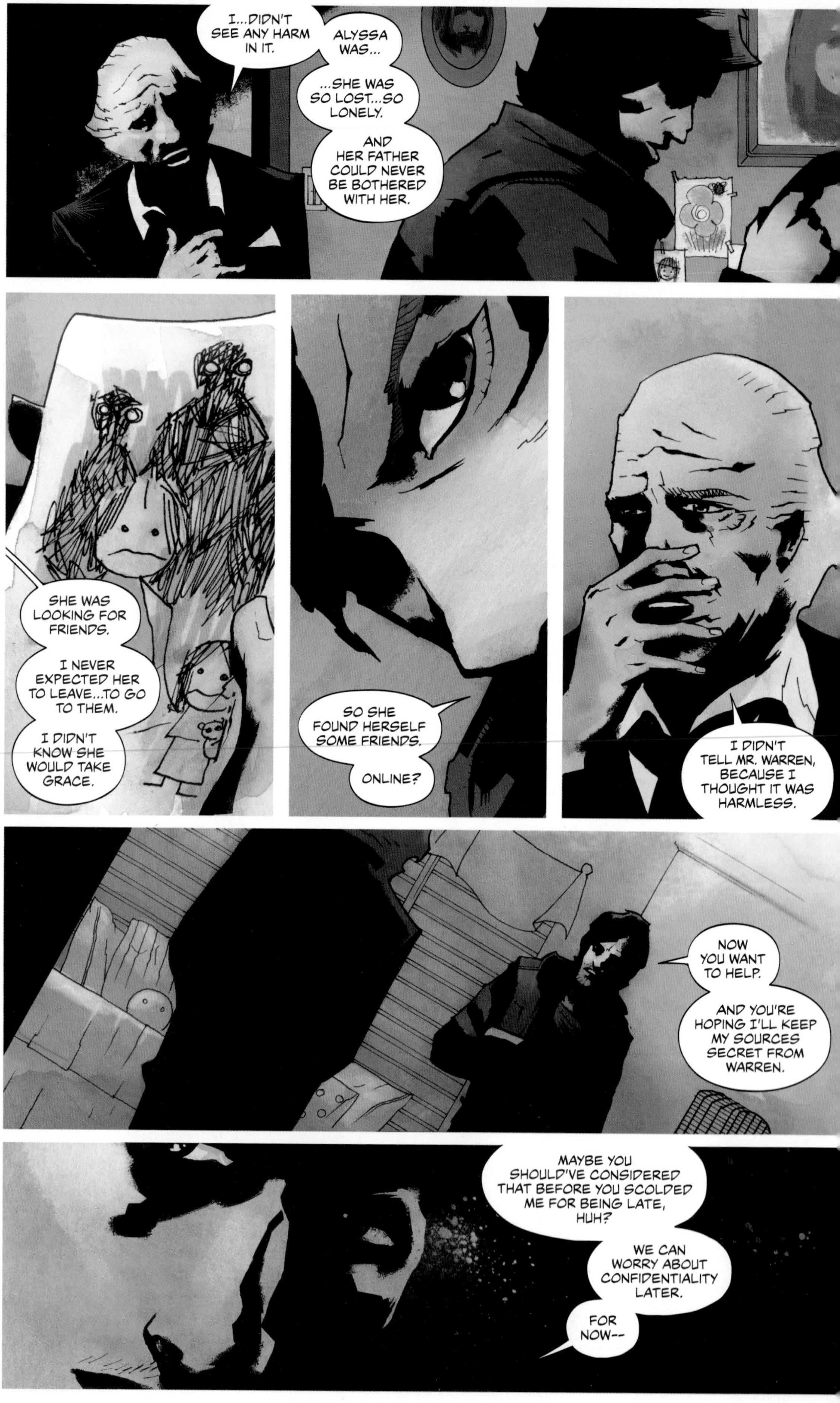
I...DIDN'T SEE ANY HARM IN IT.
ALYSSA WAS...
...SHE WAS SO LOST...SO LONELY.
AND HER FATHER COULD NEVER BE BOTHERED WITH HER.
SHE WAS LOOKING FOR FRIENDS.
I NEVER EXPECTED HER TO LEAVE...TO GO TO THEM.
I DIDN'T KNOW SHE WOULD TAKE GRACE.
SO SHE FOUND HERSELF SOME FRIENDS.
ONLINE?
I DIDN'T TELL MR. WARREN, BECAUSE I THOUGHT IT WAS HARMLESS.
NOW YOU WANT TO HELP.
AND YOU'RE HOPING I'LL KEEP MY SOURCES SECRET FROM WARREN.
MAYBE YOU SHOULD'VE CONSIDERED THAT BEFORE YOU SCOLDED ME FOR BEING LATE, HUH?
WE CAN WORRY ABOUT CONFIDENTIALITY LATER.
FOR NOW--

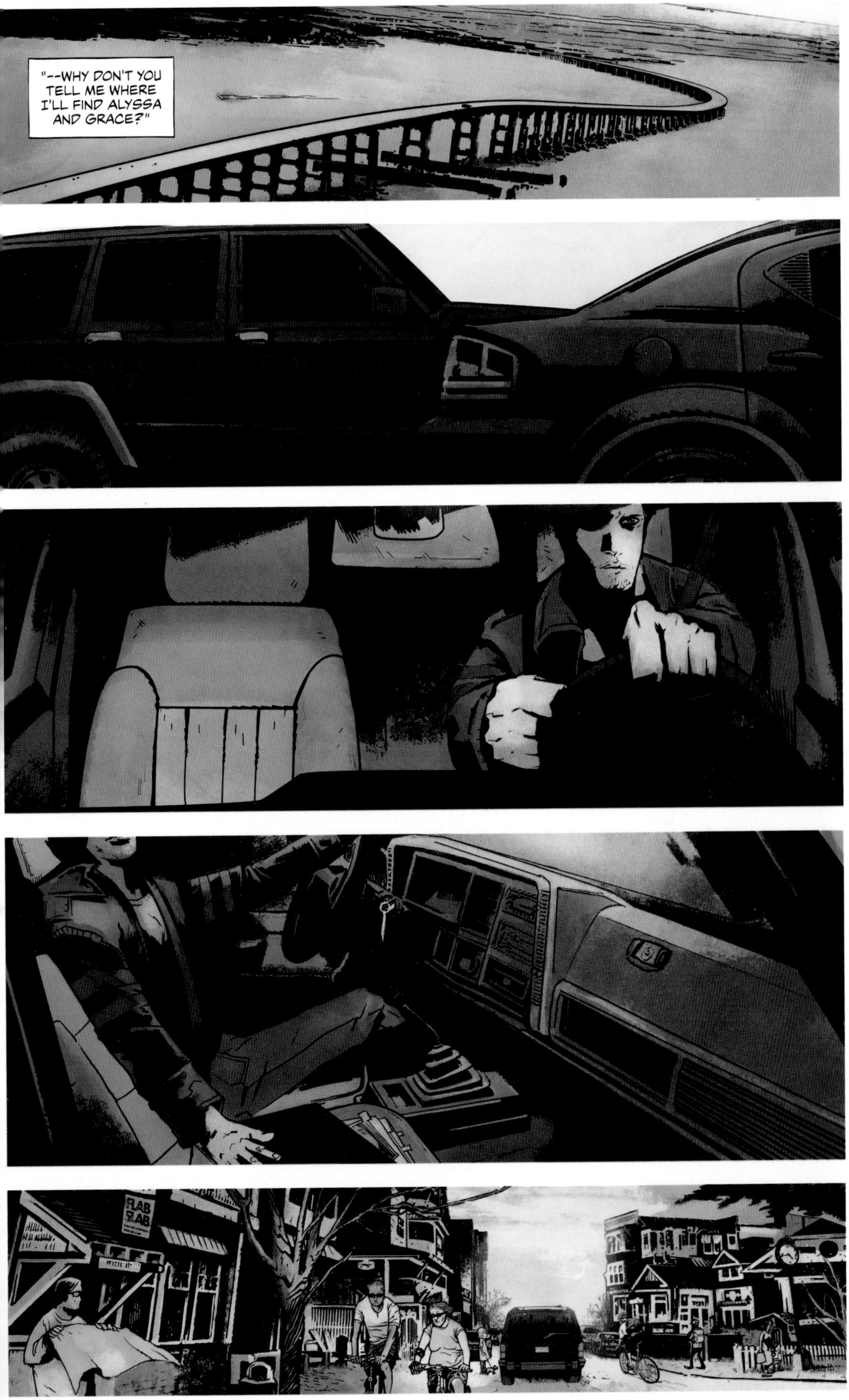
"--WHY DON'T YOU TELL ME WHERE I'LL FIND ALYSSA AND GRACE?"

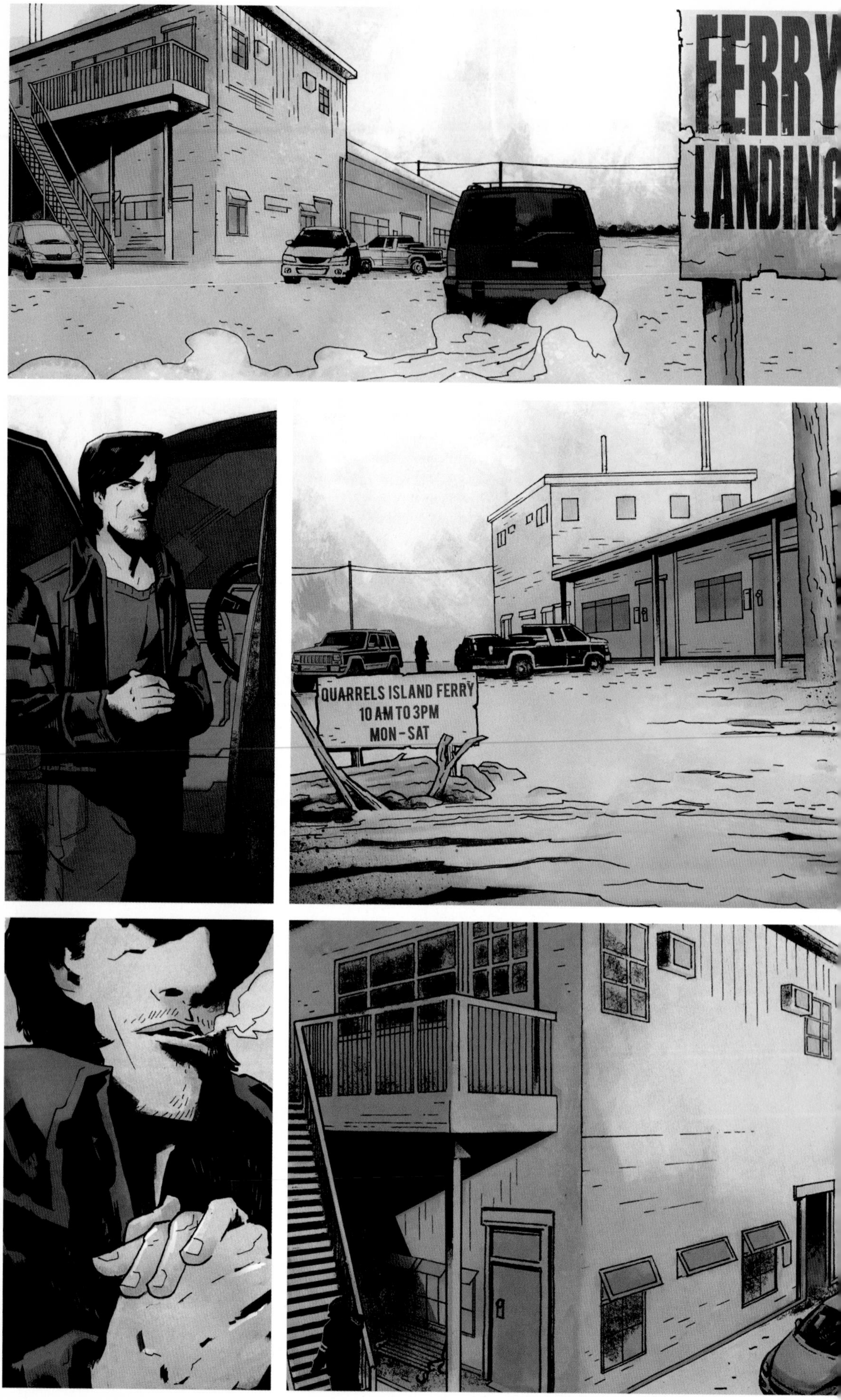
FERRY
LANDING
QUARRELS ISLAND FERRY
10 AM TO 3PM
MON-SAT

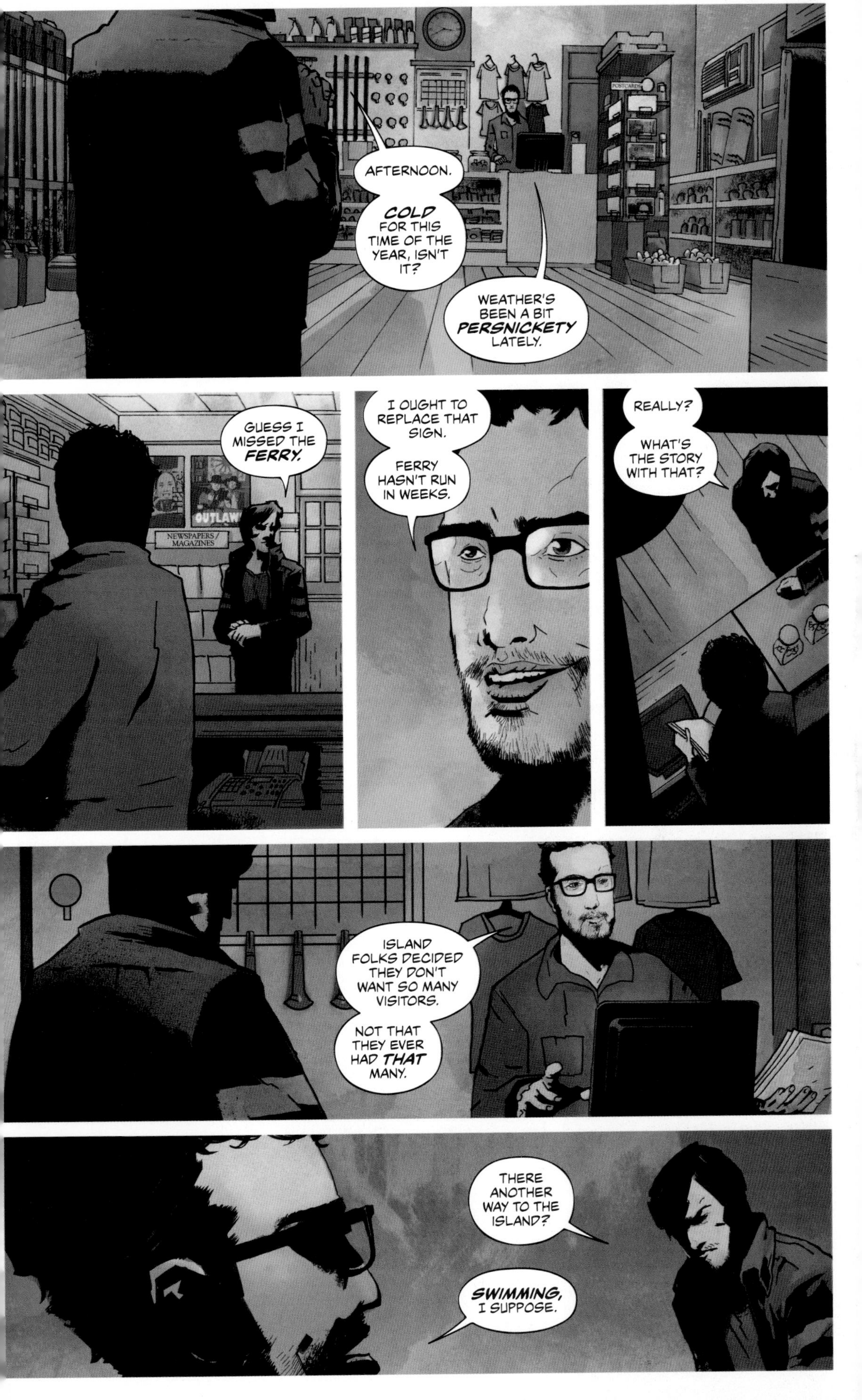
AFTERNOON.
COLD FOR THIS TIME OF THE YEAR, ISN'T IT?
WEATHER'S BEEN A BIT PERSNICKETY LATELY.
OUTLAW
NEWSPAPERS / MAGAZINES
GUESS I MISSED THE FERRY.
I OUGHT TO REPLACE THAT SIGN.
FERRY HASN'T RUN IN WEEKS.
REALLY?
WHAT'S THE STORY WITH THAT?
ISLAND FOLKS DECIDED THEY DON'T WANT SO MANY VISITORS.
NOT THAT THEY EVER HAD THAT MANY.
THERE ANOTHER WAY TO THE ISLAND?
SWIMMING, I SUPPOSE.

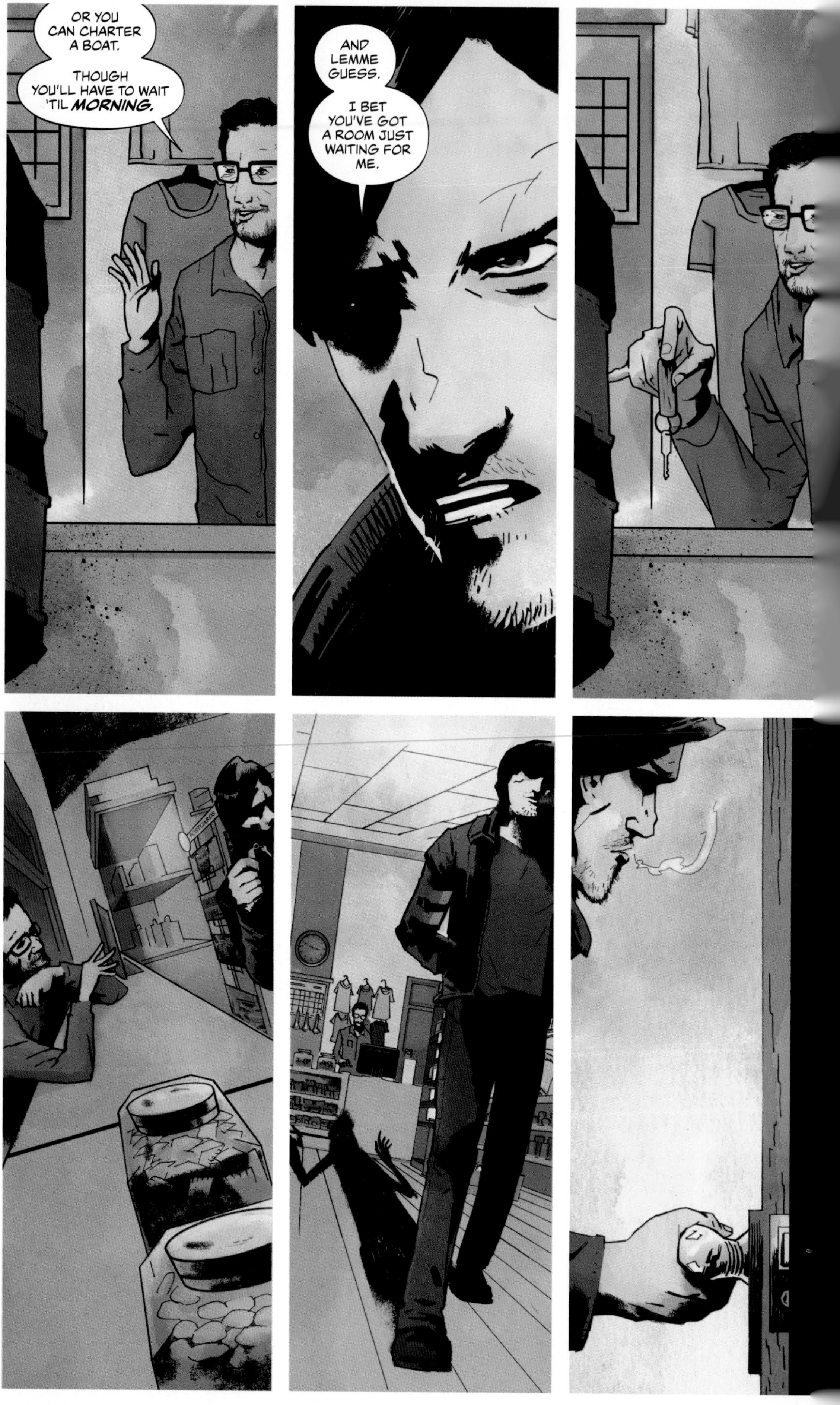
OR YOU CAN CHARTER A BOAT.
THOUGH YOU'LL HAVE TO WAIT 'TIL ***MORNING.***
AND LEMME GUESS.
I BET YOU'VE GOT A ROOM JUST WAITING FOR ME.
POSTCARDS

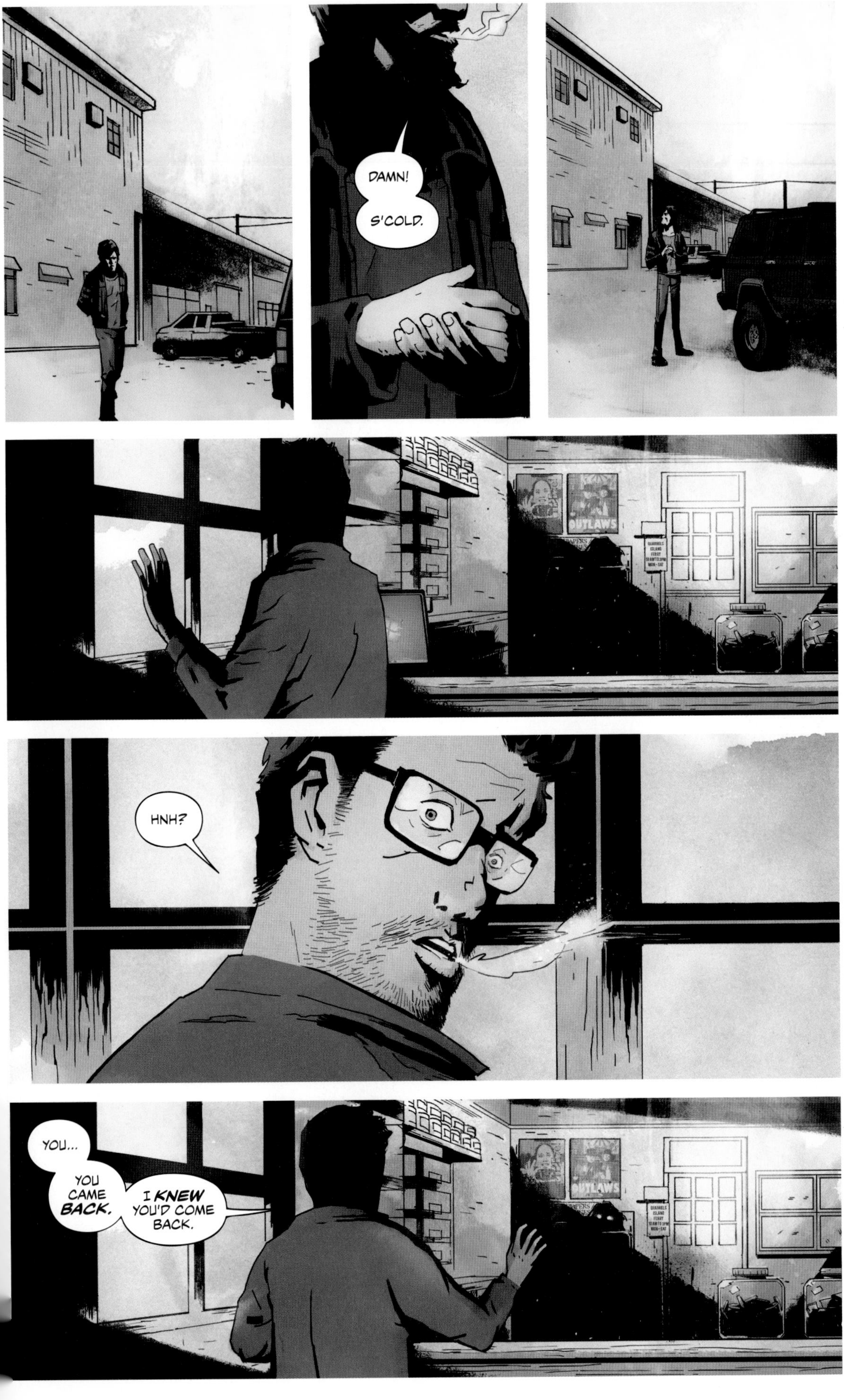
DAMN!
S'COLD.
OUTLAWS
HNH?
YOU...
YOU CAME BACK.
I KNEW YOU'D COME BACK.

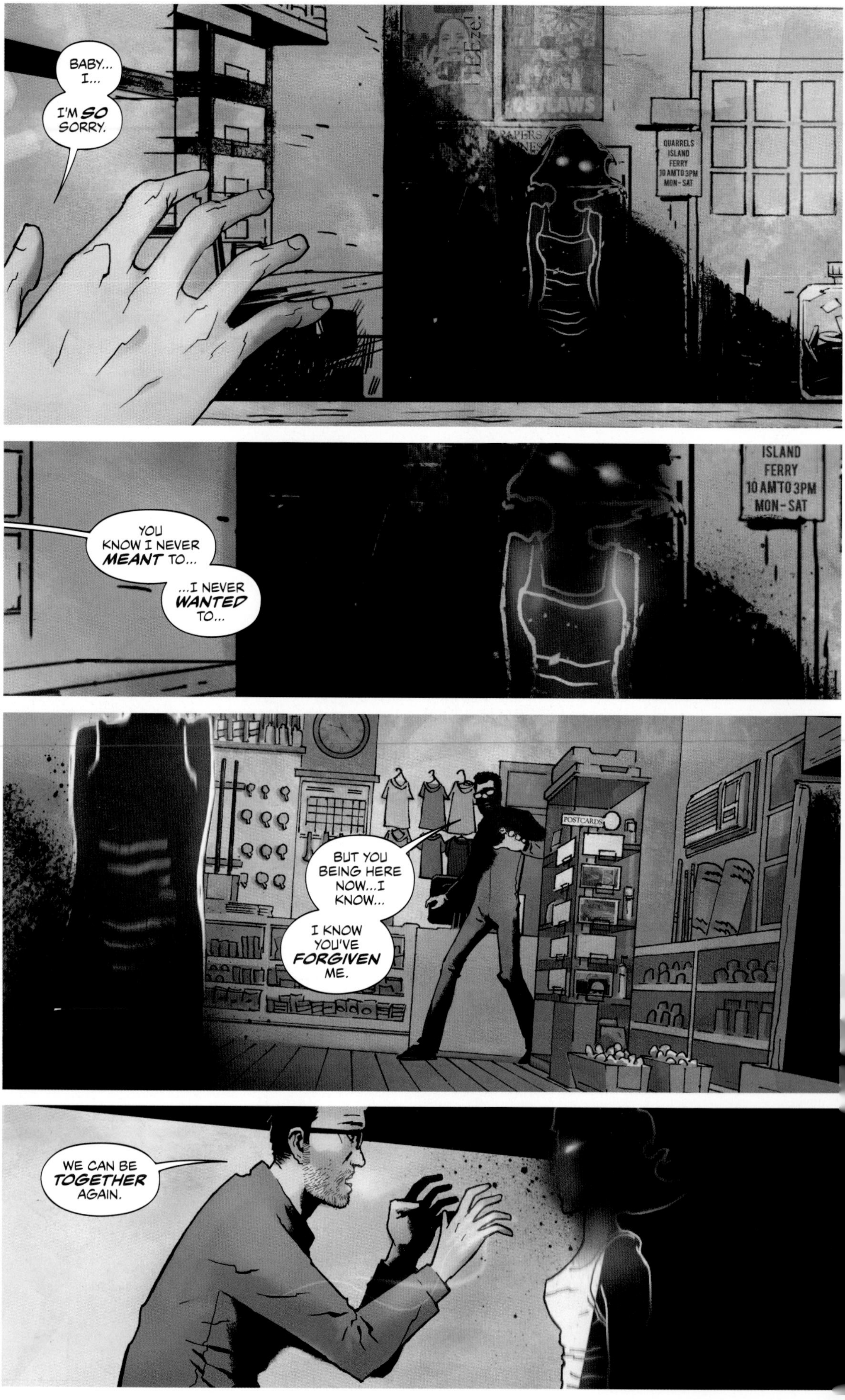
BABY... I...
I'M **SO** SORRY.
QUARRELS ISLAND FERRY 10 AM TO 3PM MON-SAT
YOU KNOW I NEVER **MEANT** TO...
...I NEVER **WANTED** TO...
ISLAND FERRY 10 AM TO 3PM MON-SAT
POSTCARDS
BUT YOU BEING HERE NOW...I KNOW...
I KNOW YOU'VE **FORGIVEN** ME.
WE CAN BE **TOGETHER** AGAIN.

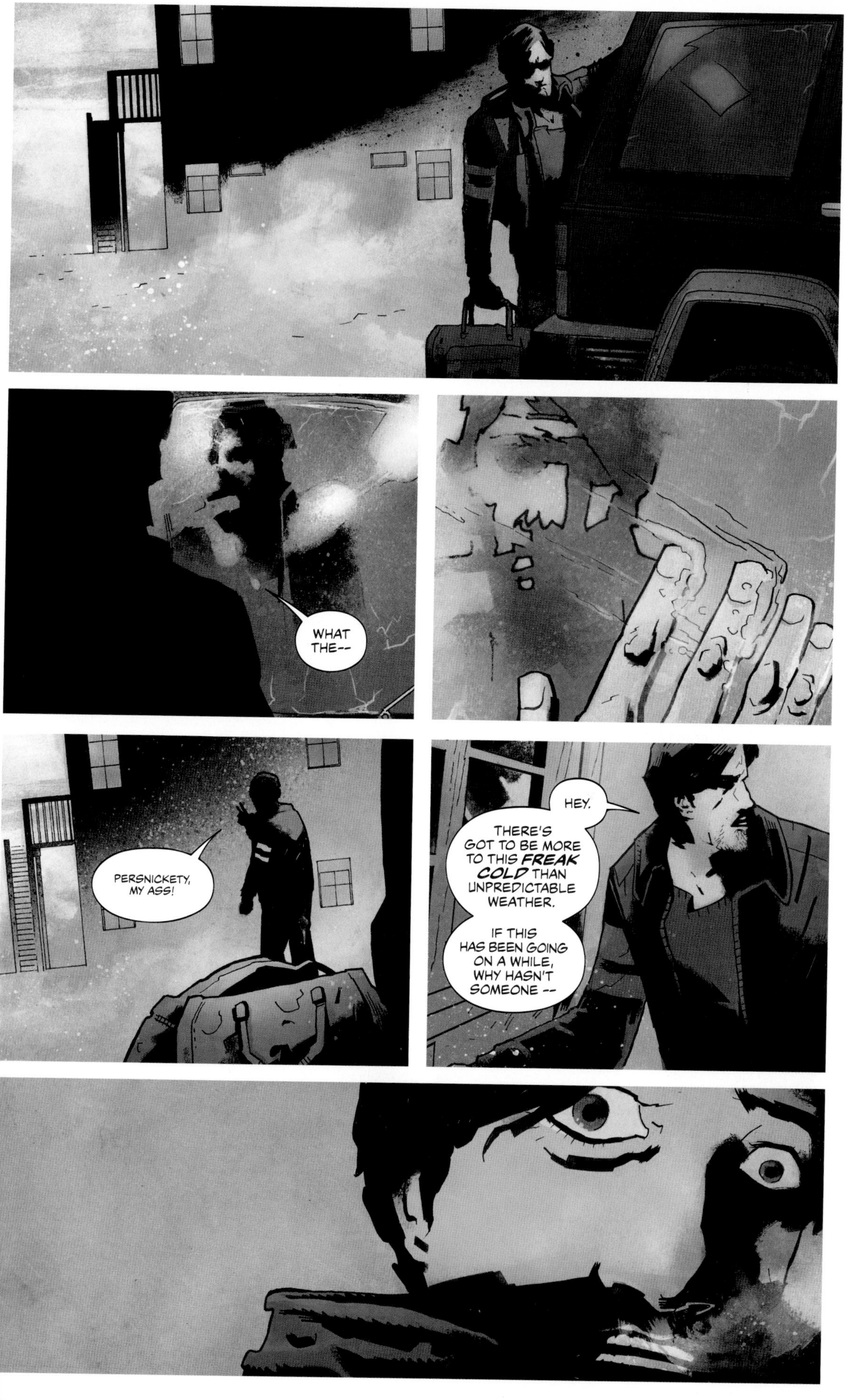
WHAT THE--
PERSNICKETY, MY ASS!
HEY.
THERE'S GOT TO BE MORE TO THIS FREAK COLD THAN UNPREDICTABLE WEATHER.
IF THIS HAS BEEN GOING ON A WHILE, WHY HASN'T SOMEONE --

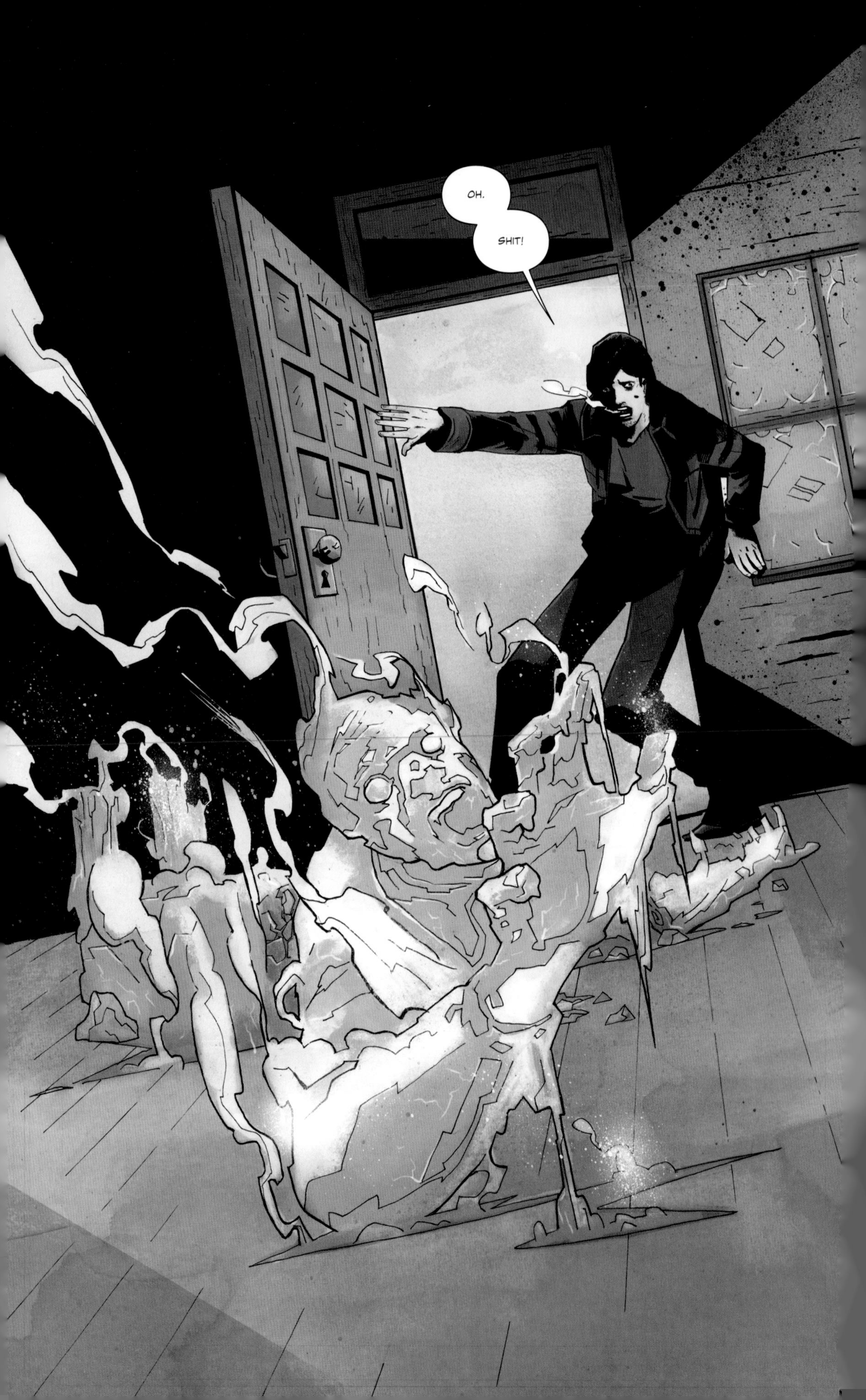
OH.
SHIT!

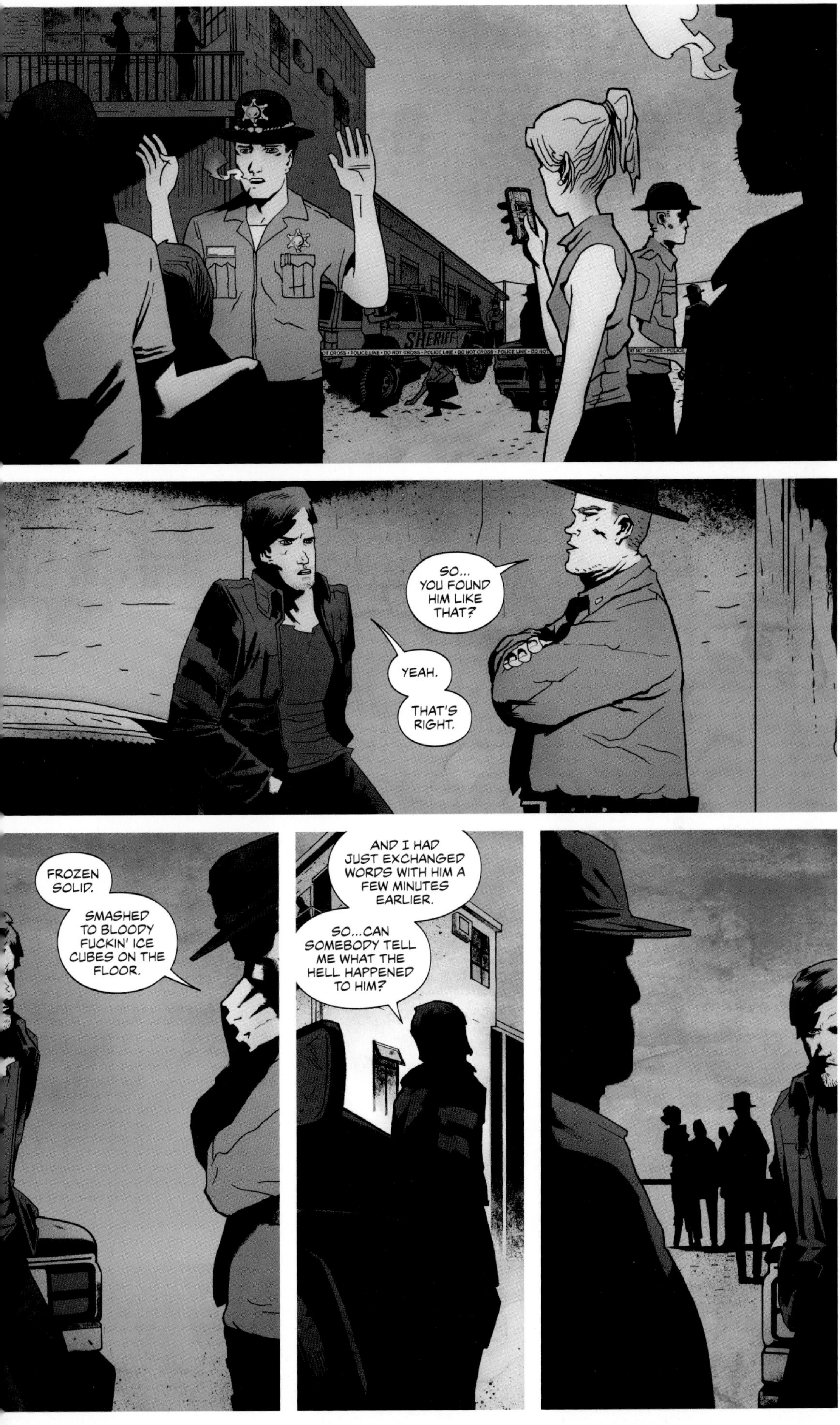
SHERIFF
SO... YOU FOUND HIM LIKE THAT?
YEAH.
THAT'S RIGHT.
FROZEN SOLID.
SMASHED TO BLOODY FUCKIN' ICE CUBES ON THE FLOOR.
AND I HAD JUST EXCHANGED WORDS WITH HIM A FEW MINUTES EARLIER.
SO...CAN SOMEBODY TELL ME WHAT THE HELL HAPPENED TO HIM?

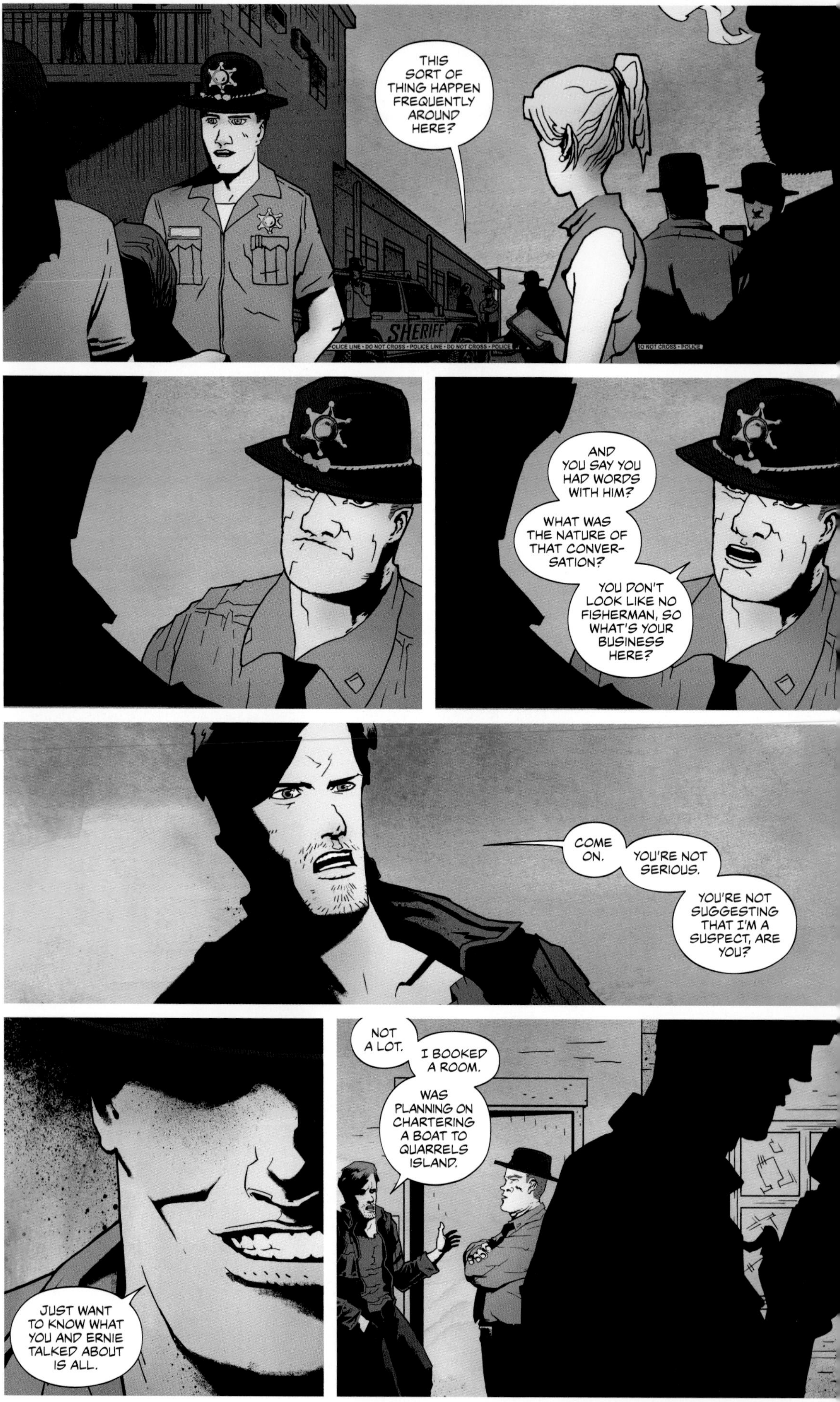
THIS SORT OF THING HAPPEN FREQUENTLY AROUND HERE?
SHERIFF
POLICE LINE • DO NOT CROSS • POLICE LINE • DO NOT CROSS • POLICE
DO NOT CROSS • POLICE
AND YOU SAY YOU HAD WORDS WITH HIM?
WHAT WAS THE NATURE OF THAT CONVERSATION?
YOU DON'T LOOK LIKE NO FISHERMAN, SO WHAT'S YOUR BUSINESS HERE?
COME ON.
YOU'RE NOT SERIOUS.
YOU'RE NOT SUGGESTING THAT I'M A SUSPECT, ARE YOU?
JUST WANT TO KNOW WHAT YOU AND ERNIE TALKED ABOUT IS ALL.
NOT A LOT.
I BOOKED A ROOM.
WAS PLANNING ON CHARTERING A BOAT TO QUARRELS ISLAND.

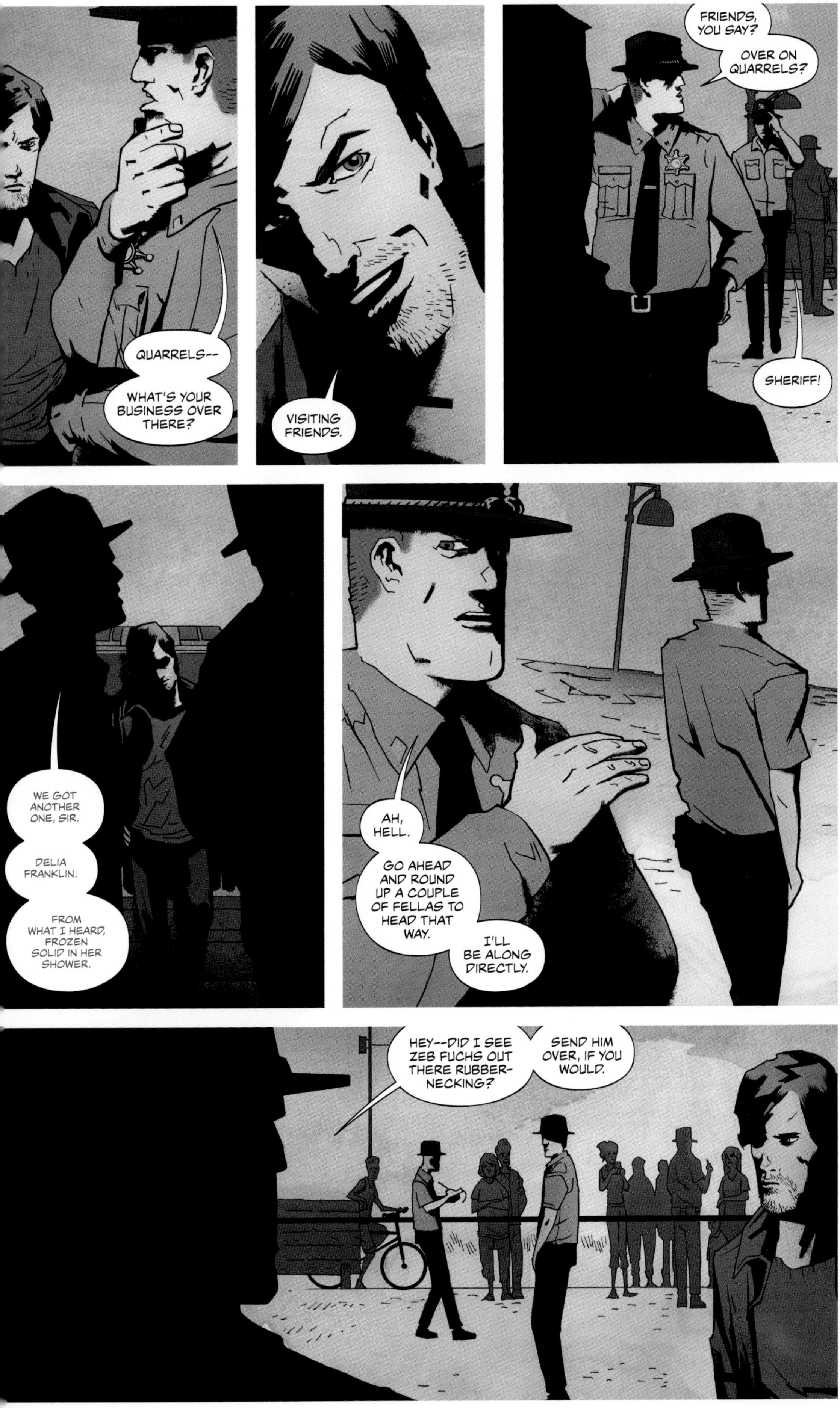
QUARRELS--
WHAT'S YOUR BUSINESS OVER THERE?
VISITING FRIENDS.
FRIENDS, YOU SAY?
OVER ON QUARRELS?
SHERIFF!
WE GOT ANOTHER ONE, SIR.
DELIA FRANKLIN.
FROM WHAT I HEARD, FROZEN SOLID IN HER SHOWER.
AH, HELL.
GO AHEAD AND ROUND UP A COUPLE OF FELLAS TO HEAD THAT WAY.
I'LL BE ALONG DIRECTLY.
HEY--DID I SEE ZEB FUCHS OUT THERE RUBBER-NECKING?
SEND HIM OVER, IF YOU WOULD.

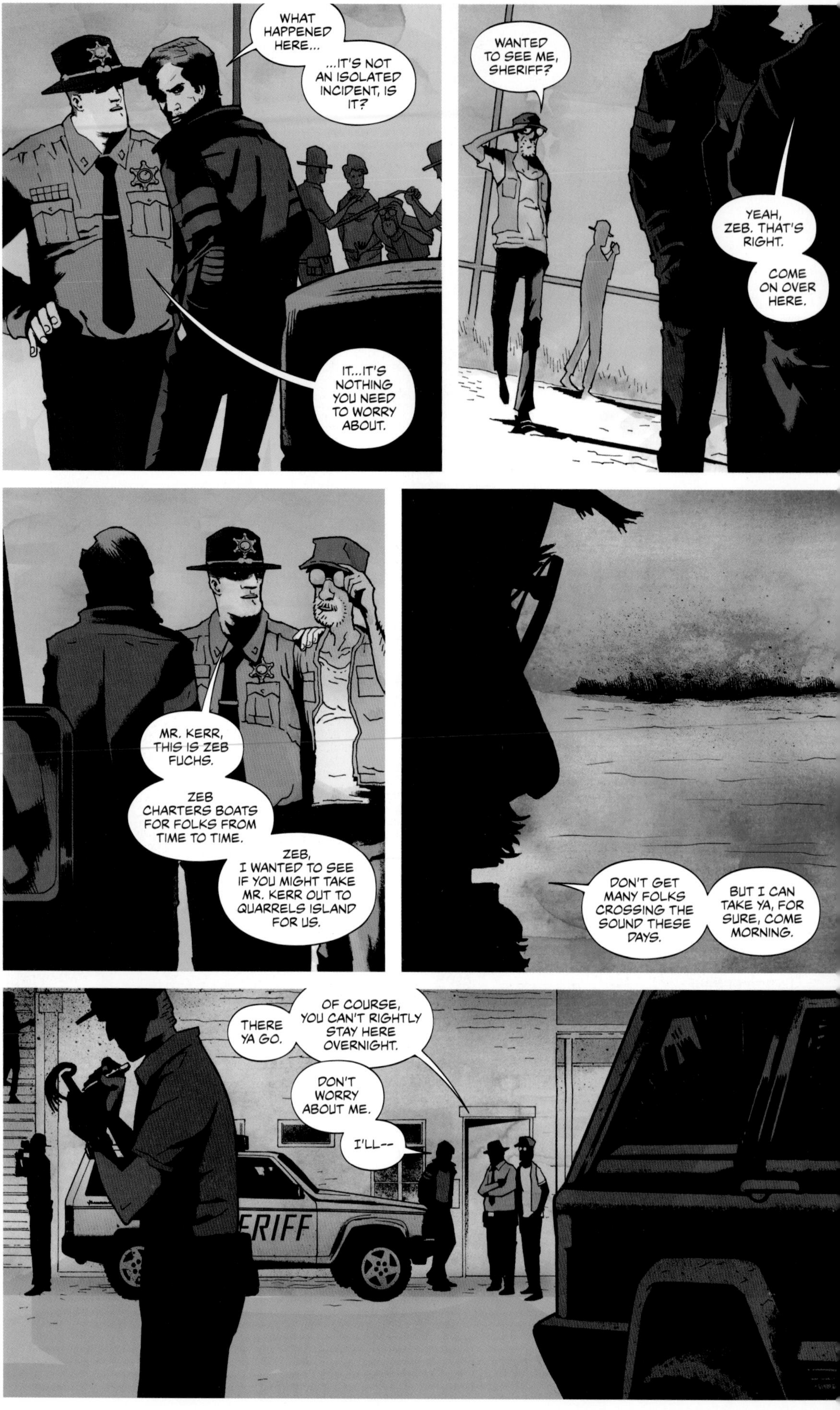
WHAT HAPPENED HERE...
...IT'S NOT AN ISOLATED INCIDENT, IS IT?
IT...IT'S NOTHING YOU NEED TO WORRY ABOUT.
WANTED TO SEE ME, SHERIFF?
YEAH, ZEB. THAT'S RIGHT.
COME ON OVER HERE.
MR. KERR, THIS IS ZEB FUCHS.
ZEB CHARTERS BOATS FOR FOLKS FROM TIME TO TIME.
ZEB, I WANTED TO SEE IF YOU MIGHT TAKE MR. KERR OUT TO QUARRELS ISLAND FOR US.
DON'T GET MANY FOLKS CROSSING THE SOUND THESE DAYS.
BUT I CAN TAKE YA, FOR SURE, COME MORNING.
THERE YA GO.
OF COURSE, YOU CAN'T RIGHTLY STAY HERE OVERNIGHT.
DON'T WORRY ABOUT ME.
I'LL--
ERIFF

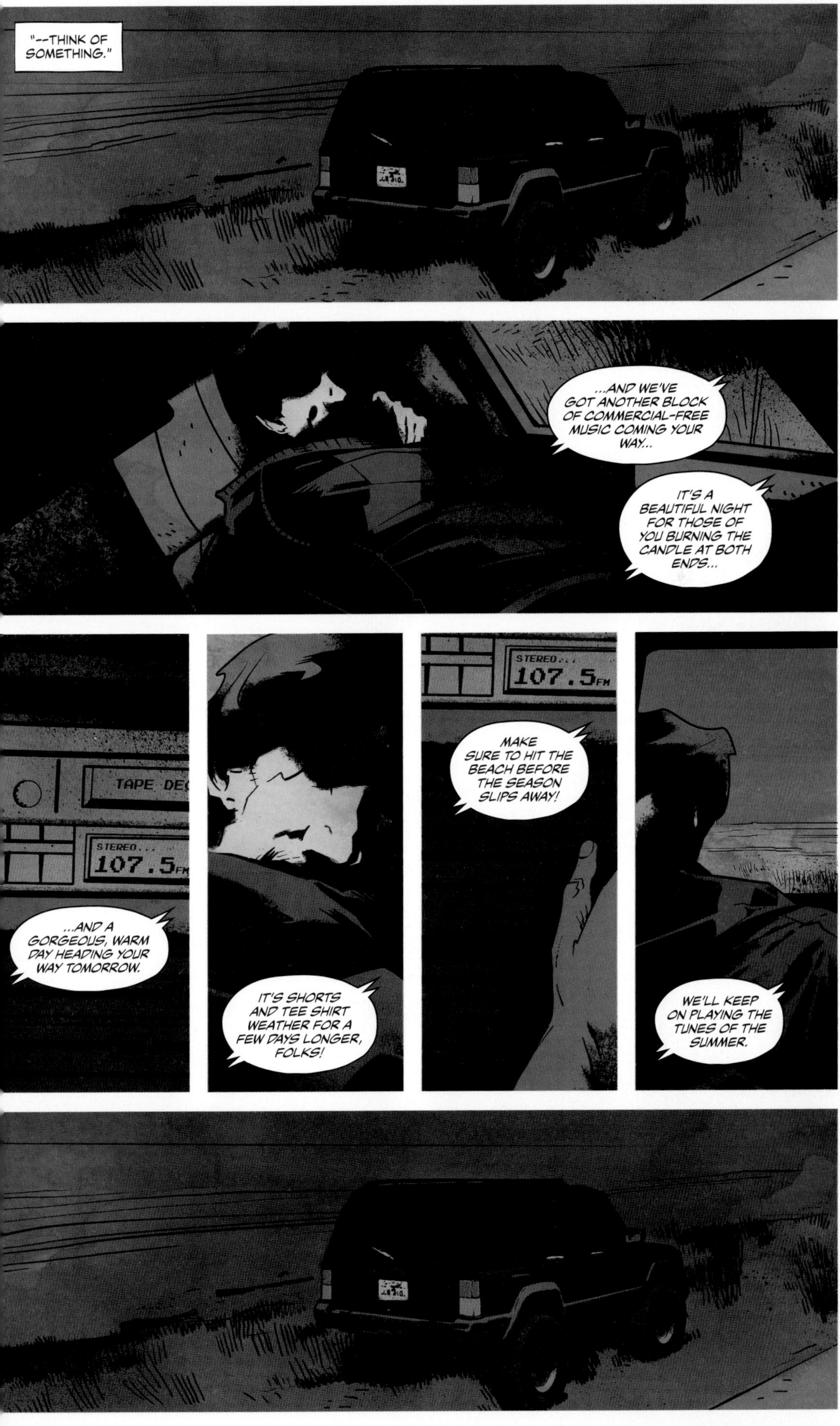
"--THINK OF SOMETHING."
...AND WE'VE GOT ANOTHER BLOCK OF COMMERCIAL-FREE MUSIC COMING YOUR WAY...
IT'S A BEAUTIFUL NIGHT FOR THOSE OF YOU BURNING THE CANDLE AT BOTH ENDS...
TAPE DEC
STEREO...
107.5FM
...AND A GORGEOUS, WARM DAY HEADING YOUR WAY TOMORROW.
IT'S SHORTS AND TEE SHIRT WEATHER FOR A FEW DAYS LONGER, FOLKS!
STEREO...
107.5FM
MAKE SURE TO HIT THE BEACH BEFORE THE SEASON SLIPS AWAY!
WE'LL KEEP ON PLAYING THE TUNES OF THE SUMMER.

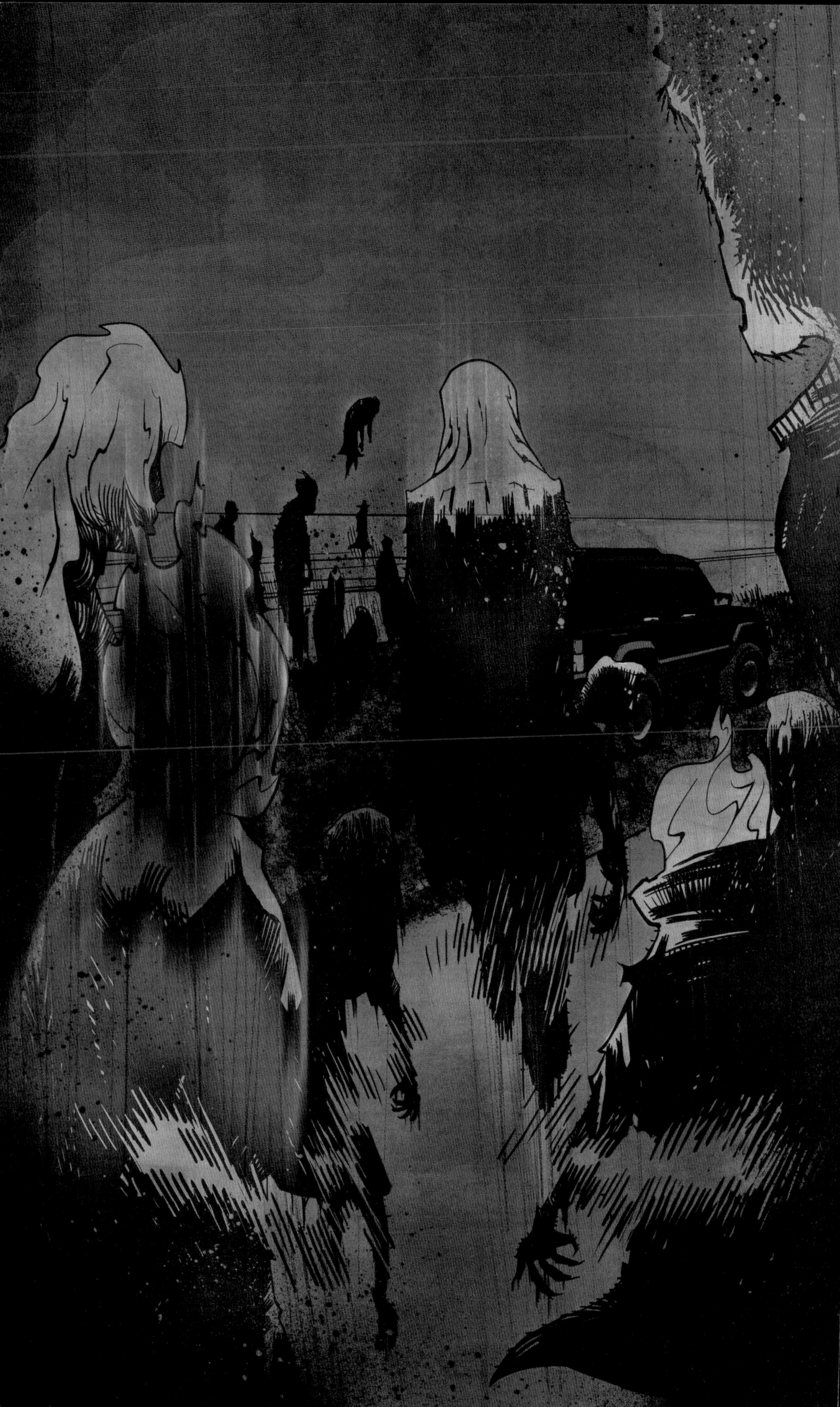

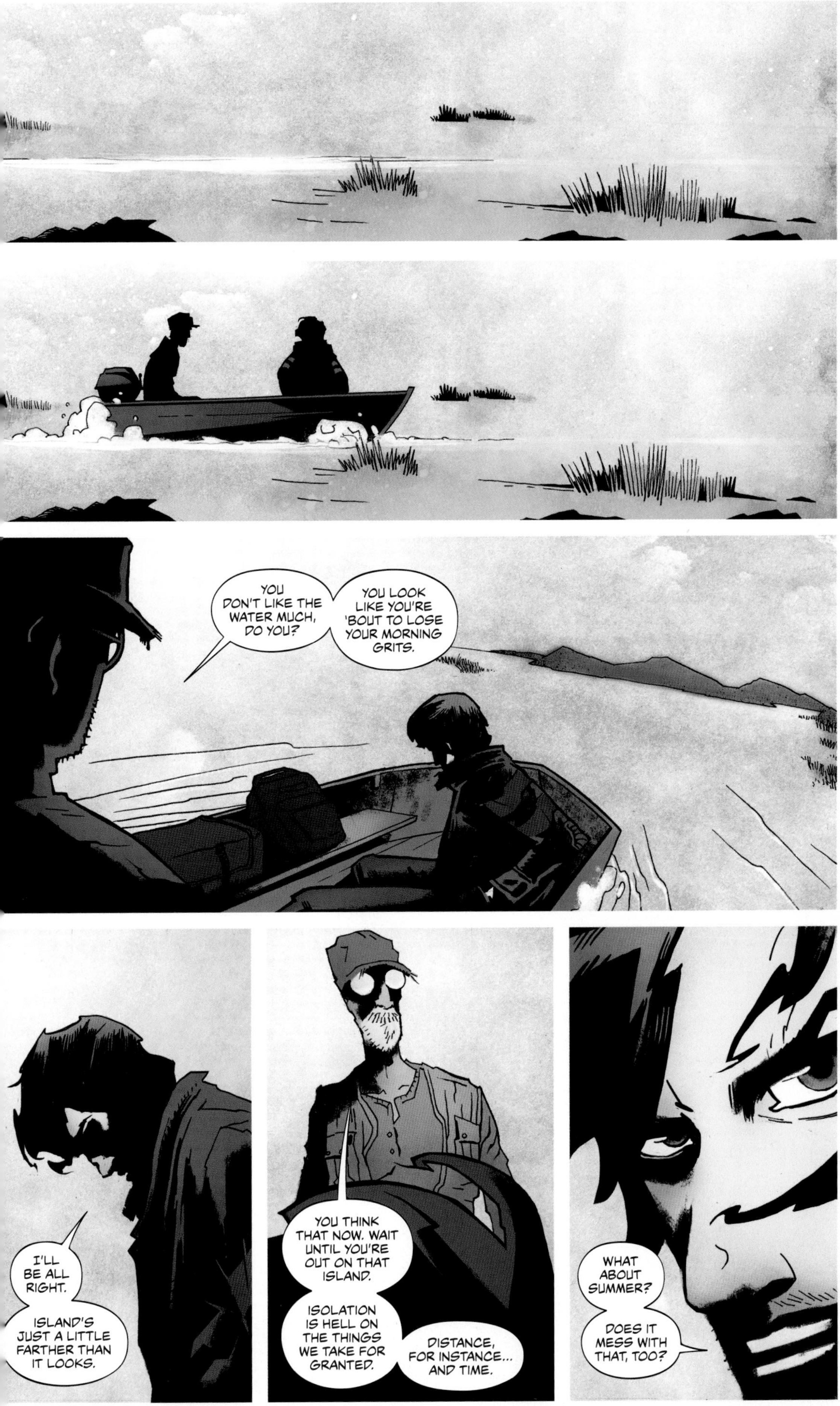
YOU DON'T LIKE THE WATER MUCH, DO YOU?
YOU LOOK LIKE YOU'RE 'BOUT TO LOSE YOUR MORNING GRITS.
I'LL BE ALL RIGHT.
ISLAND'S JUST A LITTLE FARTHER THAN IT LOOKS.
YOU THINK THAT NOW. WAIT UNTIL YOU'RE OUT ON THAT ISLAND.
ISOLATION IS HELL ON THE THINGS WE TAKE FOR GRANTED.
DISTANCE, FOR INSTANCE... AND TIME.
WHAT ABOUT SUMMER?
DOES IT MESS WITH THAT, TOO?

I WAS LISTENING TO THE RADIO LAST NIGHT.

NOT A LOCAL STATION.

MAYBE AN HOUR OR TWO AWAY.

THE WEATHER REPORT WAS CALLING FOR HIGH TEMPERATURES.

JUST AN HOUR AWAY.

SO WHY IS IT SO COLD HERE?

I DON'T KNOW WHAT TO TELL YOU.

BUT WE'RE HERE.

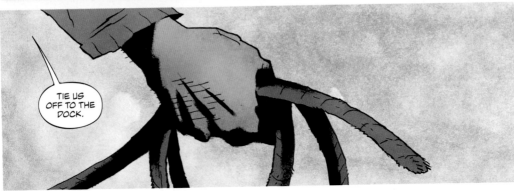

TIE US OFF TO THE DOCK.

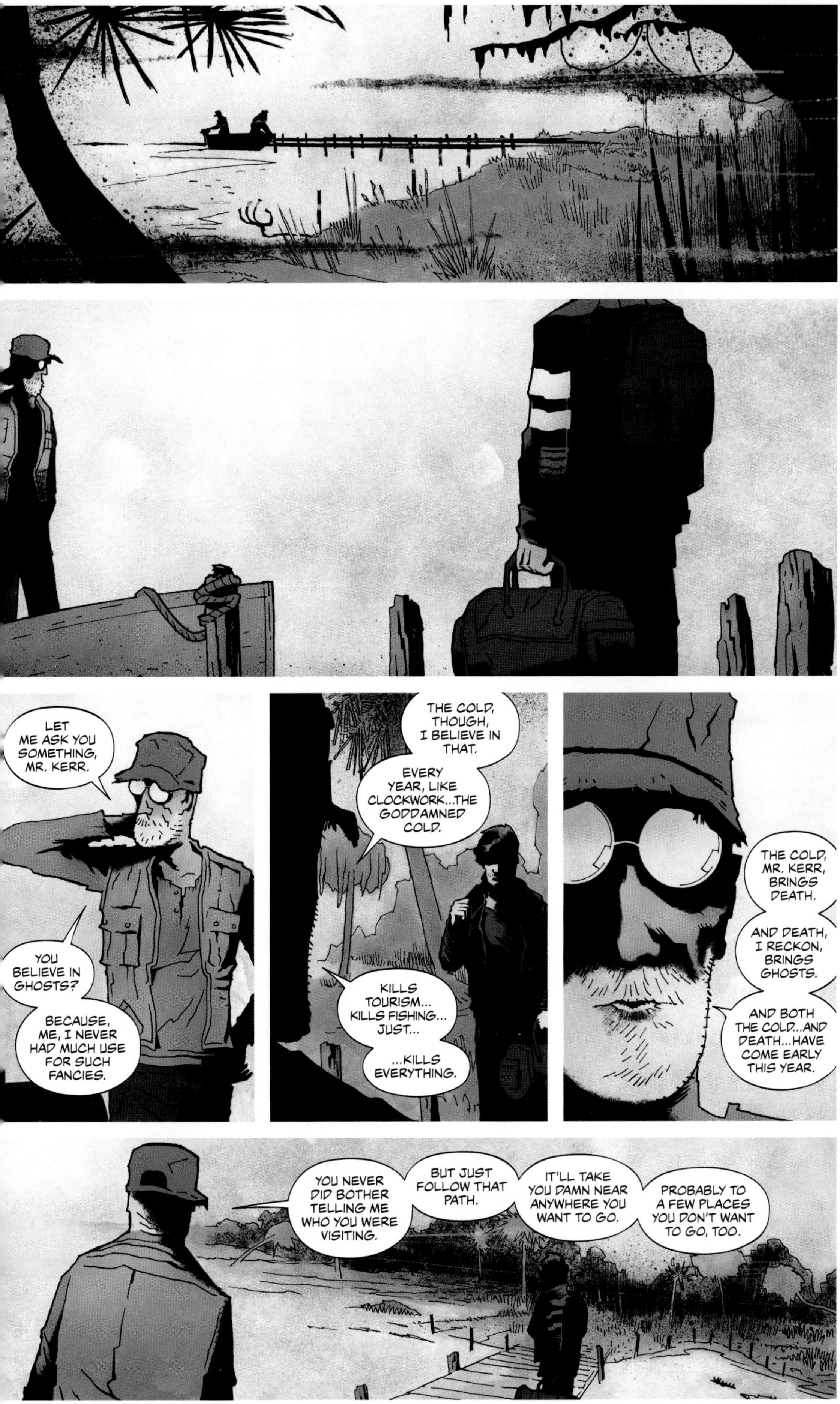
LET ME ASK YOU SOMETHING, MR. KERR.
YOU BELIEVE IN GHOSTS?
BECAUSE, ME, I NEVER HAD MUCH USE FOR SUCH FANCIES.
THE COLD, THOUGH, I BELIEVE IN THAT.
EVERY YEAR, LIKE CLOCKWORK...THE GODDAMNED COLD.
KILLS TOURISM... KILLS FISHING... JUST...
...KILLS EVERYTHING.
THE COLD, MR. KERR, BRINGS DEATH.
AND DEATH, I RECKON, BRINGS GHOSTS.
AND BOTH THE COLD...AND DEATH...HAVE COME EARLY THIS YEAR.
YOU NEVER DID BOTHER TELLING ME WHO YOU WERE VISITING.
BUT JUST FOLLOW THAT PATH.
IT'LL TAKE YOU DAMN NEAR ANYWHERE YOU WANT TO GO.
PROBABLY TO A FEW PLACES YOU DON'T WANT TO GO, TOO.

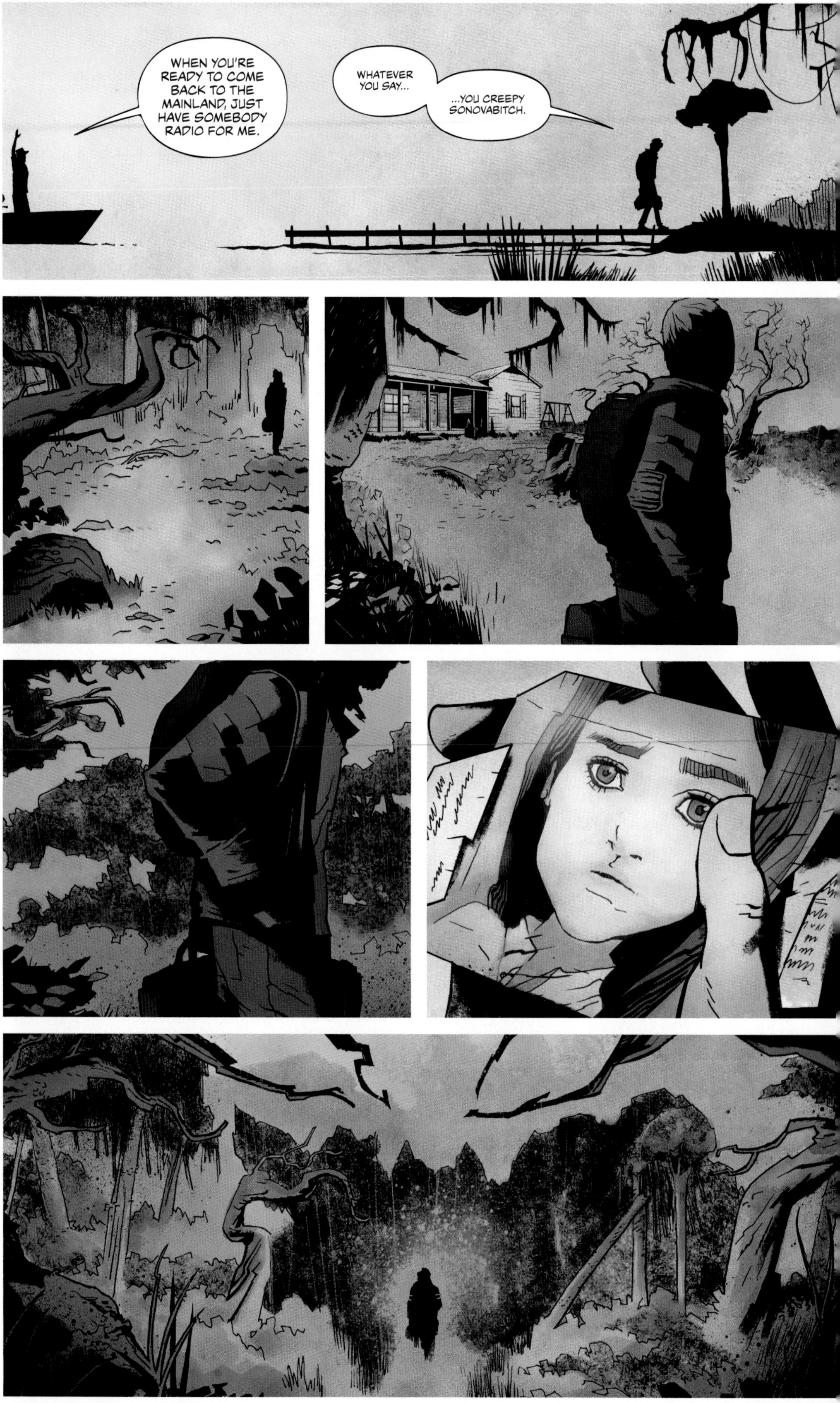
WHEN YOU'RE READY TO COME BACK TO THE MAINLAND, JUST HAVE SOMEBODY RADIO FOR ME.
WHATEVER YOU SAY...
...YOU CREEPY SONOVABITCH.

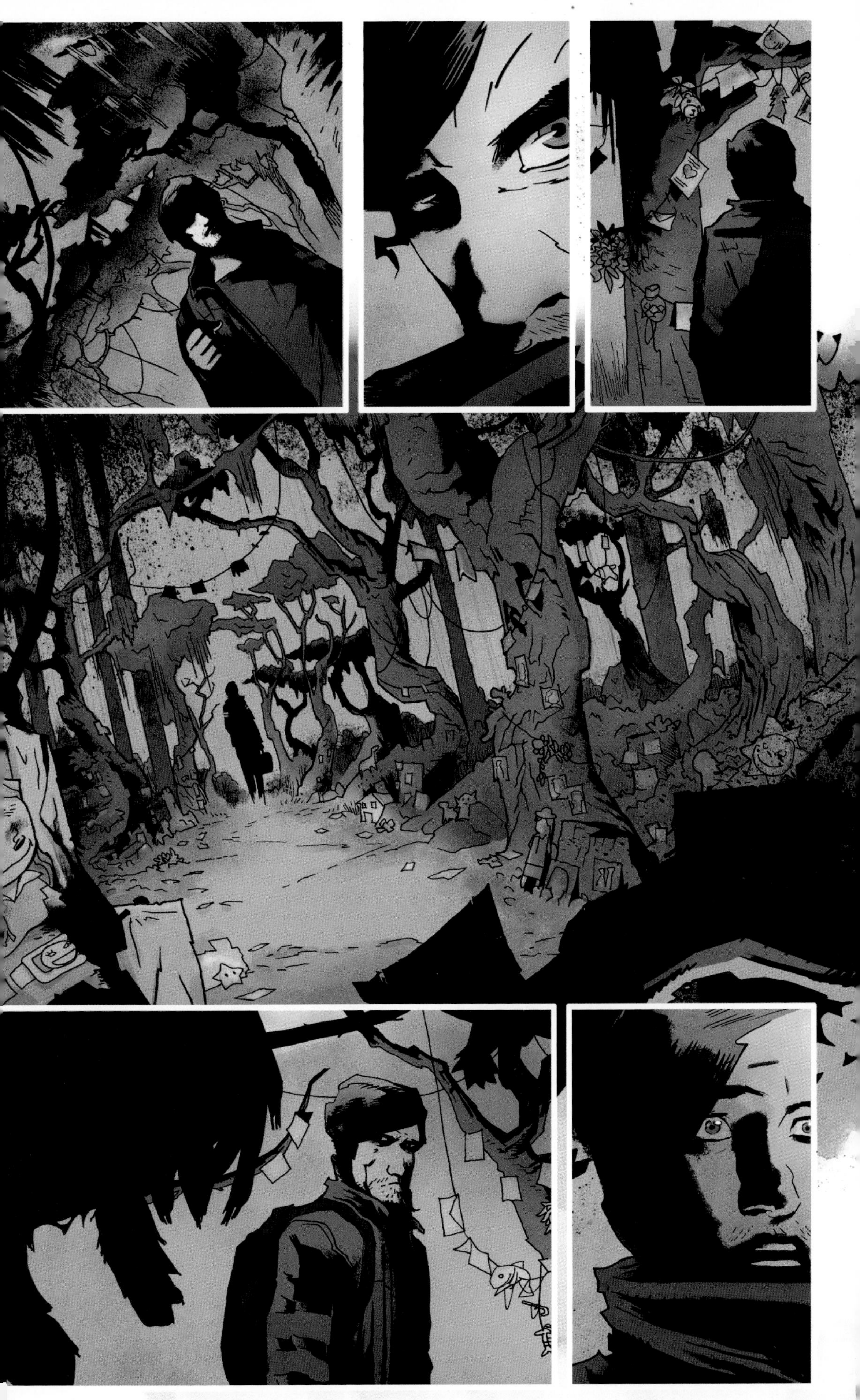

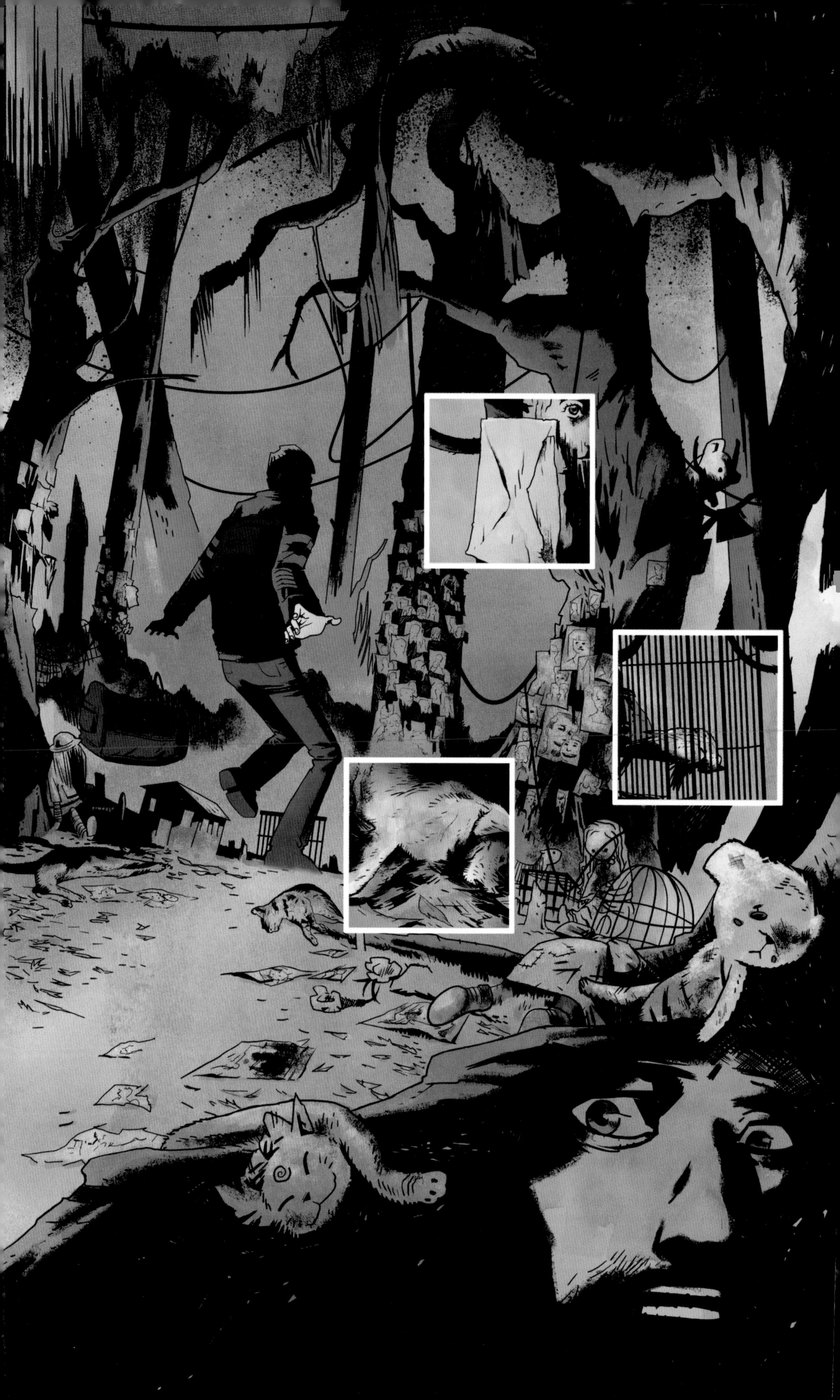

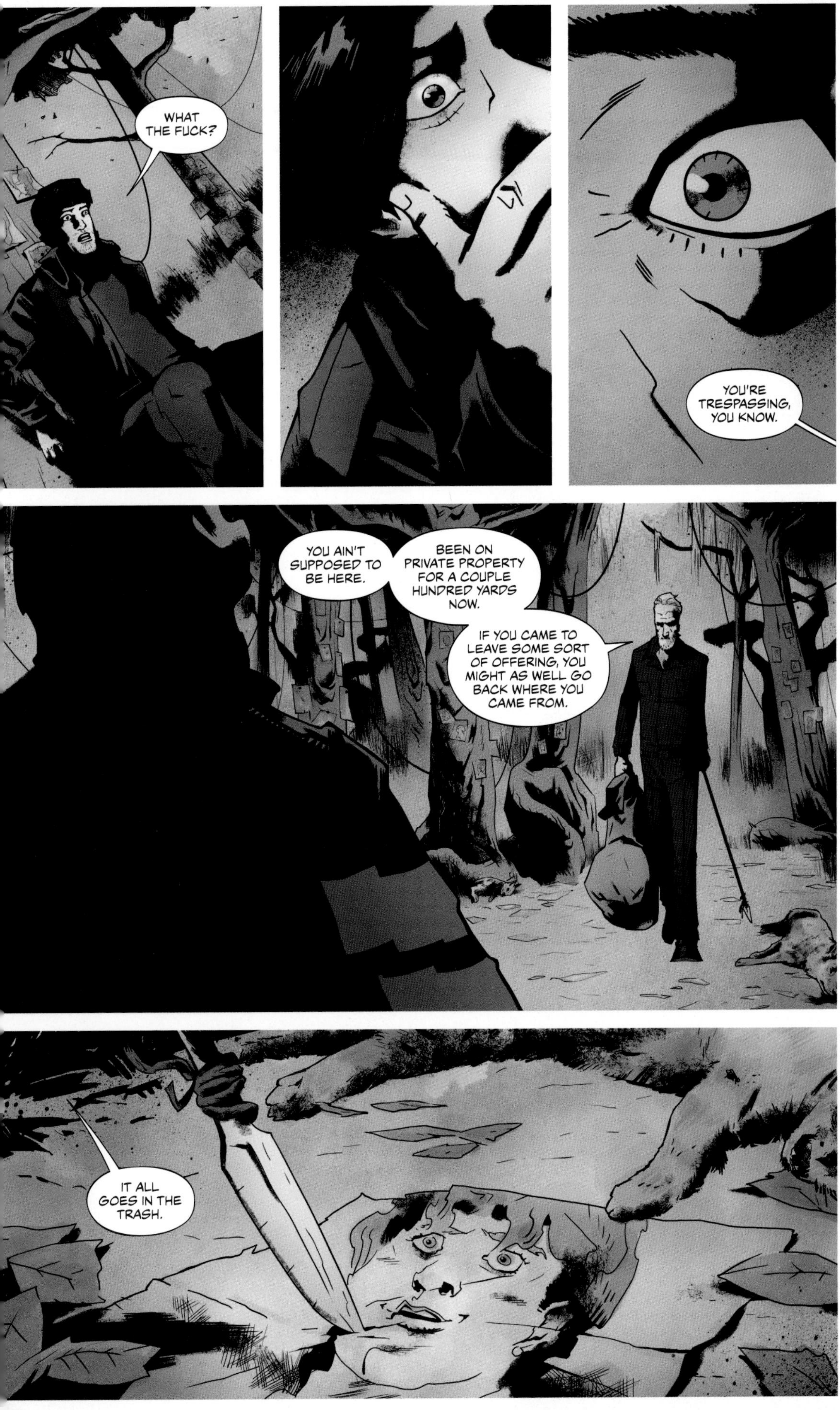
WHAT THE FUCK?
YOU'RE TRESPASSING, YOU KNOW.
YOU AIN'T SUPPOSED TO BE HERE.
BEEN ON PRIVATE PROPERTY FOR A COUPLE HUNDRED YARDS NOW.
IF YOU CAME TO LEAVE SOME SORT OF OFFERING, YOU MIGHT AS WELL GO BACK WHERE YOU CAME FROM.
IT ALL GOES IN THE TRASH.

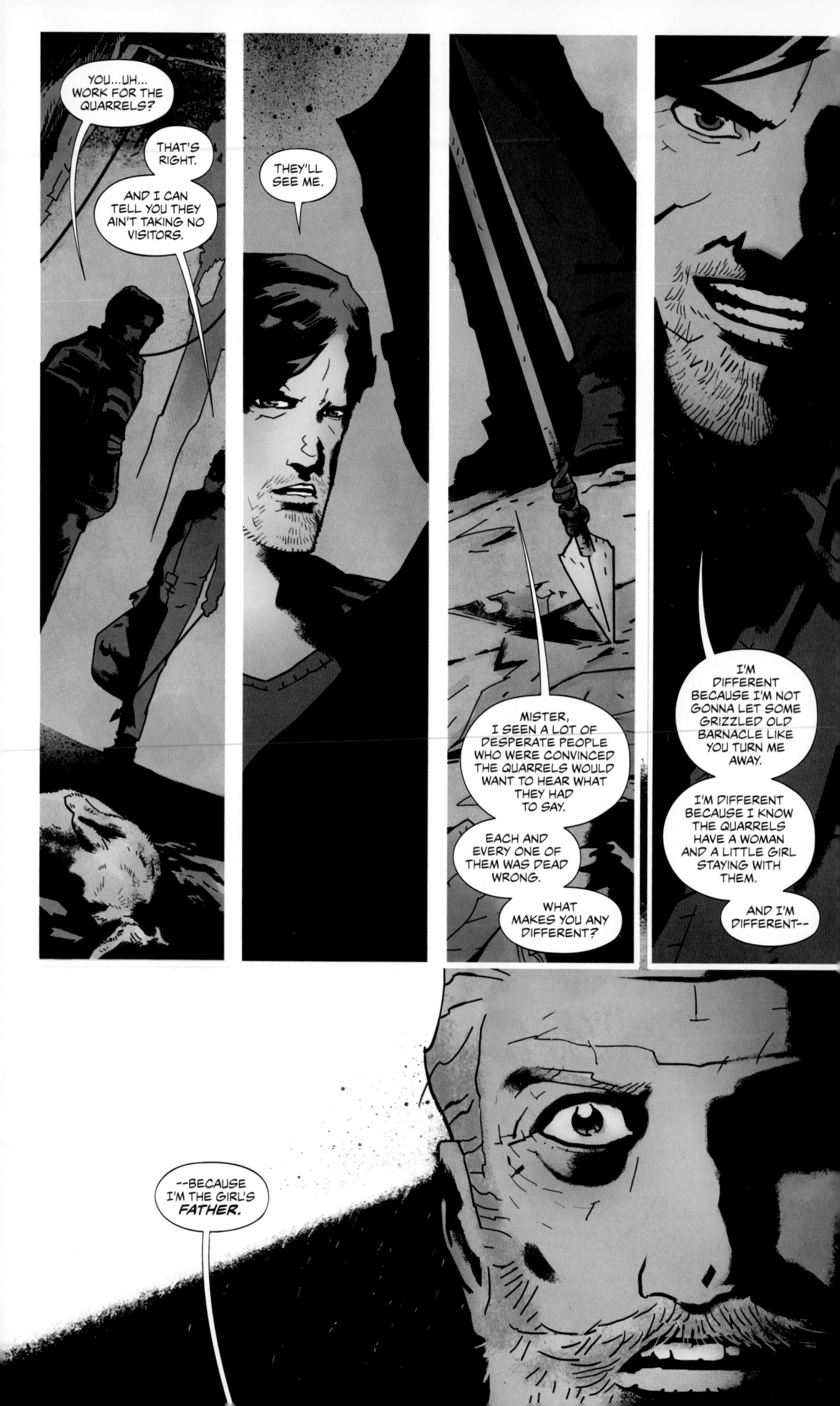
YOU...UH... WORK FOR THE QUARRELS?
THAT'S RIGHT.
AND I CAN TELL YOU THEY AIN'T TAKING NO VISITORS.
THEY'LL SEE ME.
MISTER, I SEEN A LOT OF DESPERATE PEOPLE WHO WERE CONVINCED THE QUARRELS WOULD WANT TO HEAR WHAT THEY HAD TO SAY.
EACH AND EVERY ONE OF THEM WAS DEAD WRONG.
WHAT MAKES YOU ANY DIFFERENT?
I'M DIFFERENT BECAUSE I'M NOT GONNA LET SOME GRIZZLED OLD BARNACLE LIKE YOU TURN ME AWAY.
I'M DIFFERENT BECAUSE I KNOW THE QUARRELS HAVE A WOMAN AND A LITTLE GIRL STAYING WITH THEM.
AND I'M DIFFERENT--
--BECAUSE I'M THE GIRL'S **FATHER.**

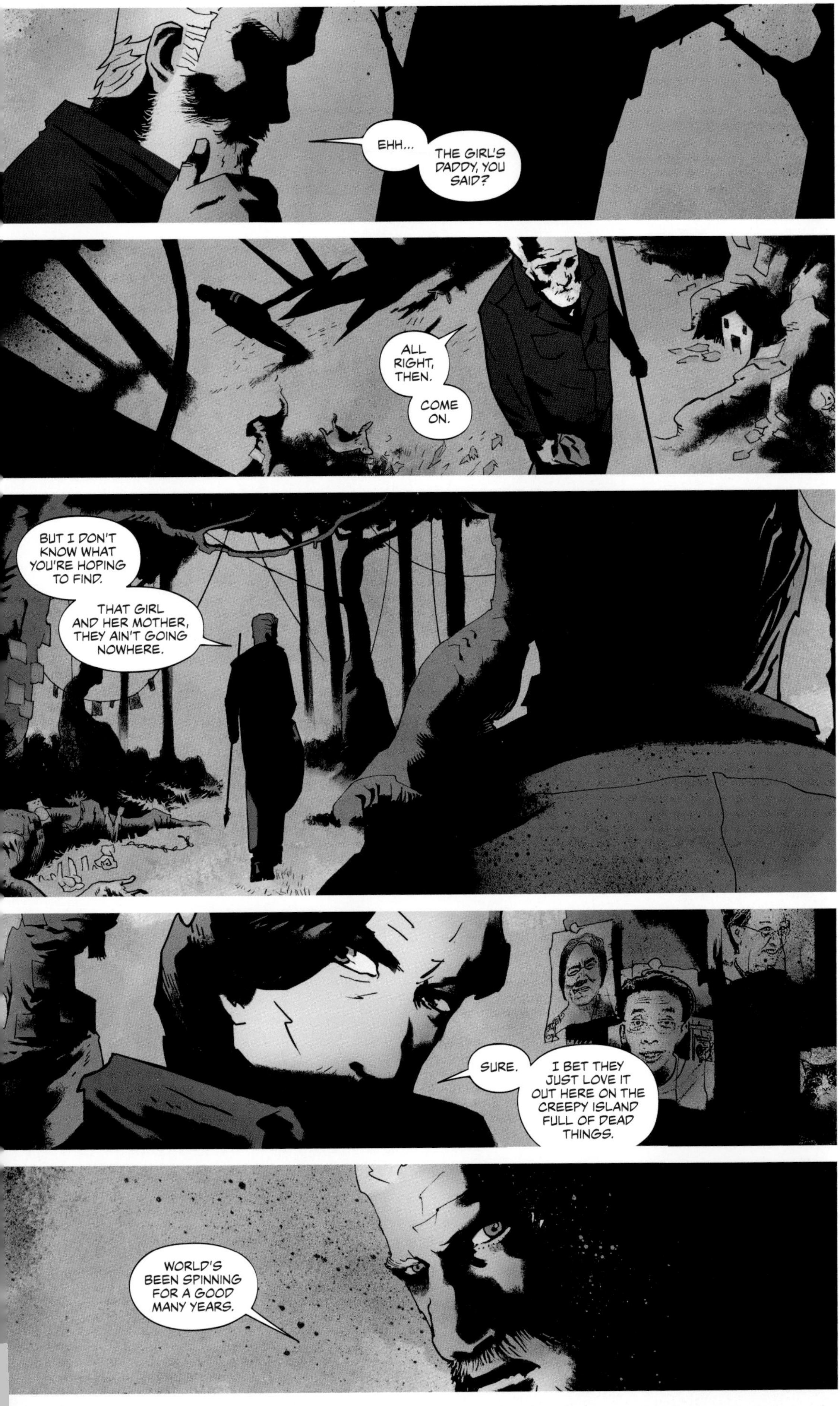
EHH...
THE GIRL'S DADDY, YOU SAID?
ALL RIGHT, THEN.
COME ON.
BUT I DON'T KNOW WHAT YOU'RE HOPING TO FIND.
THAT GIRL AND HER MOTHER, THEY AIN'T GOING NOWHERE.
SURE.
I BET THEY JUST LOVE IT OUT HERE ON THE CREEPY ISLAND FULL OF DEAD THINGS.
WORLD'S BEEN SPINNING FOR A GOOD MANY YEARS.

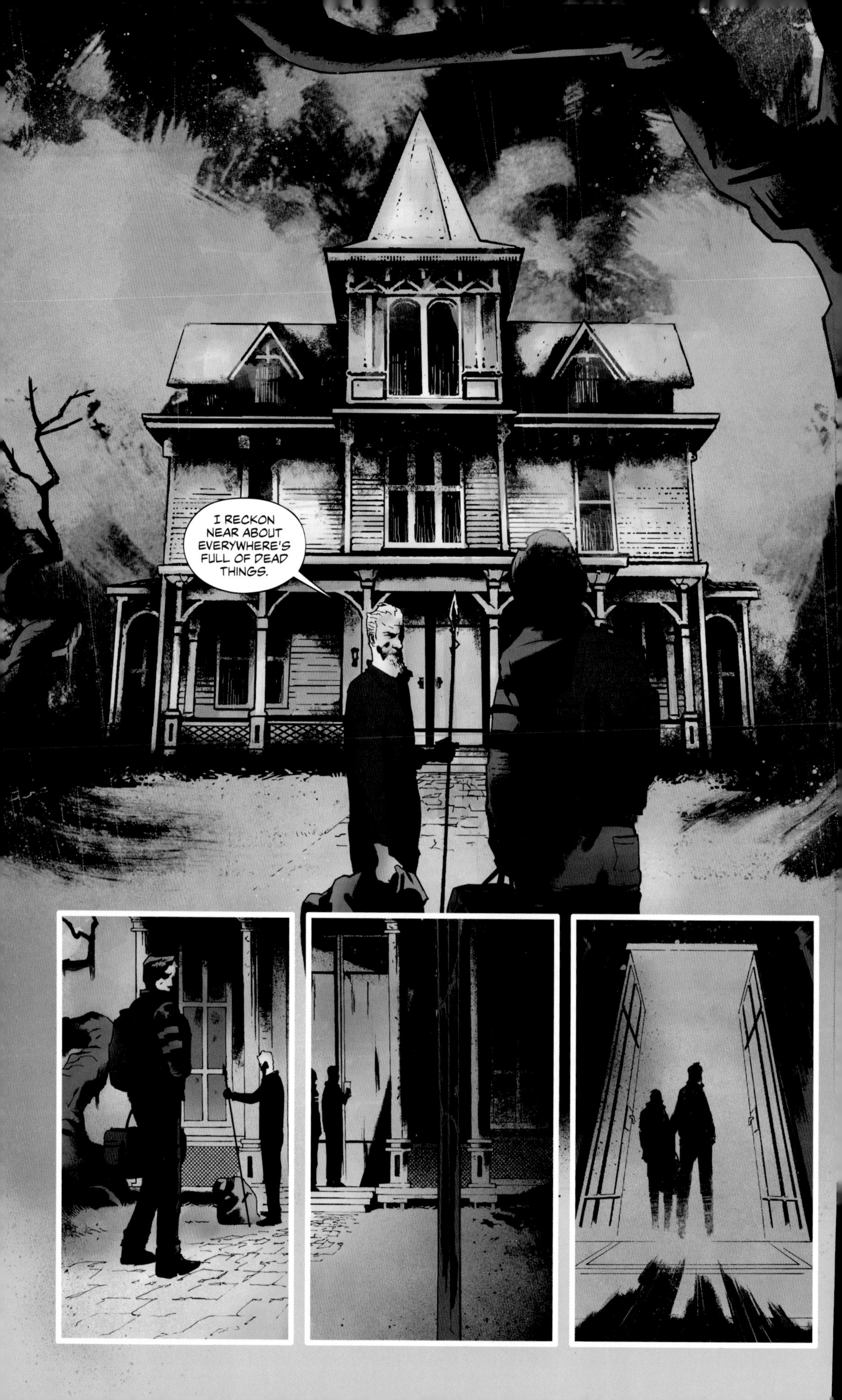
I RECKON NEAR ABOUT EVERYWHERE'S FULL OF DEAD THINGS.

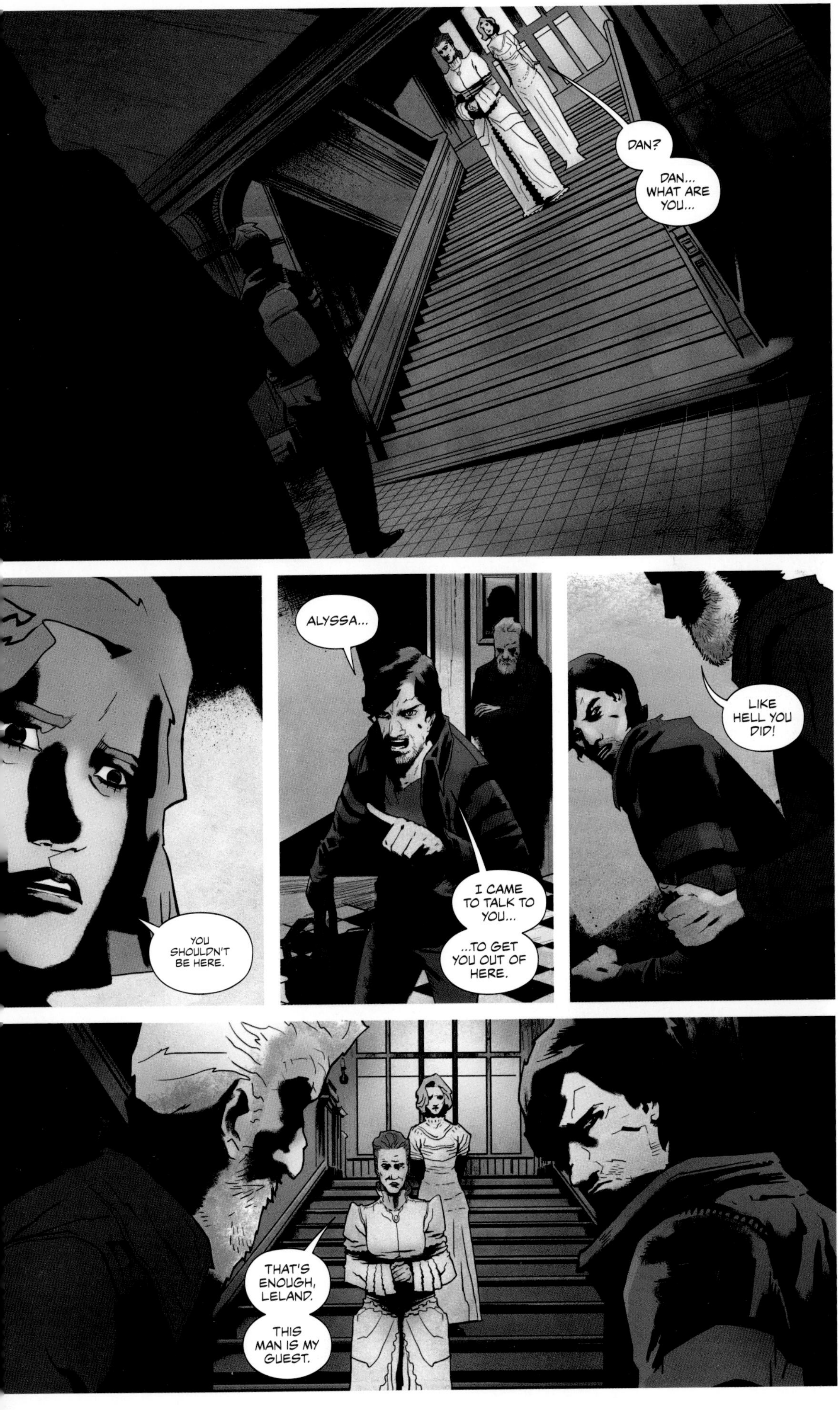
DAN?
DAN... WHAT ARE YOU...
YOU SHOULDN'T BE HERE.
ALYSSA...
I CAME TO TALK TO YOU...
...TO GET YOU OUT OF HERE.
LIKE HELL YOU DID!
THAT'S ENOUGH, LELAND.
THIS MAN IS MY GUEST.

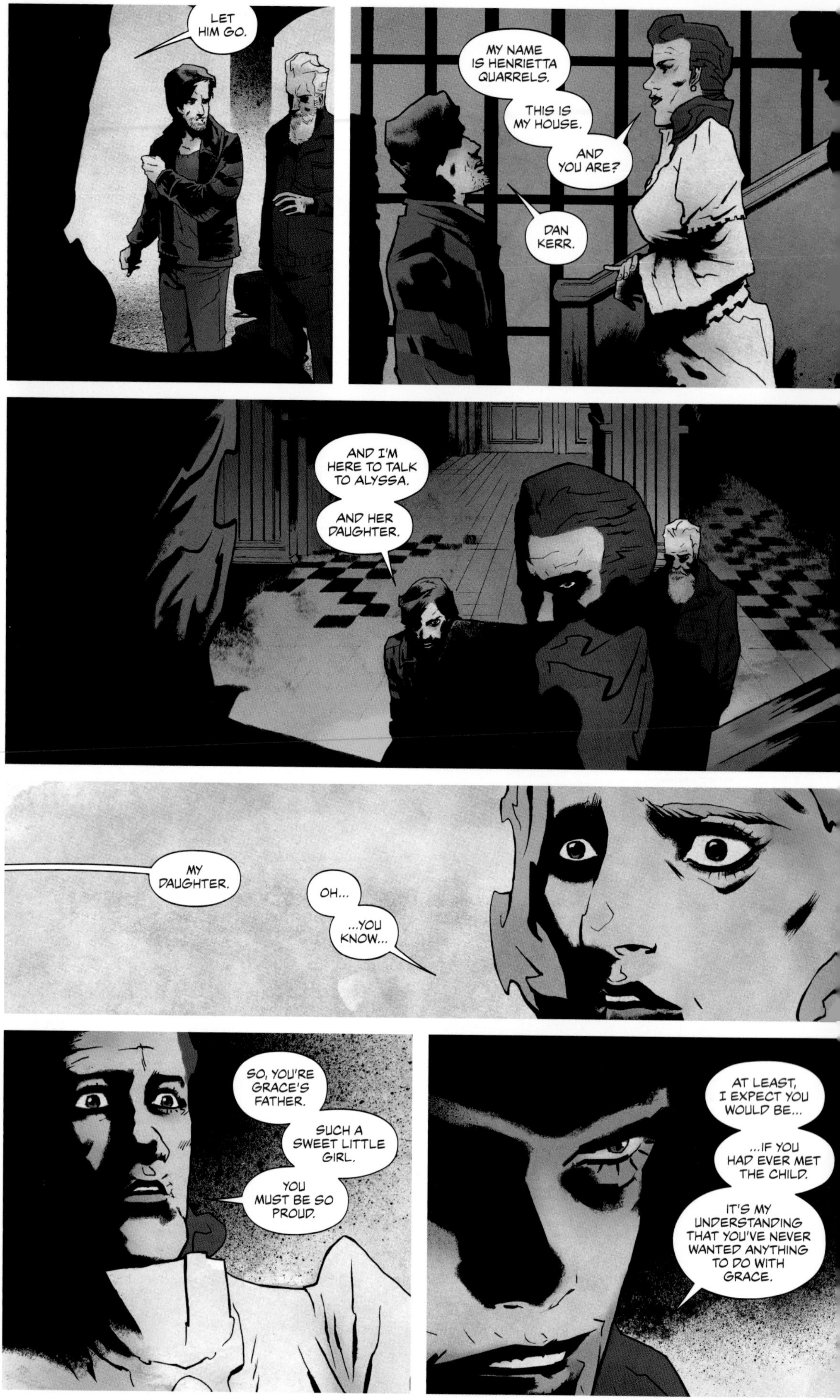
LET HIM GO.
MY NAME IS HENRIETTA QUARRELS.
THIS IS MY HOUSE.
AND YOU ARE?
DAN KERR.
AND I'M HERE TO TALK TO ALYSSA.
AND HER DAUGHTER.
MY DAUGHTER.
OH...
...YOU KNOW...
SO, YOU'RE GRACE'S FATHER.
SUCH A SWEET LITTLE GIRL.
YOU MUST BE SO PROUD.
AT LEAST, I EXPECT YOU WOULD BE...
...IF YOU HAD EVER MET THE CHILD.
IT'S MY UNDERSTANDING THAT YOU'VE NEVER WANTED ANYTHING TO DO WITH GRACE.

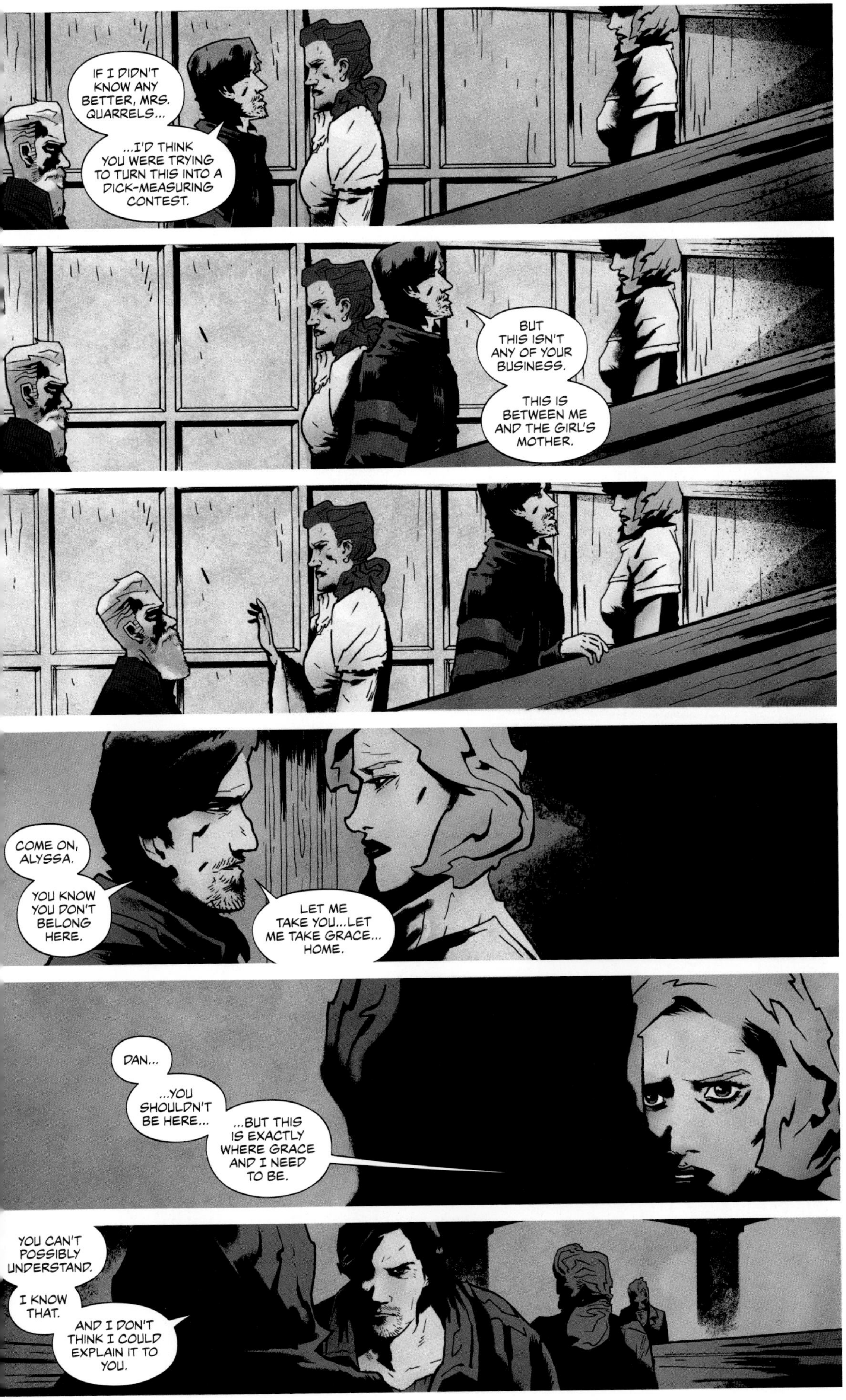
IF I DIDN'T KNOW ANY BETTER, MRS. QUARRELS...
...I'D THINK YOU WERE TRYING TO TURN THIS INTO A DICK-MEASURING CONTEST.
BUT THIS ISN'T ANY OF YOUR BUSINESS.
THIS IS BETWEEN ME AND THE GIRL'S MOTHER.
COME ON, ALYSSA.
YOU KNOW YOU DON'T BELONG HERE.
LET ME TAKE YOU...LET ME TAKE GRACE... HOME.
DAN...
...YOU SHOULDN'T BE HERE...
...BUT THIS IS EXACTLY WHERE GRACE AND I NEED TO BE.
YOU CAN'T POSSIBLY UNDERSTAND.
I KNOW THAT.
AND I DON'T THINK I COULD EXPLAIN IT TO YOU.

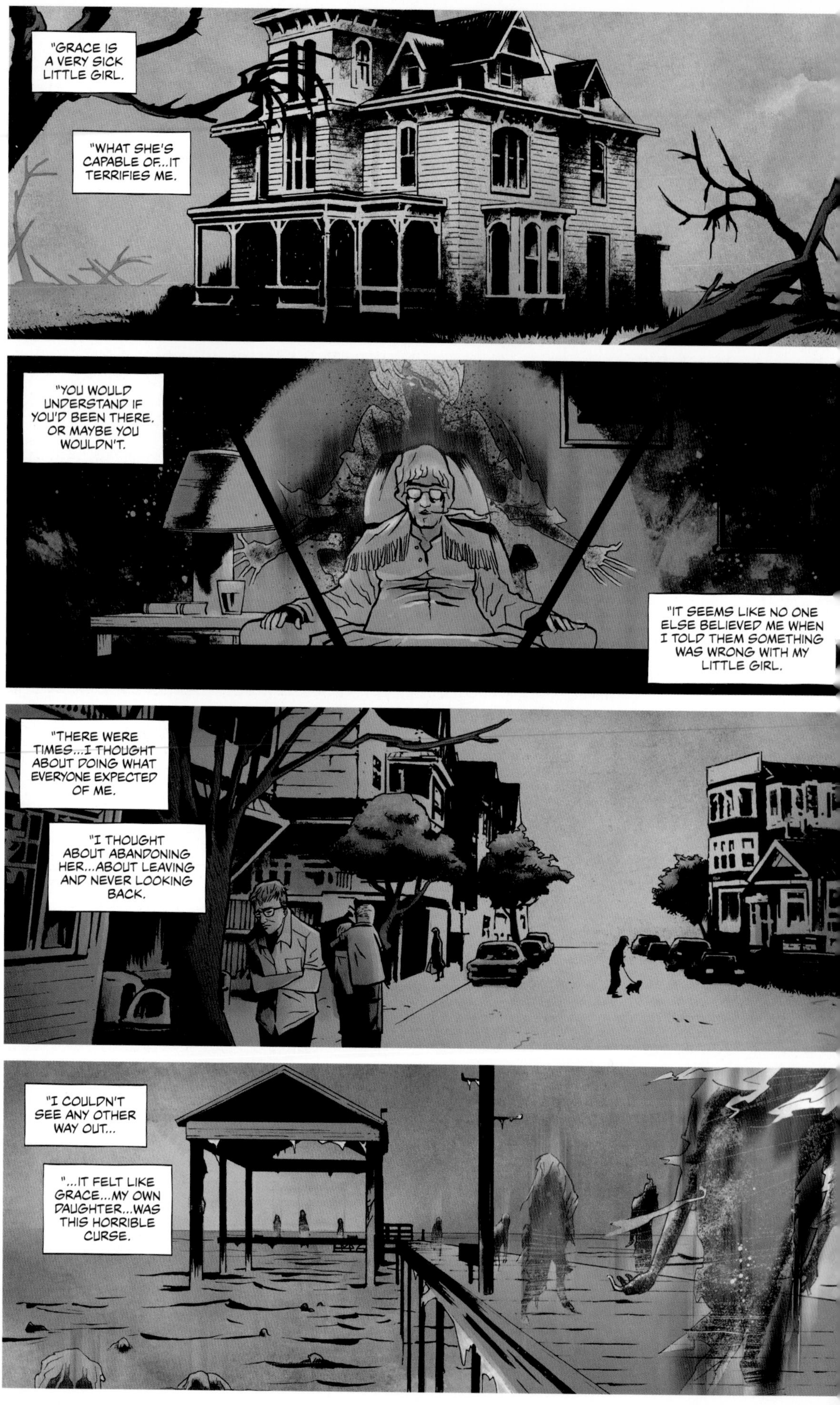
"GRACE IS A VERY SICK LITTLE GIRL.
"WHAT SHE'S CAPABLE OF...IT TERRIFIES ME.
"YOU WOULD UNDERSTAND IF YOU'D BEEN THERE. OR MAYBE YOU WOULDN'T.
"IT SEEMS LIKE NO ONE ELSE BELIEVED ME WHEN I TOLD THEM SOMETHING WAS WRONG WITH MY LITTLE GIRL.
"THERE WERE TIMES...I THOUGHT ABOUT DOING WHAT EVERYONE EXPECTED OF ME.
"I THOUGHT ABOUT ABANDONING HER...ABOUT LEAVING AND NEVER LOOKING BACK.
"I COULDN'T SEE ANY OTHER WAY OUT...
"...IT FELT LIKE GRACE...MY OWN DAUGHTER...WAS THIS HORRIBLE CURSE.

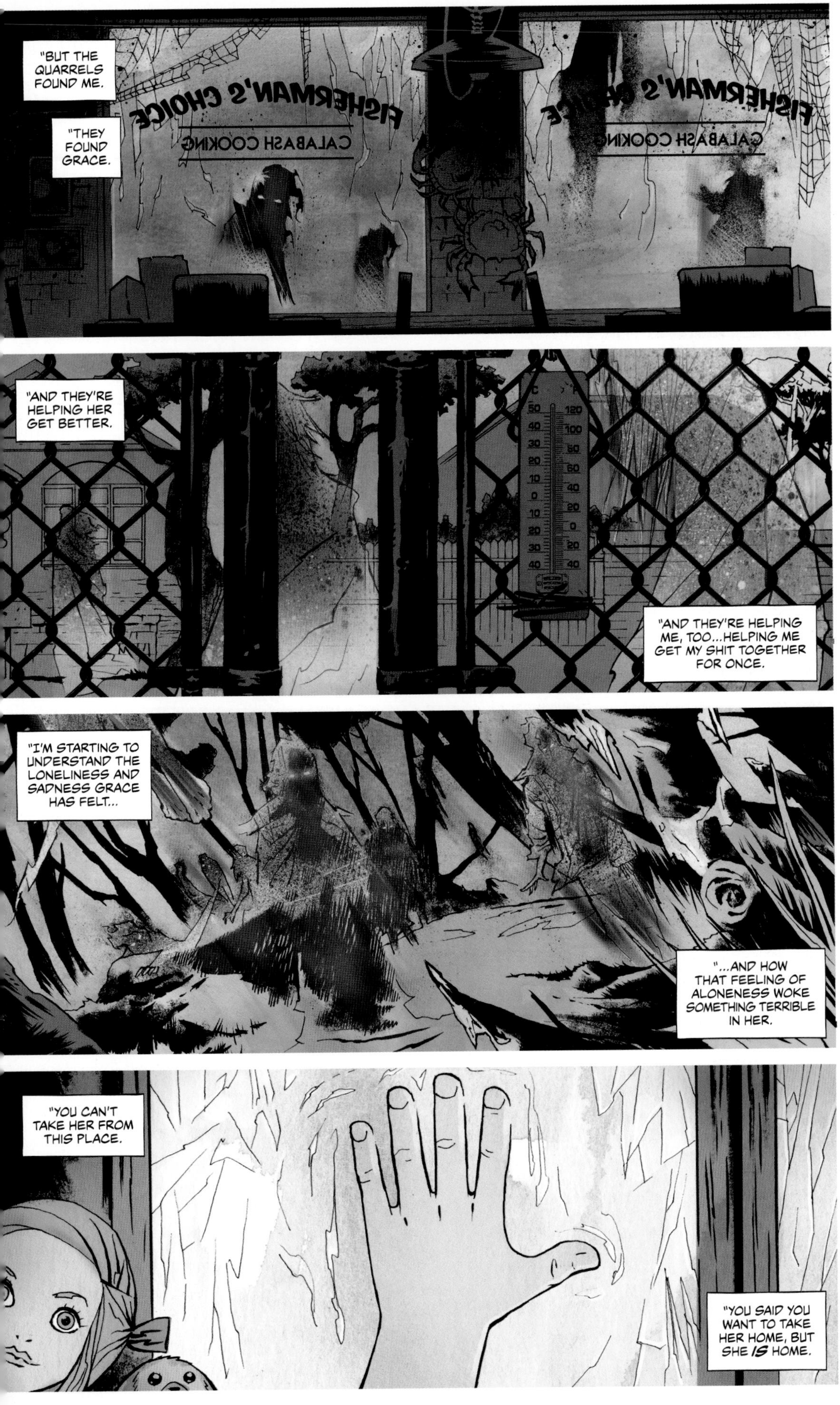
"BUT THE QUARRELS FOUND ME.
"THEY FOUND GRACE.
FISHERMAN'S CHOICE
CALABASH COOKING
"AND THEY'RE HELPING HER GET BETTER.
"AND THEY'RE HELPING ME, TOO...HELPING ME GET MY SHIT TOGETHER FOR ONCE.
"I'M STARTING TO UNDERSTAND THE LONELINESS AND SADNESS GRACE HAS FELT...
"...AND HOW THAT FEELING OF ALONENESS WOKE SOMETHING TERRIBLE IN HER.
"YOU CAN'T TAKE HER FROM THIS PLACE.
"YOU SAID YOU WANT TO TAKE HER HOME, BUT SHE *IS* HOME.

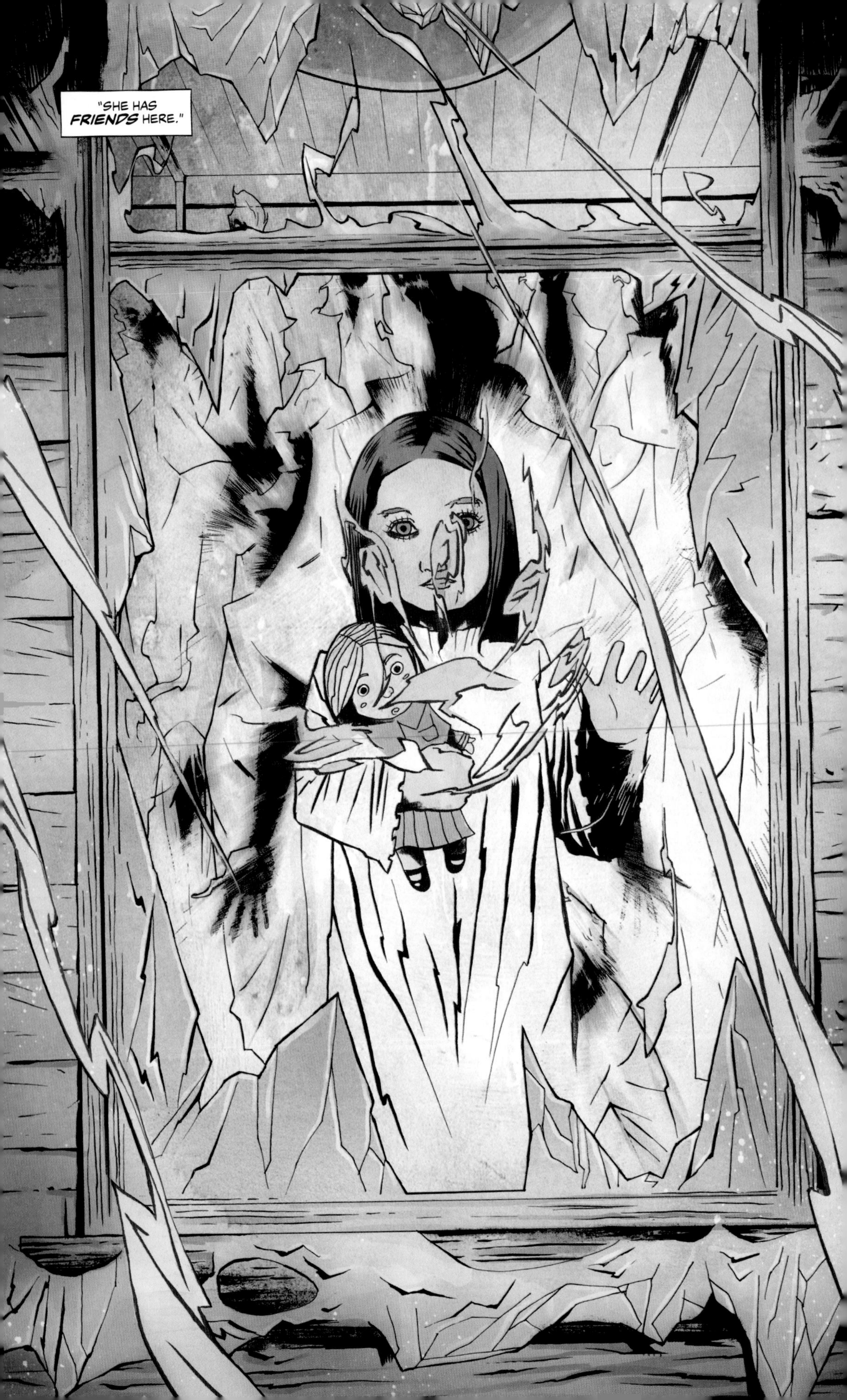
"SHE HAS FRIENDS HERE."

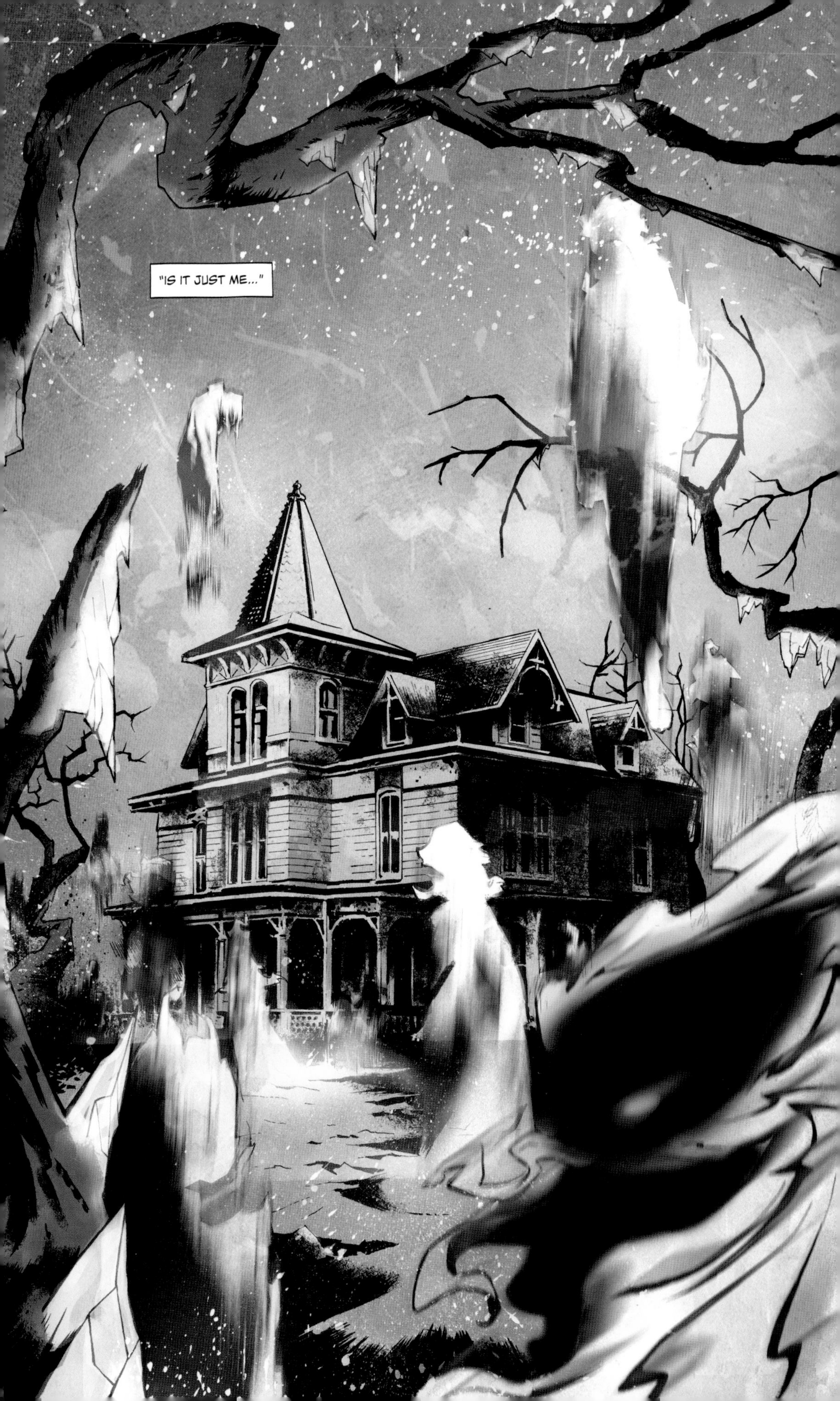
"IS IT JUST ME..."

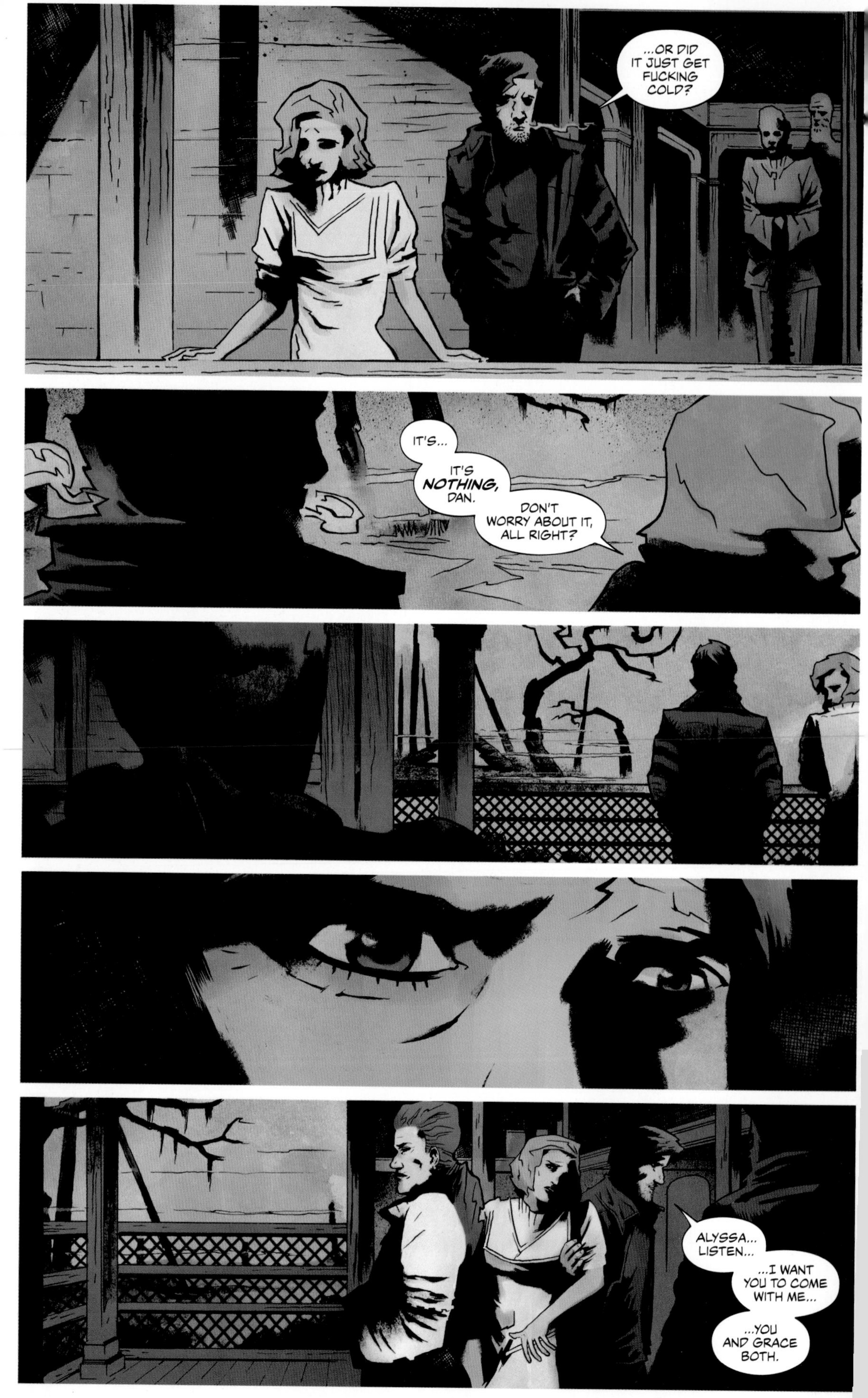
...OR DID IT JUST GET FUCKING COLD?
IT'S...
IT'S **NOTHING,** DAN.
DON'T WORRY ABOUT IT, ALL RIGHT?
ALYSSA... LISTEN...
...I WANT YOU TO COME WITH ME...
...YOU AND GRACE BOTH.

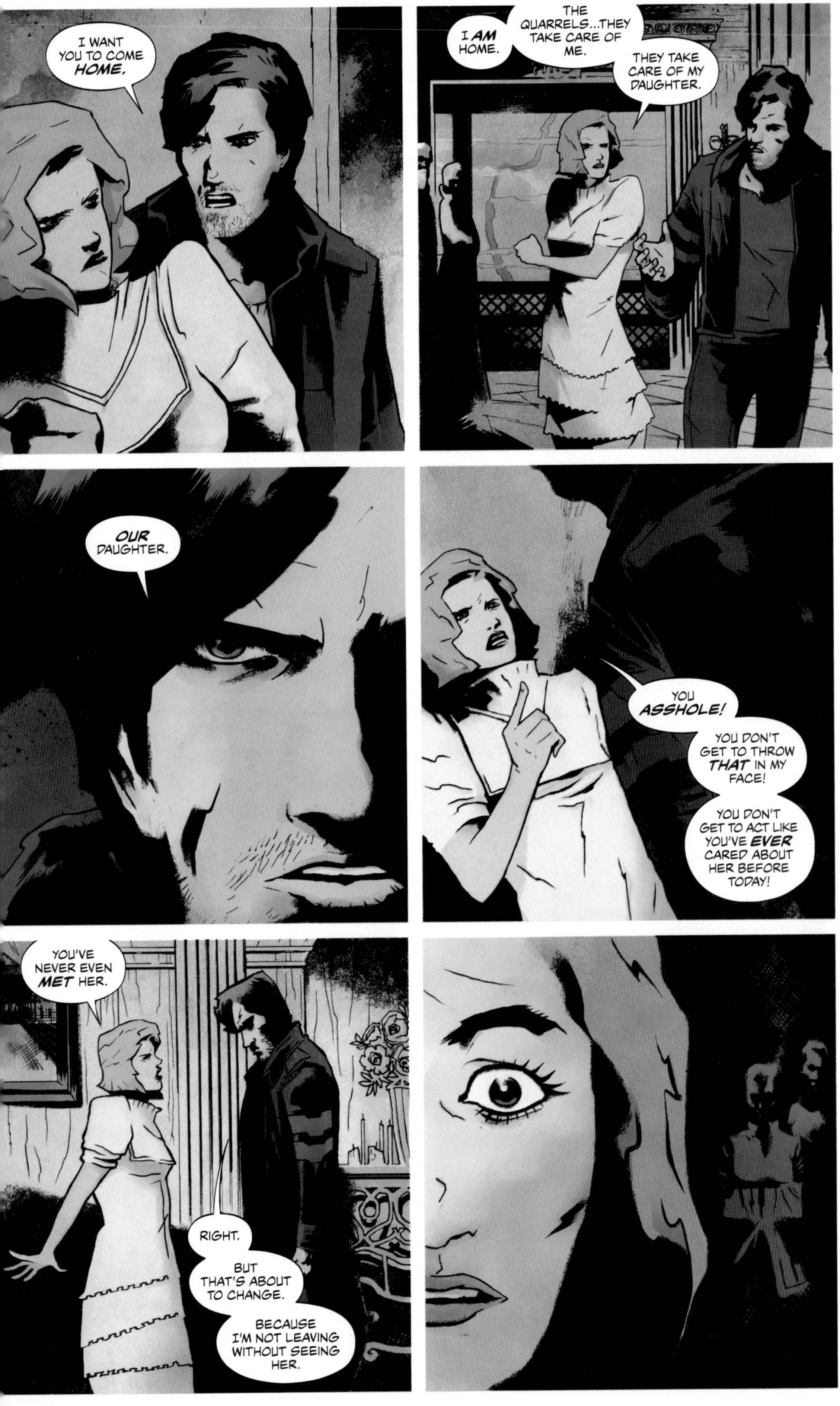

I WANT YOU TO COME HOME.
I AM HOME.
THE QUARRELS...THEY TAKE CARE OF ME.
THEY TAKE CARE OF MY DAUGHTER.
OUR DAUGHTER.
YOU ASSHOLE!
YOU DON'T GET TO THROW THAT IN MY FACE!
YOU DON'T GET TO ACT LIKE YOU'VE EVER CARED ABOUT HER BEFORE TODAY!
YOU'VE NEVER EVEN MET HER.
RIGHT.
BUT THAT'S ABOUT TO CHANGE.
BECAUSE I'M NOT LEAVING WITHOUT SEEING HER.

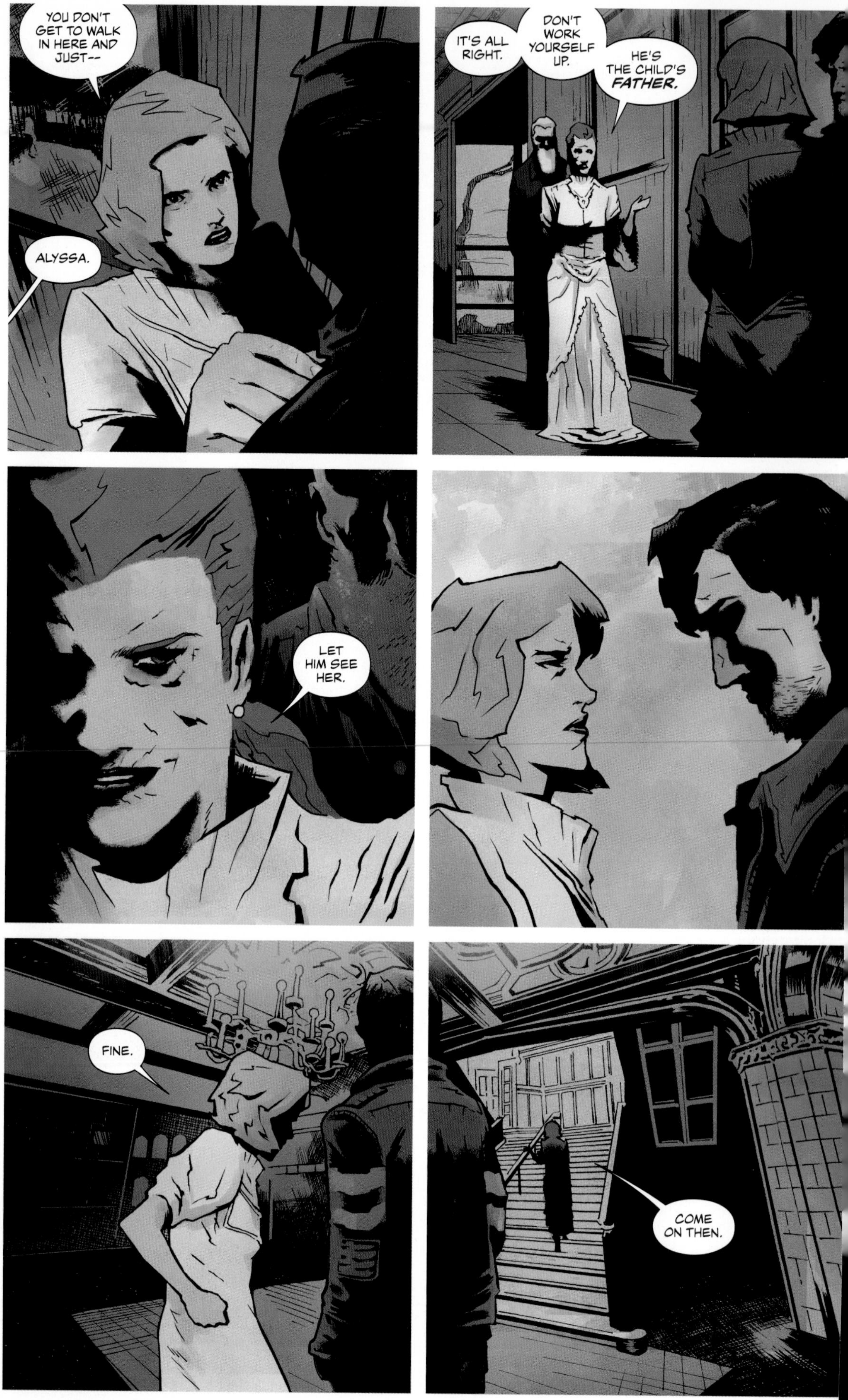
YOU DON'T GET TO WALK IN HERE AND JUST--
ALYSSA.
IT'S ALL RIGHT.
DON'T WORK YOURSELF UP.
HE'S THE CHILD'S **FATHER.**
LET HIM SEE HER.
FINE.
COME ON THEN.

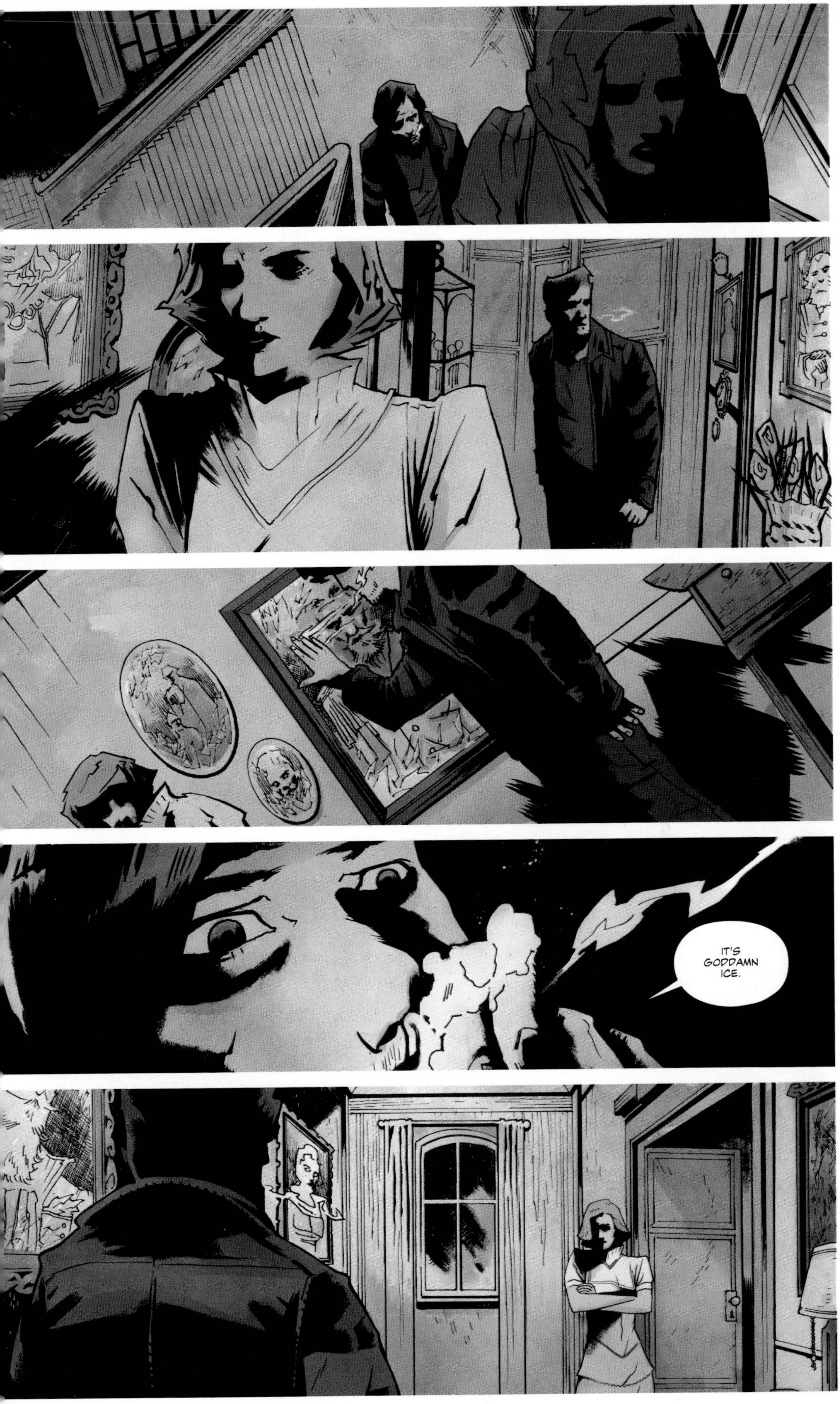
IT'S GODDAMN ICE.

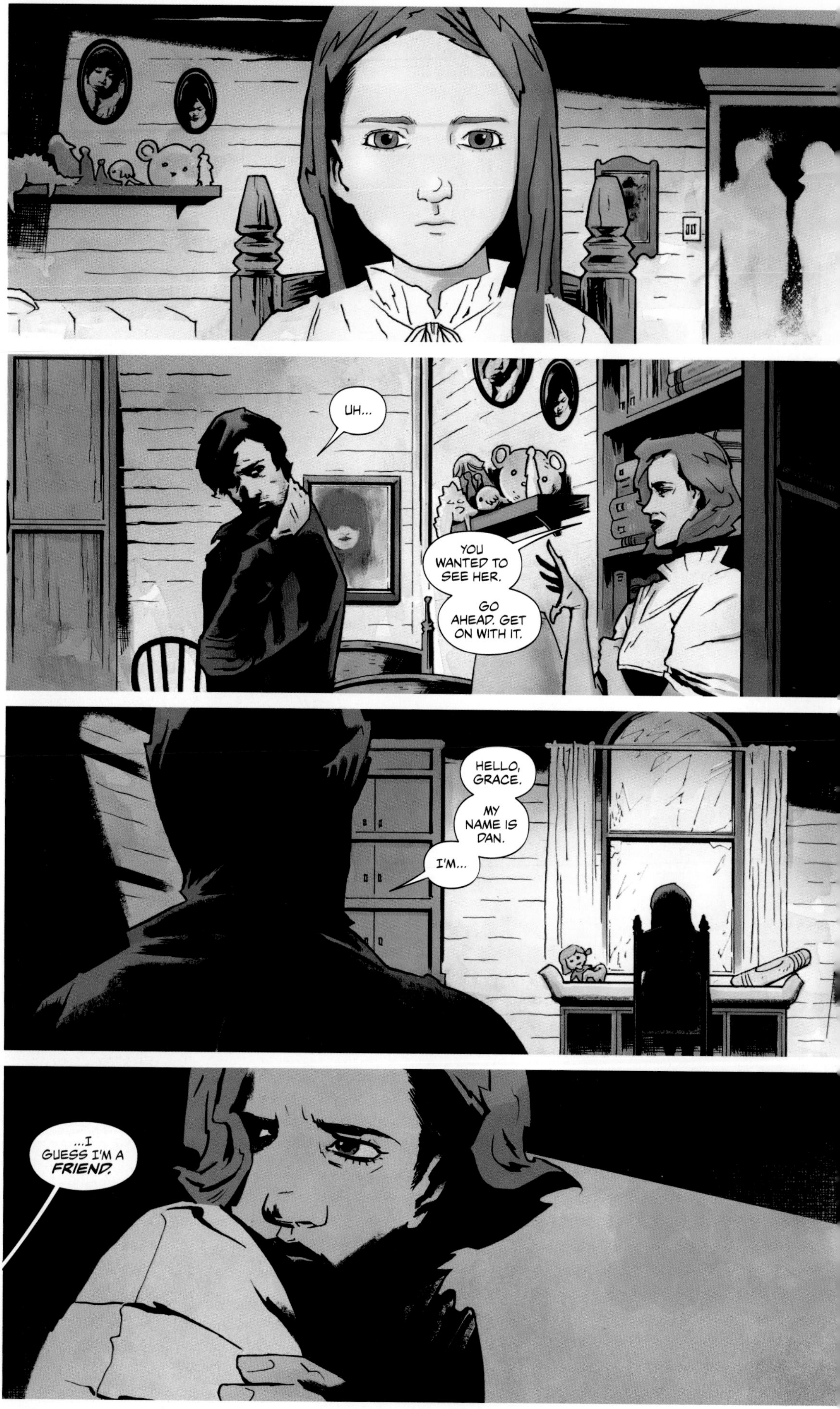
UH...
YOU WANTED TO SEE HER.
GO AHEAD. GET ON WITH IT.
HELLO, GRACE.
MY NAME IS DAN.
I'M...
...I GUESS I'M A FRIEND.

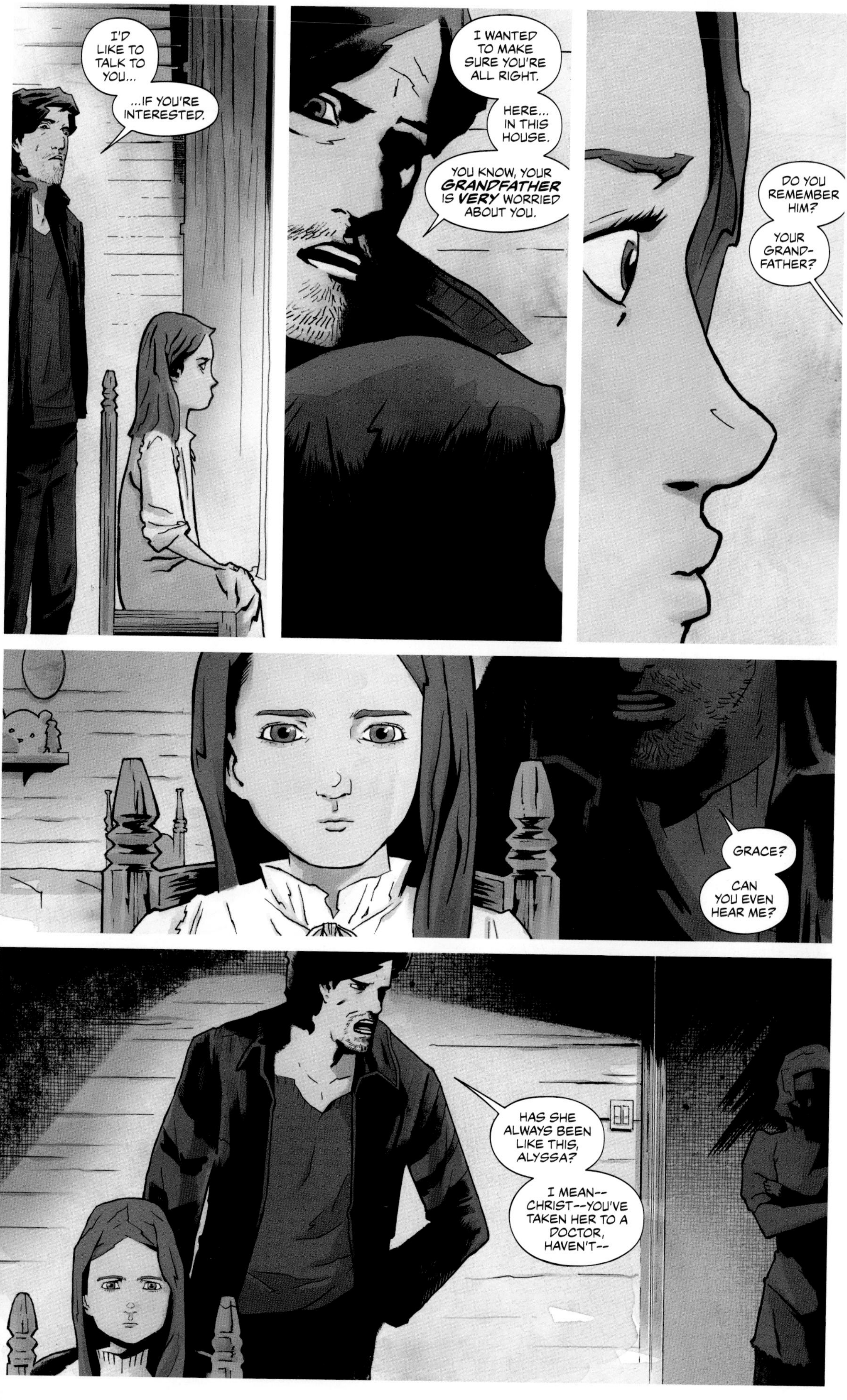
I'D LIKE TO TALK TO YOU...
...IF YOU'RE INTERESTED.
I WANTED TO MAKE SURE YOU'RE ALL RIGHT.
HERE... IN THIS HOUSE.
YOU KNOW, YOUR GRANDFATHER IS VERY WORRIED ABOUT YOU.
DO YOU REMEMBER HIM?
YOUR GRAND-FATHER?
GRACE?
CAN YOU EVEN HEAR ME?
HAS SHE ALWAYS BEEN LIKE THIS, ALYSSA?
I MEAN-- CHRIST--YOU'VE TAKEN HER TO A DOCTOR, HAVEN'T--

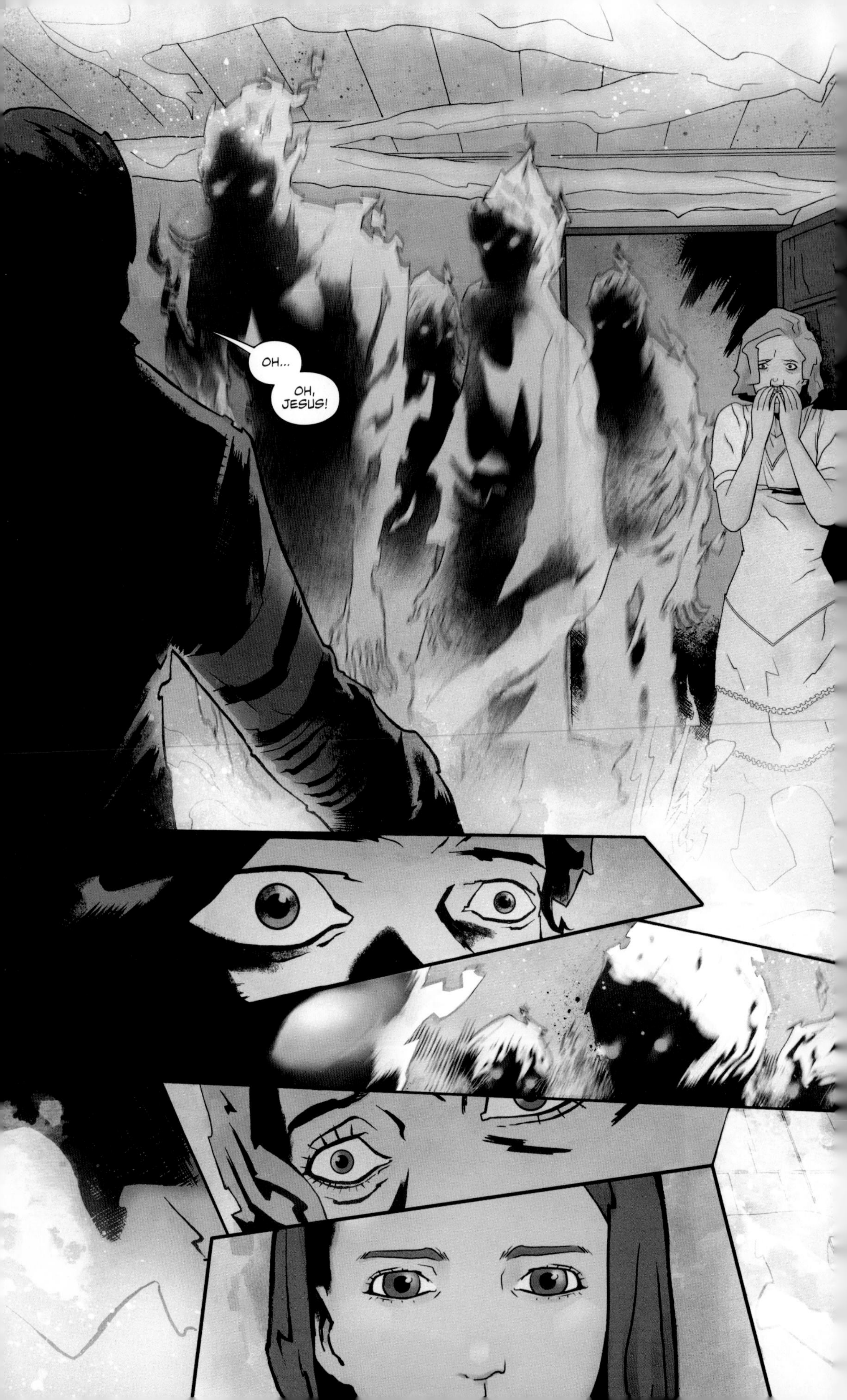
OH...
OH, JESUS!

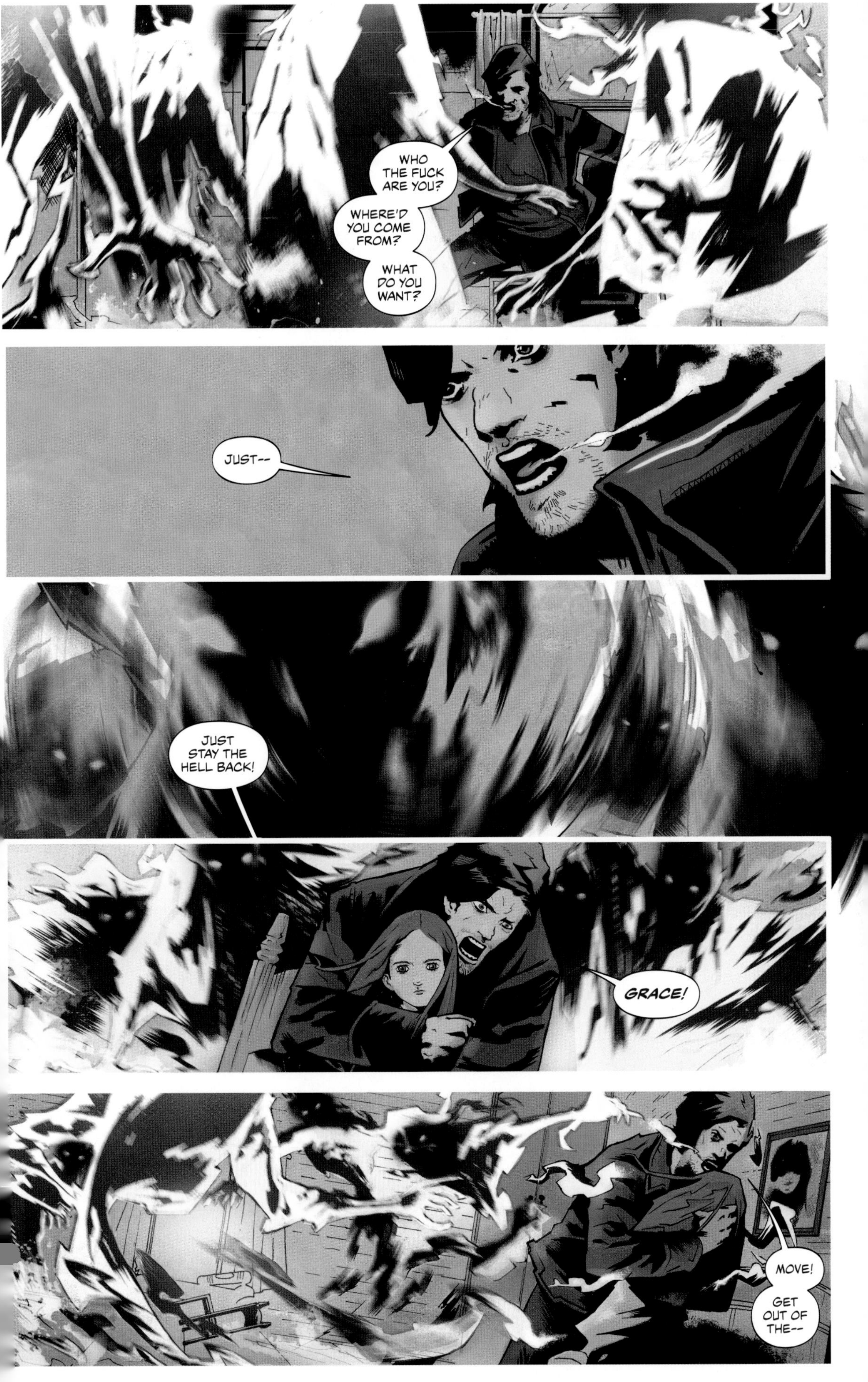
WHO THE FUCK ARE YOU?
WHERE'D YOU COME FROM?
WHAT DO YOU WANT?
JUST--
JUST STAY THE HELL BACK!
GRACE!
MOVE!
GET OUT OF THE--

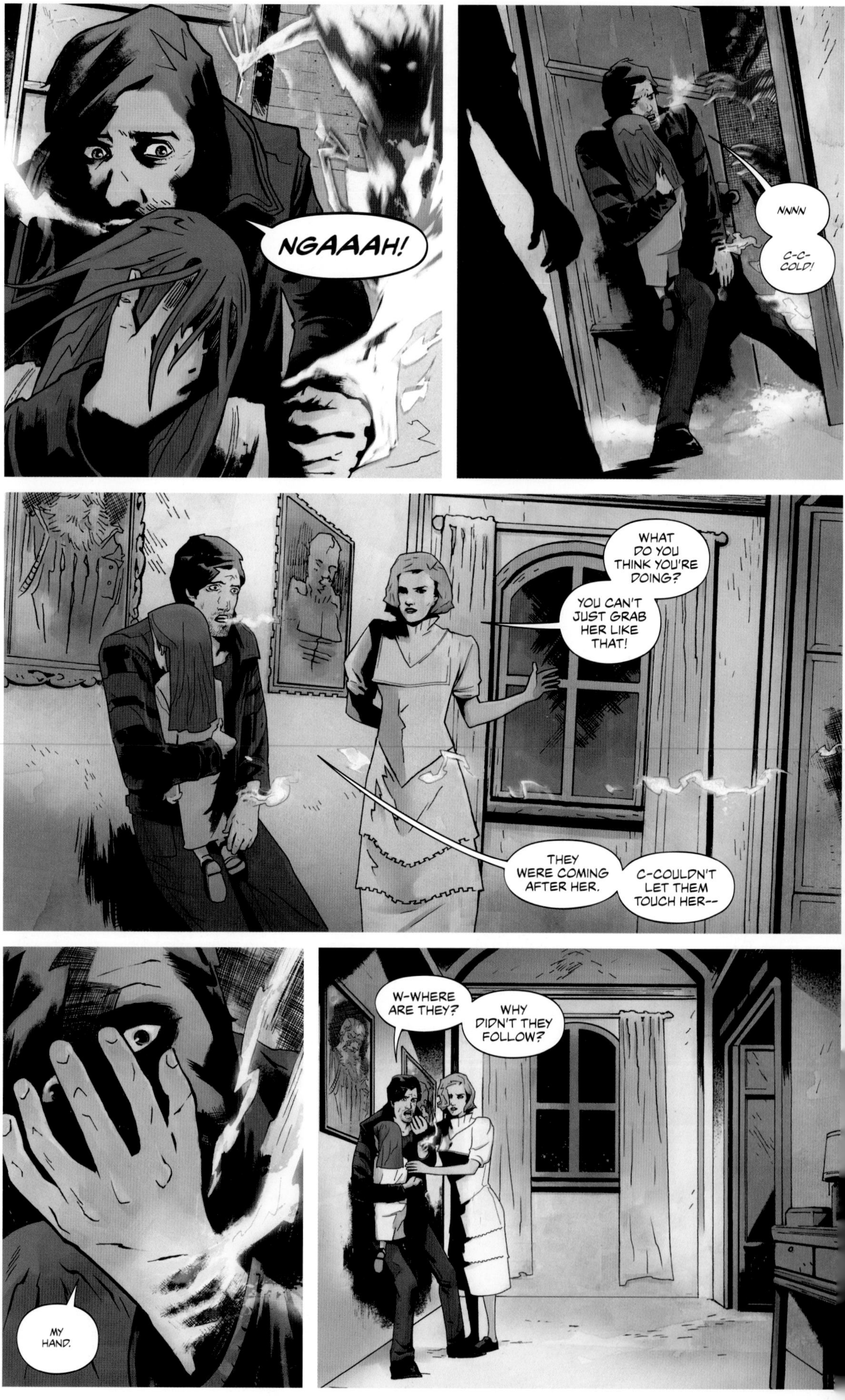
NGAAAH!
NNNN
C-C-COLD!
WHAT DO YOU THINK YOU'RE DOING?
YOU CAN'T JUST GRAB HER LIKE THAT!
THEY WERE COMING AFTER HER.
C-COULDN'T LET THEM TOUCH HER--
MY HAND.
W-WHERE ARE THEY?
WHY DIDN'T THEY FOLLOW?

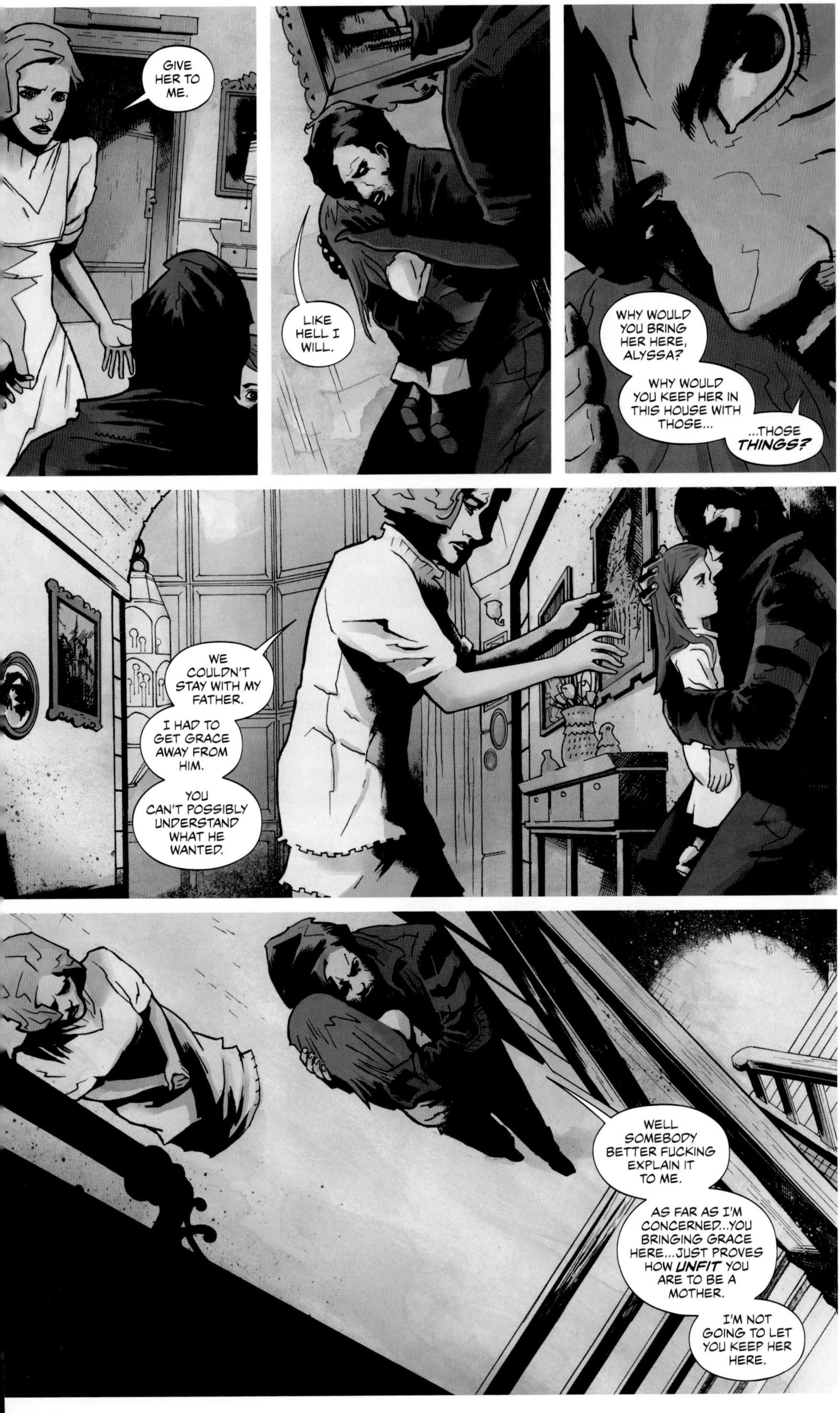
GIVE HER TO ME.
LIKE HELL I WILL.
WHY WOULD YOU BRING HER HERE, ALYSSA?
WHY WOULD YOU KEEP HER IN THIS HOUSE WITH THOSE...
...THOSE *THINGS?*
WE COULDN'T STAY WITH MY FATHER.
I HAD TO GET GRACE AWAY FROM HIM.
YOU CAN'T POSSIBLY UNDERSTAND WHAT HE WANTED.
WELL SOMEBODY BETTER FUCKING EXPLAIN IT TO ME.
AS FAR AS I'M CONCERNED...YOU BRINGING GRACE HERE...JUST PROVES HOW *UNFIT* YOU ARE TO BE A MOTHER.
I'M NOT GOING TO LET YOU KEEP HER HERE.

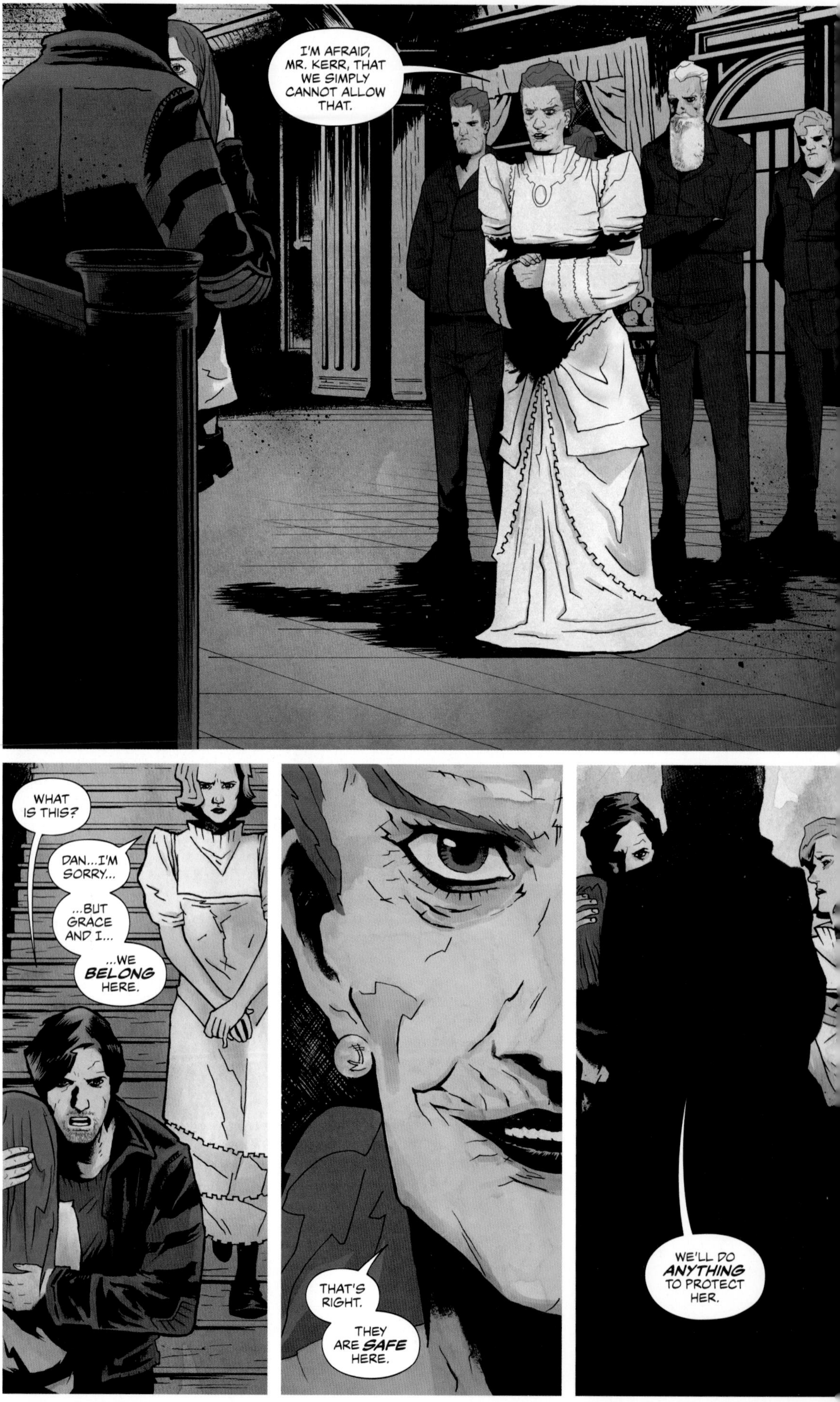

I'M AFRAID, MR. KERR, THAT WE SIMPLY CANNOT ALLOW THAT.
WHAT IS THIS?
DAN...I'M SORRY...
...BUT GRACE AND I...
...WE *BELONG* HERE.
THAT'S RIGHT.
THEY ARE *SAFE* HERE.
WE'LL DO *ANYTHING* TO PROTECT HER.

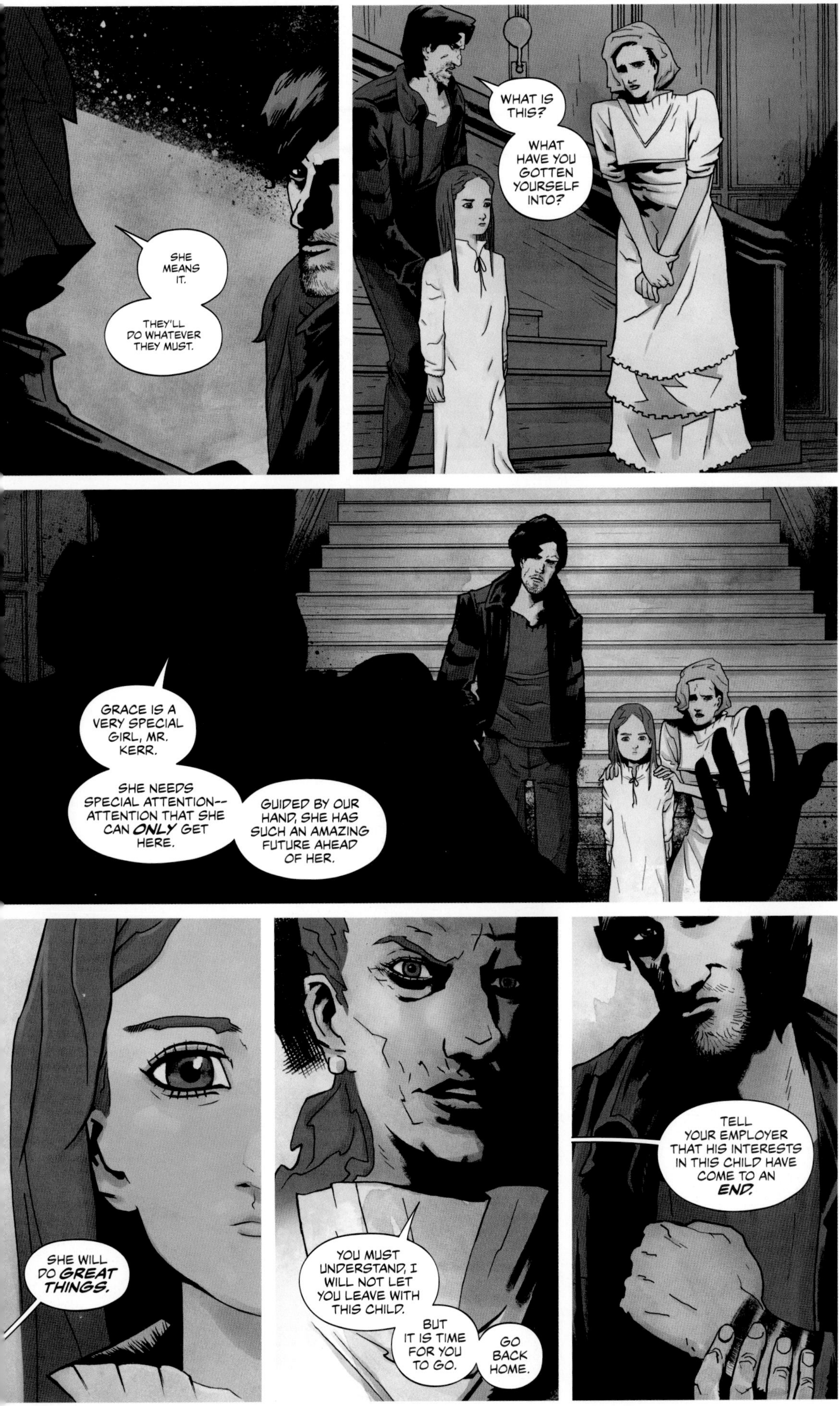
SHE MEANS IT.
THEY'LL DO WHATEVER THEY MUST.
WHAT IS THIS?
WHAT HAVE YOU GOTTEN YOURSELF INTO?
GRACE IS A VERY SPECIAL GIRL, MR. KERR.
SHE NEEDS SPECIAL ATTENTION-- ATTENTION THAT SHE CAN ONLY GET HERE.
GUIDED BY OUR HAND, SHE HAS SUCH AN AMAZING FUTURE AHEAD OF HER.
SHE WILL DO GREAT THINGS.
YOU MUST UNDERSTAND, I WILL NOT LET YOU LEAVE WITH THIS CHILD.
BUT IT IS TIME FOR YOU TO GO.
GO BACK HOME.
TELL YOUR EMPLOYER THAT HIS INTERESTS IN THIS CHILD HAVE COME TO AN END.

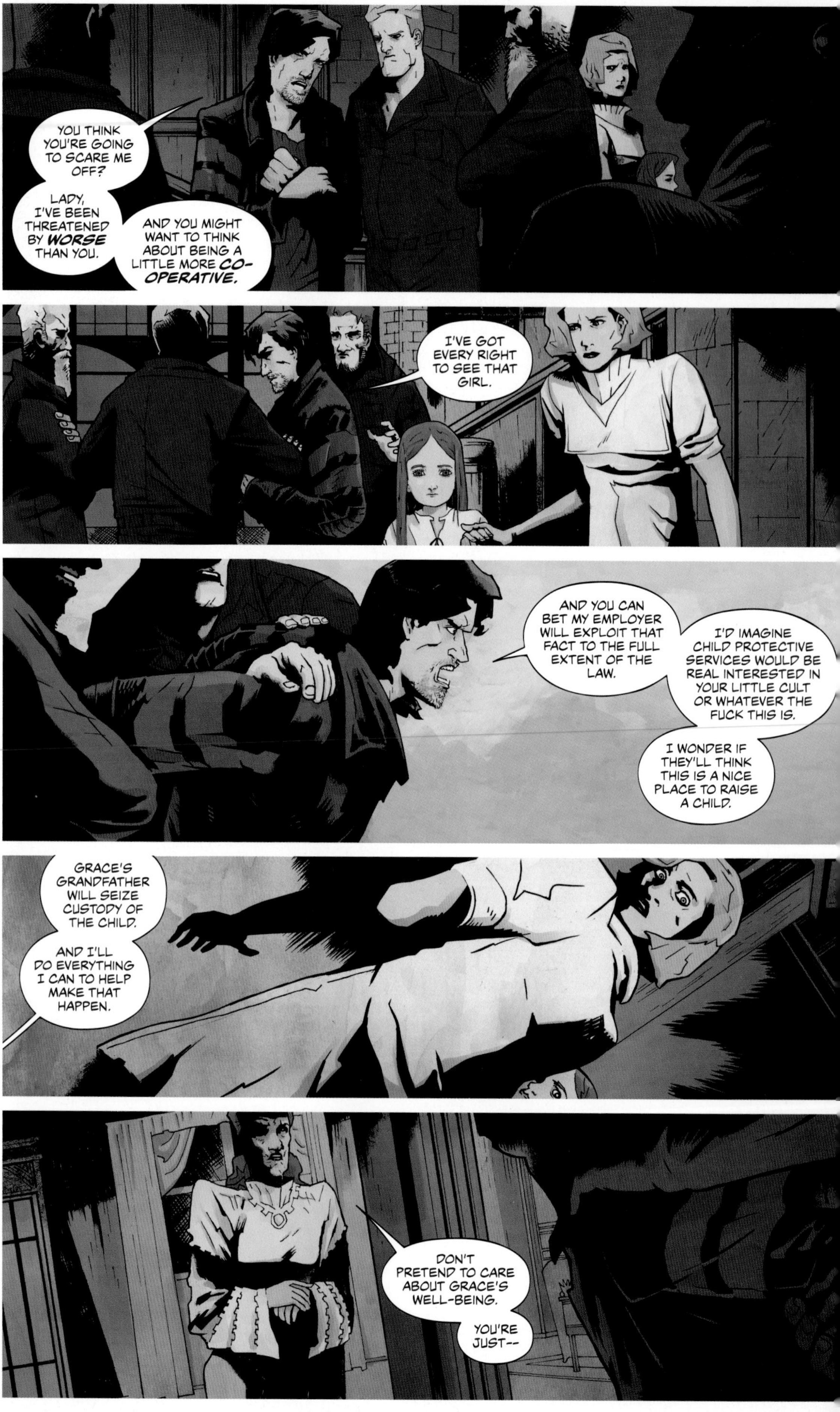
YOU THINK YOU'RE GOING TO SCARE ME OFF?
LADY, I'VE BEEN THREATENED BY WORSE THAN YOU.
AND YOU MIGHT WANT TO THINK ABOUT BEING A LITTLE MORE CO-OPERATIVE.
I'VE GOT EVERY RIGHT TO SEE THAT GIRL.
AND YOU CAN BET MY EMPLOYER WILL EXPLOIT THAT FACT TO THE FULL EXTENT OF THE LAW.
I'D IMAGINE CHILD PROTECTIVE SERVICES WOULD BE REAL INTERESTED IN YOUR LITTLE CULT OR WHATEVER THE FUCK THIS IS.
I WONDER IF THEY'LL THINK THIS IS A NICE PLACE TO RAISE A CHILD.
GRACE'S GRANDFATHER WILL SEIZE CUSTODY OF THE CHILD.
AND I'LL DO EVERYTHING I CAN TO HELP MAKE THAT HAPPEN.
DON'T PRETEND TO CARE ABOUT GRACE'S WELL-BEING.
YOU'RE JUST--

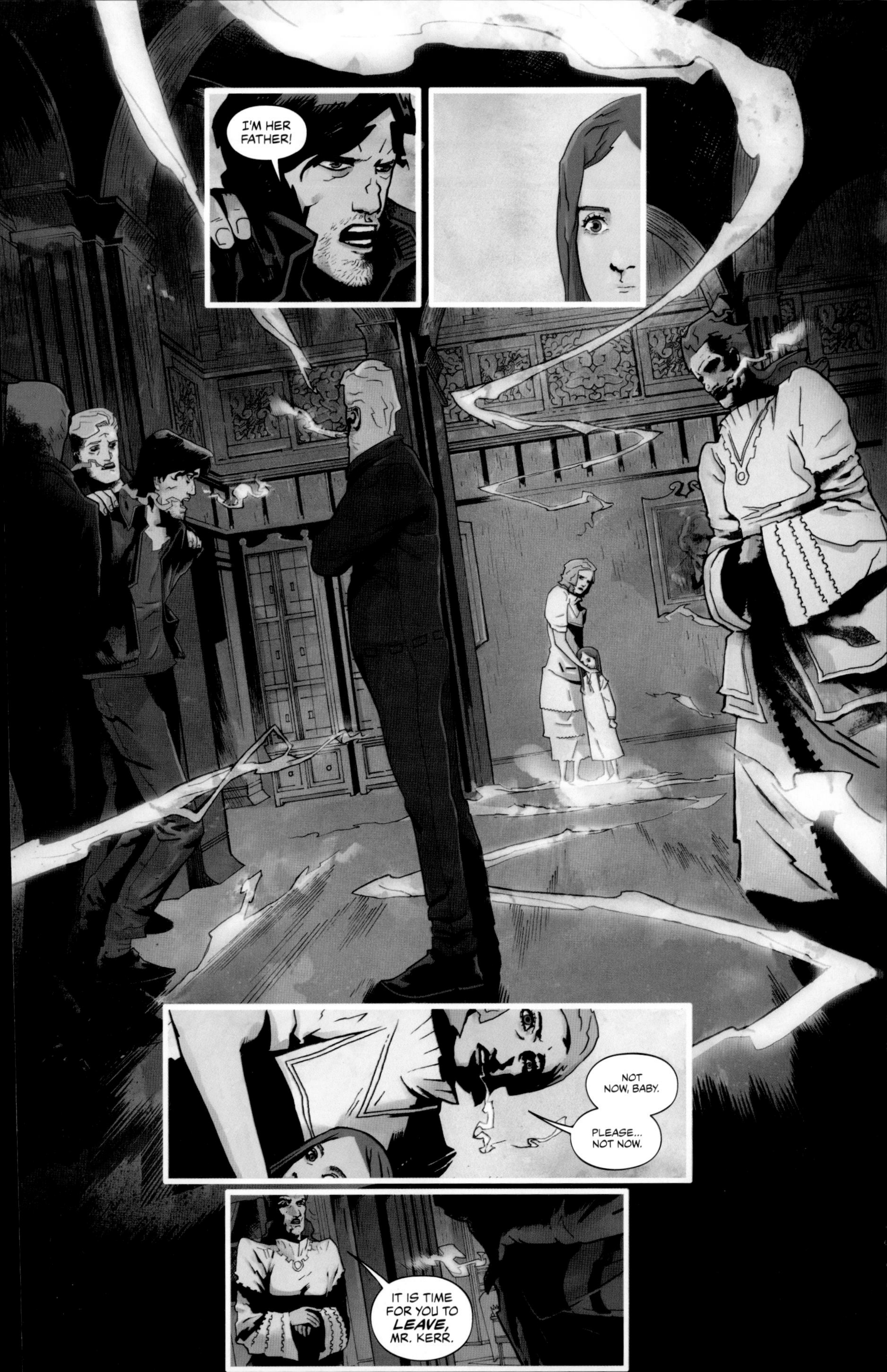
I'M HER FATHER!
NOT NOW, BABY.
PLEASE... NOT NOW.
IT IS TIME FOR YOU TO LEAVE, MR. KERR.

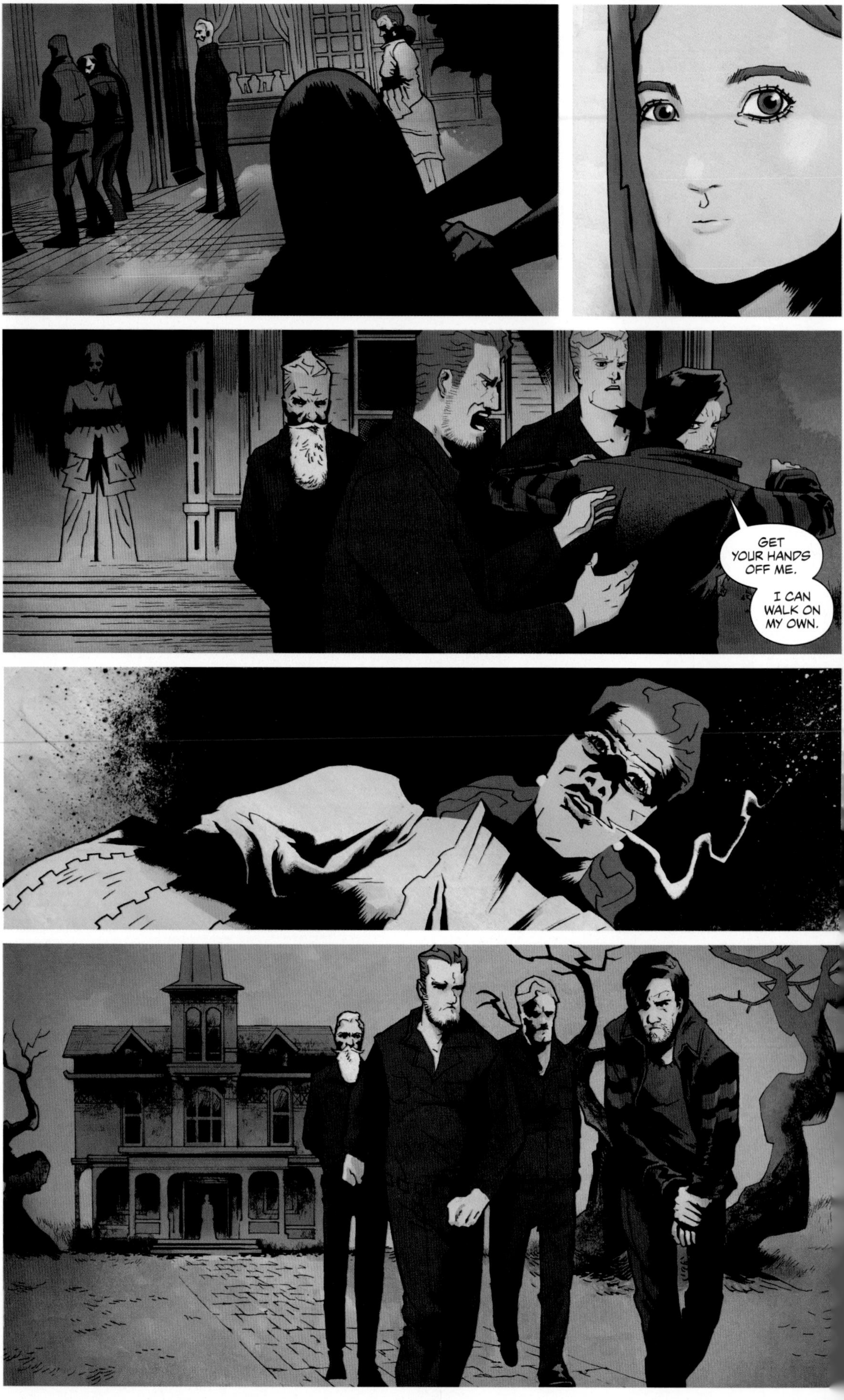
GET YOUR HANDS OFF ME.
I CAN WALK ON MY OWN.

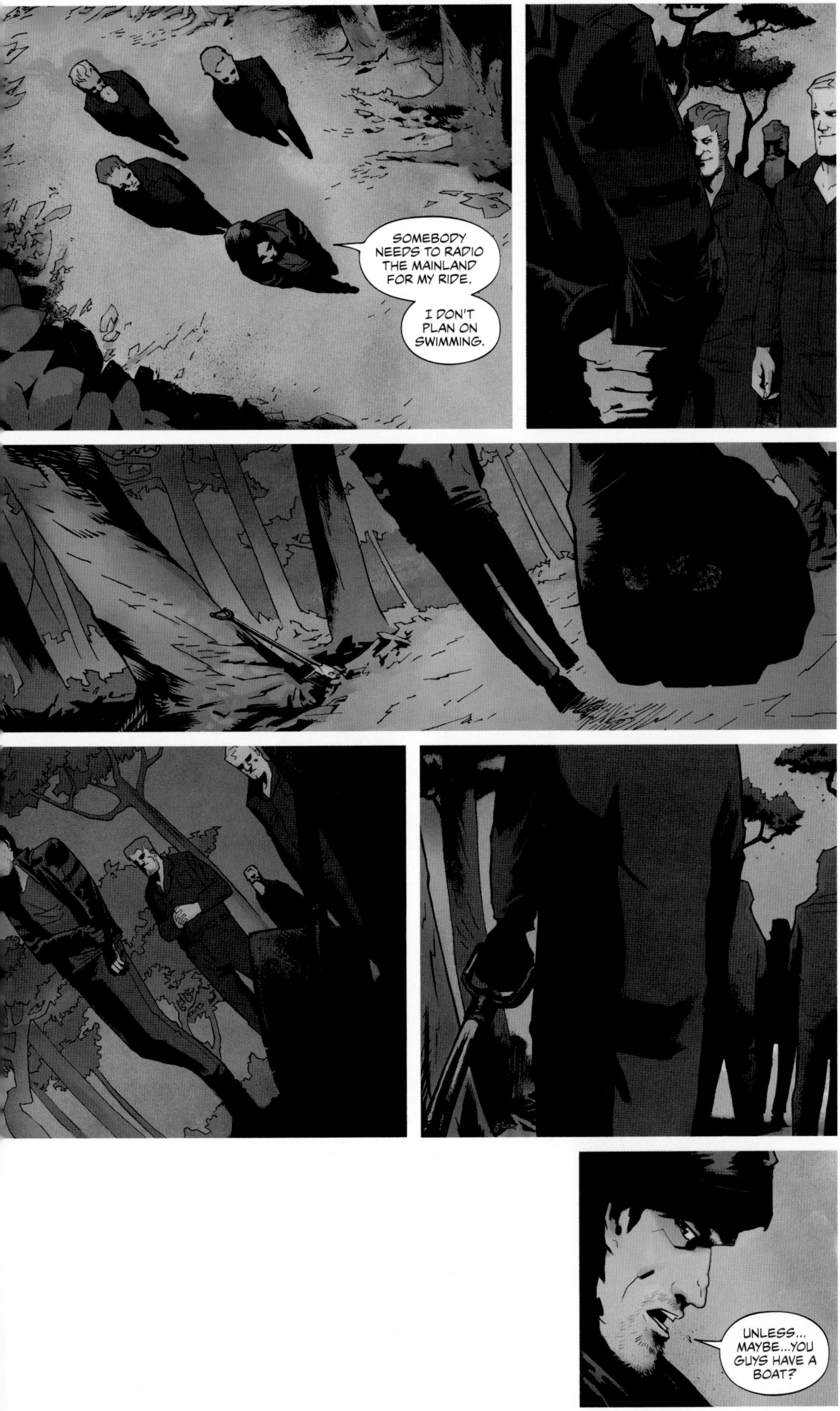
SOMEBODY NEEDS TO RADIO THE MAINLAND FOR MY RIDE.
I DON'T PLAN ON SWIMMING.
UNLESS... MAYBE...YOU GUYS HAVE A BOAT?

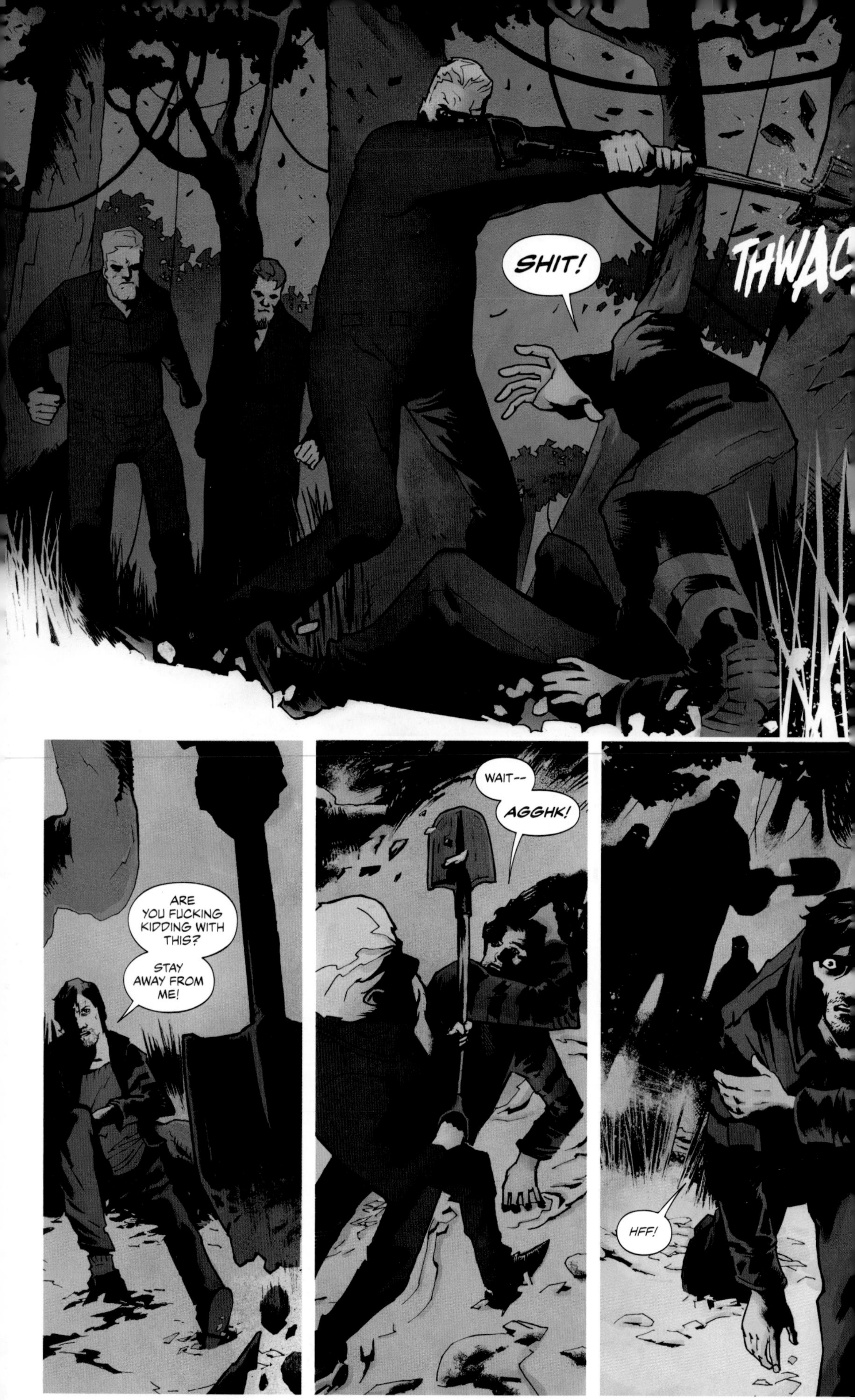
SHIT!
THWAC
ARE YOU FUCKING KIDDING WITH THIS?
STAY AWAY FROM ME!
WAIT--
AGGHK!
HFF!

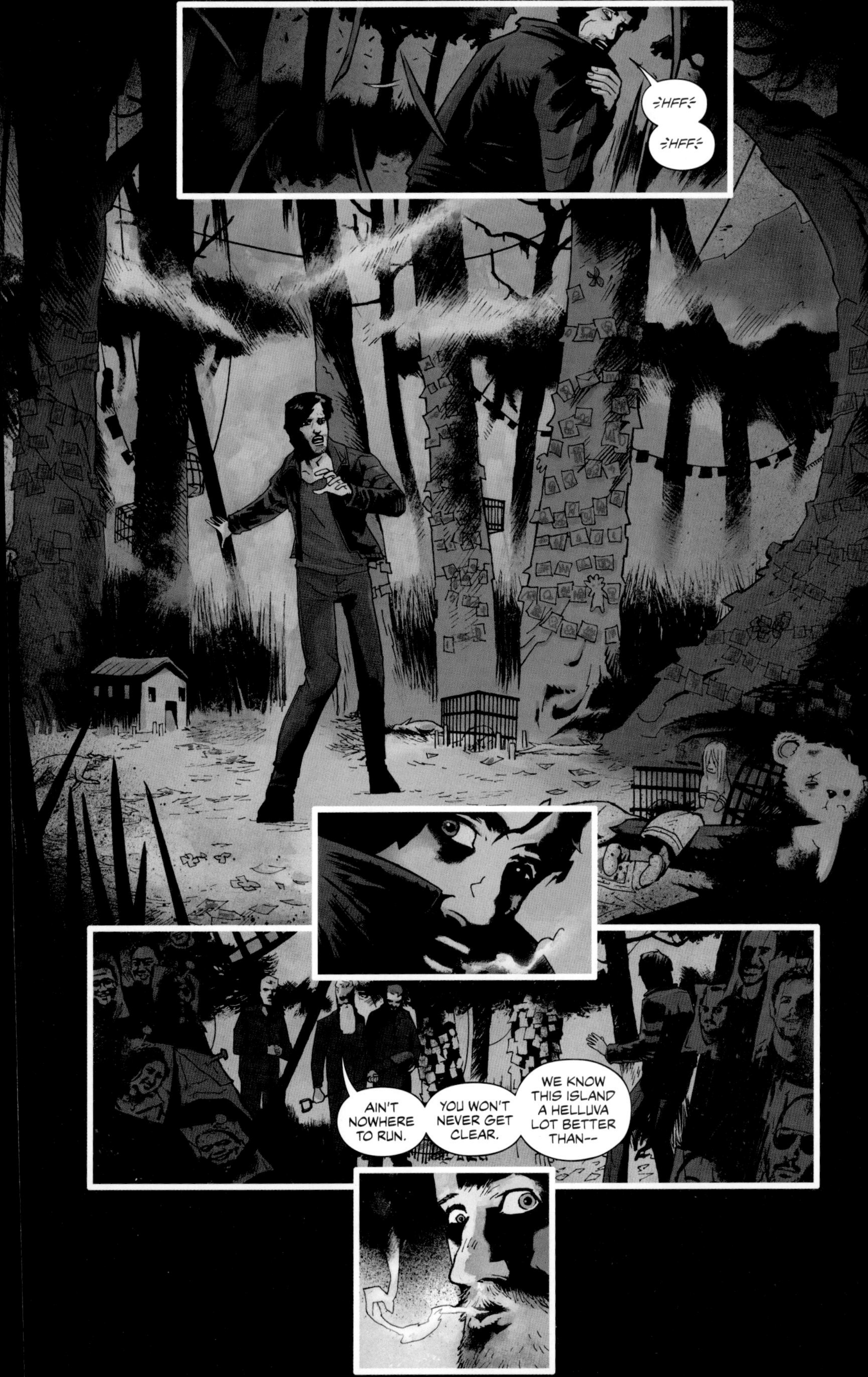
HFF
HFF
AIN'T NOWHERE TO RUN.
YOU WON'T NEVER GET CLEAR.
WE KNOW THIS ISLAND A HELLUVA LOT BETTER THAN--

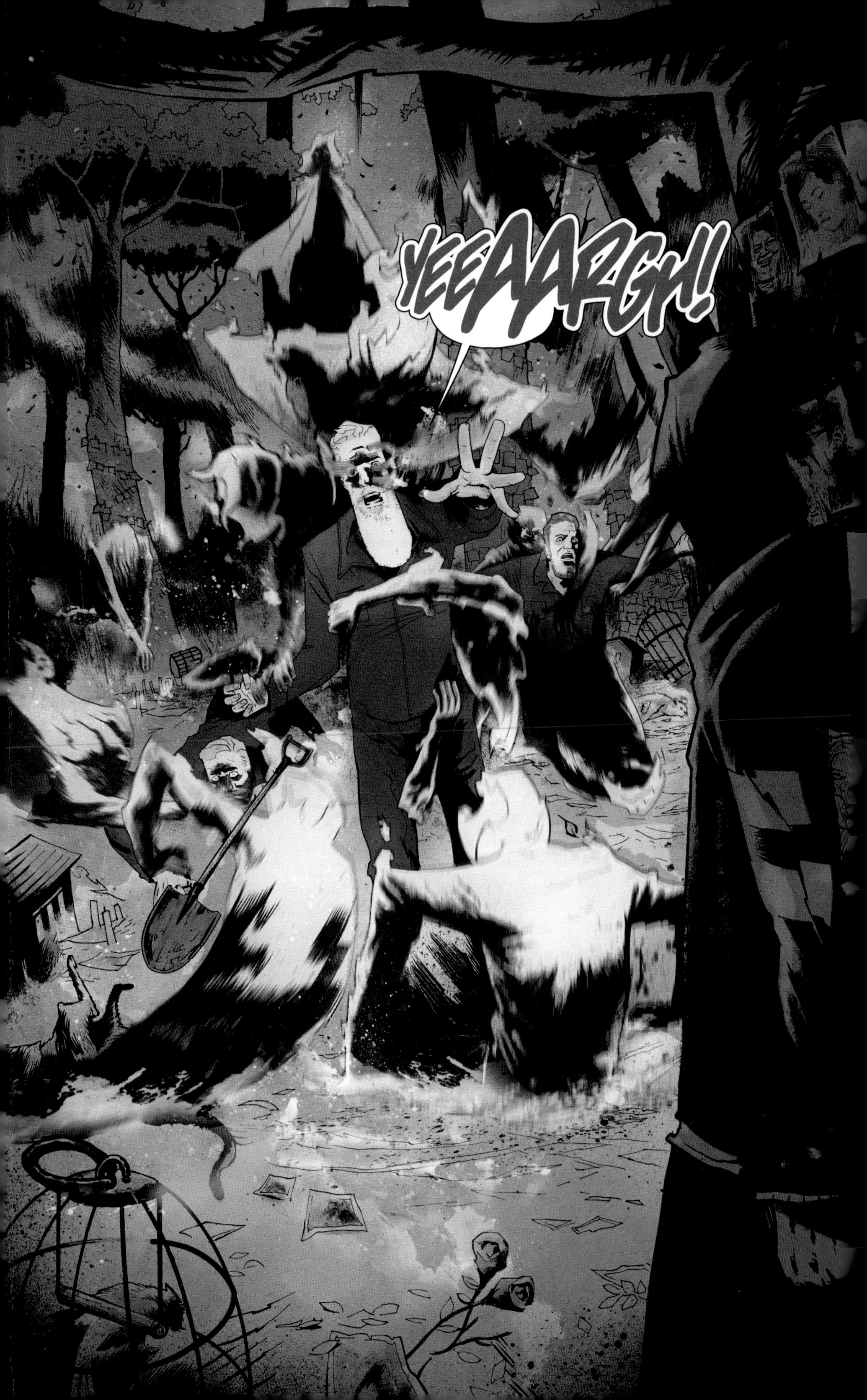
YEEAARGH!

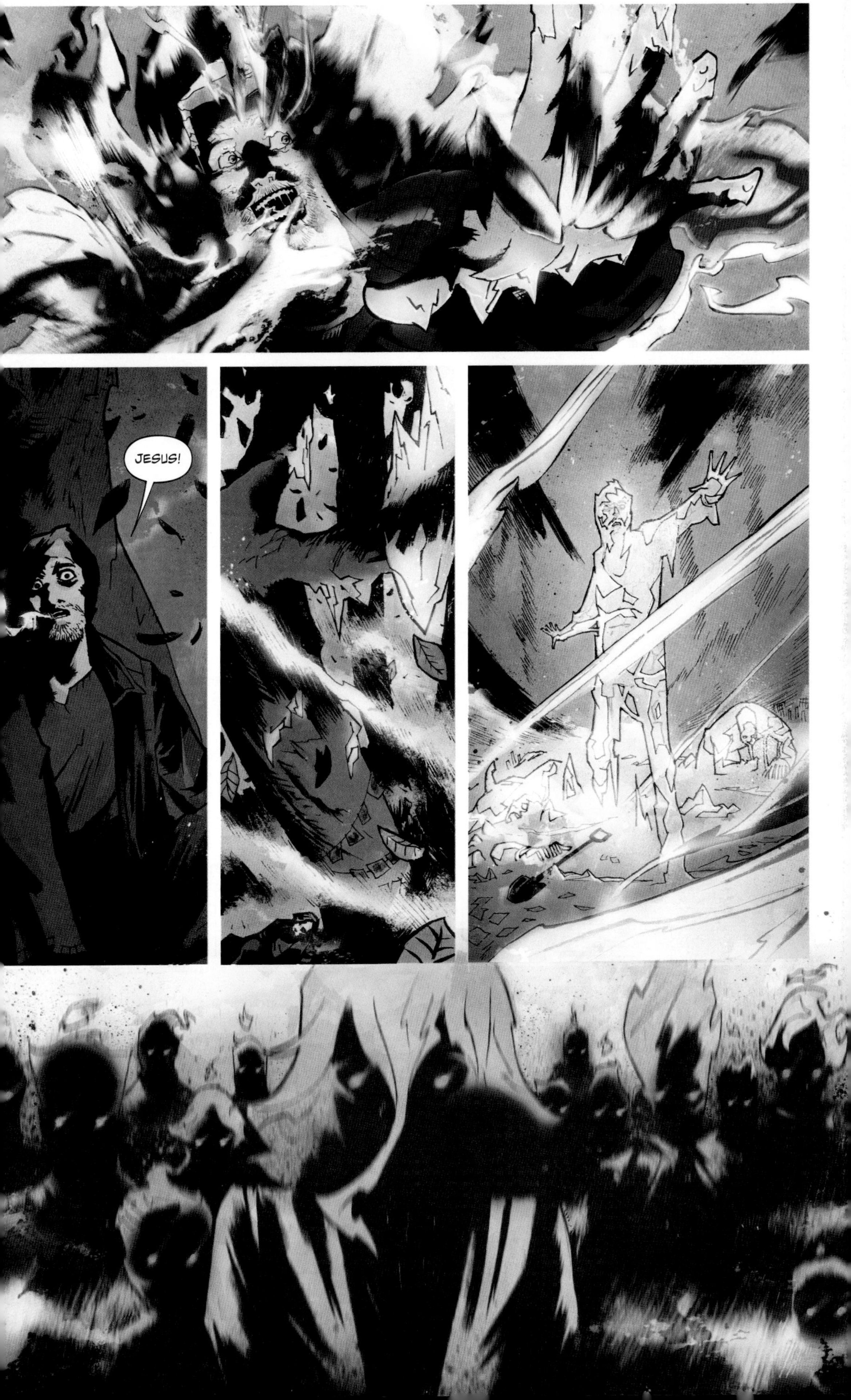
JESUS!

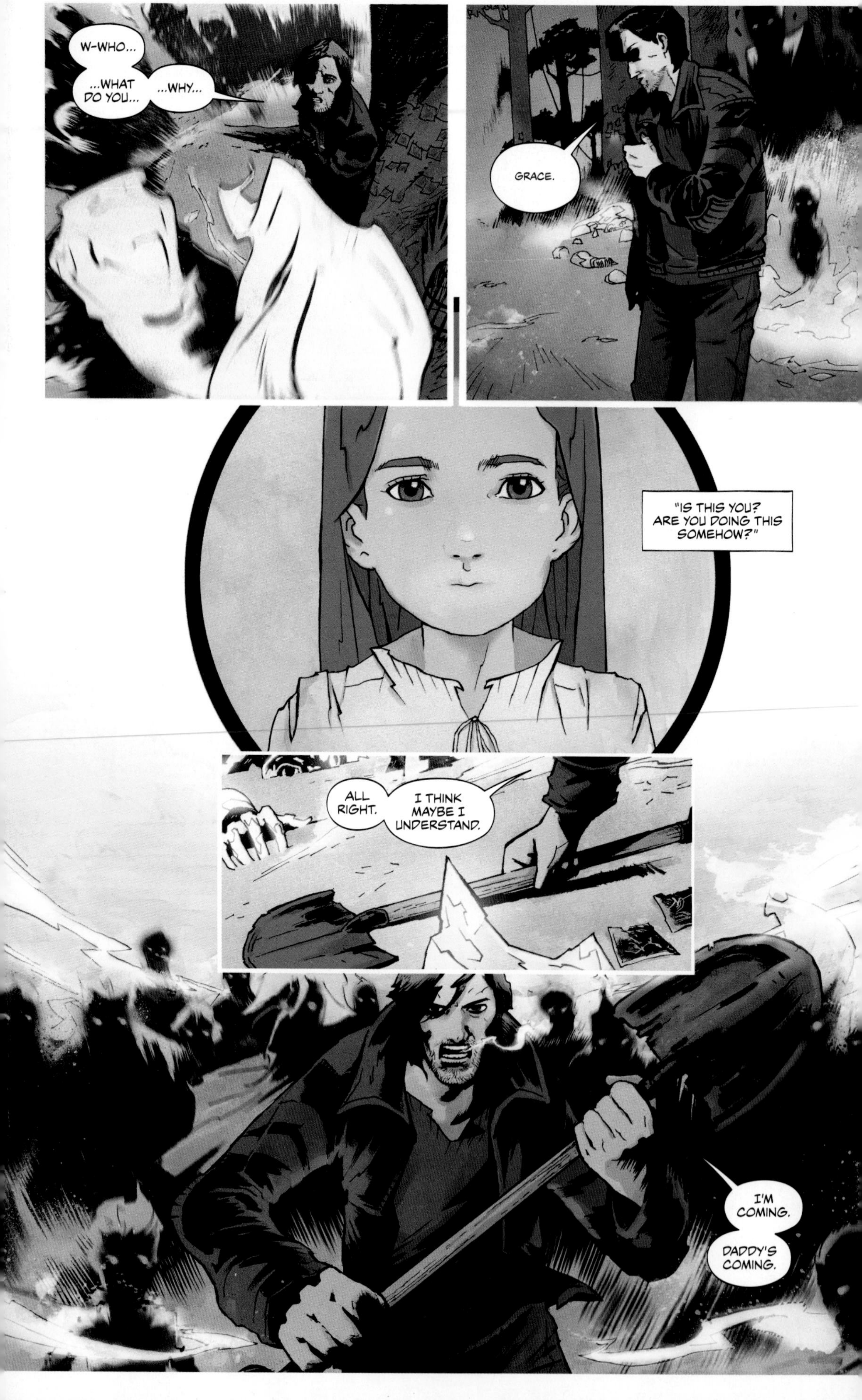
W-WHO...
...WHAT DO YOU...
...WHY...
GRACE.
"IS THIS YOU? ARE YOU DOING THIS SOMEHOW?"
ALL RIGHT.
I THINK MAYBE I UNDERSTAND.
I'M COMING.
DADDY'S COMING.

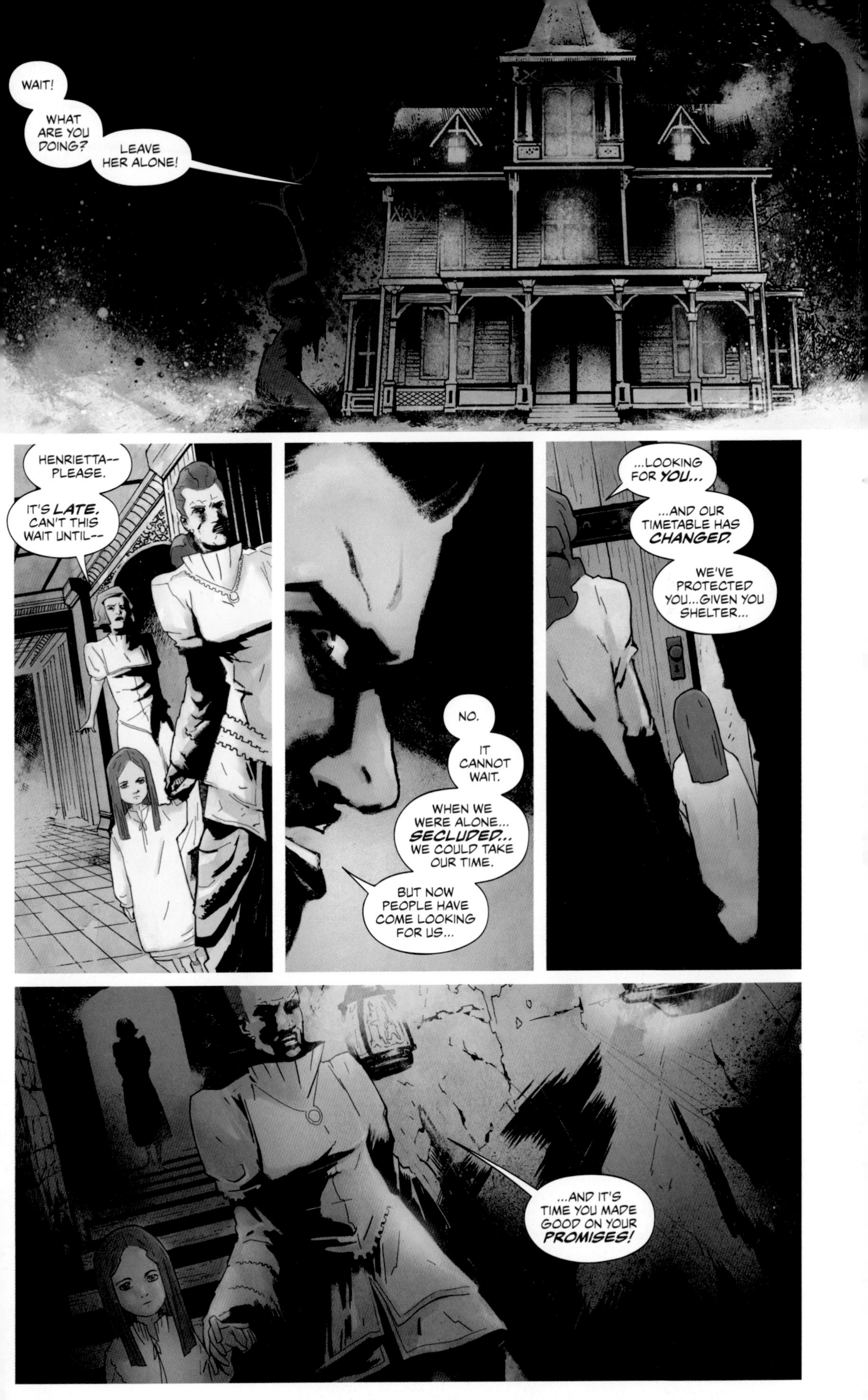
WAIT!
WHAT ARE YOU DOING?
LEAVE HER ALONE!
HENRIETTA-- PLEASE.
IT'S LATE. CAN'T THIS WAIT UNTIL--
NO.
IT CANNOT WAIT.
WHEN WE WERE ALONE... SECLUDED... WE COULD TAKE OUR TIME.
BUT NOW PEOPLE HAVE COME LOOKING FOR US...
...LOOKING FOR YOU...
...AND OUR TIMETABLE HAS CHANGED.
WE'VE PROTECTED YOU...GIVEN YOU SHELTER...
...AND IT'S TIME YOU MADE GOOD ON YOUR PROMISES!

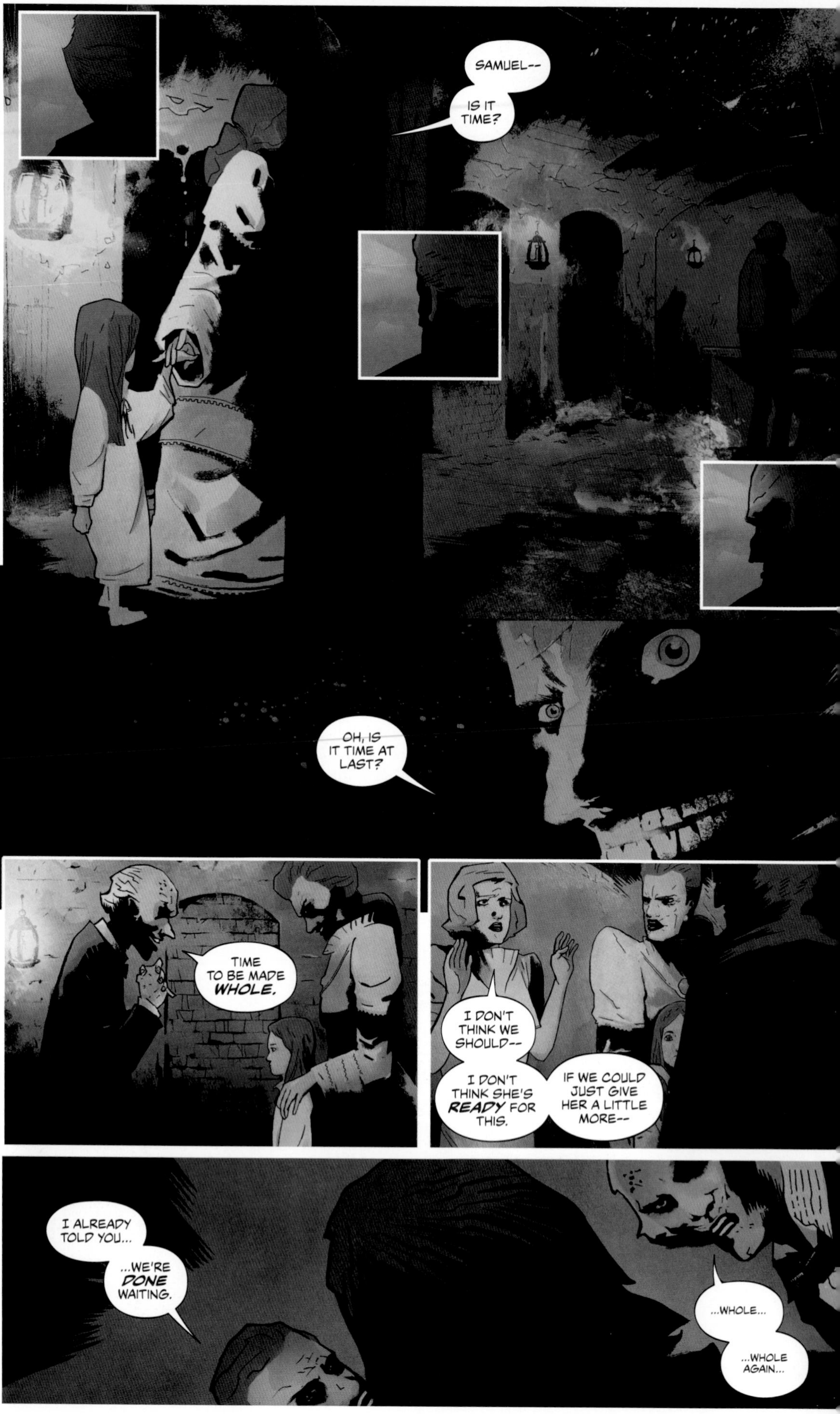
SAMUEL--
IS IT TIME?
OH, IS IT TIME AT LAST?
TIME TO BE MADE WHOLE.
I DON'T THINK WE SHOULD--
I DON'T THINK SHE'S READY FOR THIS.
IF WE COULD JUST GIVE HER A LITTLE MORE--
I ALREADY TOLD YOU...
...WE'RE DONE WAITING.
...WHOLE...
...WHOLE AGAIN...

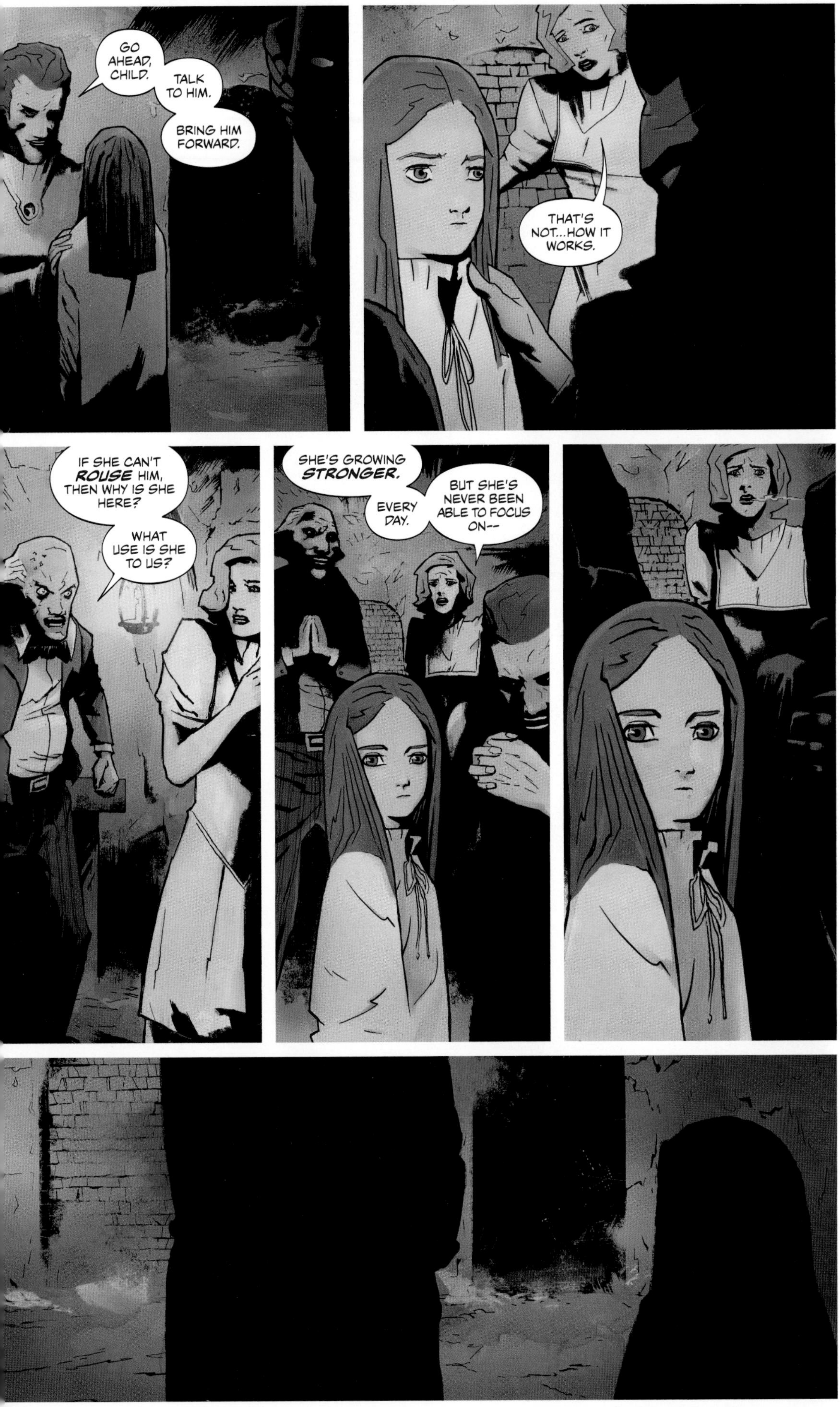
GO AHEAD, CHILD.
TALK TO HIM.
BRING HIM FORWARD.
THAT'S NOT...HOW IT WORKS.
IF SHE CAN'T ROUSE HIM, THEN WHY IS SHE HERE?
WHAT USE IS SHE TO US?
SHE'S GROWING STRONGER.
EVERY DAY.
BUT SHE'S NEVER BEEN ABLE TO FOCUS ON--

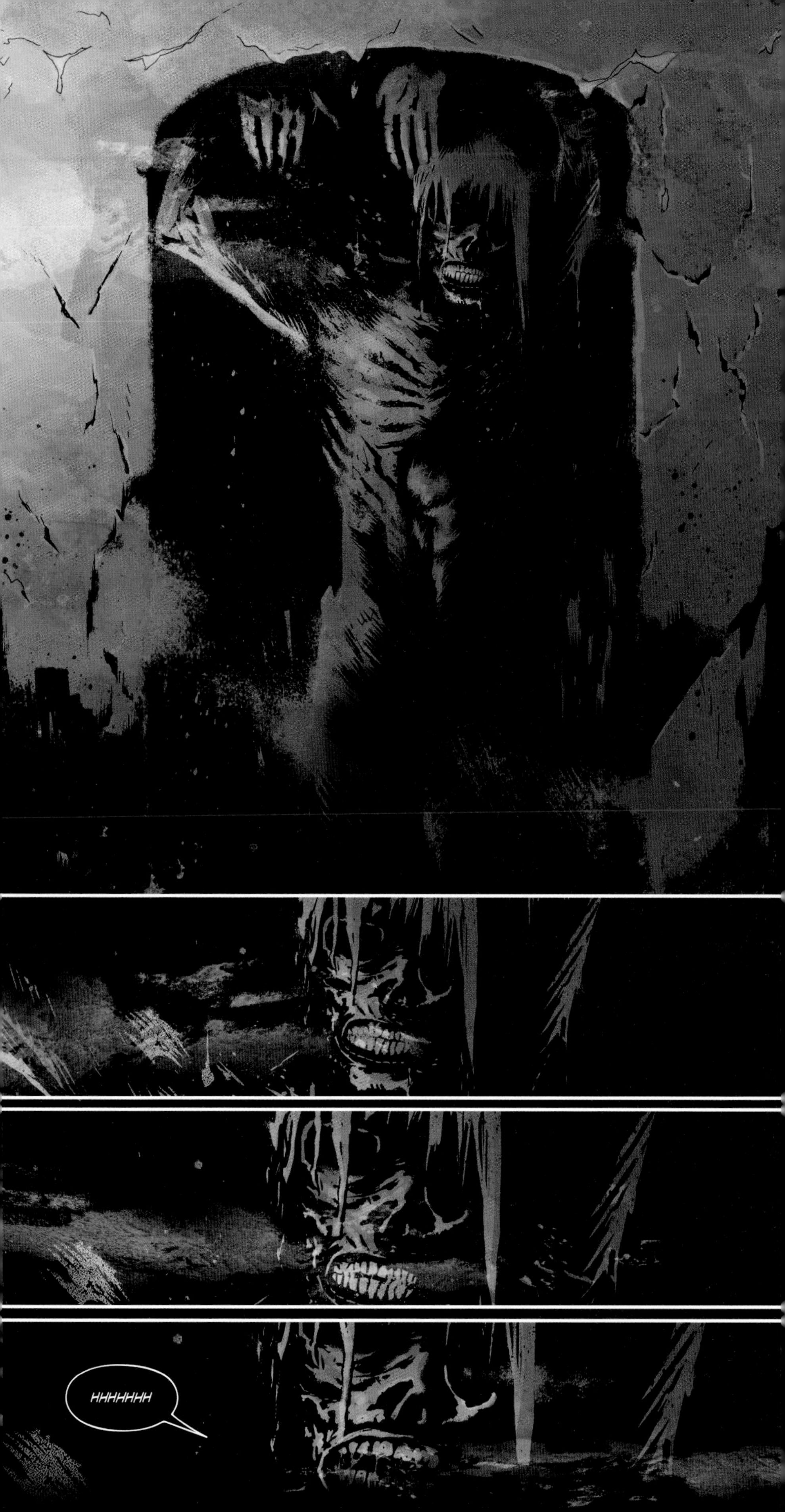
HHHHHHH

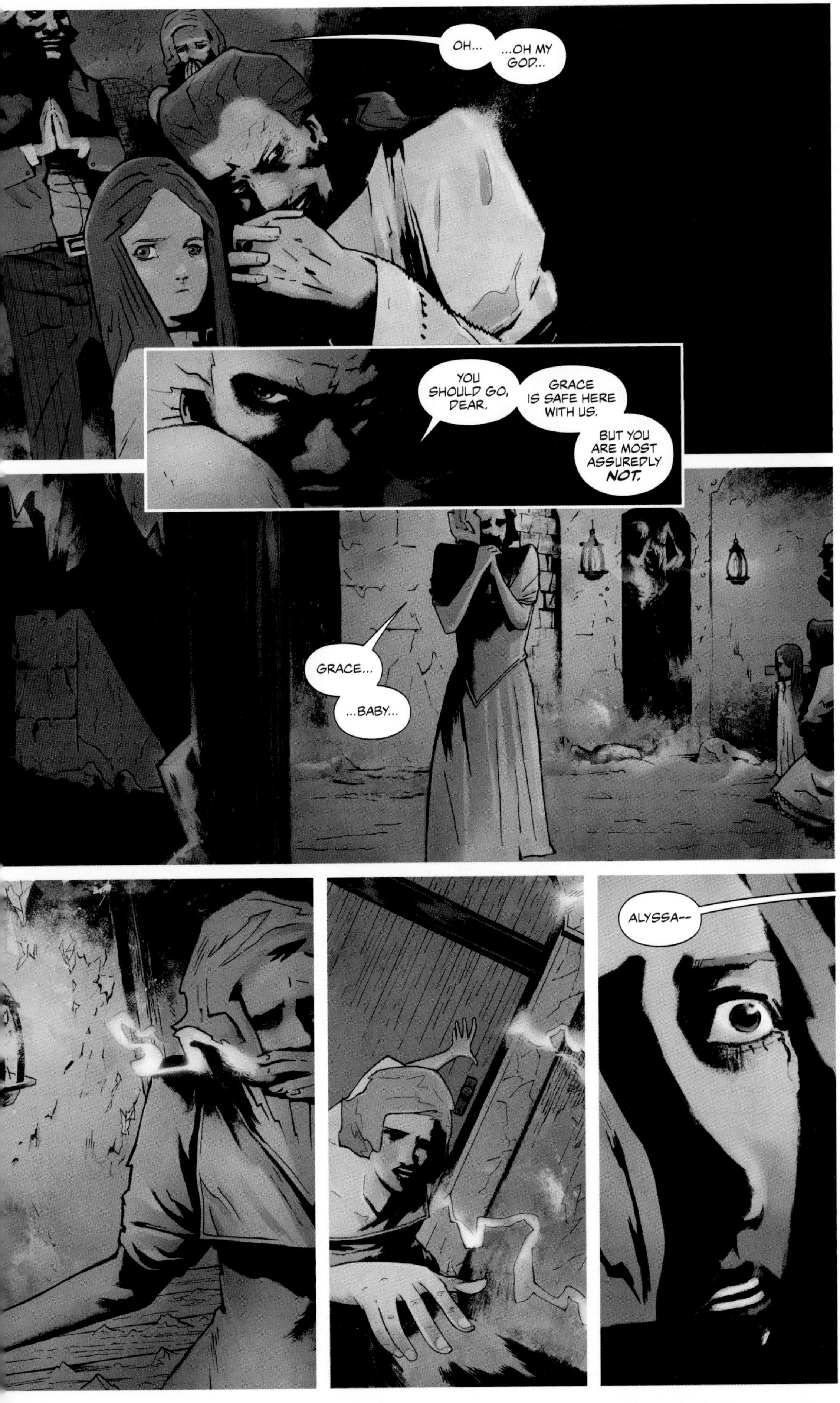
OH...
...OH MY GOD...
YOU SHOULD GO, DEAR.
GRACE IS SAFE HERE WITH US.
BUT YOU ARE MOST ASSUREDLY ***NOT.***
GRACE...
...BABY...
ALYSSA--

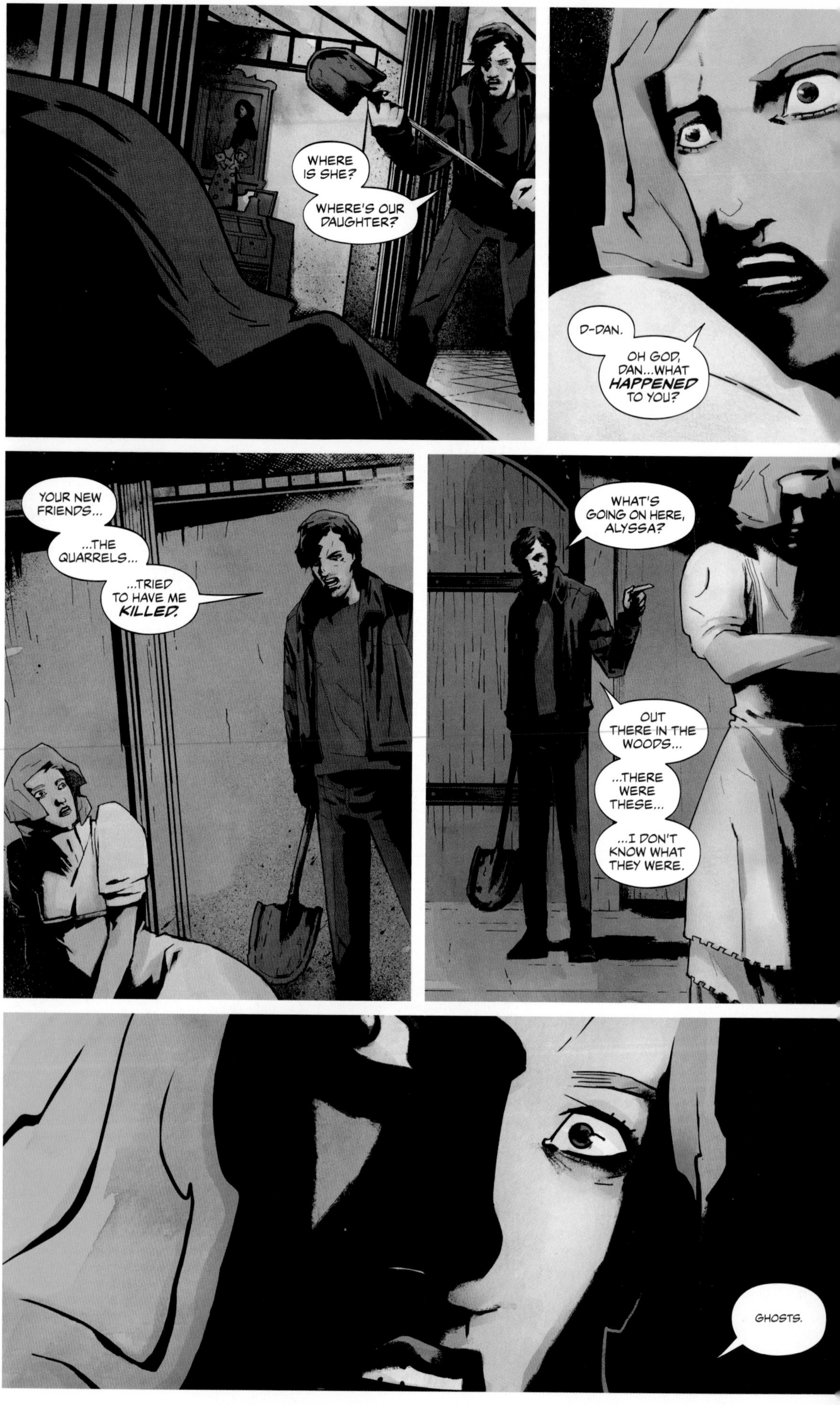
WHERE IS SHE?
WHERE'S OUR DAUGHTER?
D-DAN.
OH GOD, DAN...WHAT *HAPPENED* TO YOU?
YOUR NEW FRIENDS...
...THE QUARRELS...
...TRIED TO HAVE ME *KILLED.*
WHAT'S GOING ON HERE, ALYSSA?
OUT THERE IN THE WOODS...
...THERE WERE THESE...
...I DON'T KNOW WHAT THEY WERE.
GHOSTS.

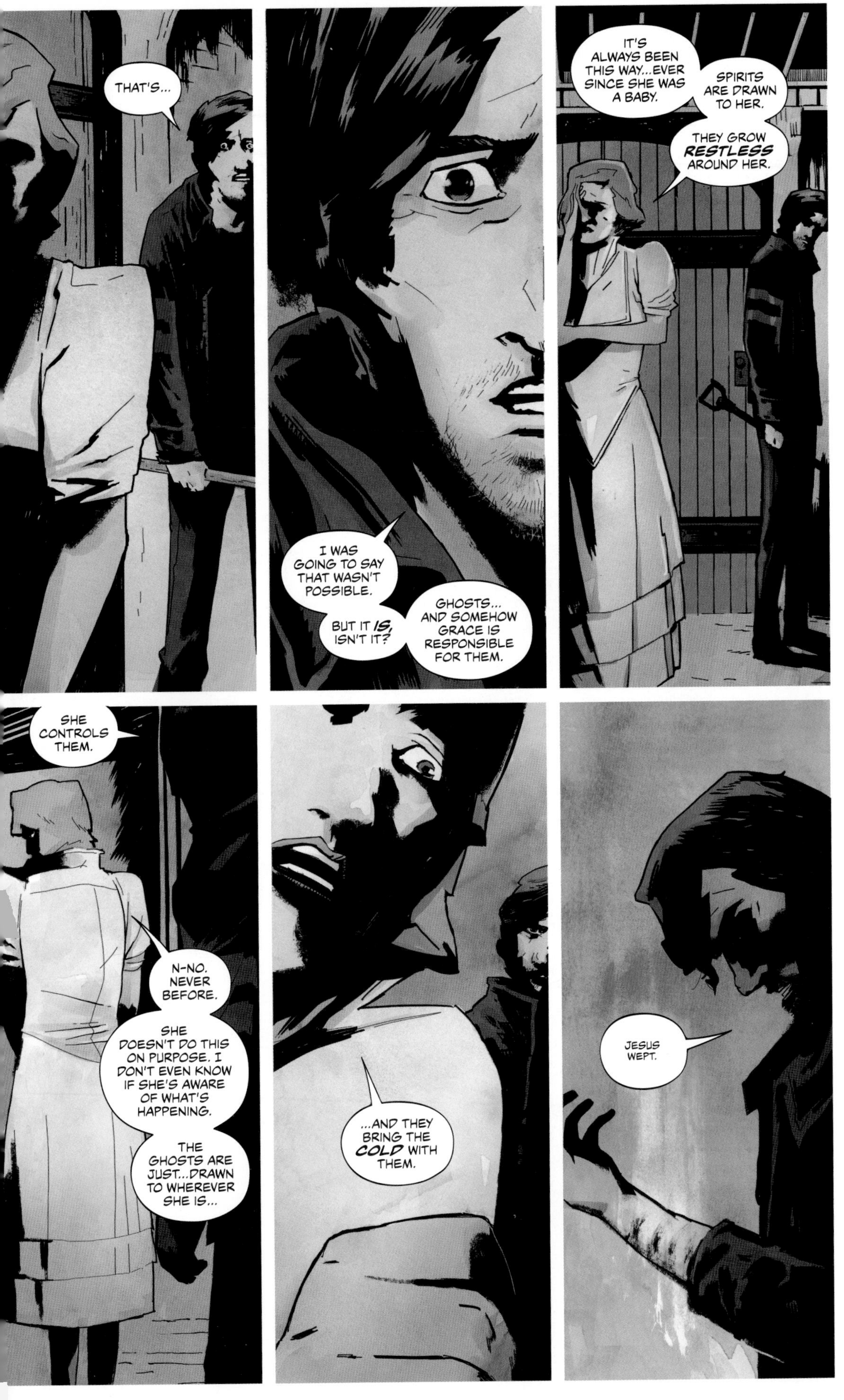
THAT'S...
I WAS GOING TO SAY THAT WASN'T POSSIBLE.
BUT IT *IS,* ISN'T IT?
GHOSTS... AND SOMEHOW GRACE IS RESPONSIBLE FOR THEM.
IT'S ALWAYS BEEN THIS WAY...EVER SINCE SHE WAS A BABY.
SPIRITS ARE DRAWN TO HER.
THEY GROW ***RESTLESS*** AROUND HER.
SHE CONTROLS THEM.
N-NO. NEVER BEFORE.
SHE DOESN'T DO THIS ON PURPOSE. I DON'T EVEN KNOW IF SHE'S AWARE OF WHAT'S HAPPENING.
THE GHOSTS ARE JUST...DRAWN TO WHEREVER SHE IS...
...AND THEY BRING THE ***COLD*** WITH THEM.
JESUS WEPT.

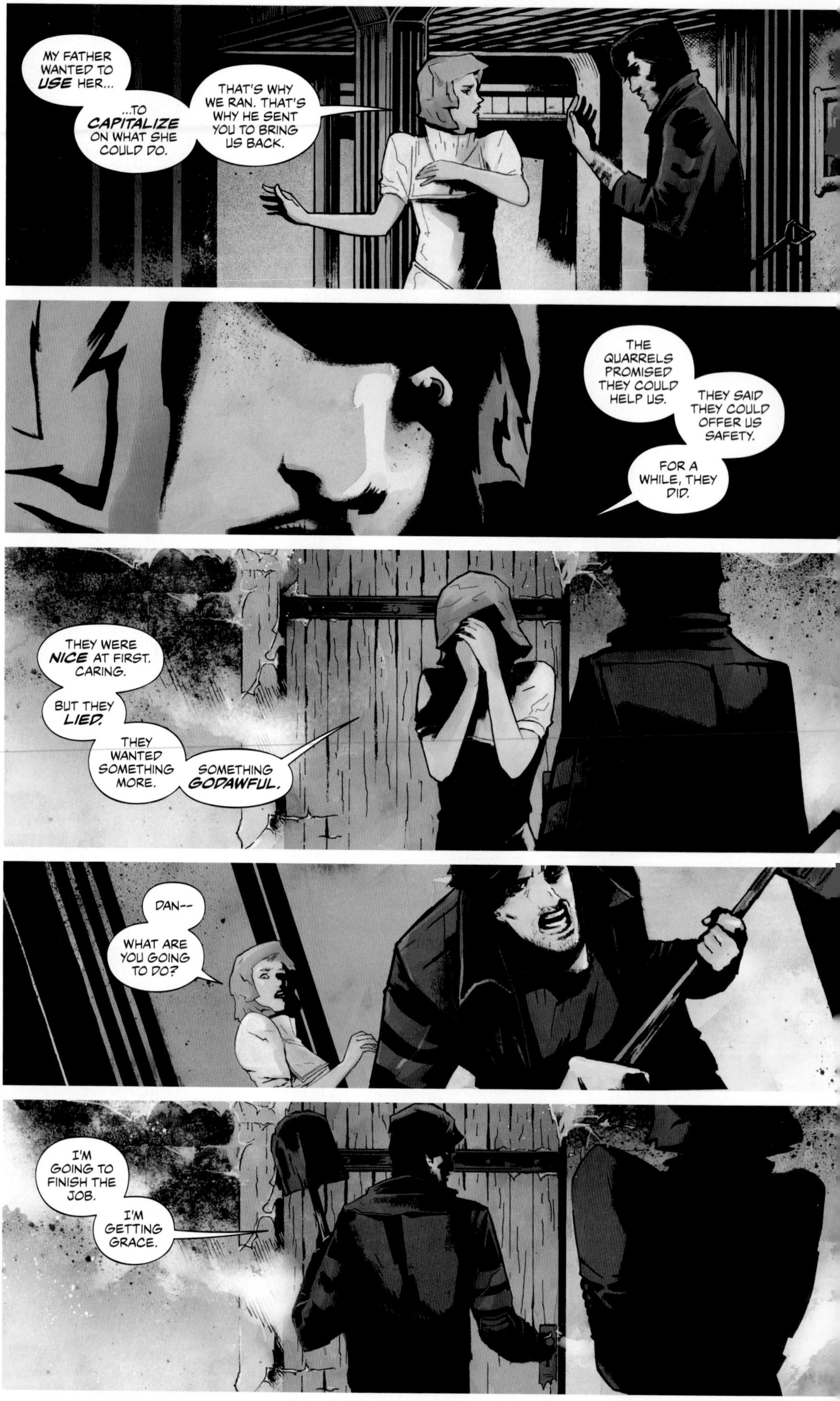
MY FATHER WANTED TO USE HER...
...TO CAPITALIZE ON WHAT SHE COULD DO.
THAT'S WHY WE RAN. THAT'S WHY HE SENT YOU TO BRING US BACK.
THE QUARRELS PROMISED THEY COULD HELP US.
THEY SAID THEY COULD OFFER US SAFETY.
FOR A WHILE, THEY DID.
THEY WERE NICE AT FIRST. CARING.
BUT THEY LIED.
THEY WANTED SOMETHING MORE.
SOMETHING GODAWFUL.
DAN--
WHAT ARE YOU GOING TO DO?
I'M GOING TO FINISH THE JOB.
I'M GETTING GRACE.

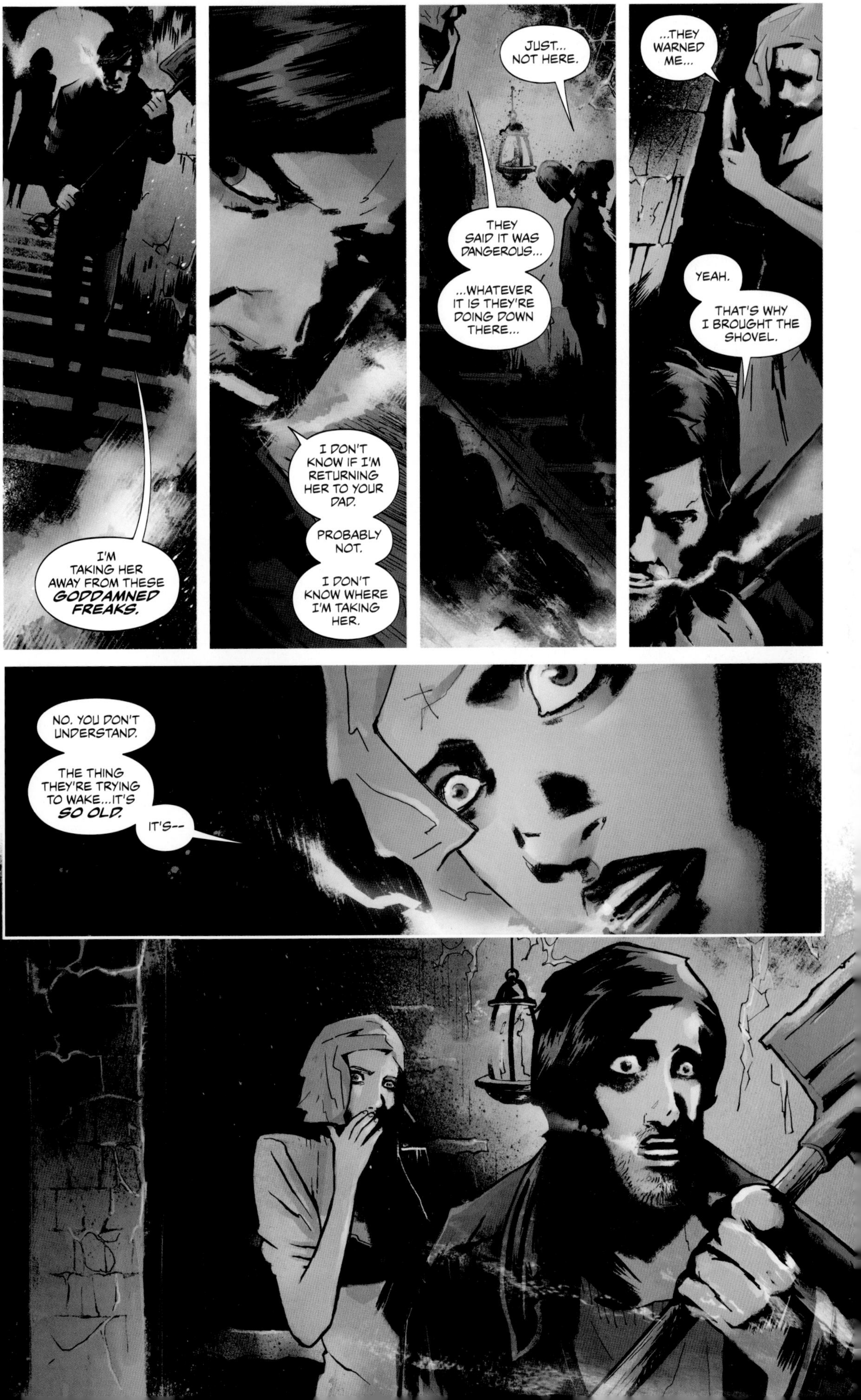
I'M TAKING HER AWAY FROM THESE GODDAMNED FREAKS.
I DON'T KNOW IF I'M RETURNING HER TO YOUR DAD.
PROBABLY NOT.
I DON'T KNOW WHERE I'M TAKING HER.
JUST... NOT HERE.
THEY SAID IT WAS DANGEROUS...
...WHATEVER IT IS THEY'RE DOING DOWN THERE...
...THEY WARNED ME...
YEAH.
THAT'S WHY I BROUGHT THE SHOVEL.
NO. YOU DON'T UNDERSTAND.
THE THING THEY'RE TRYING TO WAKE...IT'S SO OLD.
IT'S--

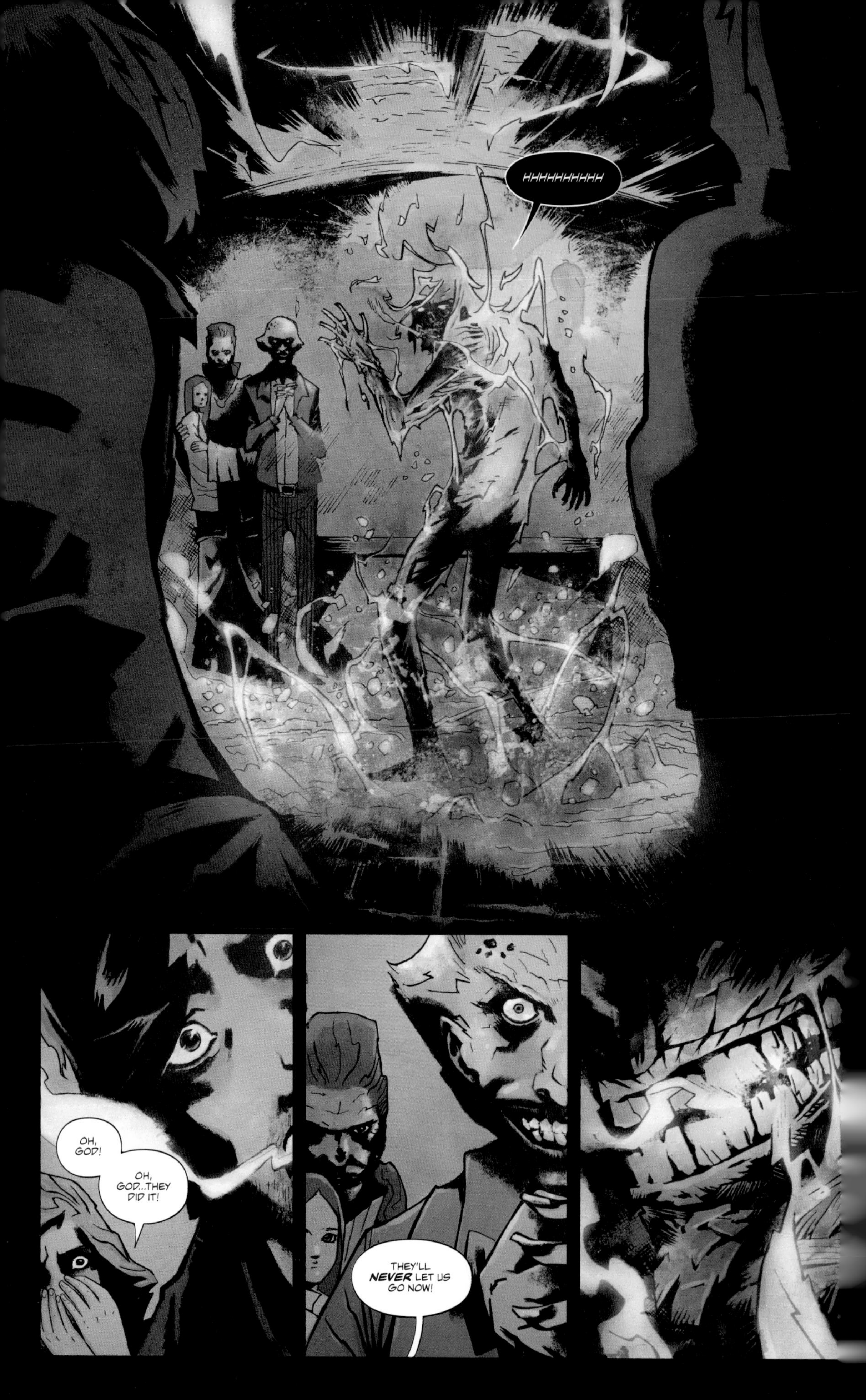
HHHHHHHHHH
OH, GOD!
OH, GOD...THEY DID IT!
THEY'LL NEVER LET US GO NOW!

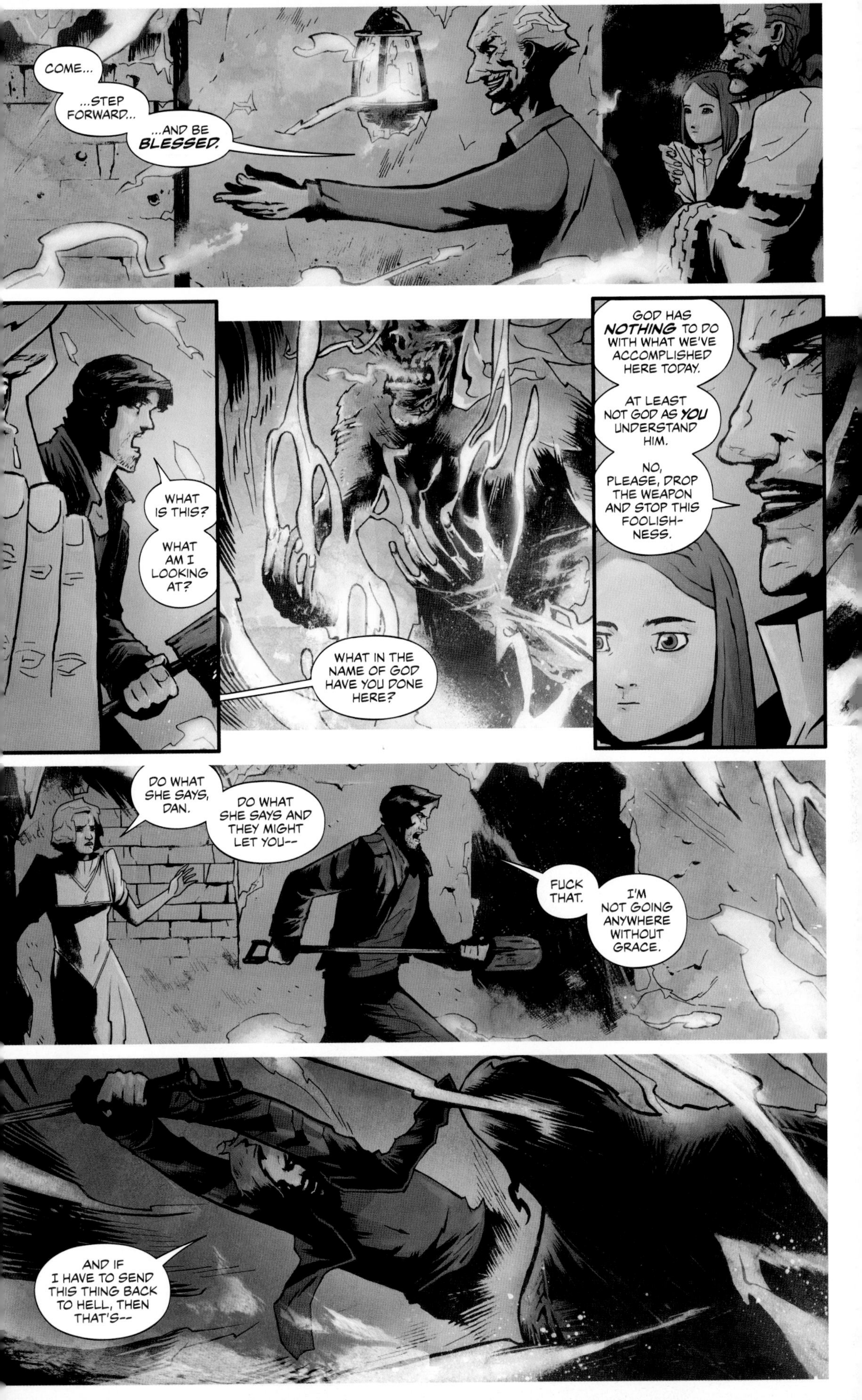
COME...
...STEP FORWARD...
...AND BE BLESSED.
WHAT IS THIS?
WHAT AM I LOOKING AT?
WHAT IN THE NAME OF GOD HAVE YOU DONE HERE?
GOD HAS NOTHING TO DO WITH WHAT WE'VE ACCOMPLISHED HERE TODAY.
AT LEAST NOT GOD AS YOU UNDERSTAND HIM.
NO, PLEASE, DROP THE WEAPON AND STOP THIS FOOLISH-NESS.
DO WHAT SHE SAYS, DAN.
DO WHAT SHE SAYS AND THEY MIGHT LET YOU--
FUCK THAT.
I'M NOT GOING ANYWHERE WITHOUT GRACE.
AND IF I HAVE TO SEND THIS THING BACK TO HELL, THEN THAT'S--

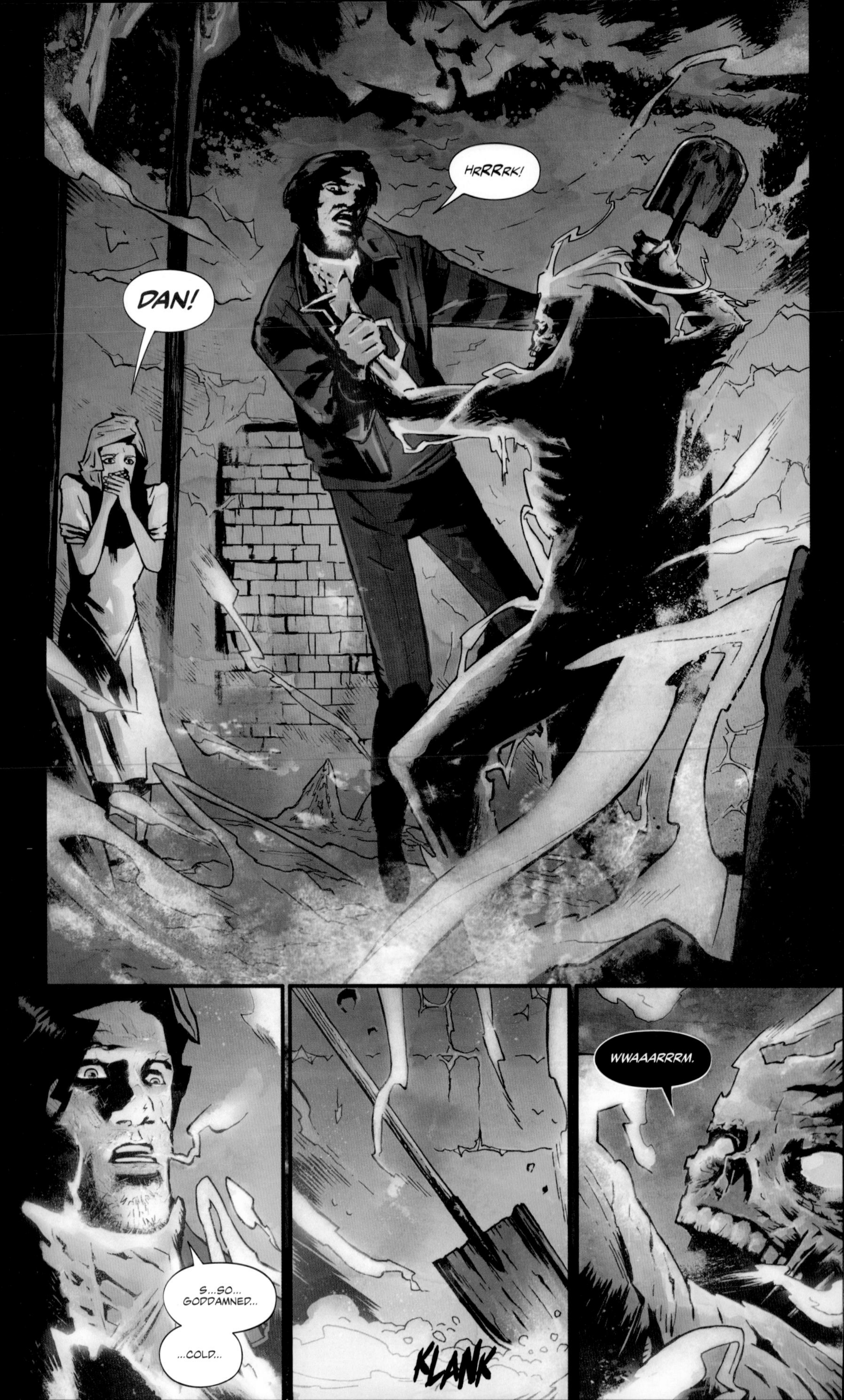
HRRRRK!
DAN!
S...SO... GODDAMNED...
...COLD...
KLANK
WWAAARRRM.

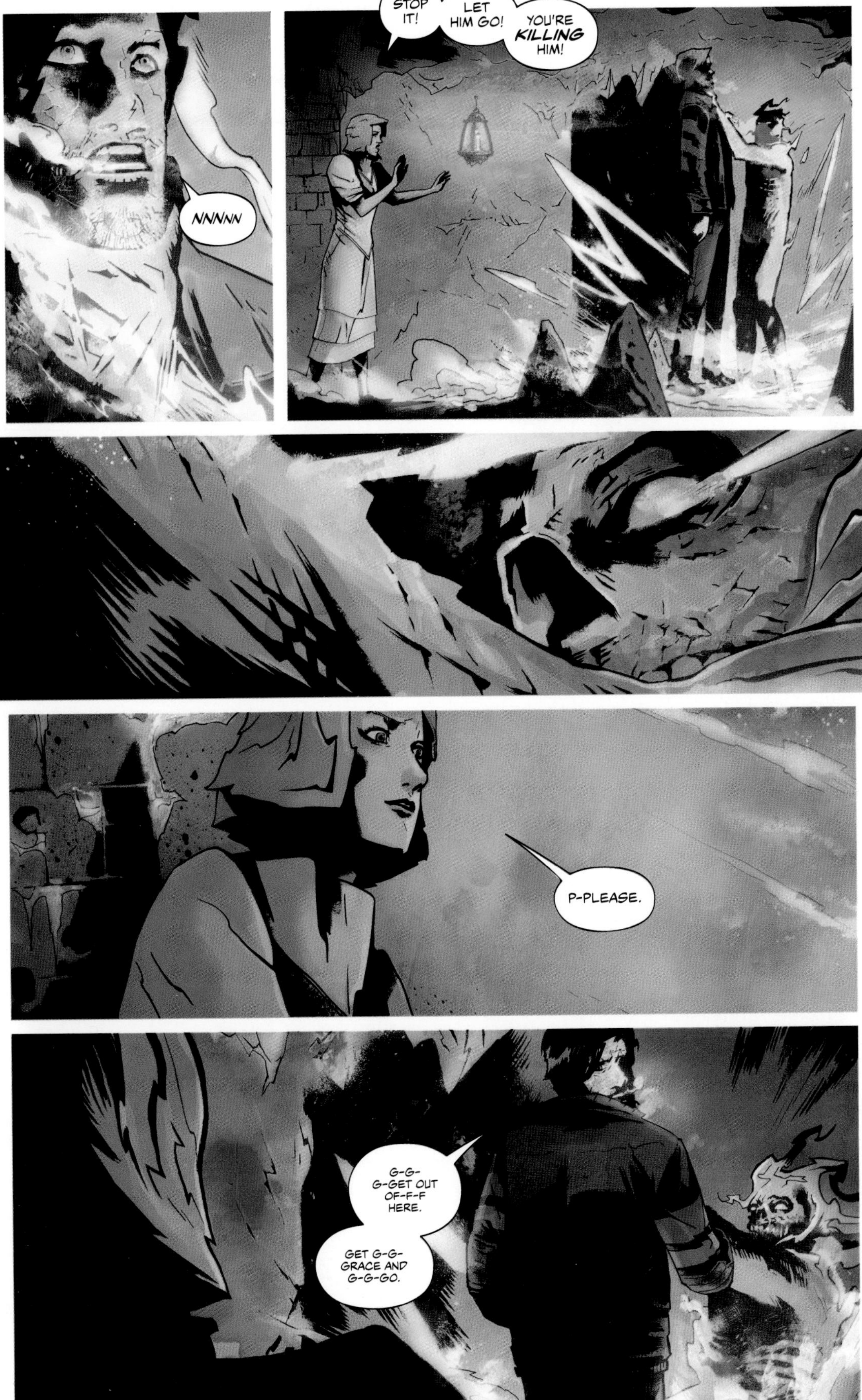
NNNNN
STOP IT!
LET HIM GO!
YOU'RE KILLING HIM!
P-PLEASE.
G-G-G-GET OUT OF-F-F HERE.
GET G-G-GRACE AND G-G-GO.

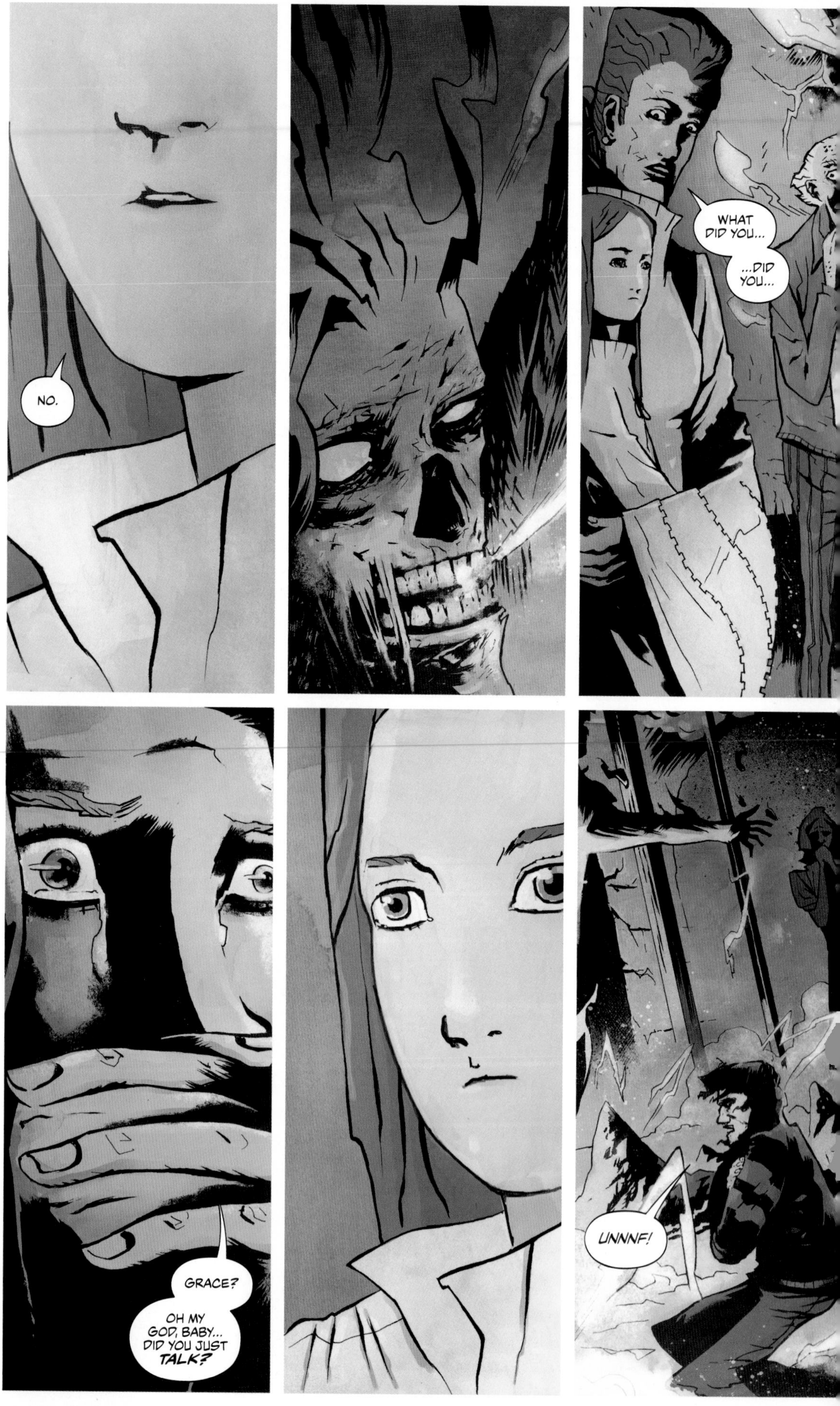
NO.
WHAT DID YOU...
...DID YOU...
GRACE?
OH MY GOD, BABY... DID YOU JUST TALK?
UNNNF!

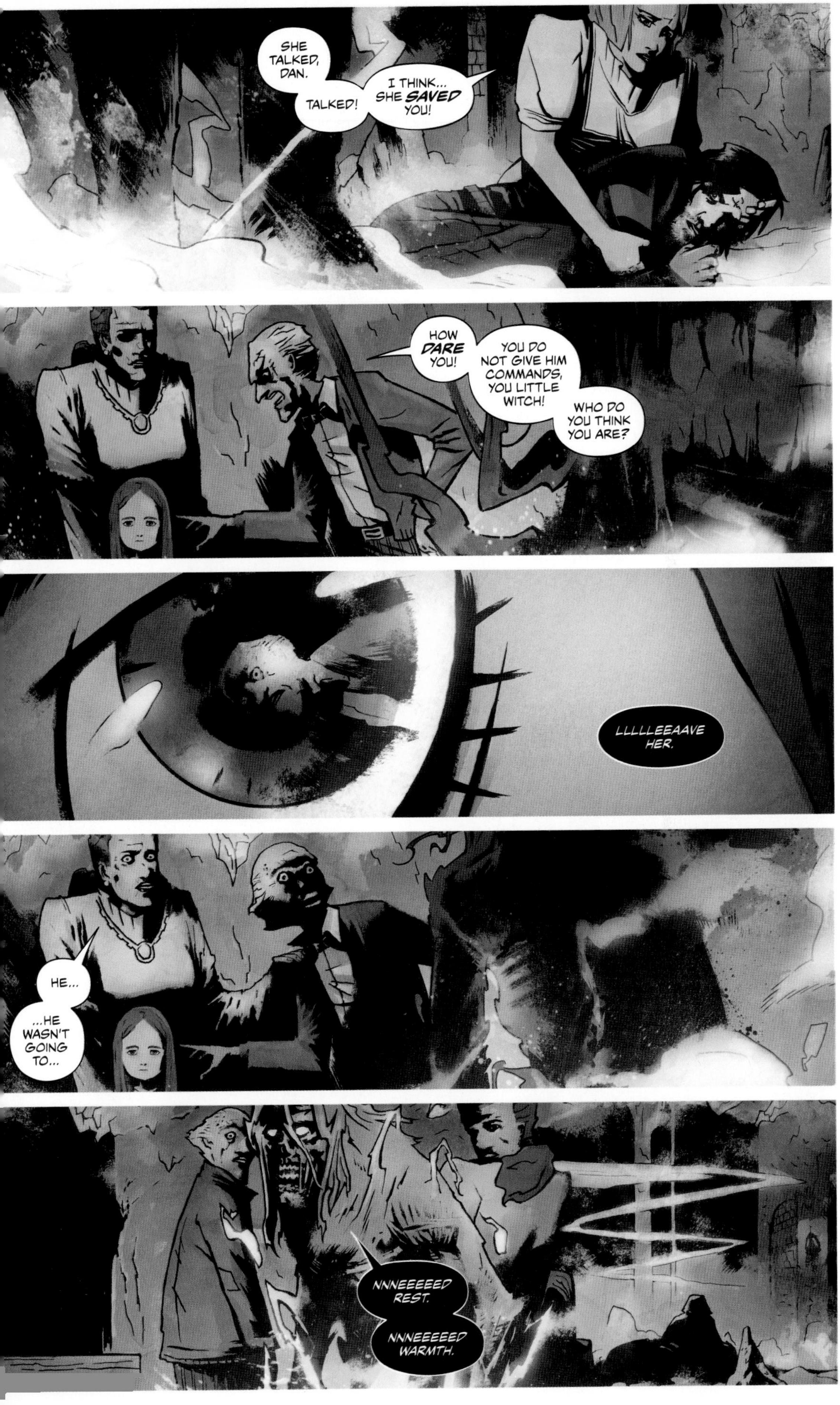

SHE TALKED, DAN.
TALKED!
I THINK... SHE SAVED YOU!
HOW DARE YOU!
YOU DO NOT GIVE HIM COMMANDS, YOU LITTLE WITCH!
WHO DO YOU THINK YOU ARE?
LLLLLEEAAVE HER.
HE...
...HE WASN'T GOING TO...
NNNEEEEED REST.
NNNEEEEED WARMTH.

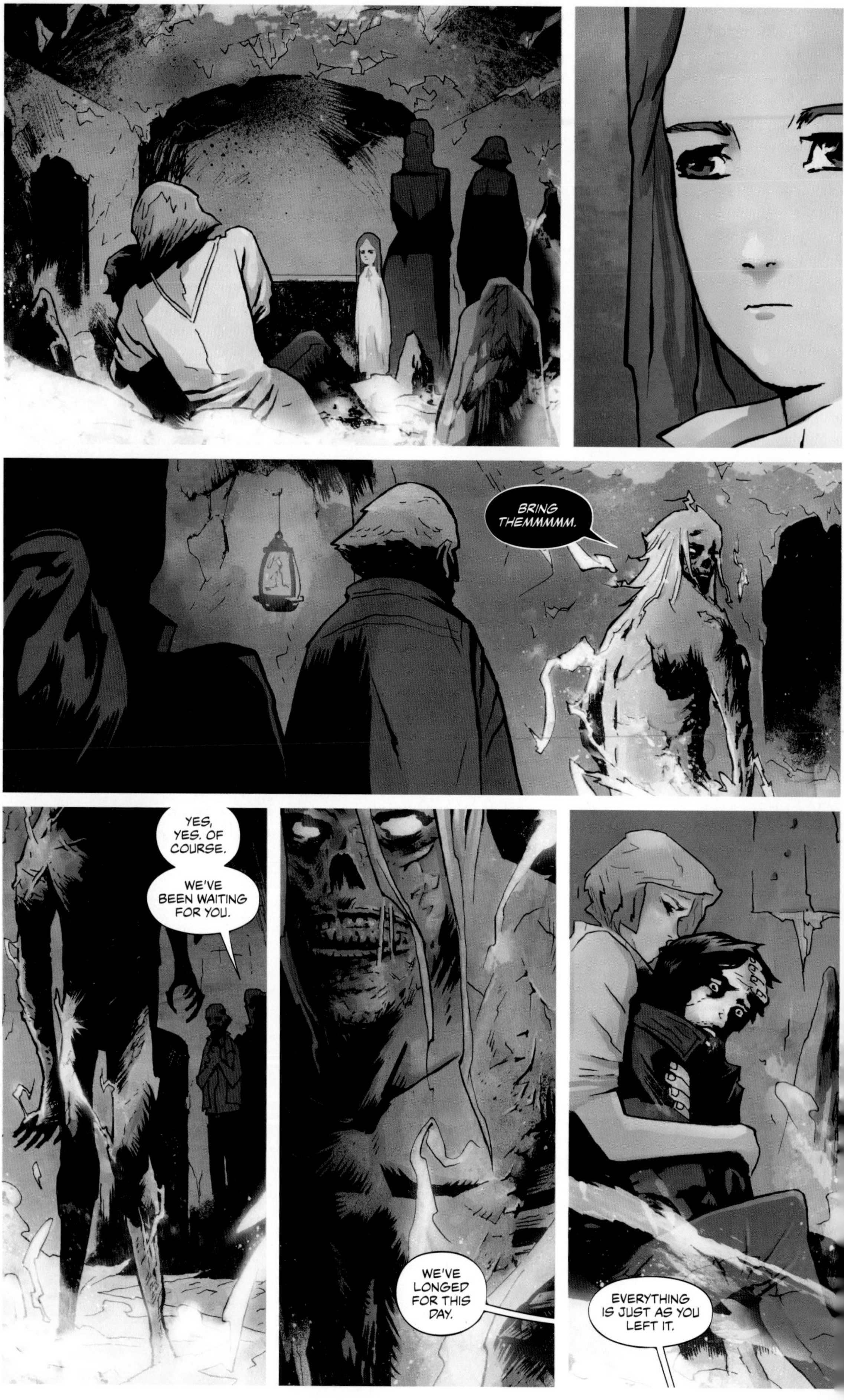
BRING THEMMMMM.
YES, YES. OF COURSE.
WE'VE BEEN WAITING FOR YOU.
WE'VE LONGED FOR THIS DAY.
EVERYTHING IS JUST AS YOU LEFT IT.

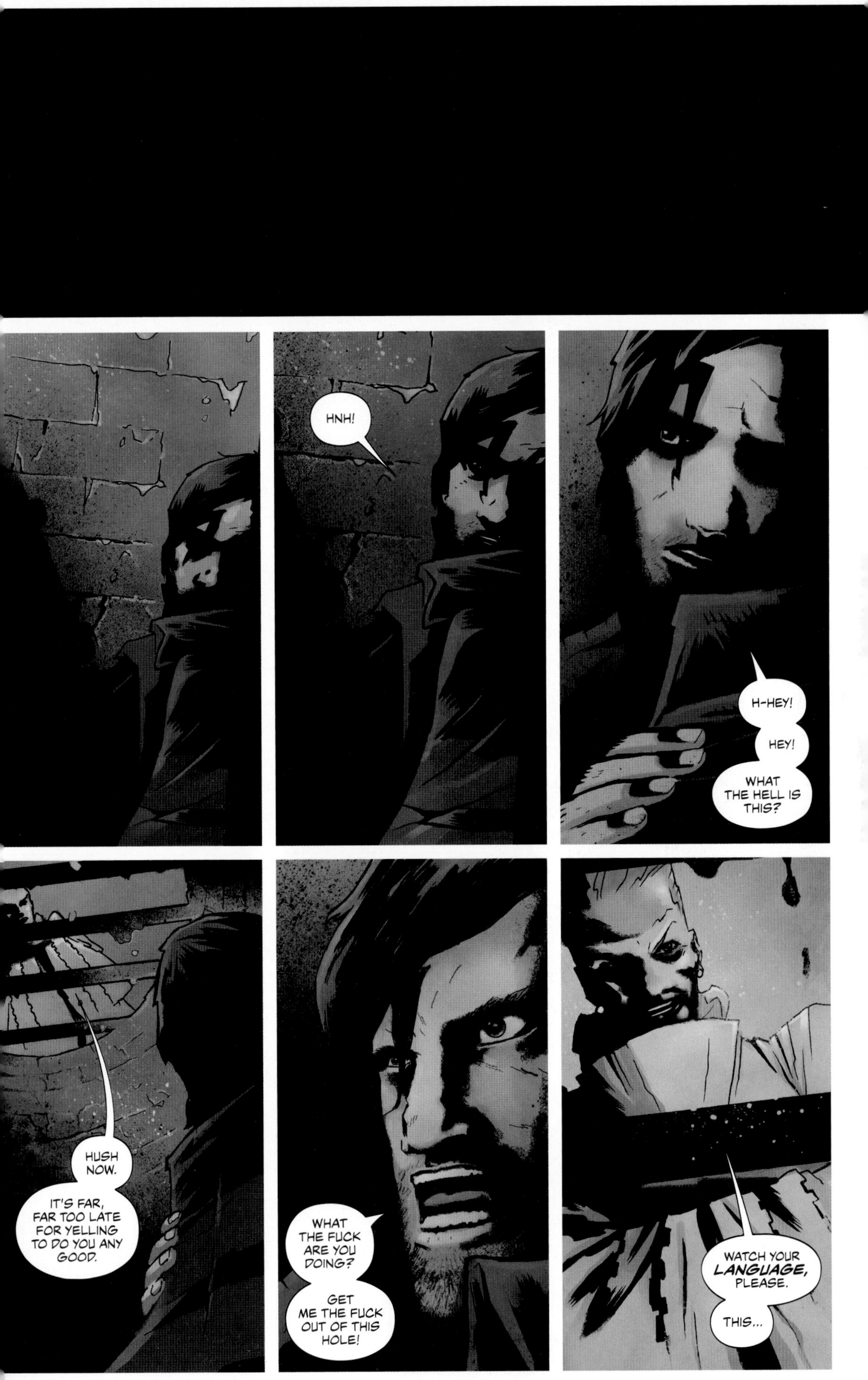
HNH!
H-HEY!
HEY!
WHAT THE HELL IS THIS?
HUSH NOW.
IT'S FAR, FAR TOO LATE FOR YELLING TO DO YOU ANY GOOD.
WHAT THE FUCK ARE YOU DOING?
GET ME THE FUCK OUT OF THIS HOLE!
WATCH YOUR *LANGUAGE,* PLEASE.
THIS...

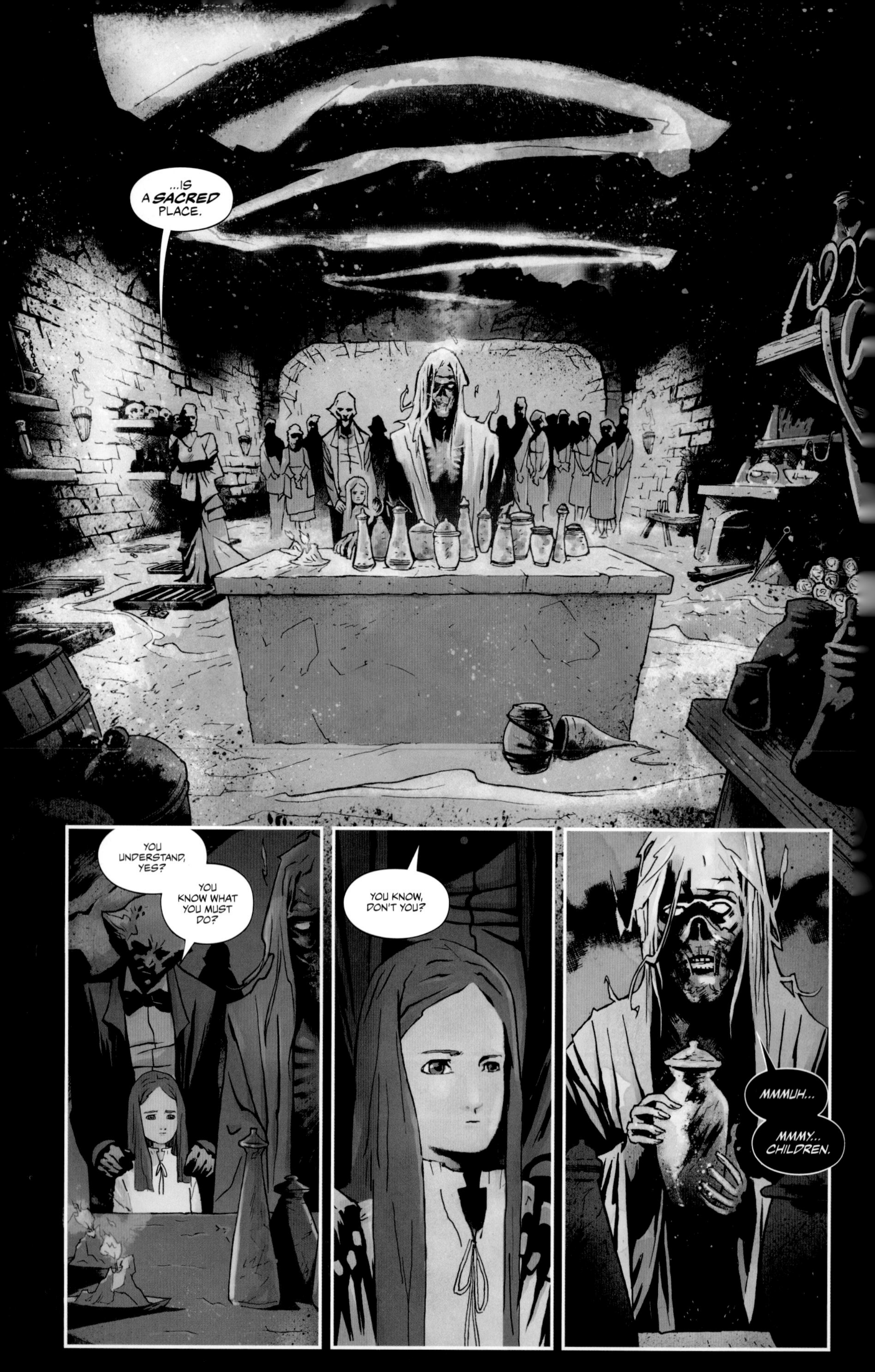

...IS A SACRED PLACE.
YOU UNDERSTAND, YES?
YOU KNOW WHAT YOU MUST DO?
YOU KNOW, DON'T YOU?
MMMUH...
MMMY... CHILDREN.

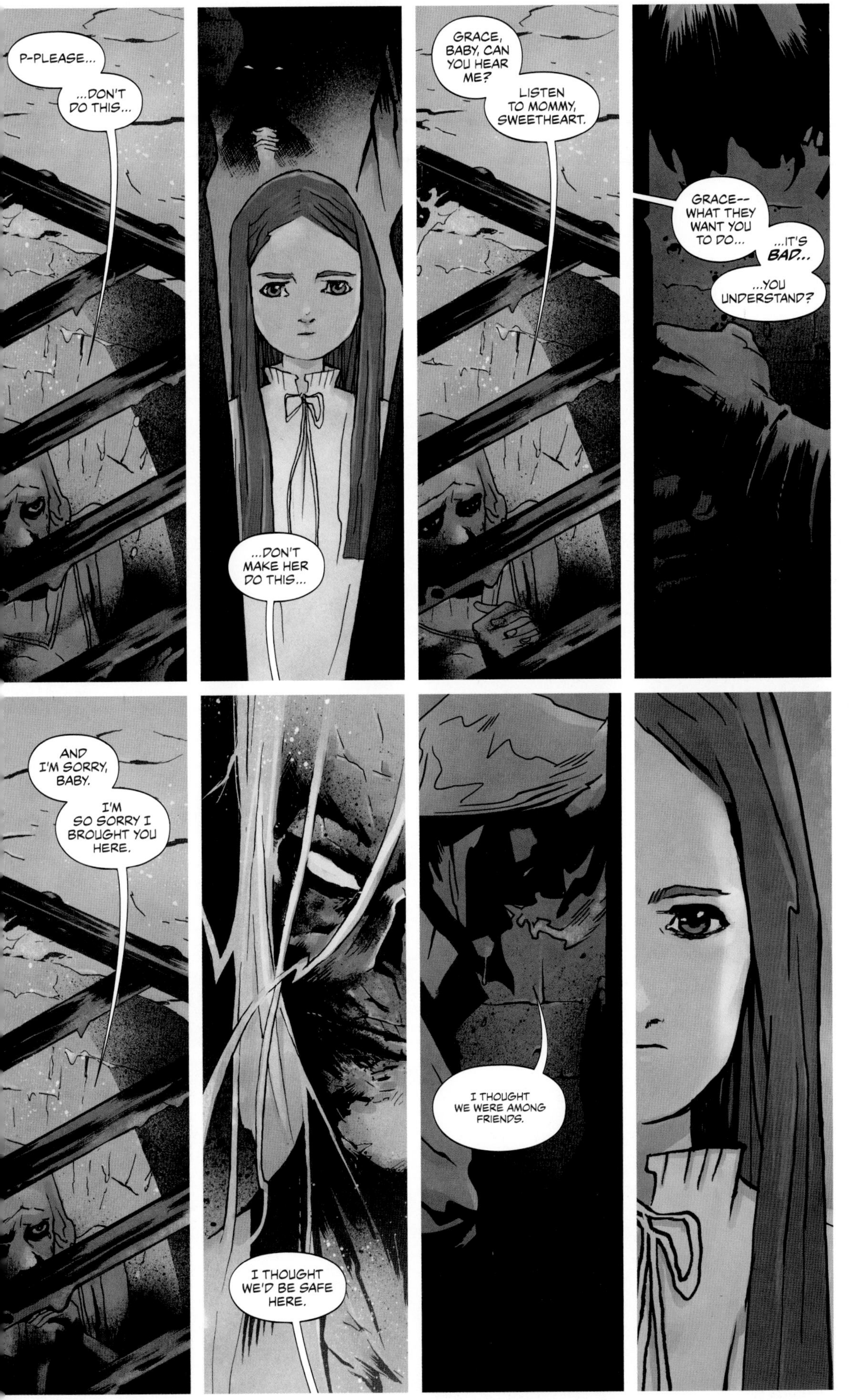
P-PLEASE...
...DON'T DO THIS...
...DON'T MAKE HER DO THIS...
GRACE, BABY, CAN YOU HEAR ME?
LISTEN TO MOMMY, SWEETHEART.
GRACE--WHAT THEY WANT YOU TO DO...
...IT'S BAD...
...YOU UNDERSTAND?
AND I'M SORRY, BABY.
I'M SO SORRY I BROUGHT YOU HERE.
I THOUGHT WE'D BE SAFE HERE.
I THOUGHT WE WERE AMONG FRIENDS.

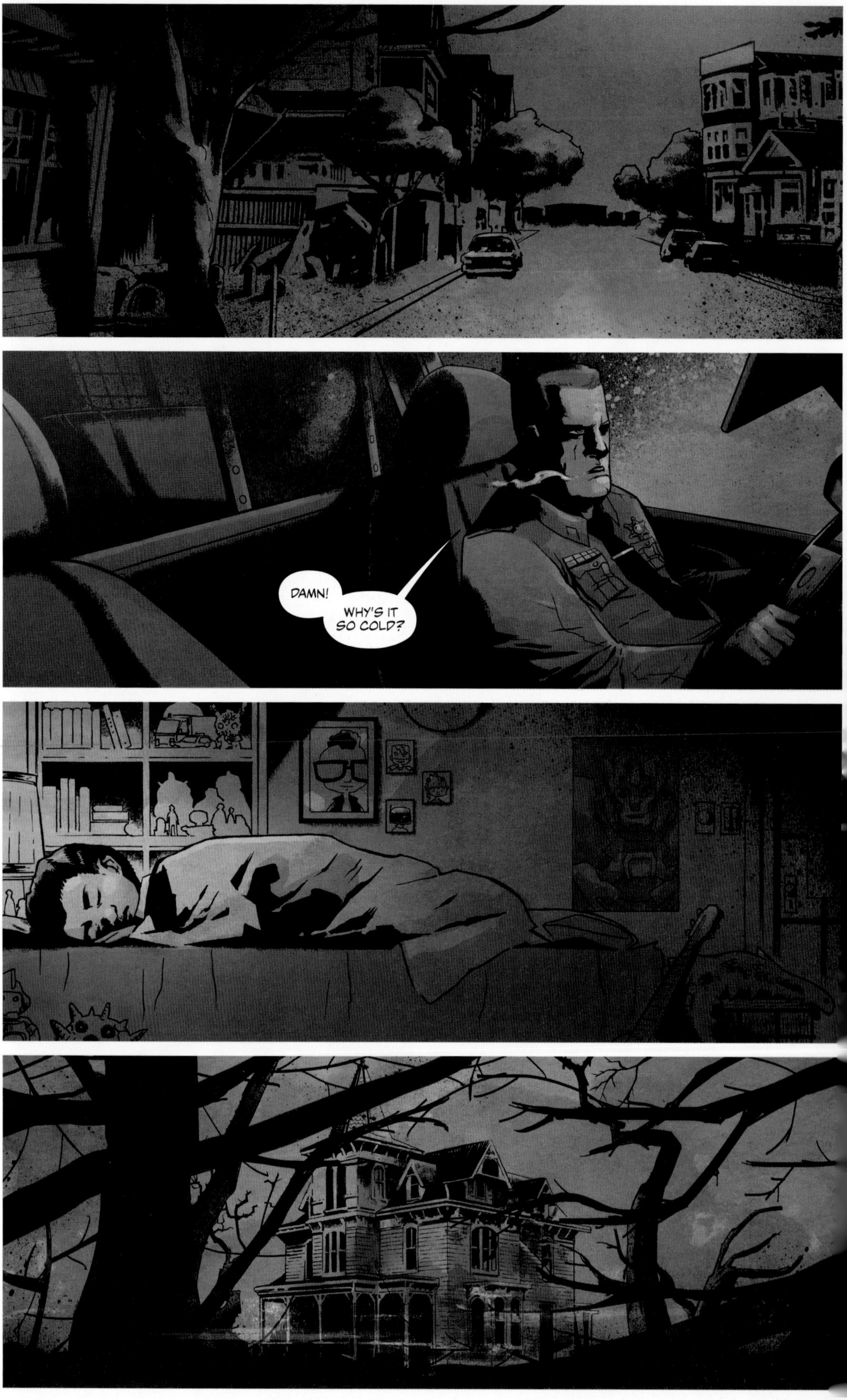
DAMN! WHY'S IT SO COLD?

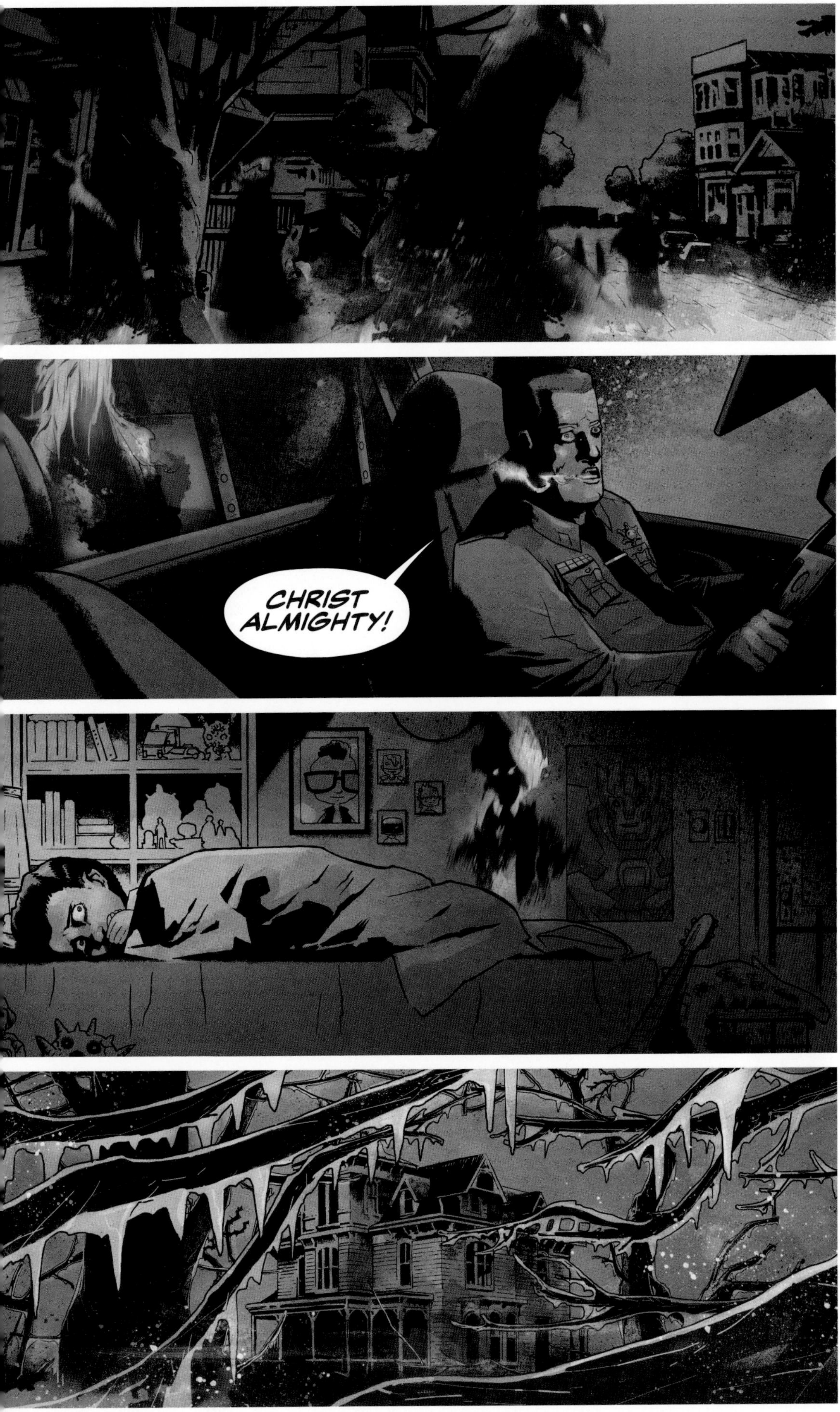
CHRIST ALMIGHTY!

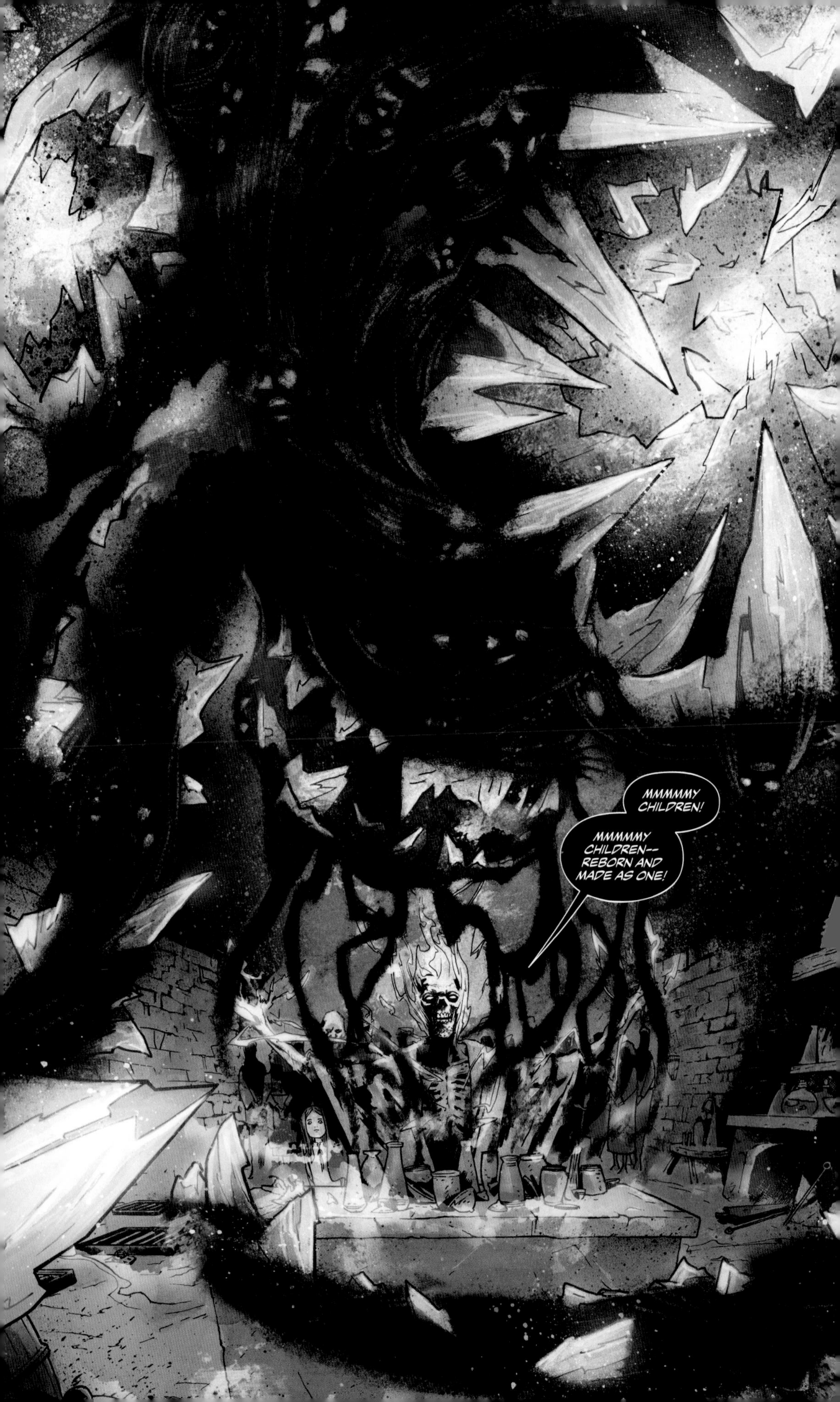
MMMMMY CHILDREN!
MMMMMY CHILDREN-- REBORN AND MADE AS ONE!

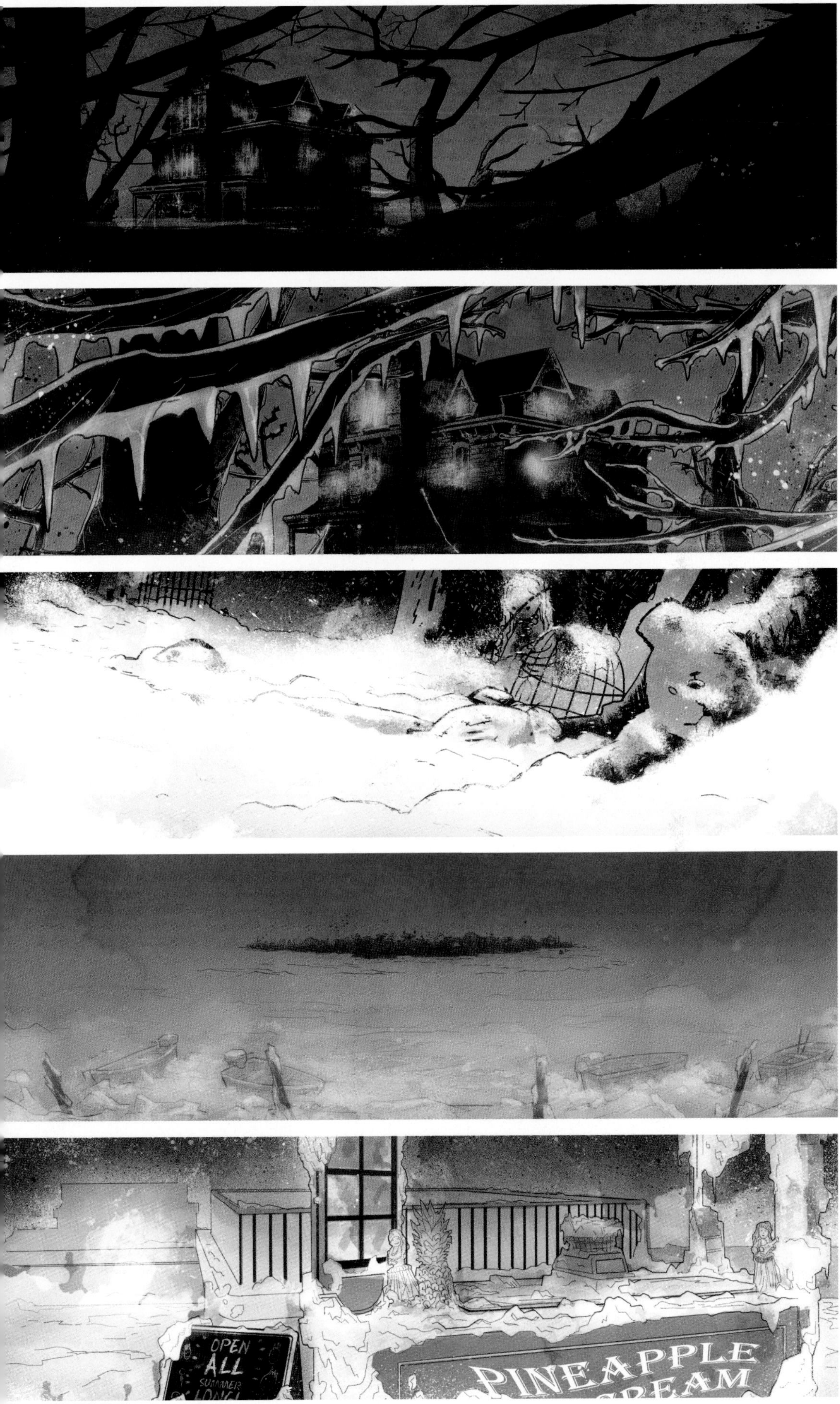
OPEN
ALL
SUMMER
PINEAPPLE

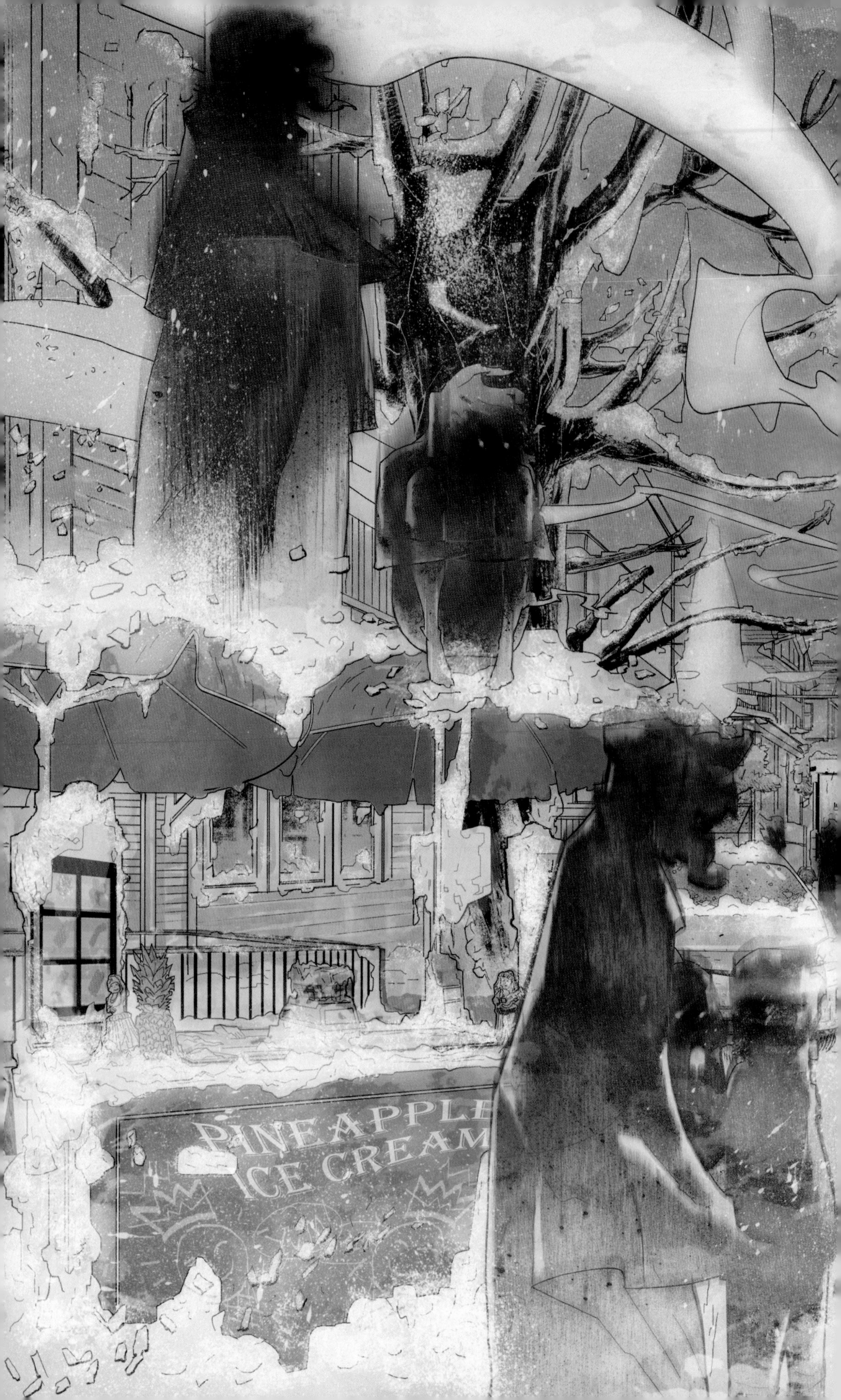
PINEAPPLE
ICE CREAM

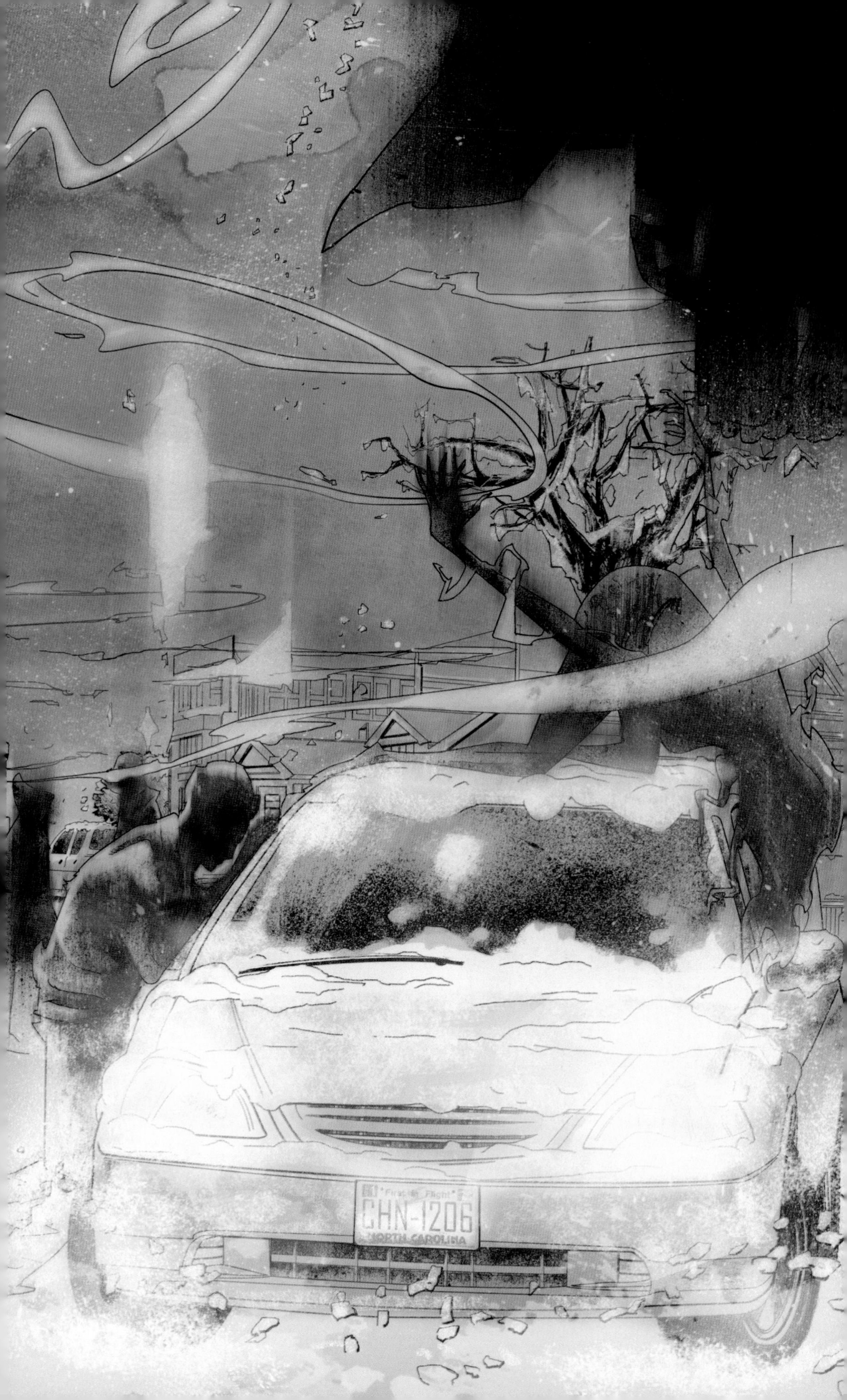
CHN-1206
NORTH CAROLINA

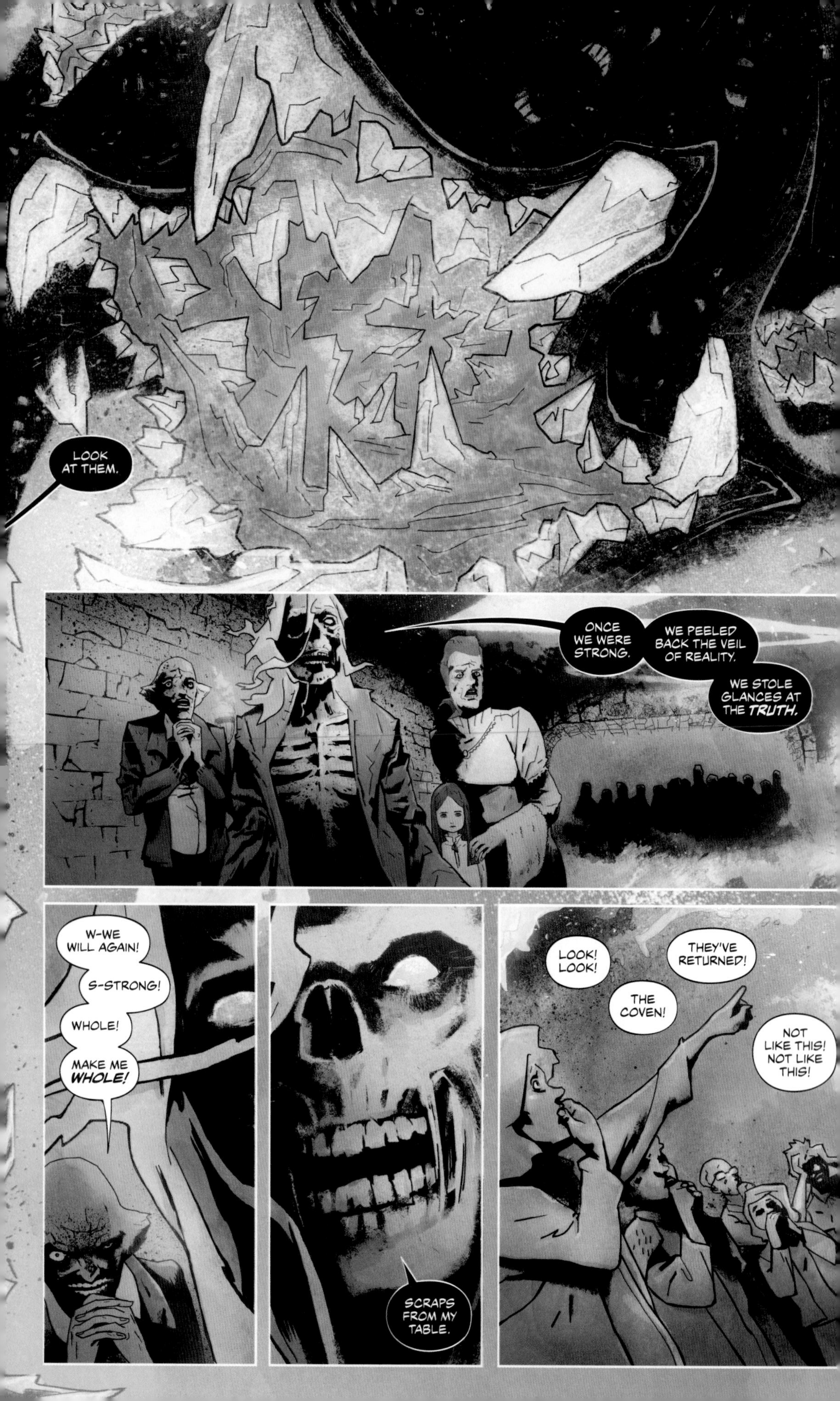
LOOK AT THEM.
ONCE WE WERE STRONG.
WE PEELED BACK THE VEIL OF REALITY.
WE STOLE GLANCES AT THE *TRUTH.*
W-WE WILL AGAIN!
S-STRONG!
WHOLE!
MAKE ME ***WHOLE!***
SCRAPS FROM MY TABLE.
LOOK! LOOK!
THEY'VE RETURNED!
THE COVEN!
NOT LIKE THIS! NOT LIKE THIS!

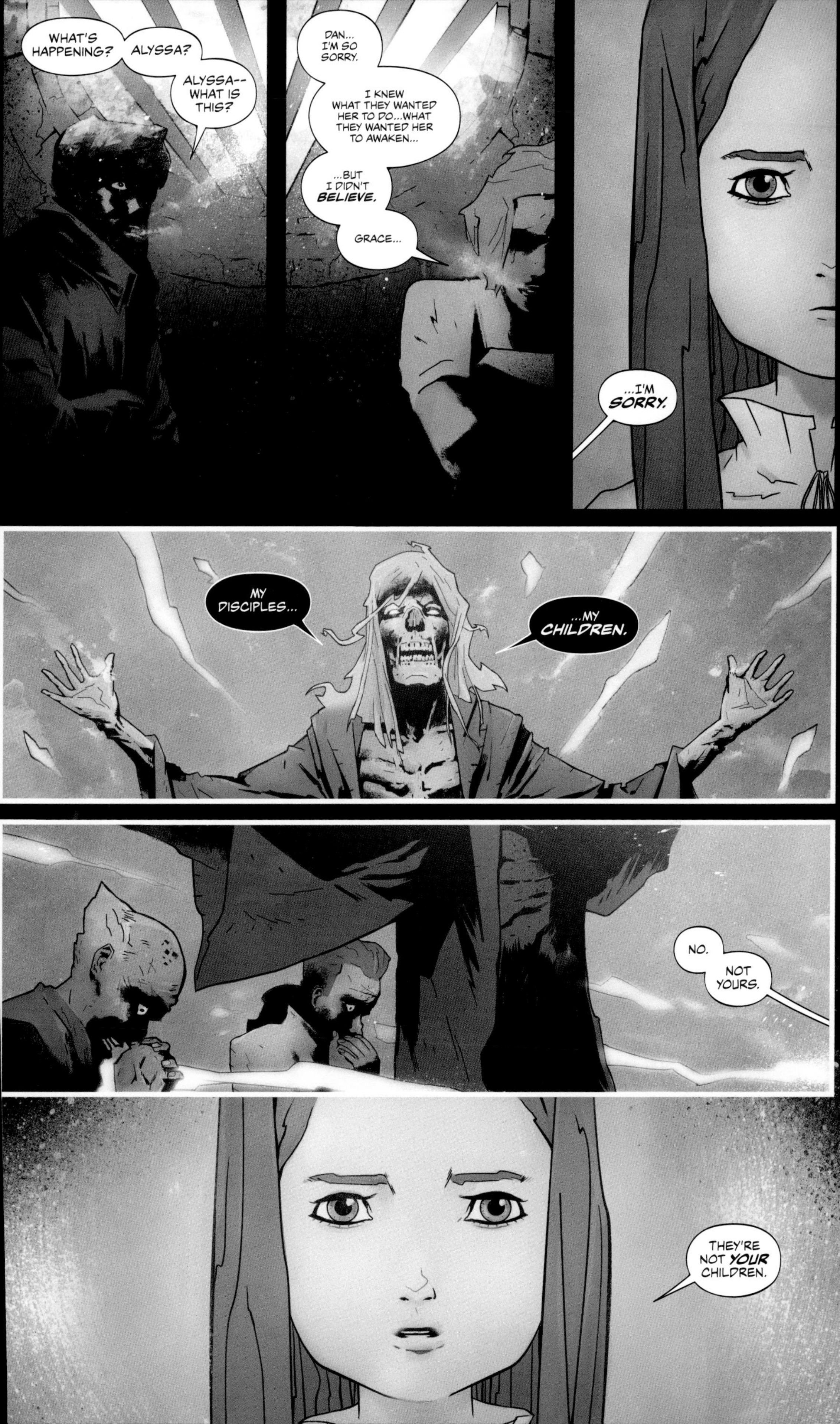
WHAT'S HAPPENING?
ALYSSA?
ALYSSA-- WHAT IS THIS?
DAN... I'M SO SORRY.
I KNEW WHAT THEY WANTED HER TO DO...WHAT THEY WANTED HER TO AWAKEN...
...BUT I DIDN'T BELIEVE.
GRACE...
...I'M SORRY.
MY DISCIPLES...
...MY CHILDREN.
NO.
NOT YOURS.
THEY'RE NOT YOUR CHILDREN.

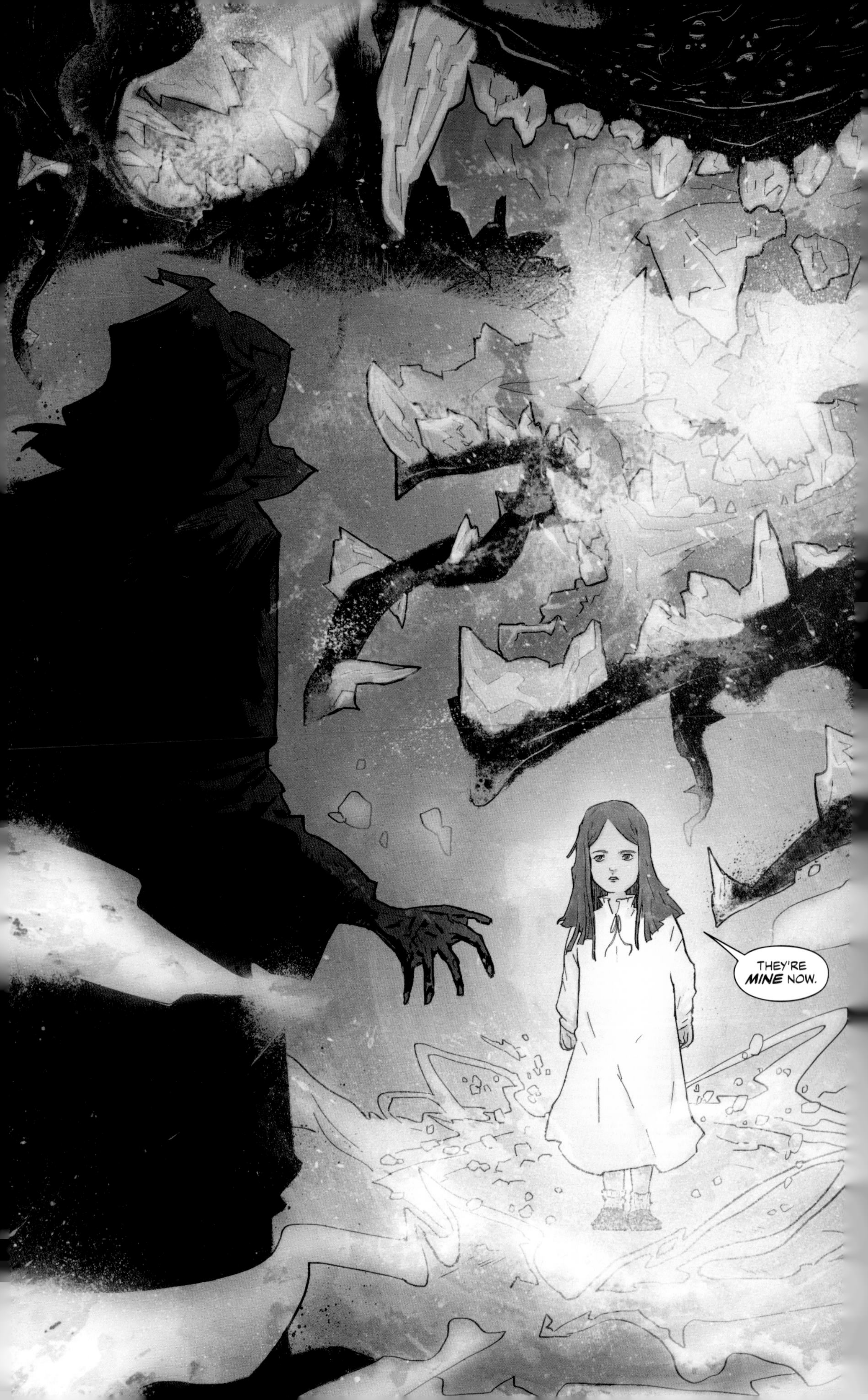
THEY'RE *MINE* NOW.

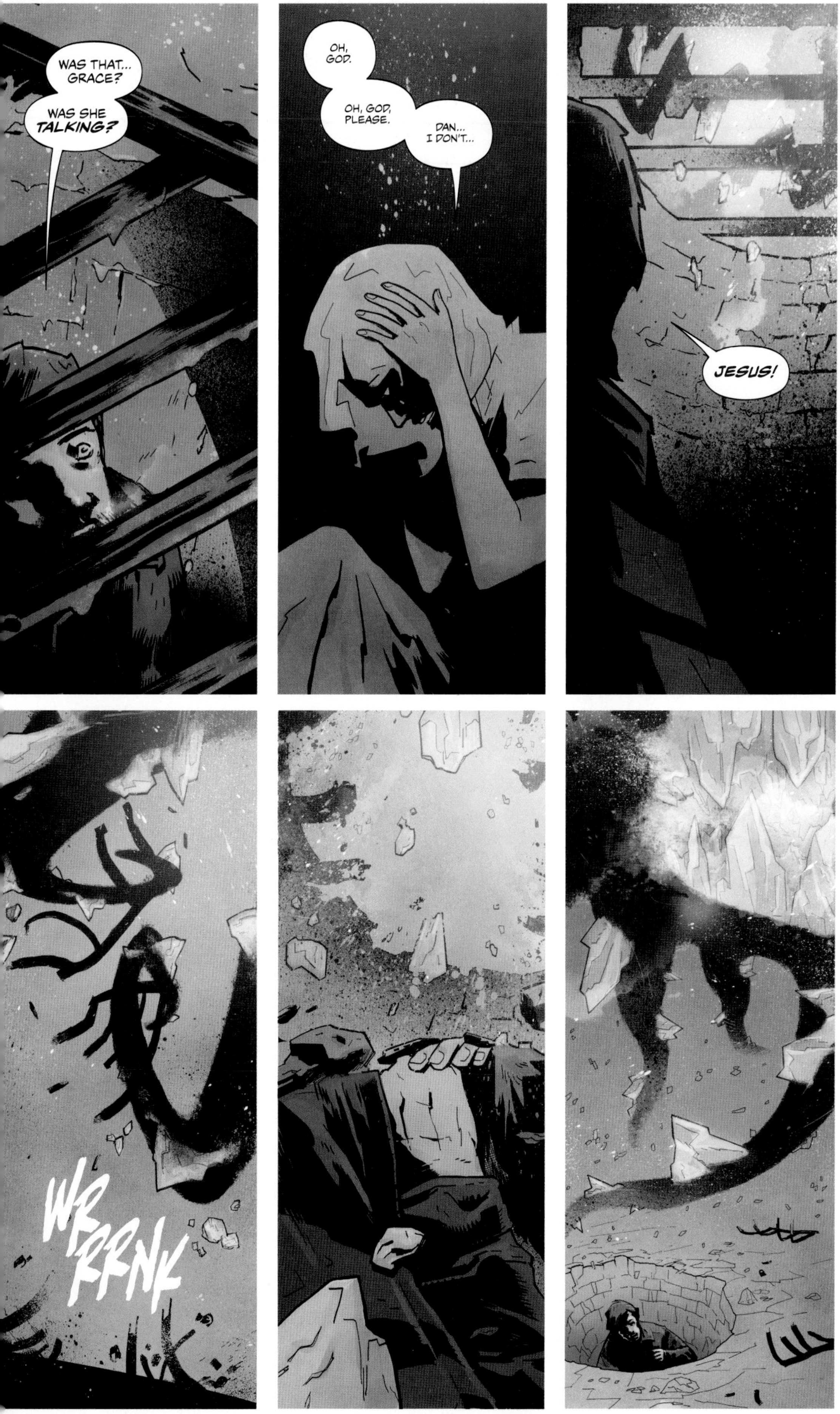
WAS THAT... GRACE?
WAS SHE *TALKING?*
OH, GOD.
OH, GOD, PLEASE.
DAN... I DON'T...
JESUS!
WRRRNK

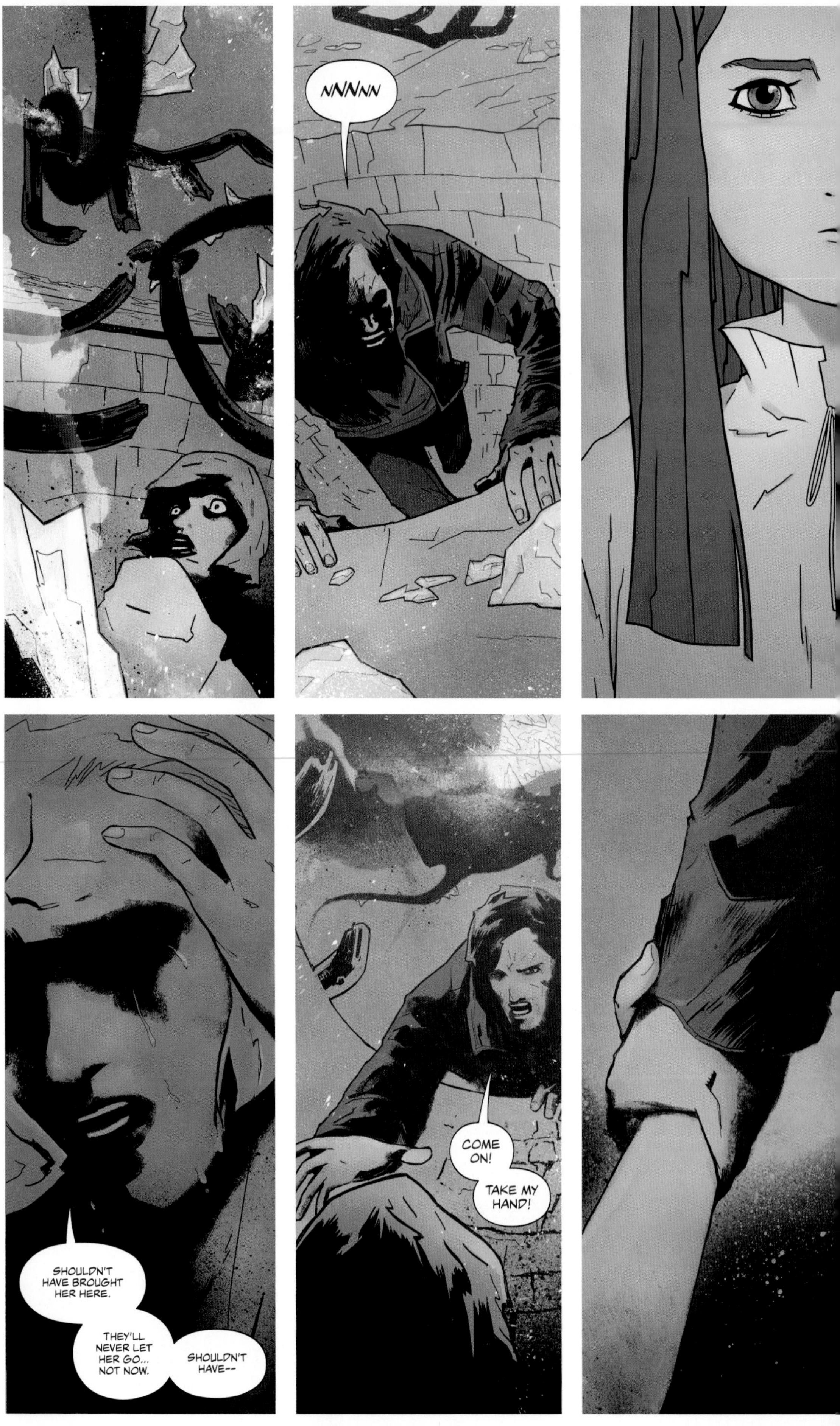
NNNNN
SHOULDN'T HAVE BROUGHT HER HERE.
THEY'LL NEVER LET HER GO... NOT NOW.
SHOULDN'T HAVE--
COME ON!
TAKE MY HAND!

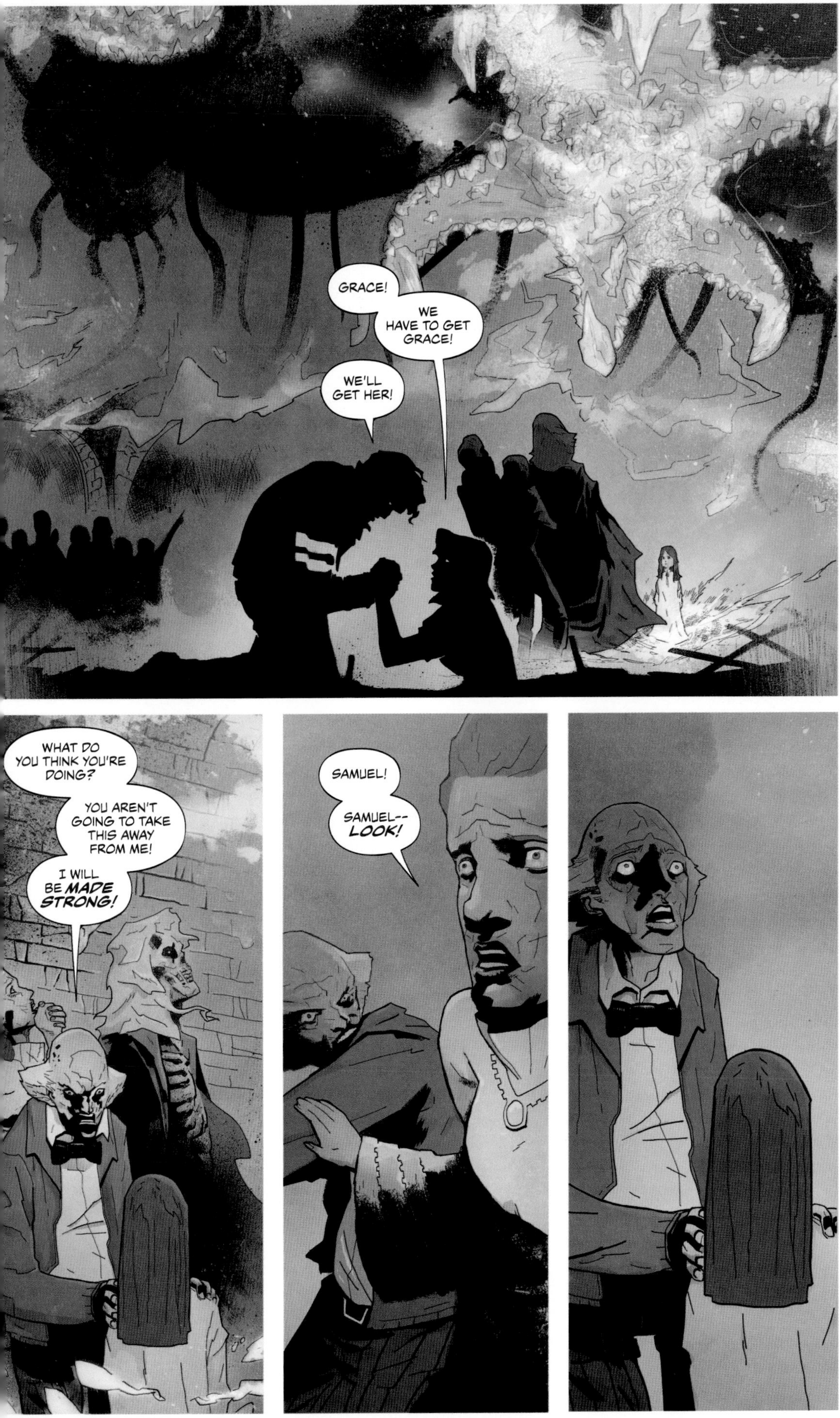
GRACE!
WE HAVE TO GET GRACE!
WE'LL GET HER!
WHAT DO YOU THINK YOU'RE DOING?
YOU AREN'T GOING TO TAKE THIS AWAY FROM ME!
I WILL BE MADE STRONG!
SAMUEL!
SAMUEL-- LOOK!

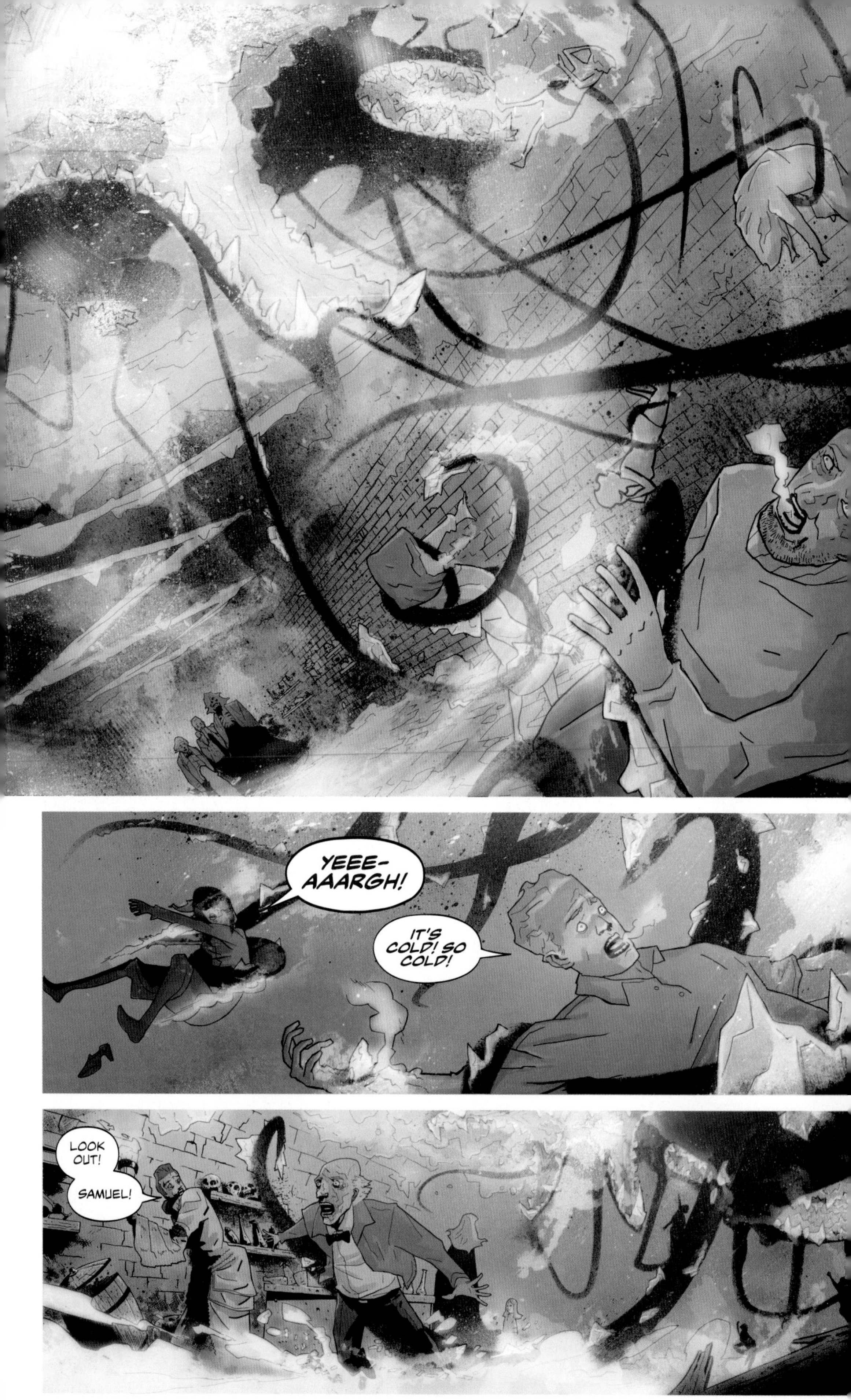
YEEE-AAARGH!
IT'S COLD! SO COLD!
LOOK OUT!
SAMUEL!

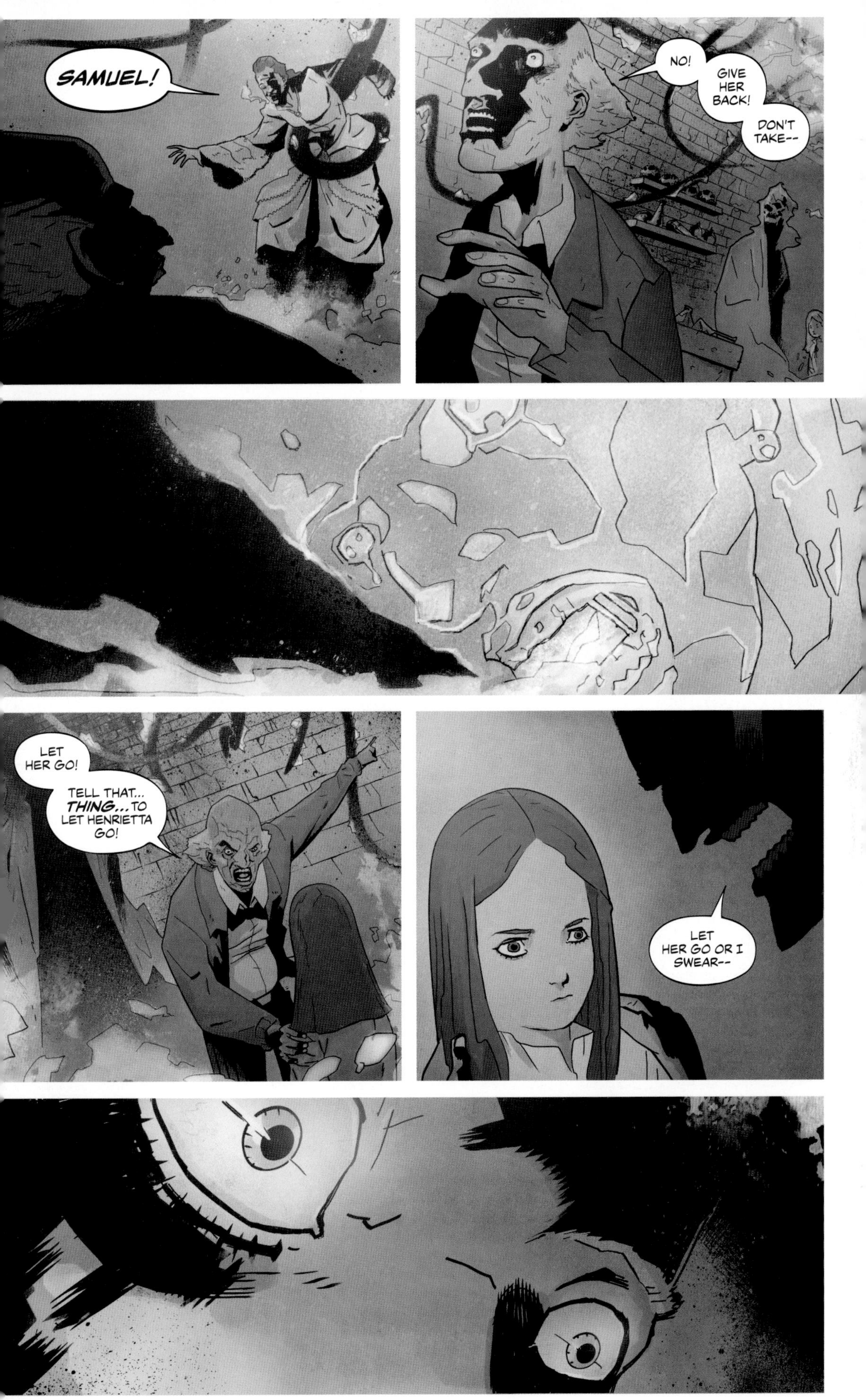
SAMUEL!
NO!
GIVE HER BACK!
DON'T TAKE--
LET HER GO!
TELL THAT... THING... TO LET HENRIETTA GO!
LET HER GO OR I SWEAR--

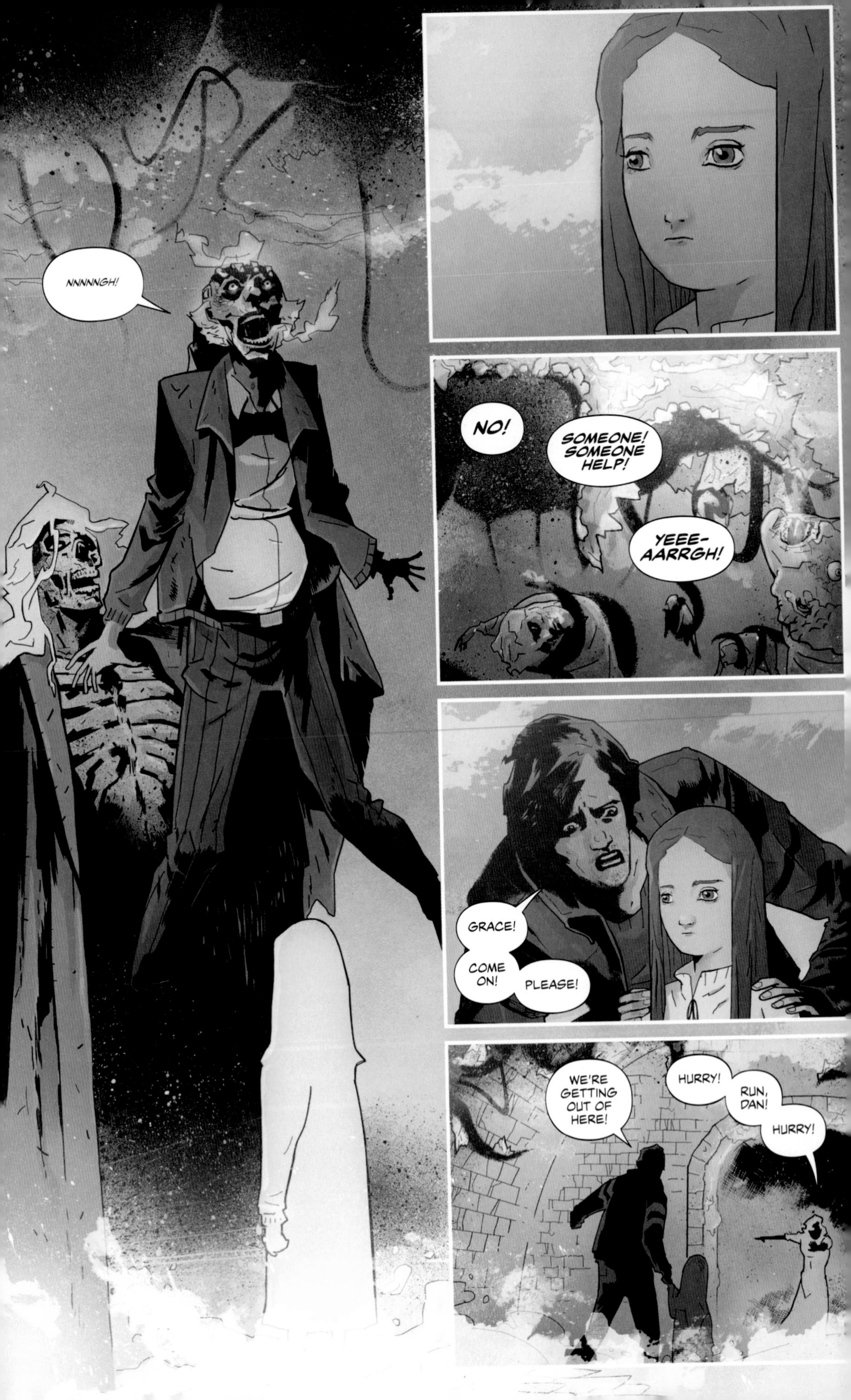
NNNNNGH!
NO!
SOMEONE! SOMEONE HELP!
YEEE-AARRGH!
GRACE!
COME ON!
PLEASE!
WE'RE GETTING OUT OF HERE!
HURRY!
RUN, DAN!
HURRY!

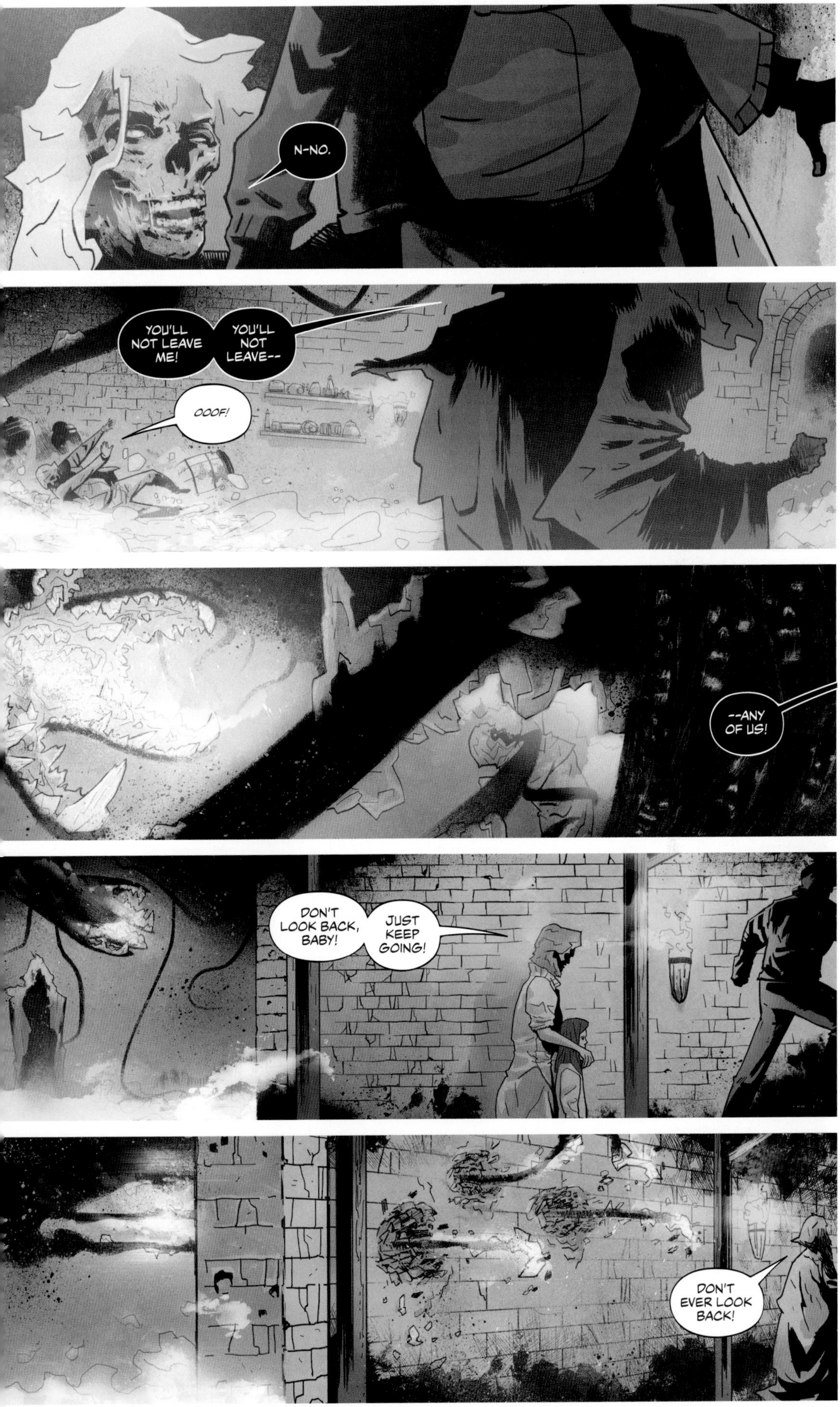
N-NO.
YOU'LL NOT LEAVE ME!
YOU'LL NOT LEAVE--
OOOF!
--ANY OF US!
DON'T LOOK BACK, BABY!
JUST KEEP GOING!
DON'T EVER LOOK BACK!

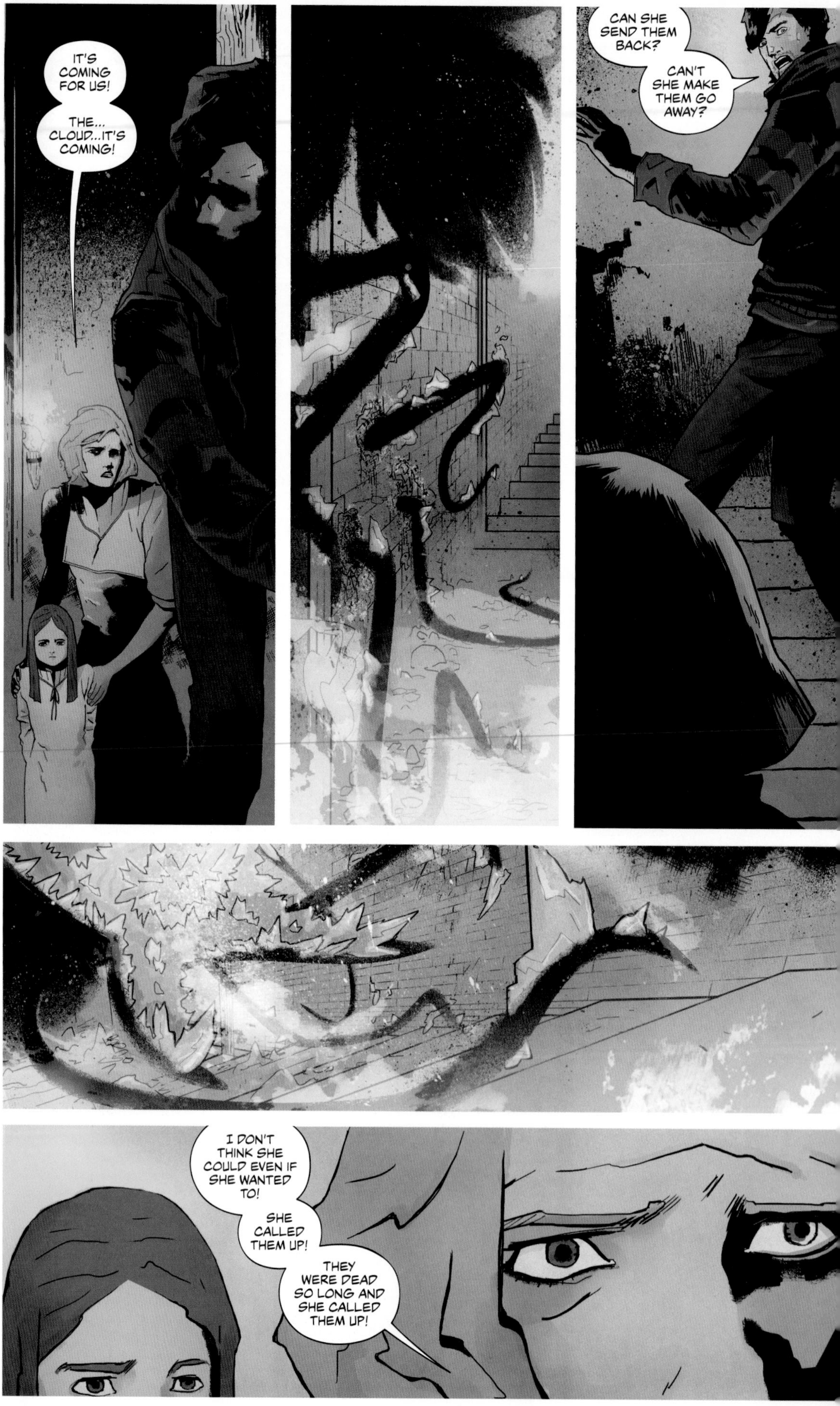
IT'S COMING FOR US!
THE... CLOUD...IT'S COMING!
CAN SHE SEND THEM BACK?
CAN'T SHE MAKE THEM GO AWAY?
I DON'T THINK SHE COULD EVEN IF SHE WANTED TO!
SHE CALLED THEM UP!
THEY WERE DEAD SO LONG AND SHE CALLED THEM UP!

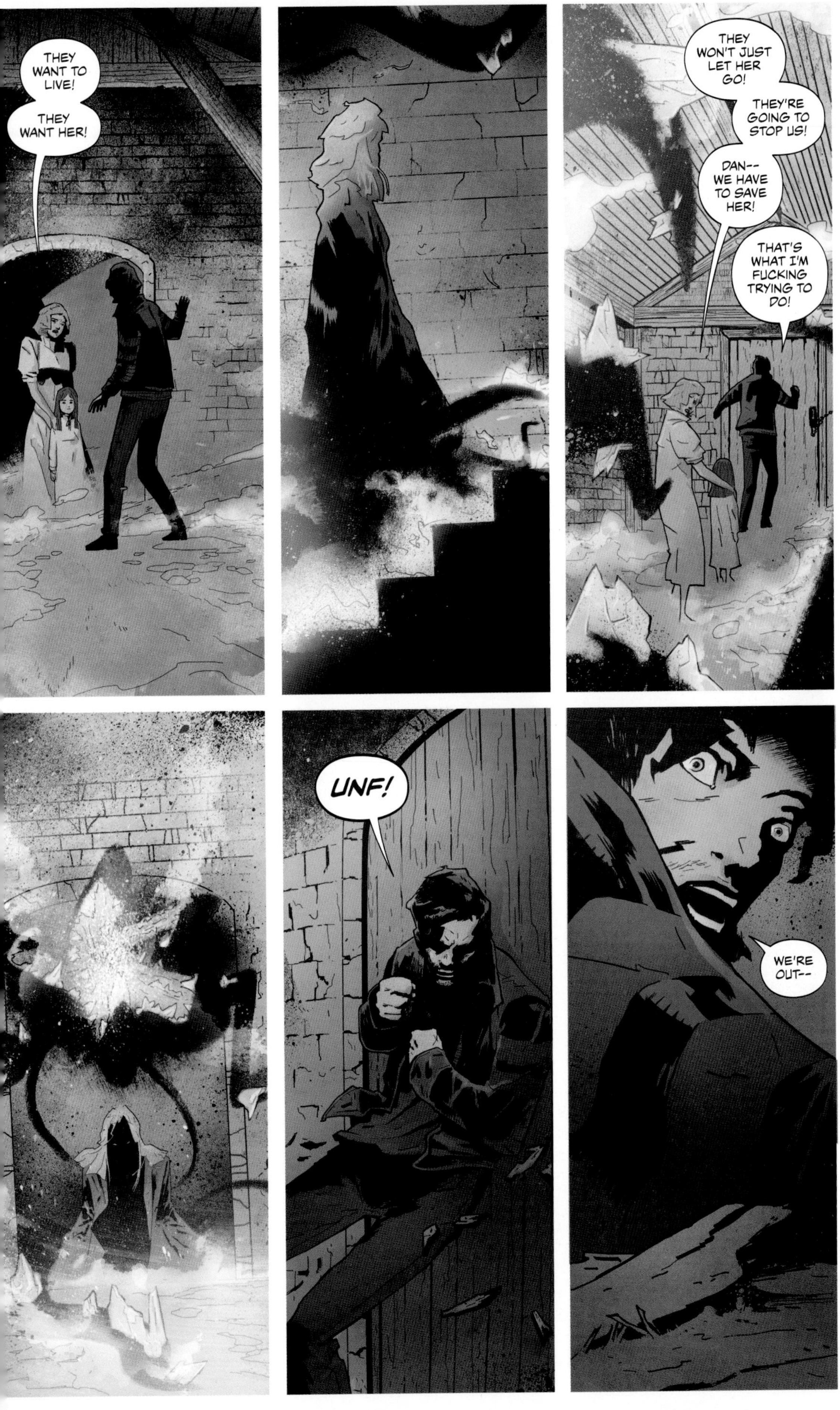
THEY WANT TO LIVE!
THEY WANT HER!
THEY WON'T JUST LET HER GO!
THEY'RE GOING TO STOP US!
DAN-- WE HAVE TO SAVE HER!
THAT'S WHAT I'M FUCKING TRYING TO DO!
UNF!
WE'RE OUT--

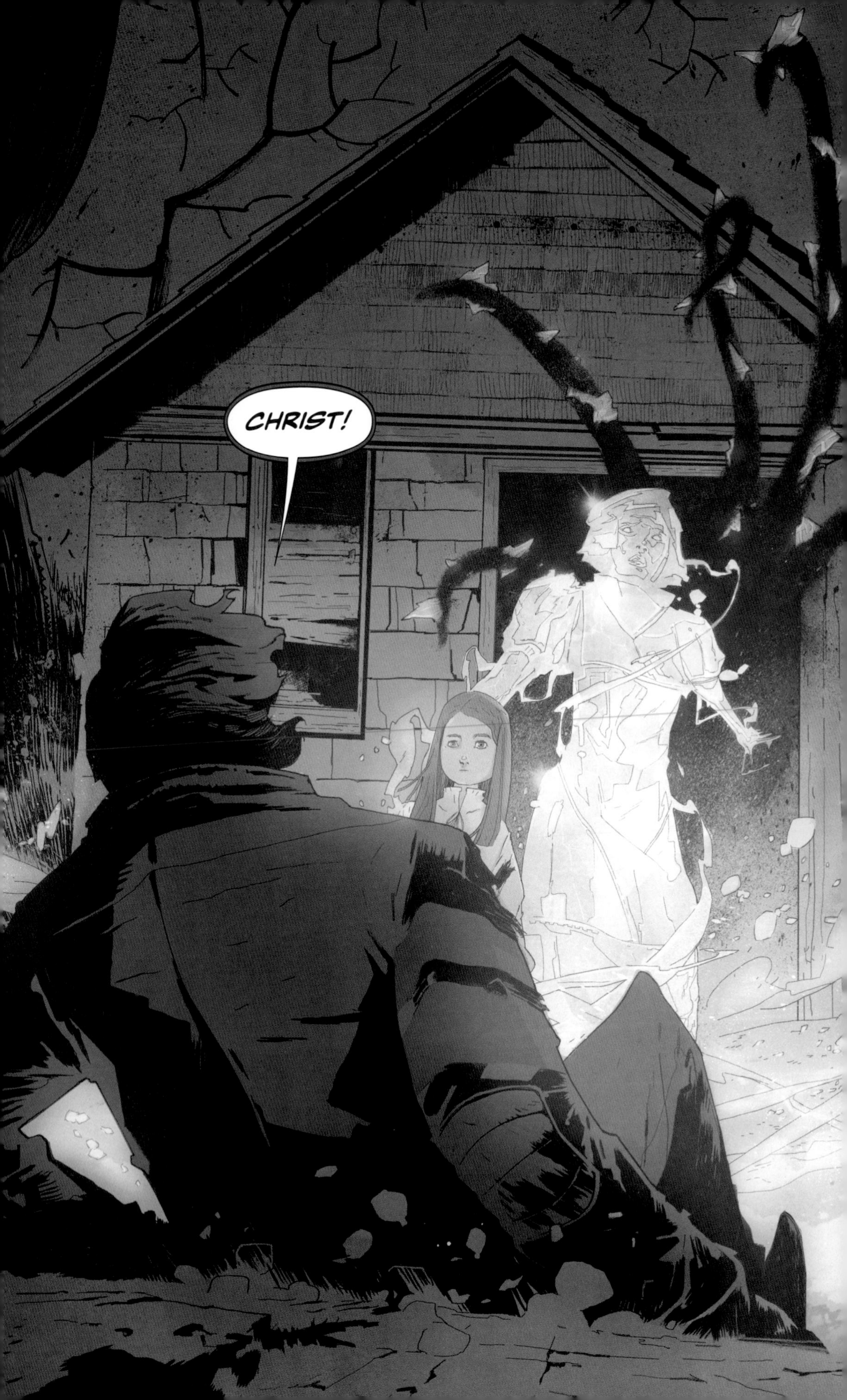
CHRIST!

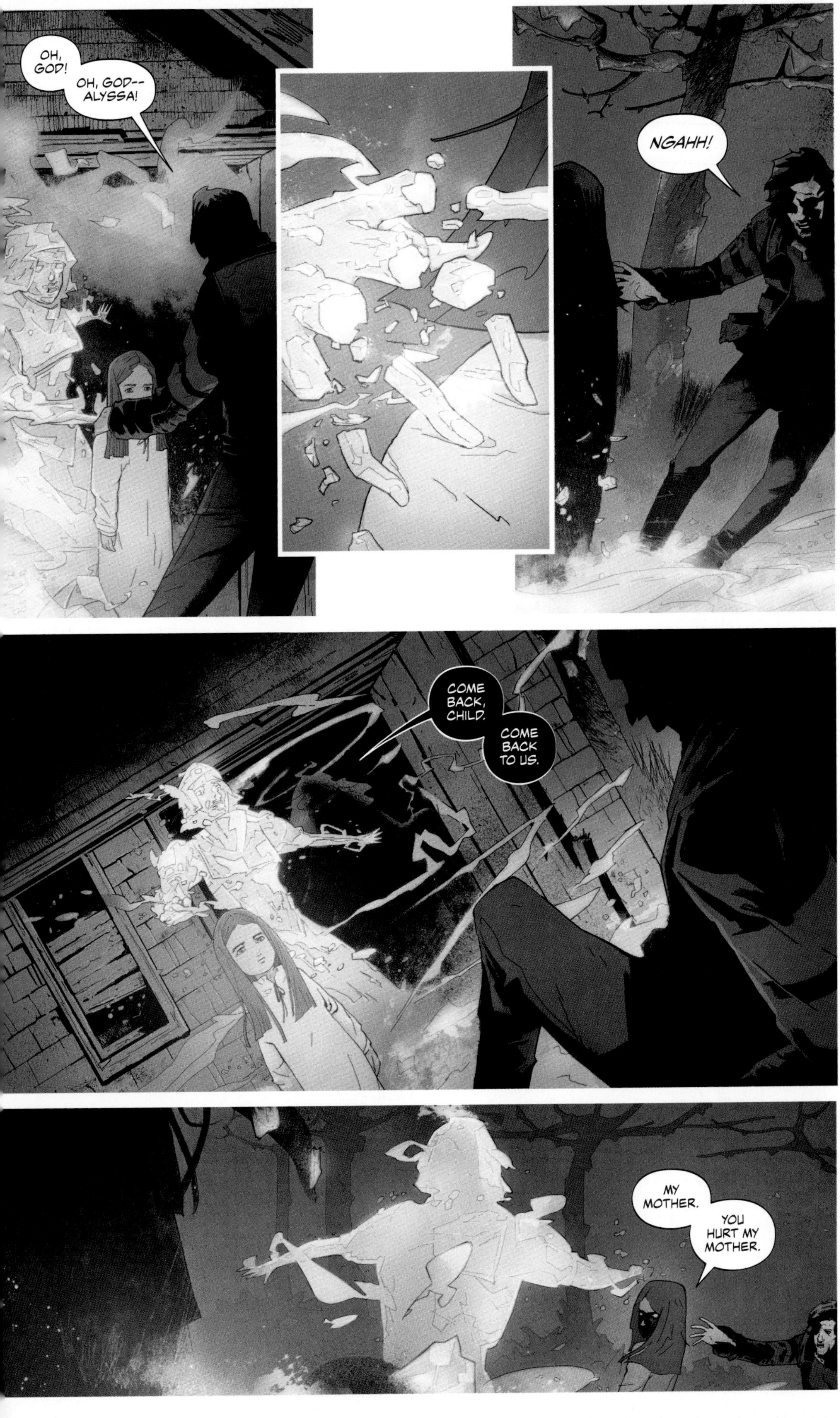
OH, GOD!
OH, GOD-- ALYSSA!
NGAHH!
COME BACK, CHILD.
COME BACK TO US.
MY MOTHER.
YOU HURT MY MOTHER.

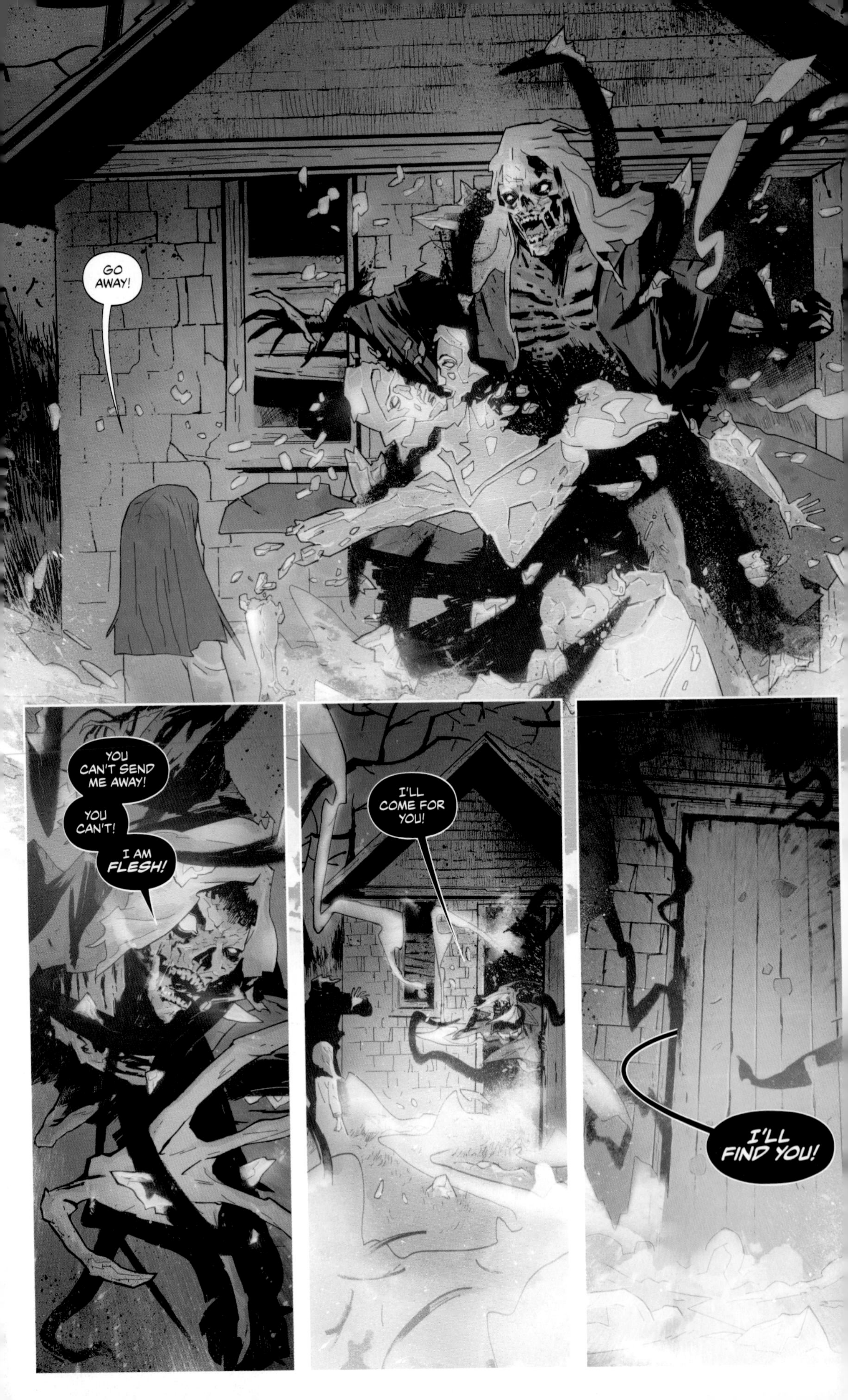
GO AWAY!
YOU CAN'T SEND ME AWAY!
YOU CAN'T!
I AM FLESH!
I'LL COME FOR YOU!
I'LL FIND YOU!

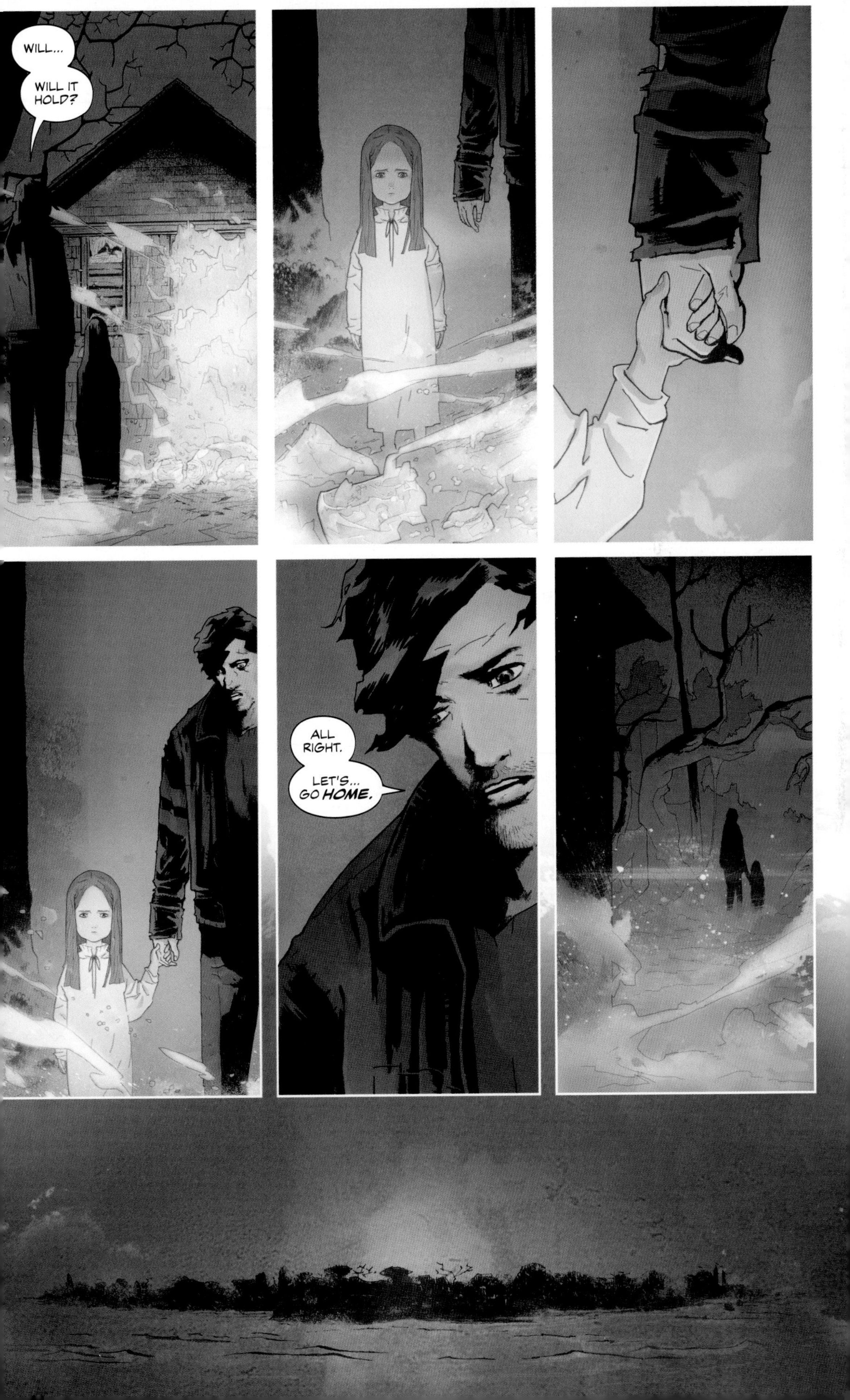
WILL...
WILL IT HOLD?
ALL RIGHT.
LET'S... GO HOME.

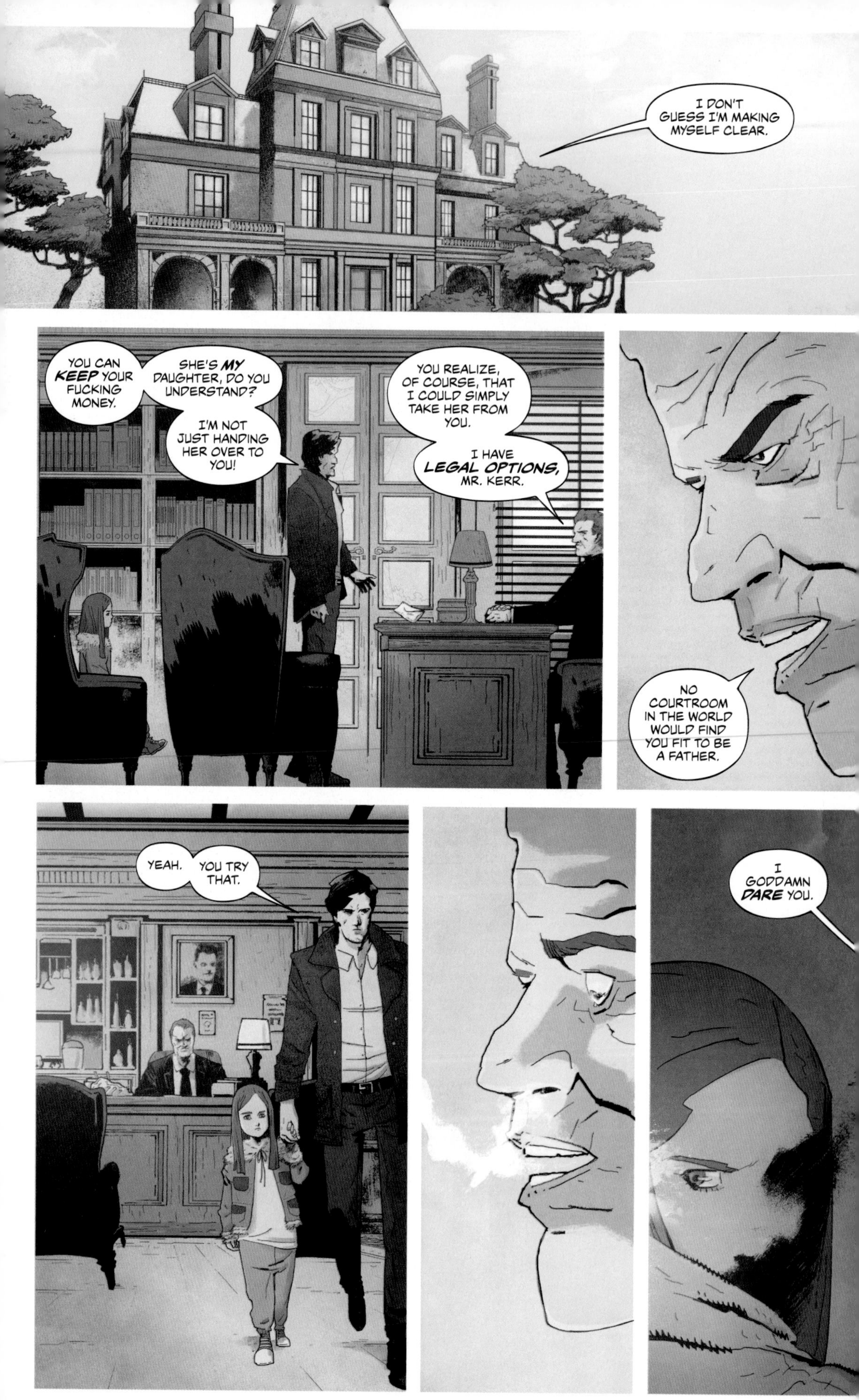

I DON'T GUESS I'M MAKING MYSELF CLEAR.
YOU CAN KEEP YOUR FUCKING MONEY.
SHE'S MY DAUGHTER, DO YOU UNDERSTAND?
I'M NOT JUST HANDING HER OVER TO YOU!
YOU REALIZE, OF COURSE, THAT I COULD SIMPLY TAKE HER FROM YOU.
I HAVE LEGAL OPTIONS, MR. KERR.
NO COURTROOM IN THE WORLD WOULD FIND YOU FIT TO BE A FATHER.
YEAH.
YOU TRY THAT.
I GODDAMN DARE YOU.

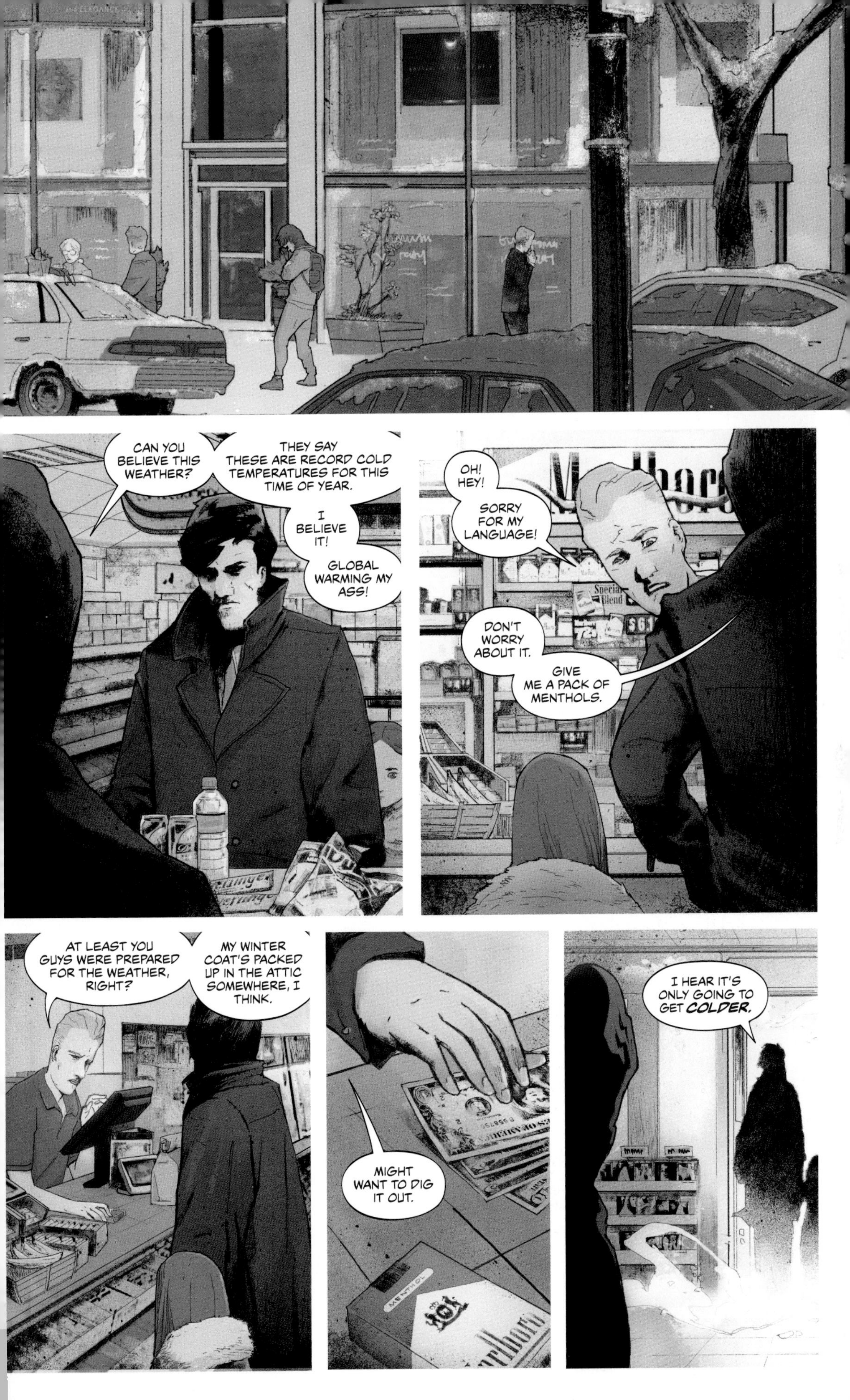

CAN YOU BELIEVE THIS WEATHER?
THEY SAY THESE ARE RECORD COLD TEMPERATURES FOR THIS TIME OF YEAR.
I BELIEVE IT!
GLOBAL WARMING MY ASS!
OH! HEY!
SORRY FOR MY LANGUAGE!
DON'T WORRY ABOUT IT.
GIVE ME A PACK OF MENTHOLS.
AT LEAST YOU GUYS WERE PREPARED FOR THE WEATHER, RIGHT?
MY WINTER COAT'S PACKED UP IN THE ATTIC SOMEWHERE, I THINK.
MIGHT WANT TO DIG IT OUT.
I HEAR IT'S ONLY GOING TO GET COLDER.

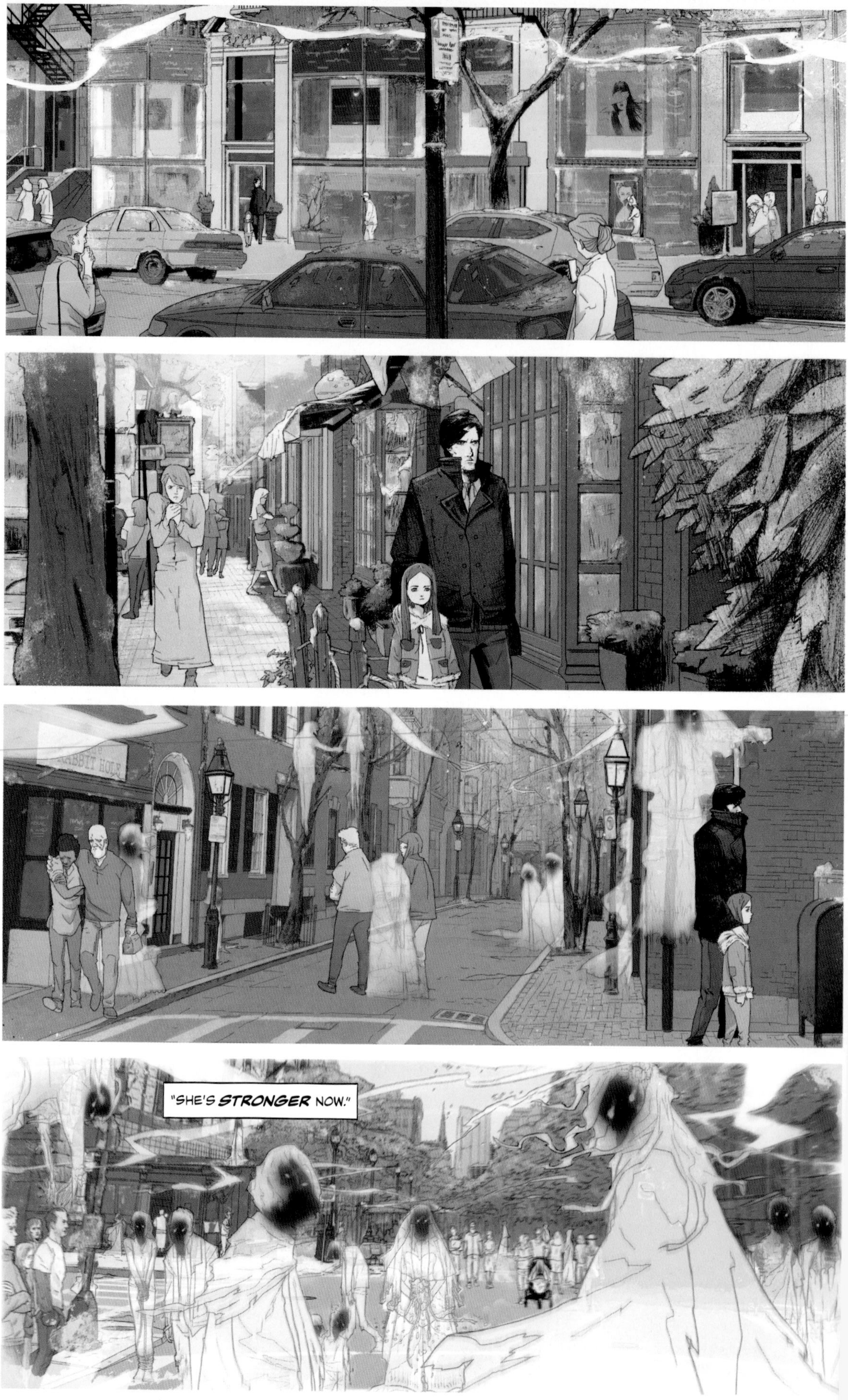
"SHE'S **STRONGER** NOW."

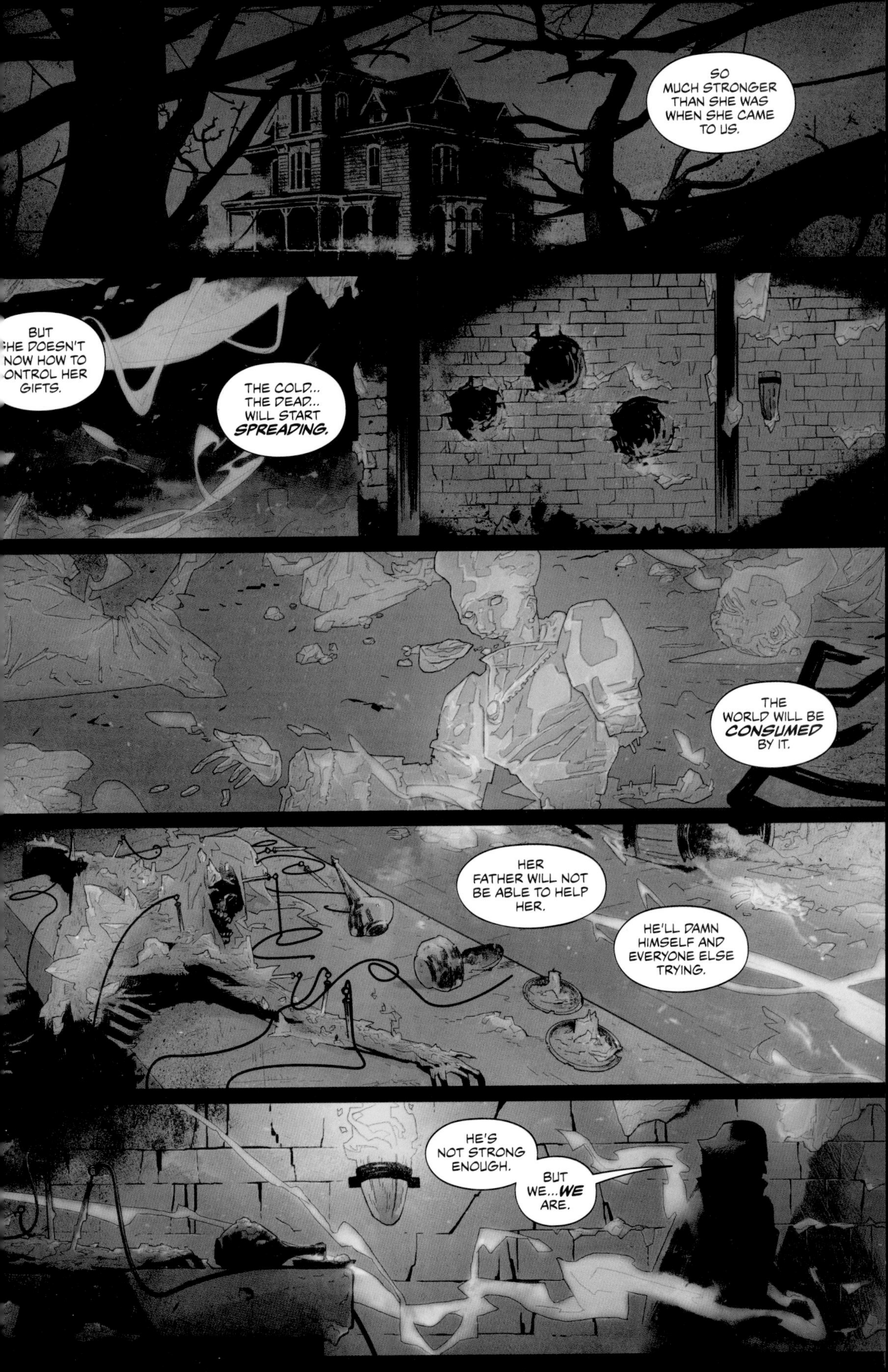
SO MUCH STRONGER THAN SHE WAS WHEN SHE CAME TO US.
BUT HE DOESN'T NOW HOW TO ONTROL HER GIFTS.
THE COLD... THE DEAD... WILL START SPREADING.
THE WORLD WILL BE CONSUMED BY IT.
HER FATHER WILL NOT BE ABLE TO HELP HER.
HE'LL DAMN HIMSELF AND EVERYONE ELSE TRYING.
HE'S NOT STRONG ENOUGH.
BUT WE...WE ARE.

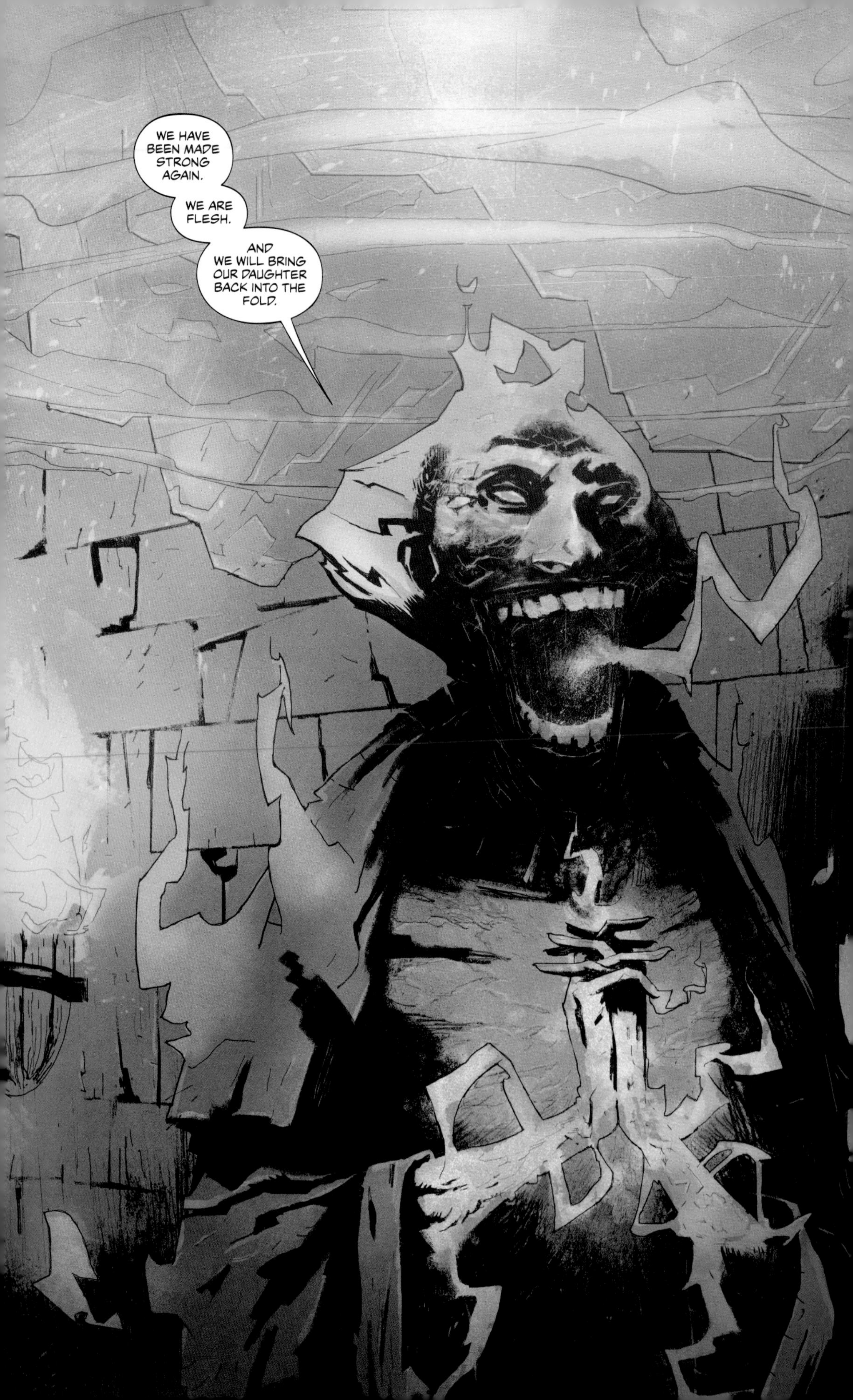
WE HAVE BEEN MADE STRONG AGAIN.
WE ARE FLESH.
AND WE WILL BRING OUR DAUGHTER BACK INTO THE FOLD.

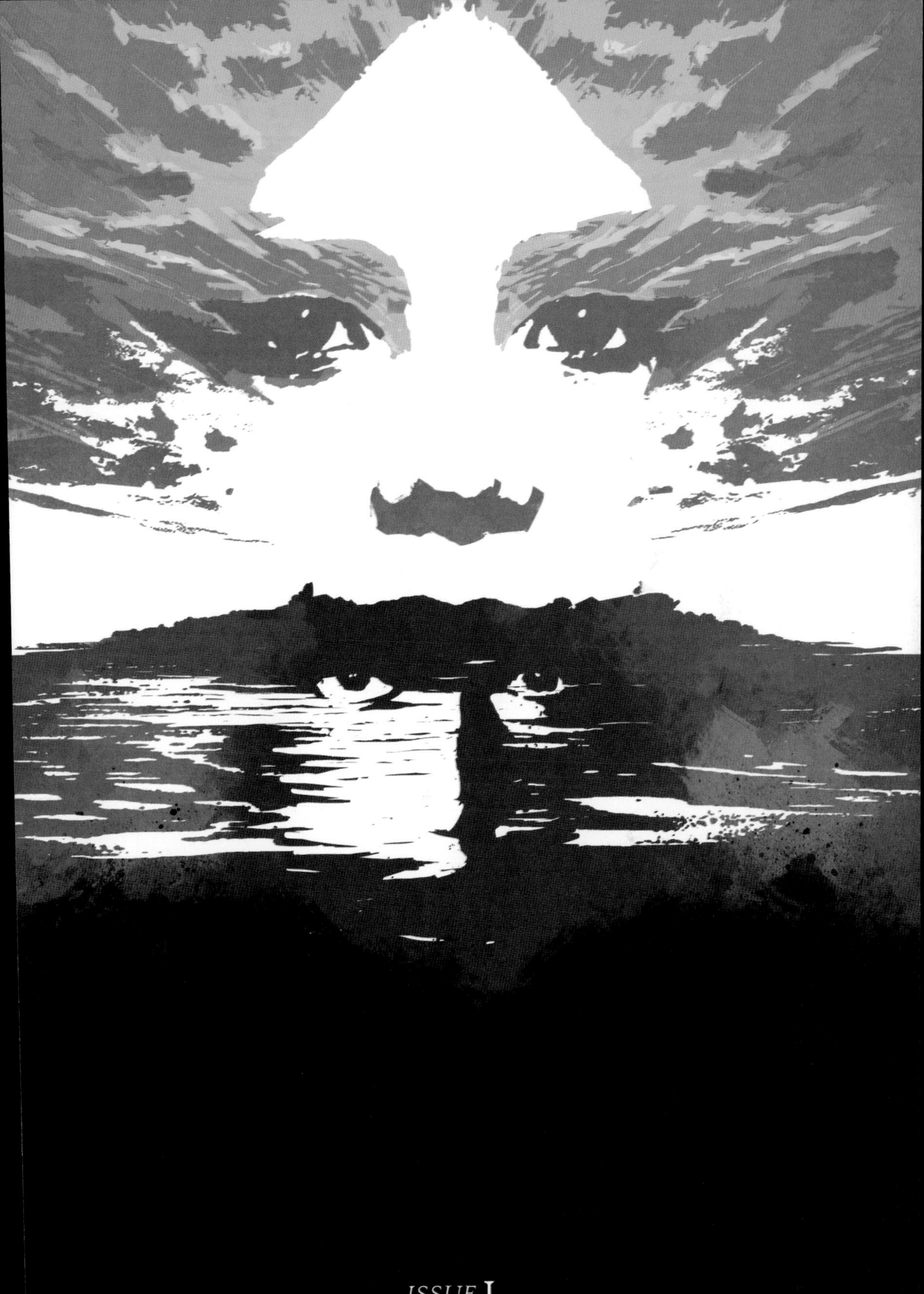

ISSUE I

MARK TORRES

COVER GALLERY

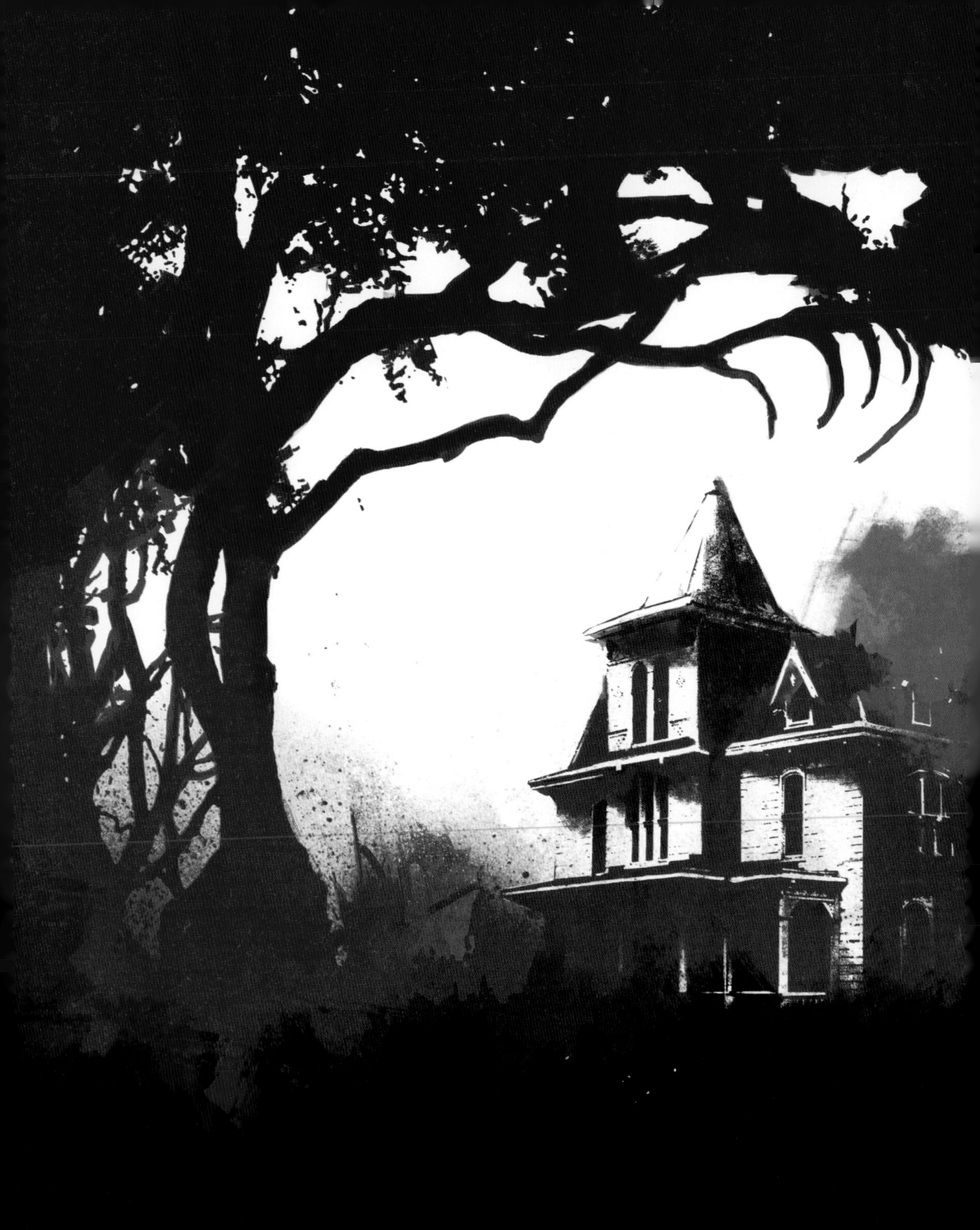

ISSUE **2**

MARK TORRES

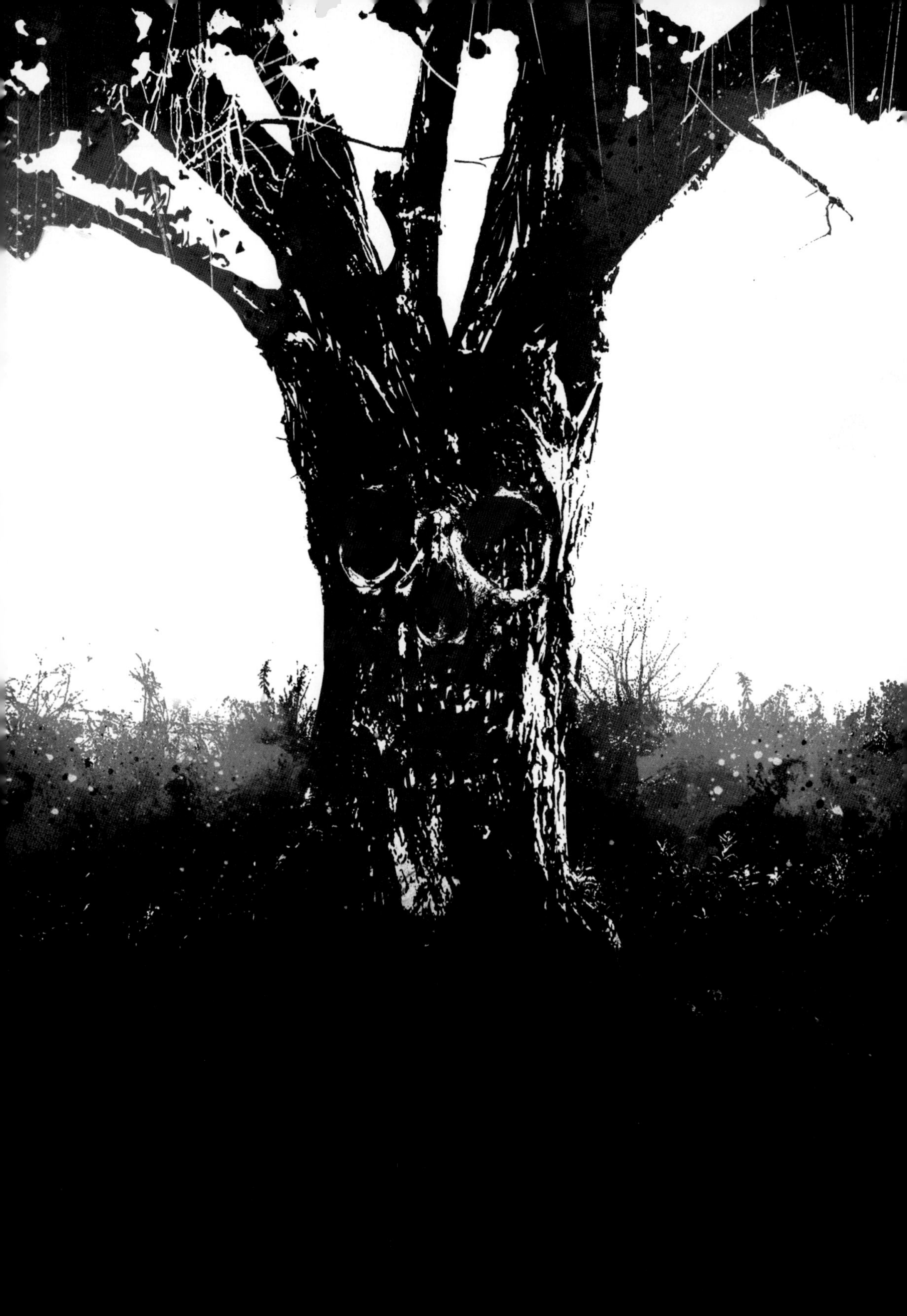

ISSUE 3

MARK TORRES

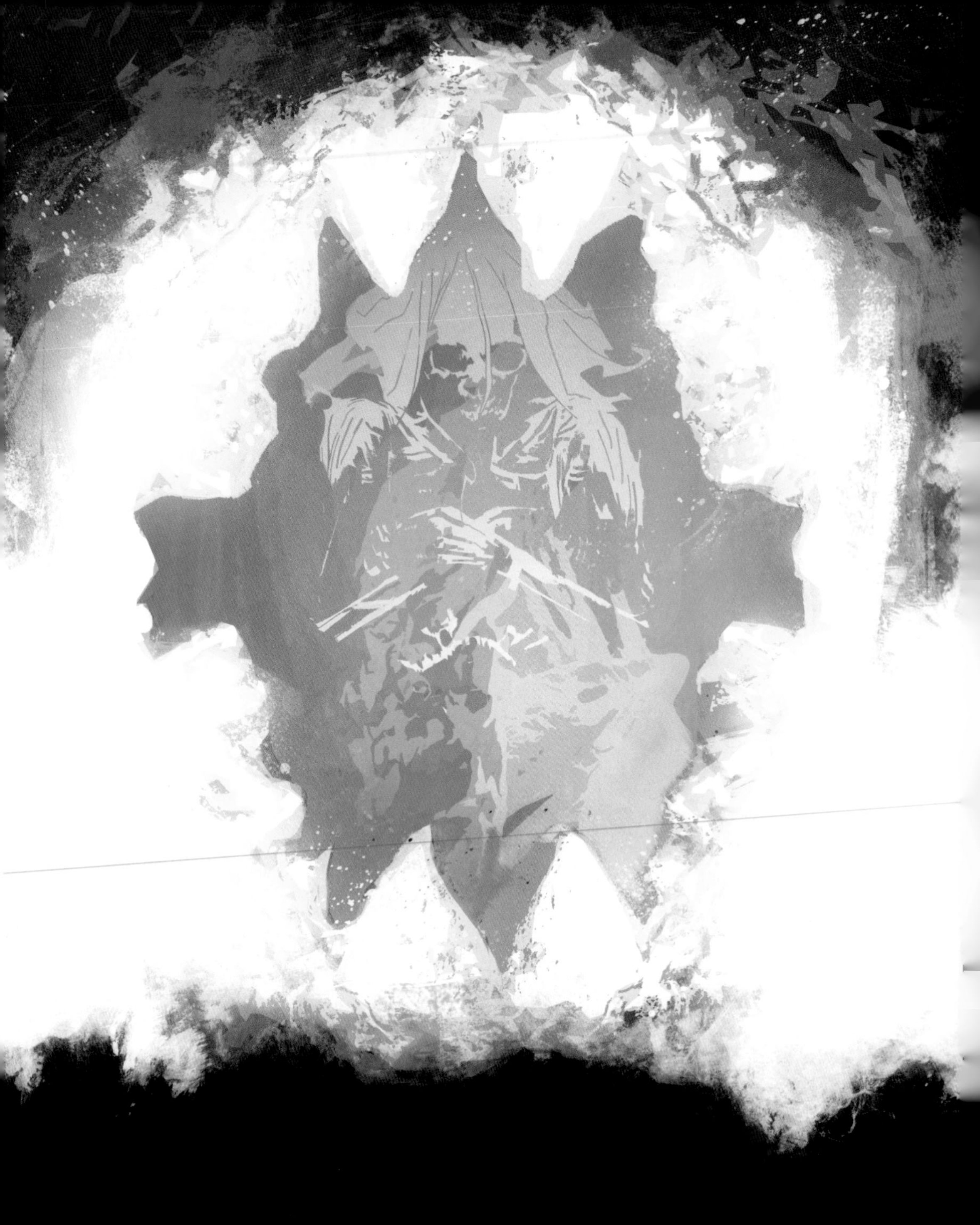

ISSUE 4

MARK TORRES

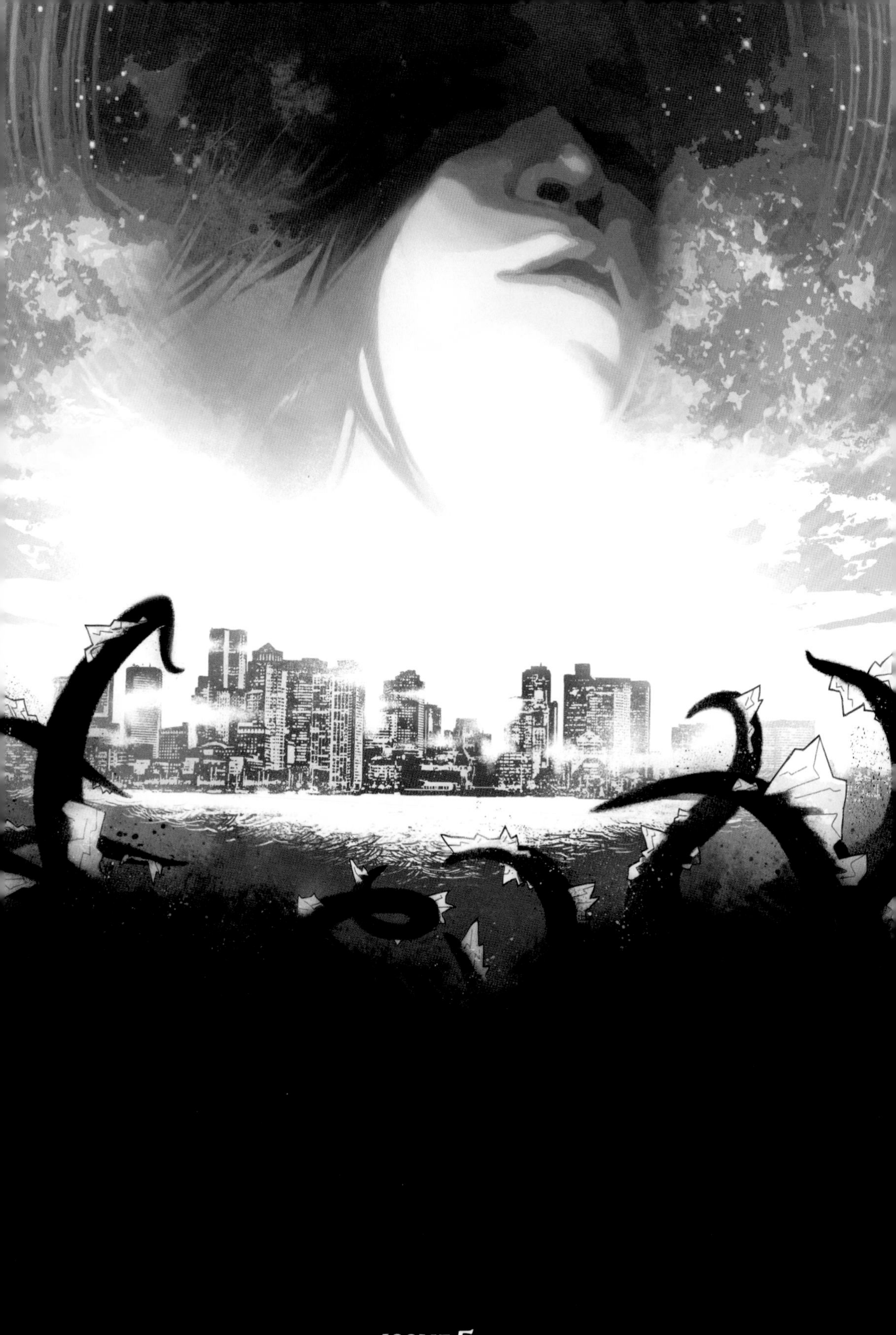

ISSUE 5

MARK TORRES

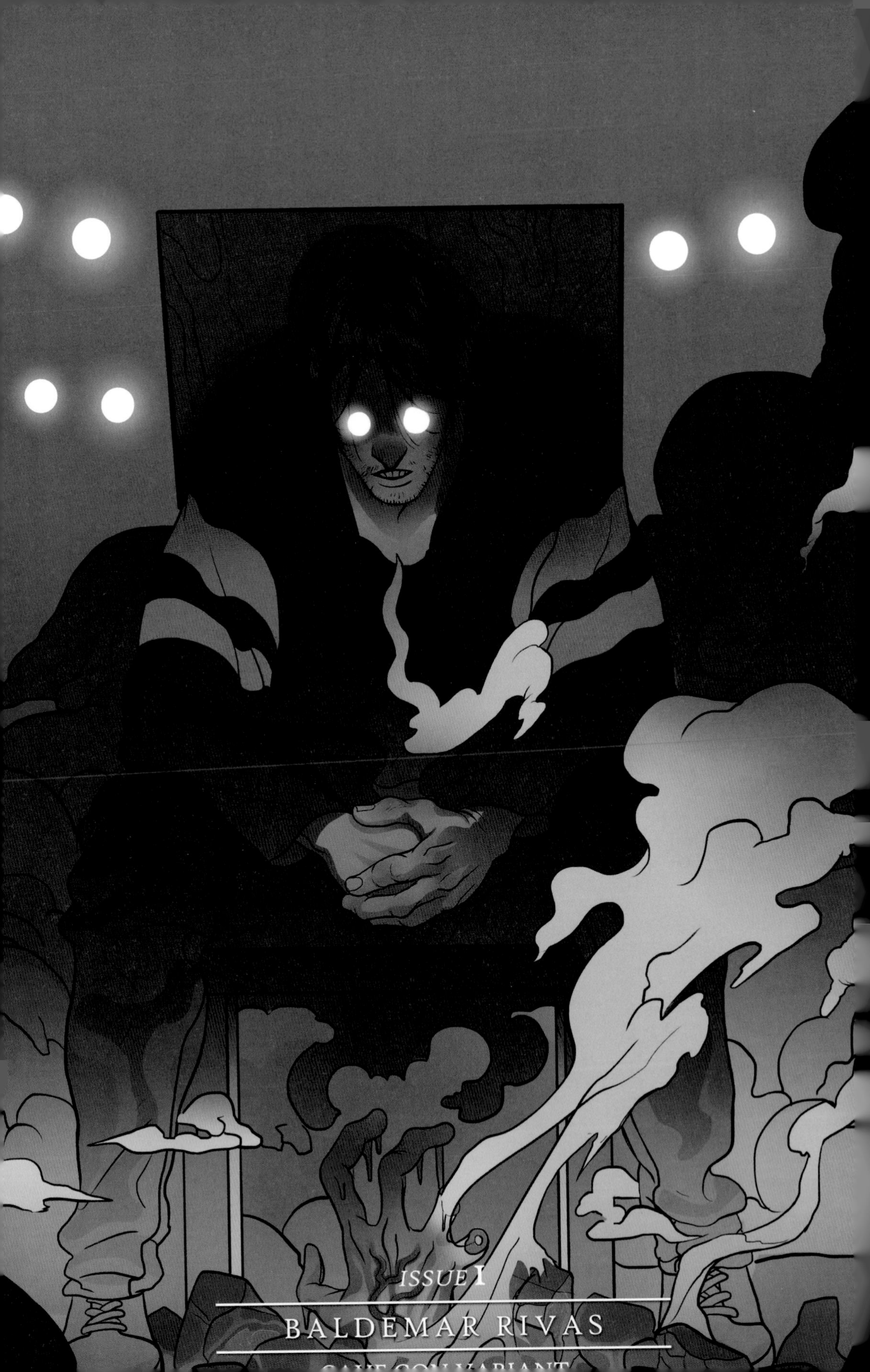
ISSUE 1
BALDEMAR RIVAS

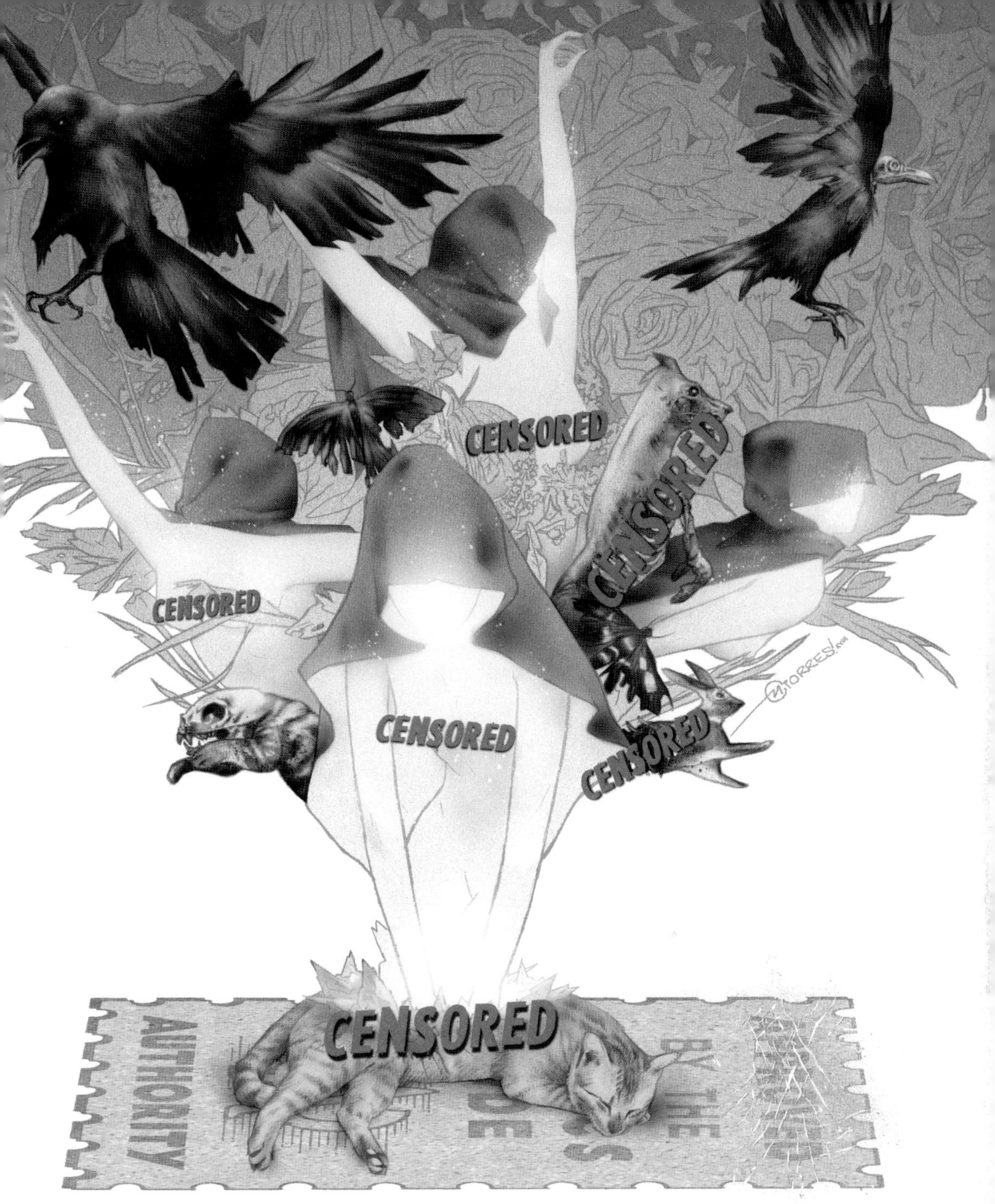
CENSORED
CENSORED
CENSORED
CENSORED
CENSORED
CENSORED
AUTHORITY
BY THE

ISSUE 2

MARK TORRES

CBLDF CENSORED VARIANT

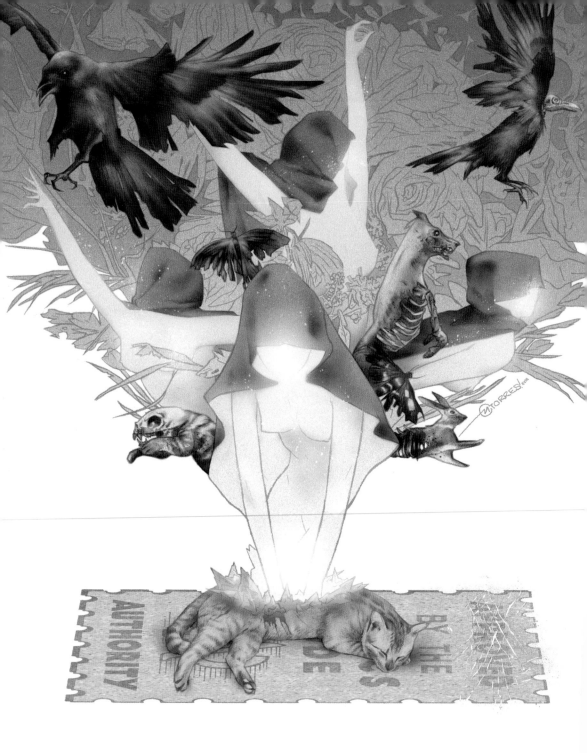

ISSUE **2**

MARK TORRES

CBLDF UNCENSORED VARIANT

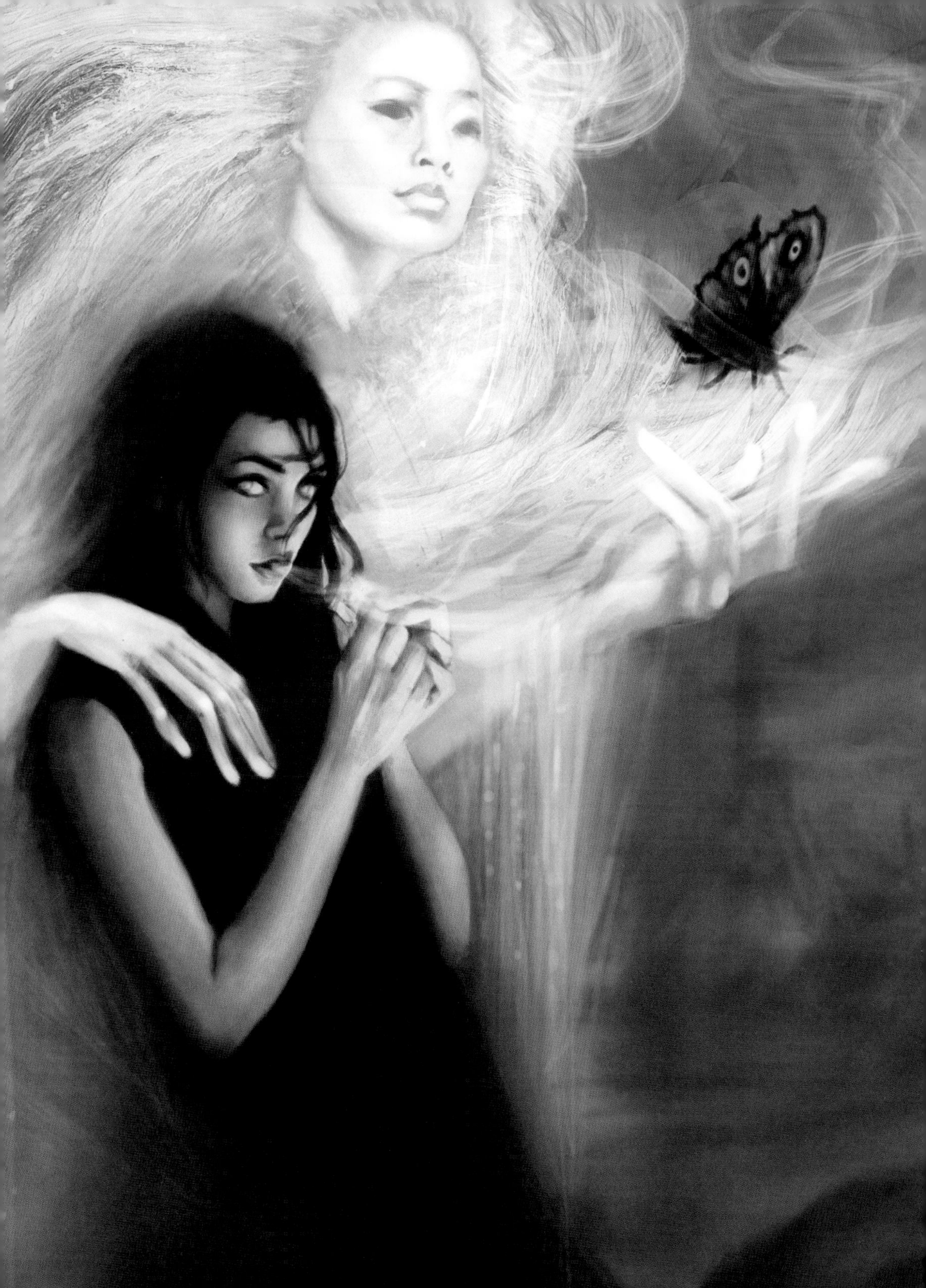

ISSUE 3

SHIUAN CHAN

ORCHESTRATIN' THE MADNESS...

- strange noises.
- cults!!
- dead body(?)

...at it through the spindly ...covered with ice, icicles

NO COPY

LOGO STUDIES

CULLEN BUNN | MARK TORRES

COLD SPOTS

COLD SPOTS

CULLEN BUNN / MARK TORRES

COLD SPOTS

CULLEN BUNN
MARK TORRES

COLD SPOTS

CHARACTER DESIGNS

MARK TORRES

COLD SPOTS Character Designs

ALYSSA WARREN

DAN KERR

Face Option A
Face Option B
Face Option C
Face Option D

HENRIETTA QUARRELS

SAMUEL QUARRELS

Face Option A
Face Option B

Face Option A
Face Option B

MARK TORRES / 07.09.2...

GRACE WARREN

ARTHUR WARREN

Face Option A
Face Option A

COLD SPOTS Character Designs

GENERAL NOTES:
Ghosts could pop up slowly across town, usually with their backs turned. Folks wouldn't think of them as ghosts, but realizes ...see the feet not touching the ground. We could probably have the ghosts slowly turn face forward as the series (and horror) p...of them are spotted, populating the island to critical mass.

GHOST EFFECT 1
- Semi corporeal,
  appears like a blur.
- Face is darkened,
  adding creepy mystery,
  with beady eyes glowing
  thru the ominous face.

GHOST EFFECT 2
- Same semi corporeal,
  blur-like state, but
  with some sort of
  "glow".

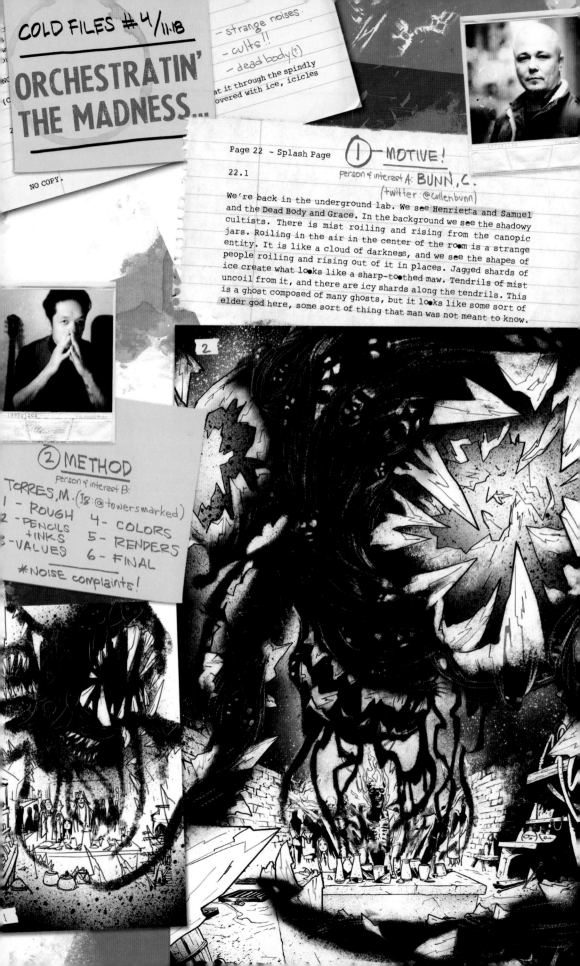

COLD FILES #4/11.18

ORCHESTRATIN' THE MADNESS...

NO COPY.

- strange noises.
- cults!!
- dead body(?)

at it through the spindly
overed with ice, icicles

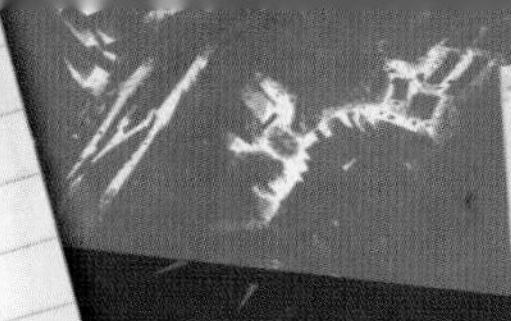

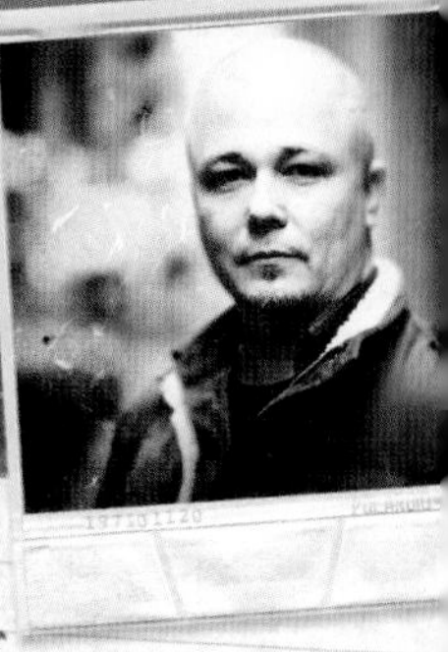

Page 22 - Splash Page

(1) MOTIVE!

person of interest A: BUNN, C.
(twitter: @cullenbunn)

22.1

We're back in the underground lab. We see Henrietta and Samuel and the Dead Body and Grace. In the background we see the shadowy cultists. There is mist roiling and rising from the canopic jars. Roiling in the air in the center of the room is a strange entity. It is like a cloud of darkness, and we see the shapes of people roiling and rising out of it in places. Jagged shards of ice create what looks like a sharp-toothed maw. Tendrils of mist uncoil from it, and there are icy shards along the tendrils. This is a ghost composed of many ghosts, but it looks like some sort of elder god here, some sort of thing that man was not meant to know.

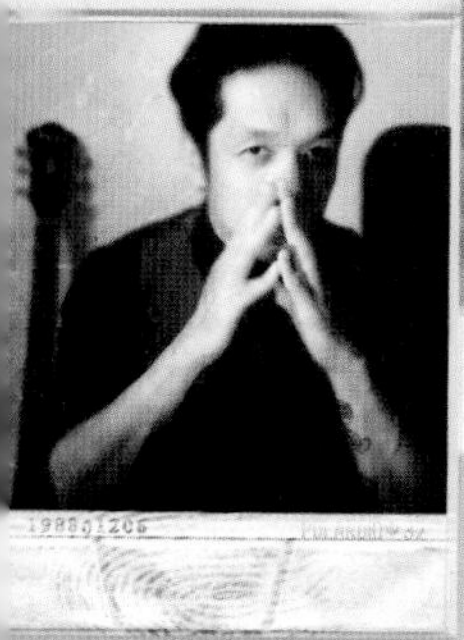

(2) METHOD

person of interest B:
TORRES, M. (IG: @towersmarked)

1 - ROUGH
2 - PENCILS +INKS
3 - VALUES
4 - COLORS
5 - RENDERS
6 - FINAL

*NOISE complaints!

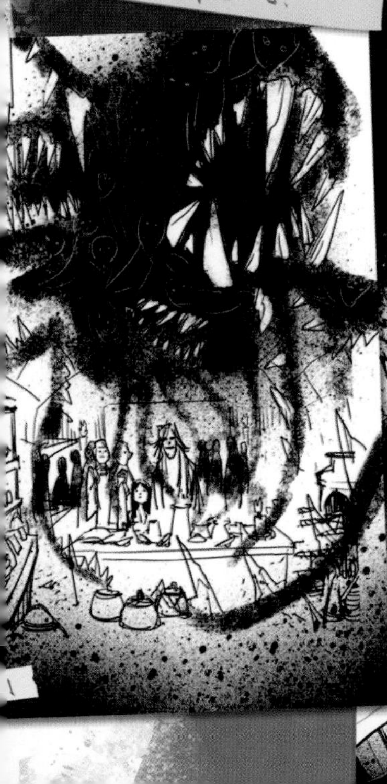
1

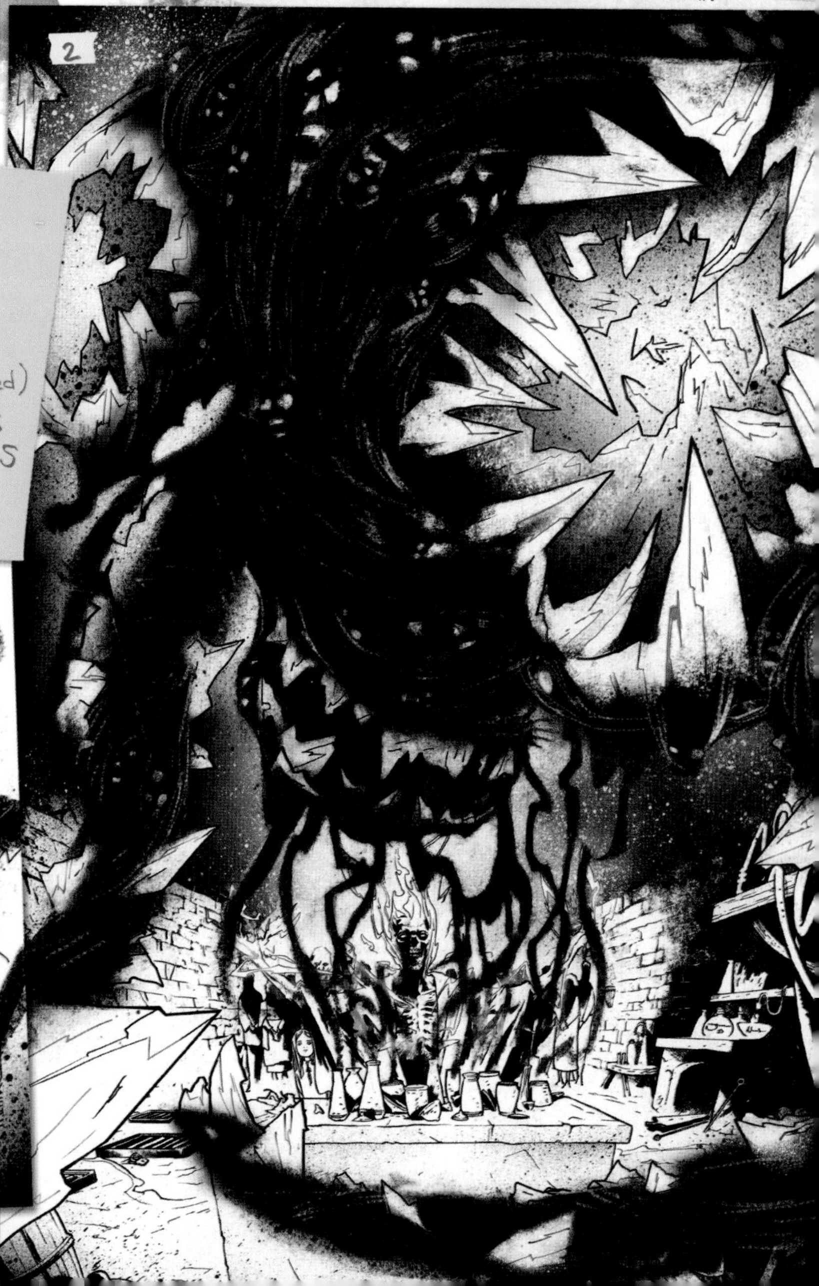
2

COLD FILES # 1/03.16

ORCHESTRATIN' THE MADNESS...

- strange noises
- cults!!
- dead body(?)

at it through the spindly
covered with ice, icicles

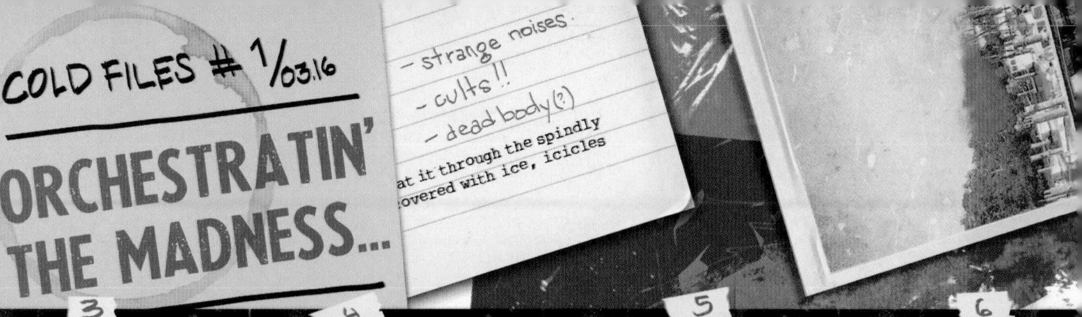

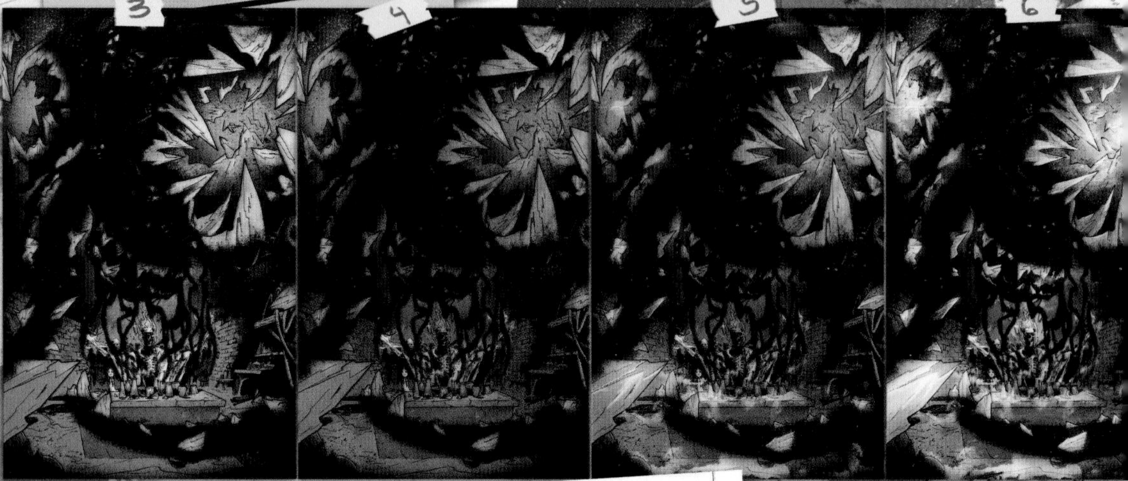
3
4
5
6

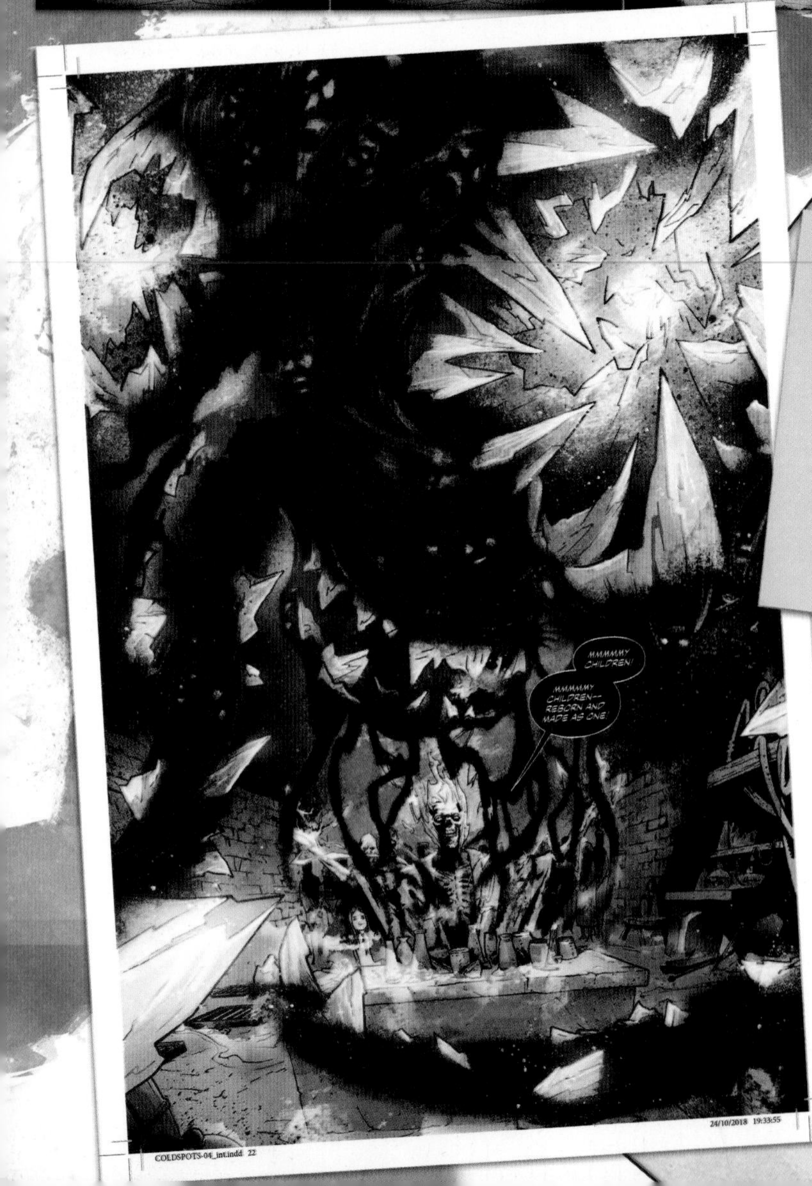
MMMMMY CHILDREN!
MMMMMY CHILDREN— REBORN AND MADE AS ONE!
COLDSPOTS-04_int.indd 22
24/10/2018 19:33:55

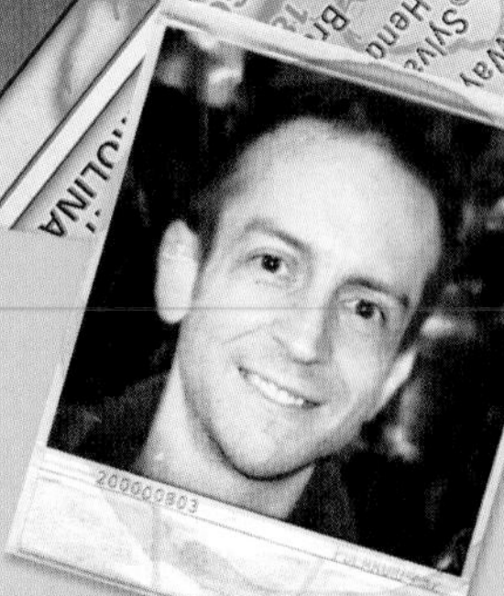

③ GETAWAY

Accomplice: BOWLAND, S.
(twitter: @SimonBowland)

- VANDALISM!!!

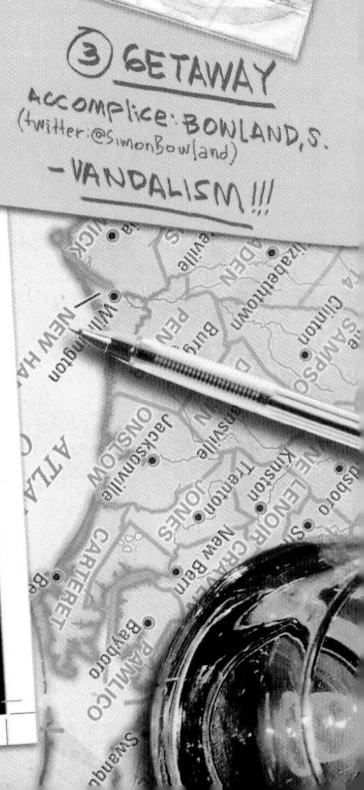

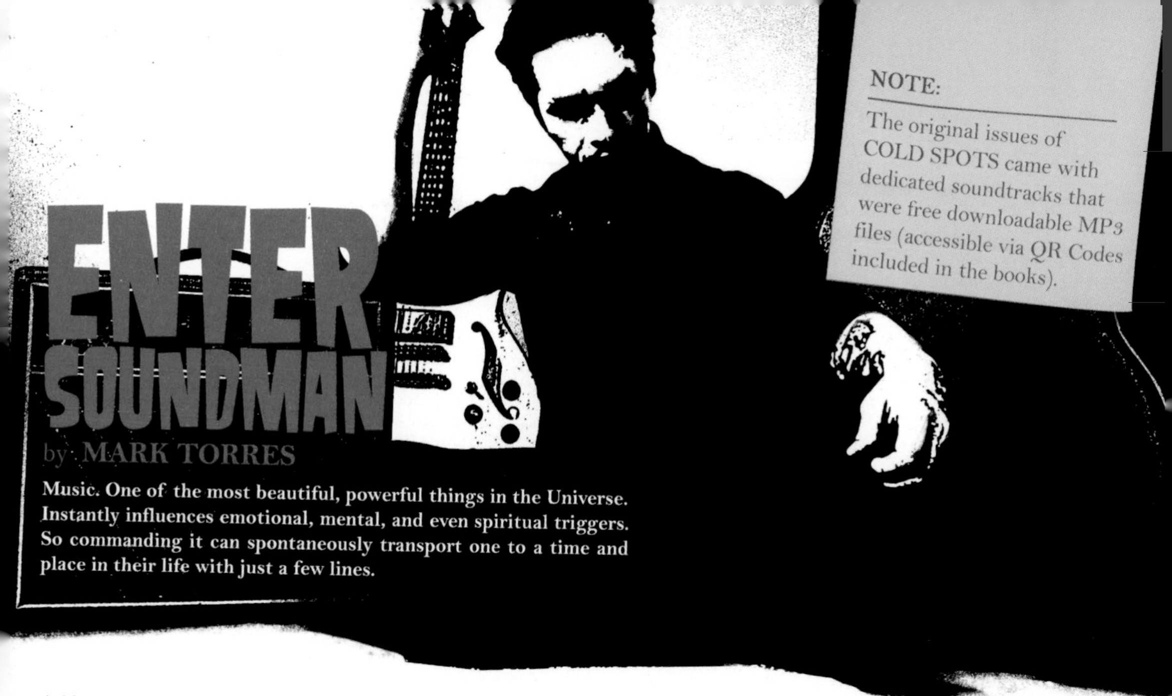

NOTE:

The original issues of COLD SPOTS came with dedicated soundtracks that were free downloadable MP3 files (accessible via QR Codes included in the books).

ENTER SOUNDMAN

by MARK TORRES

Music. One of the most beautiful, powerful things in the Universe. Instantly influences emotional, mental, and even spiritual triggers. So commanding it can spontaneously transport one to a time and place in their life with just a few lines.

Aside from Art and Design, Music has always been a constant in my life. Fortunate to have grown in a household that appreciated this magical thing. As kids, we'd wake up (at 5am!) to the tunes of The Beatles, The Beach Boys, etc., energizing us as we prep for school. Dad was a voracious collector of cassette tapes, introduced me to Queen, The Doors, Led Zep, Pink Floyd, The Police, Toto, Dire Straits, and other seminal legends of decades gone. From Glam, New Wave/80s Pop, to the Grunge, Alternative, Brit / Electronica, Emo waves, down to Post / Math Rock, and with recent years re-sparking my love for Shoegaze and Ambient, existence was and continues to be landmarked by Music (good or bad), both as entertainment and pursuit.

With **COLD SPOTS**...where Cullen and I are presenting a slow-burn, supernatural drama, giving tribute and respect to the classic (horror) stuff we were weaned on…*Atmosphere* is key. A significant element very challenging in print form. I felt having a soundtrack, will not only remedy that, but also give readers a more enriched overall experience (also as a token for the support). Thankfully, both he and the rockin' guys at Image were on board with the pitch.

Being a huge Process Junkie, thought it'd be fun to show you folks how the (sonic) sausage is made. Here's a Behind-the-Scenes on how I usually go 'bout creating noises…erm, I mean, Music. Enjoy!

BUILDING A MYSTERY

It all begins by reading Cullen's script for the issue, noting down sequences that stimulate immediate emotive impulses. These will act as foundations in creating the theme from top to bottom. As with art, I try not to be too analytical/conscious with creating music, I've always perceived these activities as emotional, letting the pieces be birthed the way they want to. Hence, the assistance of Mr. Daniels as a gentle limiter on the brain.
(Also, hydration is good for the body. Heh!)

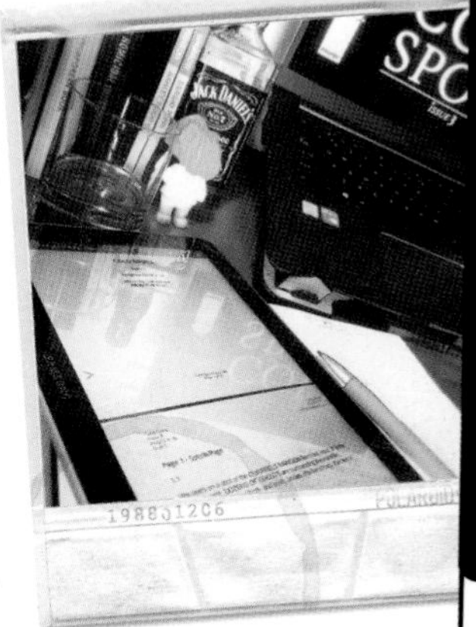

I then fire up ABLETON LIVE, my Digital Audio Workstation (DAW) of choice. Like a blank canvass, I'll start filling in sounds via:

a. Focusrite Scarlett Solo audio interface (for guitars)
b. Arturia Minilab MK2 (controller for all other sounds: Piano, synths, drums, ambients, the kitchen sink…)

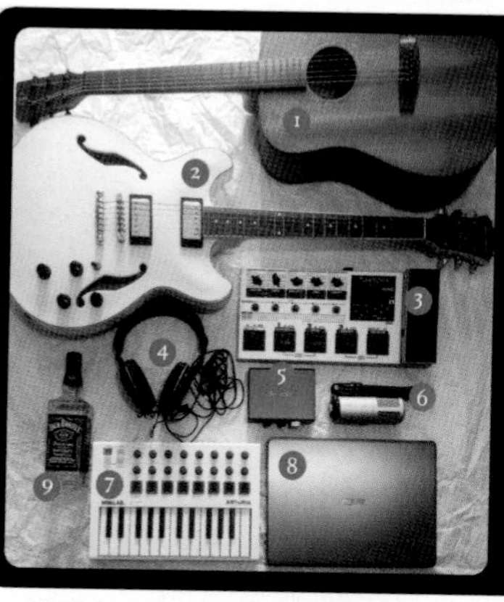

1
2
3
4
5
6
7
8
9

WEAPONS OF CHOICE

1. Phoebus PG-30N acoustic guitar w/Fishman Isys+ pickup
2. Ibanez Artcore AS73 electric guitar
3. Korg Toneworks AX1500g multi-effects processor
4. Audio-Technica headphones
5. Focusrite Scarlett Solo audio interface
6. Audio-Technica condenser mic
7. Arturia Minilab mk2 midi controller
8. ASUS VivoBook 5 laptop
9. Mr. Jack Daniel's

* *NOTE*: Not all instruments come to play, but best to always have 'em around for spontaneous inspirations.

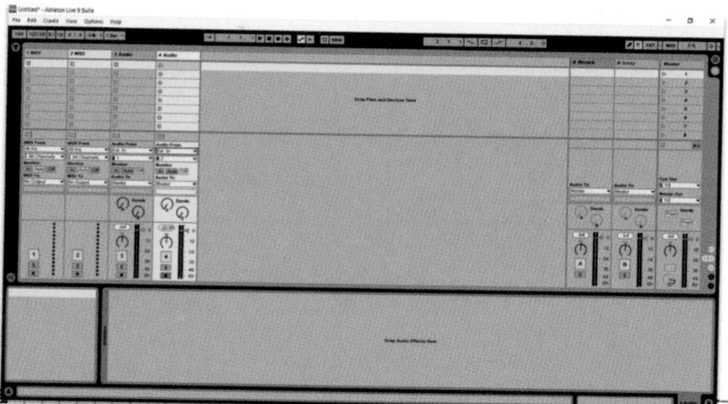

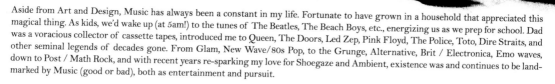

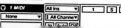

After the initial "organizing" is accomplished is where the real fun happens. Layers, notes, volume, timing, plug-ins, etc., are configured (then reconfigured), moved (sometimes returned), tweaked (eventually retweaked, or untweaked)...(huge JOY especially for *OCDs* like me), additional sounds/noises are added...more Jack is poured...time loses all sense, the outside world melts away. It's really hard work, but the fun kind, verging on addictive.

File Edit Create View Options Help

(At this point, normally, either I've written down some choices or already got a working title.)

A few more hours and work logged, finally called it in, finalizing with the title "**Lullaby for the Found and the Lost**" (though I've been endeared by the working label "*Lullaby for the Sheep and the Wolf*"). An extra step here normally will be playing the completed track as background while having the entire issue pages play on a slideshow...to "check" the cadence and emotional beats. Necessary adjustments are made if something feels off. Otherwise, It's a Wrap!

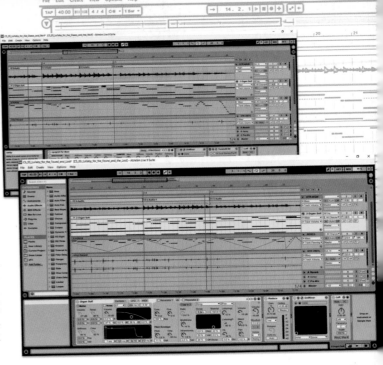

The hardest part actually is packing up a project, resisting the urge to keep on tweaking, and hitting that EXPORT button. I personally have always felt this true for any creatives (even athletes), akin to a parent wanting to keep sheltering/nurturing a child, almost not letting it go out to the world (sooooo emo!).

With **COLD SPOTS #3**, I was a bit torn what mood to anchor the track on, given the many pivotal sequences up for consideration. Eventually settled for a somber vibe, originally a hymn for Grace. In addition, felt it'd be a good rest point, as the previous 2 themes had been layers-rich creepiness messing with the mind. This one, hopefully, goes sharply for your hearts (haha!). Initially had it all-acoustic, but with my tendency for ambiance, eventually mixed in some oldie pianos and musical box-inspired bells and whistles...making the composition a little more "full bodied," but still haunting, in a way. I still love the all-acoustic, though...maybe when we get a chance to compile everything in a single album, I'd be able to add that version as bonus.

So there, hope you guys had fun with the tour, and that this will add to your further enjoyment of not only the soundtrack, but the entire **COLD SPOTS** experience. For more Art and Music behind-the-scenes, info on my solo EP "**Sounds, In the Key of S**"...and whatnots, you can find me on Instagram, **@towersmarked**. Cheers!

COLD SPOTS
SOUNDTRACK DISCOGRAPHY

1. REUNION
2. QUARRELS ISLAND
3. LULLABY FOR THE FOUND AND THE LOST
4. SACRAMENT OF DEAD STARS
5. BY NIGHT'S EMBRACE

All tracks composed, performed and produced by Mark Torres